Donald S. Olson was born in Minneapolis, Minnesota in 1950. He has had three novels published in America, and his short stories and articles have appeared in a wide variety of literary journals, anthologies and magazines. His play, *Beardsley*, was premièred in Amsterdam and has also been seen in Rotterdam and London. He lives in New York City.

The Confessions of

AVBREY BEARDSLEY

A Novel by

DONALD S. OLSON

BLACK SWAN

THE CONFESSIONS OF AUBREY BEARDSLEY
A BLACK SWAN BOOK : 0 552 99577 0

Originally published in Great Britain by Bantam Press,
a division of Transworld Publishers Ltd

PRINTING HISTORY
Bantam Press edition published 1993
Black Swan edition published 1994

Set in Garamond by Kestrel Data, Exeter

Black Swan Books are published by Transworld Publishers Ltd,
61–63 Uxbridge Road, London W5 5SA,
in Australia by Transworld Publishers (Australia) Pty Ltd,
15–25 Helles Avenue, Moorebank, NSW 2170
and in New Zealand by Transworld Publishers (NZ) Ltd,
3 William Pickering Drive, Albany, Auckland.

Reproduced, printed and bound in Great Britain by
Cox & Wyman Ltd, Reading, Berks.

To Gary Larson

Acknowledgements

Fiction has its own demands, and so has biography. This work of 'autobiographical fiction' falls somewhere between the two. I have treated Aubrey Beardsley's life as though it were fiction, but I have based my fiction on biographical facts. Some of those facts I have chronologically altered for the purposes of my story, others I have reinterpreted, and still others I have invented. My goal has not been to confuse but to clarify and create a coherent portrait of a fascinating and elusive man, and the sources of his art.

Aubrey Beardsley's last agonized letter begging Leonard Smithers to destroy 'all obscene drawings' was the catalyst for a five-year search to decipher the personality of the man who wrote it. That letter is quoted verbatim from *The Letters of Aubrey Beardsley*, ed. Henry Maas, J. L. Duncan and W. G. Good (London: Casell, 1970; Rutherford, NJ: Fairleigh Dickinson University Press, 1970). The late Dr Miriam Benkovitz, herself a biographer of Beardsley, generously lent me her copy of this essential text. Other biographies of Beardsley have been written by Stanley Weintraub, Malcolm Easton, Brigid Brophy and Brian Reade, and from each of them I have gained helpful information. *The Letters of Oscar Wilde*, ed. Rupert Hart-Davis (London: Hart-Davis, 1962; New York: Harcourt, Brace & World, 1962), and Richard Ellman's definitive *Oscar Wilde* (London: Hamish Hamilton, 1987; New York: Alfred A. Knopf, 1988) have also been invaluable.

I would like to acknowledge the generous assistance provided by the curators and custodians of original manuscript materials and drawings in the Fogg Museum, Cambridge, Massachusetts; the Berg Collection of the New York Public Library; the Metropolitan Museum Library, New York; the Princeton University Library (Gallatin Beardsley Collection); the Phillip H. and A. S. W.

Rosenbach Foundation, Philadelphia; and the Victoria and Albert Museum, London. Special thanks are also due to Michael Klein, Leslie Gardner, Patrick Janson-Smith, Ursula Mackenzie and Antonia Till. Their help and enthusiasm have been a blessing on these confessions.

ILLUSTRATIONS

The Abbé for *Under the Hill*, 1904.　　　　　　　　　12

Birth from the calf of a woman's leg design for *Vera Historia* by
Lucian of Samosata.　　　　　　　　　18

The Return of Tannhäuser to the Venusberg.　　　　　　　　　28

Design for front cover of *Pierrot's Library*, 1896.　　　　　　　40

Title page of *The Lysistrata of Aristophanes*, 1896.　　　　　　64

Portrait of Aubrey Beardsley as a child, courtesy Reading
University Library.　　　　　　　　　92

The Black Cat for *Tales of Mystery and Wonder* by
Edgar Allan Poe.　　　　　　　　　116

Portrait of Mabel Beardsley. By courtesy of the Mander and
Mitchenson Theatre Collection.　　　　　　　　　142

Hermaphroditus from *Later Work of Aubrey Beardsley*, 1901.　　168

Portrait of Aubrey Beardsley, by permission of Princeton
University Library.　　　　　　　　　196

The Achieving of the Sangreal for *Le Morte D'Arthur*, by
Thomas Mallory.　　　　　　　　　226

First design for *Salome*.　　　　　　　　　252

Design for cover of *The Yellow Book* prospectus.　　　　　　278

The Woman in the Moon for *Salome*.　　　　　　　　302

Cul-de-Lampe from the 'Ballad of a Barber' for *The Savoy*,
No. 3 1896.   324

Design for the front cover of *The Savoy*, No. 1, 1896.
Courtesy of the Fogg Art Museum, Harvard University Art
Museums, bequest of Grenville L. Winthrop.   348

The Lacedemonian Ambassadors from *The Lysistrata of
Aristophanes*, 1896.   382

Headpiece for *The Pierrot of the Minute* by
Ernest Dowson, 1897.   400

Alberich to illustrate 'Das Rheingold' for *The Savoy*,
No. 8, the last issue, 1896.   404

Initial Letter M (Venus) for *Ben Johnson and His Volpone*, 1898.   416

Last portrait of Beardsley taken in the room where he died,
1898. By Courtesy of the National Portrait Gallery, London.   423

The Confessions of Aubrey Beardsley

May 1897
Pavillon Louis XIV, rue de Pontoise,
St-Germain.

A LINE ONCE COMMITTED to paper, Père Coubé, is irrevocable. You can erase a pencil mark with india rubber, of course, but some trace of your original intention always remains. With ink, the hand must be smooth, bold, utterly certain, and consistently fearless; for nothing can cover up the blot, the smear, the tiny hesitation of flow and willpower that reveals instantly a limner's inadequacy or imperfection.

And so it is with man's spirit – or so you Roman Catholics claim. Until we are forgiven, each sin, no matter how small, is like a grimy smudge on the pure Japanese vellum of our soul. (I choose vellum for my metaphor, Father, because it is the most chaste and luxurious of papers, and holds an inked impression better and more permanently than any other.)

Each time we sin, you have told me, we hurt God and ourselves. You likened deliberate sinning – no matter how trivial – to pricking God with a needle, and mortal sin to the equivalent of delivering Him a resounding blow. And since our souls mirror our actions the hurt comes back to us, clings to us, remains forever transcribed in our spiritual ledger-book until we seek forgiveness.

Oscar Wilde hit upon this in *The Picture of Dorian Gray*, a book you may have heard of or read about at the time of his trials. In it, the outer equanimity of a fashionable man is counterpoised against his internal spiritual putrefaction; Dorian Gray's portrait is, of course, his soul; his actions in life befoul the pretty young man seen in the picture. Oscar knows better than most the filthy inner portraits the most civilized of men carry about with them, and the guilty torment they cause. It is because of Oscar that my own life changed so quickly, so irrevocably, so contemptibly, as I shall relate in the ensuing story of my life.

This notion of an unclean soul, dear Father, has been vividly in my thoughts for months and explains my desire to unburden myself to you. I am naturally meticulous – my work shows this, as does my person. No matter how ill I am, I insist on my daily toilette. The sicker I am, the more scrupulous I become. Grooming allows me to believe that I have a life beyond my illness – this wretched, stinking, eternal sickness that has, as much as anything, determined my life and, in some measure, how I have lived it. It is not easy to spend one's life rotting from within.

But now, of late, it is inner cleanliness that I seek. Nothing more than a thorough scrubbing of my soul, using the cruellest bristle-brush, will do. Yet how reluctant I am to embark on my confession! My tongue grows thick with embarrassment each time you sit so patiently at my side, waiting for me to begin. That is why your idea of writing it all down drew from me a gasp of relief.

Dear Père Coubé, I am English, and in speaking or social exchanges the English reveal *nothing* of the scarred secret soul throbbing within each of us. As a nation we have stunned the truth of our emotions into a fatal submission to the laws of class and good taste. When we would scream, we smile and nod; when we would kill, we tip our hats and bow. I have fought against this stifling national complacency in my art – some would say, to too great effect – and suffered for it. My drawings have been called obscene, immoral, sexless, unhealthy, unclean; and I myself have been portrayed in the popular press as a lubricious degenerate libertine.

At one time, I admit, I revelled in such notoriety; I throve on it; it was to me a kind of black sun that revealed me in a strange unholy light – to the envy, delight and anticipation of my admirers. The aroma of strange sins clung to me; I was a child prodigy of evil. Yes, I quite enjoyed this unsavoury reputation until it ruined me.

Yet each time I attempted to speak to you, to reveal the man behind the press cuttings, I found myself struck dumb. My *Englishness* intervened. And so did a fear of glibness, of insincerity.

You have often said that we are forgiven only if we are sincere in our contrition. Father, I am dying. My life is a misery and a torment. I seek peace, peace for my soul. It is my belief that when my soul is at peace, the *pain* will go away. You see, even the sick and dying have ulterior motives. I want to confess in the belief that it will help me to regain health.

Then, too, Father, my confession is the final road to conversion. At the end of it I shall be absolved of my sins, shall lift up my head and take upon my tongue the holy wafer. The body and blood of Christ will enter me. I shall be a Roman Catholic. I shall be of a new order. I shall blaze with the glory of a God who listens and forgives. The *English* soul, Father, *never* forgives and is *never* forgiven; my confession thus alters the very shape of my internal nationality. At the end of it what shall I be? English by birth, but Roman Catholic by design. It will put me at odds with the religious customs of my countrymen for ever. It is, Father – this confession of mine – a progress into perennial exile.

There is exaltation in martyrdom, you say. But you are not an artist. You do not possess the inner fire which heats the artist's imagination and delights in its expression, damning all consequences. I fear that the ceaseless fevered bounty of my imagination will take over in the course of this confession, Father, and impede my progress. None the less, to write it is better than to speak it. You, a Jesuit accustomed to the endless subtleties of thought, will understand that even as I stand ready (lie, rather, burning in my bed, coughing) to shed my sins and throw off the burden of my past, a dark triumphant voice within me crows: I am as proud as Lucifer of everything I have done, and I shan't repent of anything. The voice of the Devil, you say. But I say the voice of an artist!

You have not been ruined, as I have. Your life has not been an extraordinary one. Mine has. And while there is true desire for peace within me, there is also desire to explore the life of the senses still further. There is desire for defiance. Do you understand? There is desire to dance on the very precipice, to make faces, shout obscenities, blaspheme against everything holy. For the artist, Father, there is a holiness in expressing the other side of life, the shadow side, the side unseen by most because their eyes are fearfully averted.

You see, then, how complicated it is, this confession of mine. How does one begin? How does one tell the proud and glorious story of one's life when the very act of telling it is meant to be a disavowal, a sloughing-off of the past?

The idea of writing to God's representative on earth – humble though you are in your claims – floods me with shame on the one hand, and stirs up the foulest memories of my life on the other. You have led me this far, dear Father. Stand by me now, I beg you, as at last I open my eyes to look into the dark cavern and begin to unburden myself to you and to God.

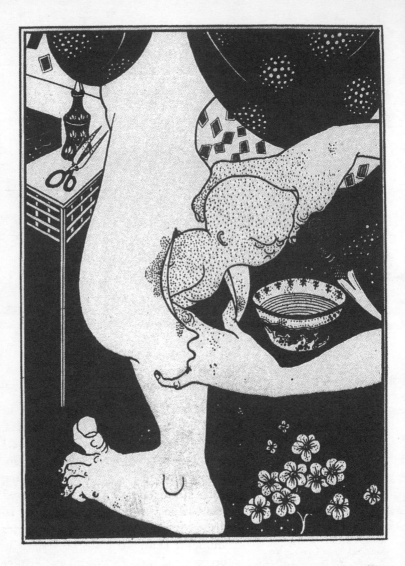

II

CCASIONALLY, IN INTERVIEWS, even in *Who's Who*, I have falsified my past, altering the date of my birth so that I will be thought younger than I am. Infant prodigies, such as I was, know only too well that they are considered remarkable because their talents are so disproportionate to their age. Prodigies are adult children; when they actually become adults, they are no longer curiosities, they are only '*former* child prodigies'. So naturally I have wanted to remain embryonic for as long as possible.

As I write this I am twenty-four years old, no longer a boy, not quite a man, and yet already an Ancient: a curious (even to myself) admixture of infancy and old age.

I was born in my grandfather's house in Brighton on 21 August 1872. (The same year, dear Father, that the Jesuits were expelled from Germany; the year Whistler's painting of his mother was completed; the year Théophile Gautier, author of the delicious Aesthetical and sexual primer, *Mademoiselle de Maupin*, which I recently illustrated, died; and the very year, and month, that my dear friend Max Beerbohm entered the world.)

My sister Mabel was born one year and three days earlier than I, so it is obvious that my parents were still locked at the hips. It is curious to imagine them so; quite unbelievable in some ways. Yet sexual imaginings have always preoccupied my thoughts. I confess it here, Father, now, so that you will not, later, be too shocked. No one – no matter how revered – escapes my Priapic fantasies.

Thus I look at my mother now, so sadly desiccated by the harsh winds of life, and attempt to imagine her in a violent embrace, her head thrown back in an agony of passion as my father sucks and fondles her tiny breasts and thrusts his flaming engine up her yielding cunt. Did it really happen thus? I would like to believe so, but more likely she lay back, eyes closed, heart drumming with fear, and let him have his way with her.

My mother has secrets, but she will not yield them up. She may now evince puzzled disgust over indelicacies of behaviour, but at one time she, too, gave way to the blind stirrings of lust. She has regretted it ever since; probably views it as madness, an unpardonable lapse in decorum. The only redeeming feature for her is that she got her children, Mabel and myself. Her life revolves entirely around us; without us she would have no justification for her obstinate martyrdom.

The truth is that my mother – Ellen Agnus Pitt as she was before marriage, teasingly called 'the bottomless Pitt' because she has always been thin as a rail – scandalized Brighton, her family, and herself, by going out unchaperoned to Brighton pier where she met Vincent Paul Beardsley, a stranger from London, and spoke to him. Yes, he picked her up. He was, my revered pater, something of a masher.

It is not difficult to imagine the scene: a bright, warm but cloud-heavy spring day, the fresh smell of the sea saturating Brighton, beckoning residents and invalids alike to the Promenade and the pier. A hectic spring gaiety bubbled in everyone's blood.

My mother, who was born in India and had lived there and in Jersey as a girl, was bored, nervous and unaccountably excited that day. She was the liveliest one in the family, and she wanted to do something. But what? The endless suffocating restraint of upper-middle-class life girdled her in like too-tight stays. She had tasted the spicy excitement of India, and known comparatively unrestrained freedom in Jersey. Here, in Brighton, twenty-four and unmarried despite her accomplishments (she played the piano beautifully, and spoke passable French), her energies were thwarted on every side by the dull-minded constraints of her station.

Her father, the retired Surgeon-Major Pitt, spent much of his time in his library, fondling his medals and dreaming about the war of 1852, in which Lower Burma was forcibly appropriated by the British Empire. Grandfather Pitt received a medal for waving a sabre in this war, as Surgeon-Major he served the Empire by joining the medical service of the Honourable East India Company in sweltering Bengal. Afterwards he practised in Jersey. His three daughters were dim abstractions to him.

Her mother and two sisters – oh, let it be admitted – were slaves to propriety. Only my mother, sniffing the sea air and absently tapping her foot, wanted something more that day than sewing and household duties and social pleasantries. Her blood was on fire. And so she slipped out for a walk to the pier.

Brighton! Dear, wet, lovely city of crescents and terraces, of fanciful excess, of Regency elegance and aristocratic *hauteur*. It comes back to haunt me, impossible not to love: Porden's Dome, where the Prince of Wales stabled his horses in grandeur; Nash's deliciously mad Royal Pavilion, where George IV gorged himself in a rococo Japanesque banqueting-hall, with dragons writhing in the chandeliers overhead. Flamboyance and style!

And sickness. A place where invalids gather, seeking health, sucking up ozone in the hope that it will fortify them, return to them their forfeit constitutions.

It was on Brighton pier that she first met him. He spoke first.

21

She answered without hesitation, smiling a little at her own daring but instinctively turning her back to the milling crowd so that she would not be seen in conversation with a lone man. The fresh sea air blew colour into their cheeks. Without looking, she could sense that his dark eyes were fixed upon her, *claiming* her. She did not mind, only her heart reminded her of the pleasant danger of it all, and she was aware of her body in a way that suggested spring, rising sap, unfolding leaves.

He coughed slightly before speaking again. Again she answered. There followed an exchange of light repartee in which the essentials were established: she was unmarried, he was unmarried; she lived in Brighton, he was visiting from London; he had no need to work, was therefore a gentleman. She smiled with relief. *At last*, she thought.

It might sound untoward, but was there any way he might meet her again? My mother awoke from her dream. How could he call when they had had no formal introduction? It was impossible; there was no way to explain him to her parents.

And yet surely – surely – there was something real, something not to be ignored, some immediate bond between them. He was respectable – a gentleman; she was a lady. They were adults, capable of making their own decisions. But now she knew the burden of life's unfairness; she was locked into a stifling prohibitive society which allowed no spontaneity, no pleasure. Pleasure was the worst sin of all.

'I often walk – almost every day – in the Pavilion gardens,' she said.

He caught her meaning instantly, and his voice became a conspiratorial whisper. 'At what time?'

'In the afternoon – before tea.'

'Will you walk there tomorrow?'

She hesitated, the magnitude of her perversity yawning. 'I will try.'

The next day it rained. My mother stood at a window of 12 Buckingham Road and stared out into the sodden greyness. Would he be there, the dark mustachioed stranger from London, waiting impatiently for her under a dripping arbour? Would she think her fickle, uninterested?

'You are distracted today, Ellen,' her mother said.

'I was thinking of London,' answered my mother.

The intrigue and deception began the following afternoon when she tried to slip out alone but was caught by her younger sister, who wished to join her. My mother lied. Amazing how easy it is to lie when your body is on fire. Once out of the house, she nearly flew. There he was, waiting. My mother knew then, with a fatal certainty, that a new life was beginning – her own.

Day after day they met in the high Regency shadows of the Pavilion gardens, seeking out lonely corners, high shielding hedges, dark fern-rich grottoes; becoming ever more entangled in the mysterious quick-growing vines of their passion. What should they do? They clasped hands in a mutual prayer of desire, my mother fearful and despairing; he touched her hair, kissed her lightly – and they looked into one another's eyes, seeing therein the wild beseeching animals caught in the trap of civilization and manners.

And then the scandal broke. They were seen. It was reported to the Surgeon-Major and Mrs Pitt. The heavens stormed, fearful lamentations rose skyward. Caught in a deception, my mother did the only thing she could: she defended her heart. Inquisitorial punishments were hinted at, threats of unending variety and unyielding severity echoed from the formerly tranquil library at Buckingham Road. Was this how the gently nurtured daughter of a surgeon-major behaved? Was this the behaviour of a young lady related – distantly, perhaps, but related none the less – to the great statesman Pitt?

I look at my mother now – her lips perennially set in a tight grimace which could indicate either pain or grim humour – in the end I suppose the two are much the same; her life an unending exercise in patience and perseverance, one eternal crisis because of me; and I try to imagine her then, twenty-four (my age now), and defending the actions of her heart. No doubt she rose to moments of high passion – those moments sublime when self-defence and moral certitude combine to form a perfect halo of eloquence around the speaker. Then, too, she pleaded, on her knees, that they might suspend their outrage until they met him, heard him avow that his intentions had been honourable from the start, that he wanted to marry her.

Marry her!

A perfect *fungus* of emotional melodrama, Father, engendered by one chance meeting.

It is strange, is it not, that chance – the only card we are dealt out daily – is never accounted for in the full pack? I have mentioned this to you before, and you objected to my use of the word *chance*. All is for you pre-ordained by the mysterious will of God. I know that I must now begin to believe this; yet at times it seems to me that our lives are chance, and nothing but chance. Every morning the dice-box rattles and our daily number is dashed out; everything depends on it, yet we have no idea what the number is. The roulette wheel spins, and the horror is that we cannot hear the croupier calling out the fateful numbers.

My mother begged her parents to meet him, to give him a chance to prove himself worthy. After all, he was of their class. He was a gentleman! He owned property. He had no need to work. And he wanted to marry her.

So it was that my father was called to Buckingham Road. Everyone was prepared to dislike him. He had usurped a rightful authority, which is the greatest sin the English know. Yet that day he managed to persuade the bemedalled Surgeon-Major to let him marry my mother. Passion must have allowed him some measure of eloquence. In the end it was best for propriety's sake to let them take their vows, which they did in the church of St Nicholas of Myra in 1870. My mother has told us that there was a terrible storm that day; every time she mentions this fact it is with a sad prophetic note which we cannot fail to recognize.

At last they were free, and indeed obliged, to consummate their love. They had entered into the legal sanctity of wedlock. They were joined for life.

I hope she enjoyed it, my mother. It did not last for long. The roseate dream shattered. Mabel was born one year afterwards, and I one year and three days after Mabel. I squeezed through the hot straining crack in my mother's loins and began to scream along with her. We had every right to scream, for a lingering fever came on and my mother could not care for me. I was wrested from her arms. I smacked my lips for breasts that were denied me. I howled for the comfort of breast-warmth in this cold new world and never received it. For weeks we were strangers longing for one another. And when at last she got me into her arms I fear she never wanted to let me go.

When the fever finally subsided and she could come downstairs, it was only to discover that my father was being sued by the young widow of a clergyman for breach of promise. He had lied. There had been others – not just flirtations, evidently, but promises of matrimony. My mother was mortally shocked to learn that she had not been the only woman in his life.

The Pitts would have no breath of scandal; my father, forced to settle out of court, had to give the aggrieved woman most of his rather small estate. We lost practically everything; *she* had the satisfaction of maintaining her good Christian name, and a comfortable sum of money.

From that day our lives changed. Where once there had been the small charming comforts – warm fires, plentiful food, servants – there was now nothing. Nothing. That horrible zero which reduces life to an anxious nullity.

I have known both, Father – poverty and wealth – and I would rather have wealth. I am no St Francis. Having no money grinds everything that is fine out of mankind; turns love sour. Yes, now I know that man is truly *Homo economicus*; that everything on our planet revolves around cash and credit; that the man with pound notes in his pocket walks differently from the man whose pockets are bare. But a child knows nothing of this and has no sympathy for it, doesn't understand how it can affect so basely those around him.

My mother, suddenly faced with the reality of raising two children on nothing, became desperate. She has been desperate ever since. Anxiety is her constant companion. I think she never stops blaming herself for talking to a dark handsome stranger that day on Brighton pier.

Of course, her family did everything possible to let her know that she had brought this catastrophe upon herself. Her insistence on marrying a man about whom they knew nothing, a man she had met in such indelicate circumstances; her flouting of their code of behaviour – yes, when one transgresses the moral code, punishment is certain to result. There is nothing more pleasant than to see another person punished for stepping outside the boundaries of propriety.

My father's father was a goldsmith who died of consumption at forty. When he was nineteen my father had a small legacy and shares in a property settled on him by his Welsh grandfather Beynon. That was why he called himself a gentleman, and wrote it as his profession on the marriage certificate. It was his good looks and his money which made him so attractive to the ladies. Perhaps, too, they saw the dark sparkle of consumption in his eyes and the flush that sits high on the cheekbones of those marked for certain death, heard the short dry intermittent cough which indicates that the disease is present but held in check, and a spark of sensual longing ignited the tinder of their high-minded sympathies. (Mabel has assured me, Father, that women *do* experience physical longings, contrary to popular belief.) Everyone loves a dying man with money, and my father took advantage of this.

Only he didn't die. To this day he has not died. He lives on and on and on, a veritable pauper, with the disease still present but in a perpetual remission. While I, his son, inheritor of his germ, as he inherited it from his father, lie dying in a foreign land of the disease engendered by his lust. My best work still before me and—

But I must not lose the line of my story—

The dice-box rattled, the roulette wheel spun, and fortune was lost. What were they to do? My father had no training: a gentleman does not work.

But now he did. Through distant connections in my mother's family, he found work in a brewery. His mouth became set, like my mother's, as the bitter pinch of financial restraint set in. My mother had married a gentleman; now she was sharing her bed with a common labourer! Their plight did not bring them closer together unfortunately; rather, it was the cause of their growing estrangement.

What he earned at the brewery was insufficient, so my mother went to work as well. And, as soon as we could, so did Mabel and I. That's the thing about prodigies, Father. Properly managed, they can earn money.

III

T-Germain is not without its charms, one being that it is less expensive than Paris, but after a few days here one begins to feel deucedly isolated. The food is excellent, but it is difficult to obtain books – an equally important form of sustenance. In Paris the superb bookshops and stalls along the quays yield up endless treasures; most recently I obtained from Gateau a complete edition of *Casanova* in six volumes, and had the pleasure of discovering that prodigious lover to be not only a great man, but also a great writer. I have been setting lures to my publisher, Smithers, to let me illustrate an English edition he is bringing out, but he does not bite.

The memoirs of great sinners fascinate me, as do the legends surrounding them. I hold especially dear that medieval legend of Tannhäuser, who entered the cave of the Venusberg and discovered therein the charmingly obscene and insatiable desires of Venus.

Do you know Wagner's opera on this subject, Father? I imagine not, although the Jesuits are far more worldly than people suspect. I have written my own imaginary version of the legend – a novel, in fact, called *Under the Hill* – which differs from Wagner's in its resolution, and which, were it ever to be published unexpurgated, would no doubt quickly find its way to the top of the *Index Librorum Prohibitorum*. I mention it here because it has troubled me of late. It troubles me because I am inordinately proud of it, and would not willingly renounce it.

There, in the humid grotto of Venus, the minstrel Tannhäuser finds an underworld of sensual abandonment, a pagan resort where guilt never sees the punishing light of day and where, as a result, love is practised in all its infinite fescennine variety.

Illness and impatience made it impossible for me to complete my novel (Smithers published expurgated chapters in *The Savoy*, along with several of my delicious illustrations), but had I finished the story I would have shown Tannhäuser, soul-sick and weary of love, leaving the Venusberg and journeying as a pilgrim to Rome. There the Pope would hurl anathema against the poor singer, and tell him that he would never be saved until his pilgrim's staff burst into flower. The abused and excommunicated Tannhäuser would return gratefully, humbly, to Venus's arms in the nether world of guiltless sin.

Thus I drew him, twice, his eyes fixed longingly on the distant mound as he stumbles through thorny thickets on his way back to the Venusberg, where his flesh will be caressed instead of mortified, and the life of physical sensation will expurgate the self-denying rituals of the Church. And there, in the Venusberg, as he is locked in a penetrating embrace with the Queen of Love, I meant to have his pilgrim staff spurt into leaf.

I suppose it amounts to heresy, but I wanted my Tannhäuser to find his spiritual salvation in physical love.

Physical love. Have you ever known it, Father? It is a constant preoccupation of my life – I should say, what's left of my life. It is the troubling irritation that produces the pearls of my art. Renounce the sins of the flesh, you say. Do not give way to evil thoughts. But why should the flesh, with its capacity to give poor miserable man his morsel of pleasure, always be considered as evil? Because it keeps us from God, you say. Is it not possible that it brings us, in some mysterious way, closer to Him?

I know. I suffer from heretical thinking. My mother complains constantly that I am 'wilful'. The critics brand me as degenerate and deliberately immoral. That is why I confess to you, who knows something of the world and the people in it. Are not most of us a tangle of contradictions?

And what is one to do with this inborn faculty of imagination? Imagination creates heresy. If you follow your imagination, you will assuredly at some point find yourself tied to a stake with flames rising to greet you. Nevertheless, an artist must follow these lonely subterranean pathways to find the meaning of his life and work; but in so doing he is certain to awaken the wrath of the mob.

I've had my brush with the mob – seen their livid hate-filled faces, had my livelihood snatched away because of their fearful misperceptions of my character, and their mean desire for revenge. I now live on the verge of a pauper's life – and death – because of the mob; because I followed the promptings of my imagination rather than the shibboleths of the middle class. And still I cannot relinquish it. Imagination is a sacred faculty, an inner fire to be tended with a vestal-like dedication.

From St-Germain there is a rather lovely view of Paris – at least, one can see the Eiffel Tower and Sacré-Cœur. A hazy mist, perhaps wood-smoke, fills the space in between. The two monuments – one to industry, one to God – summarize the miracles of this complex age of ours as we lurch and tumble towards the end of the nineteenth century. I wonder if I will live the three years until the next century. *The twentieth century* – how majestic and modern it sounds. And how quietly fearful the world is as we approach the great turning.

The healthy people stroll casually into town from our hotel, the

Pavillon Louis XIV, or into the lovely woods that begin almost at the hotel's doorway. I try not to hate them. I try not to be jealous as I creep as far as the 'terrace' with my stick, and there collapse exhausted into a chair.

It would be easier to forgive this loathsome way of life if I truly felt that it was leading towards my eventual recovery. But to go on month after month unable to turn my hand to anything; and to *welcome* these narrowing perimeters . . . it makes me think I am mentally submitting to the possibility of permanent invalidişm. I bob up and down on a sea of despair.

The endless annoyances of my diseased body, and my inability to draw – I have been forbidden to do so, and have drawn nothing since we left London, save for one (rather splendid) *couverture* for a projected *Ali Baba* for Smithers – makes me fretful and overly anxious. A painful ulcer has appeared on my tongue, and there is a horrid yellowish discharge from my *membrum virilis*. I have spat no blood since Paris, over a week ago, but my mischievous lungs, creaking like old boots, promise fresh sanguinary horrors if I am not careful. This afternoon I have an appointment with Dr Lamarre, who is said to be one of the most learned and skilful doctors in France.

You will forgive me, Father, for bringing up these details of my enfeebled daily life. I do try not to complain, but at times – often at night, when I am most utterly alone, and the healthy world snores around me, and the pain is the greatest – a black fury overcomes me. I cannot control it. I have tried, and I cannot. I pray for strength, but it eludes me.

Let me, then, return to my childhood. Let me conjure up the past.

When I was quite small my mother took me to London, where we visited Westminster Abbey. I could not have been more than five years old, yet to this day I remember the marvel of seeing stained glass for the first time – my mother pointed it out to me just as the sun was striking a rose window, and I stared in fearful rapture as the colours throbbed to life. 'Each window tells a story,' she explained, but I could not quite understand how a window 'spoke'.

'Where is Harriet?' I asked.

Mother was puzzled. 'Harriet?'

'*Harriet and the Matches*,' I said, meaning a particularly frightening cautionary tale that Mother had recently read to me. In it, Harriet is repeatedly admonished by her mother not to play with matches. The little idiot does not listen, of course, and one day she strikes the fatal match; her dress catches fire, and she dances and screams in agony as the flames consume her. If each stained-glass window 'told a story', I wanted to be shown Harriet being immolated.

'Not children's stories,' my mother said, laughing softly (how I loved hearing her laugh; it was such a rare occurrence). 'No, darling, stories from the Bible. Stories about Christ, and his mother and father, and the Tree of Jesse . . .'

Holding hands, we wandered on through the echoing vastness of the Abbey, staring at the busts and memorials of the great, stopping finally at Poets' Corner. 'Mamma, what are they?' I asked.

'They are memorials,' she whispered. 'If you are a very great man, when you die people erect a memorial to your memory. It may be a stained-glass window, or a bust like that one there, or a tablet on the wall.'

'Mamma, shall I have a bust or a stained-glass window when I am dead? For I may be a great man one day.'

'Which would you like, my darling?'

I considered for a moment. 'A bust, I think, for I am rather good-looking.'

And as a child I *was* quite handsome, nothing like the withered skeleton I have become. Mother encouraged my vanity; I was her little genius. Mabel was very clever, too, but I had the special gift, the spark from heaven. It made Mother quite adore me – except when I threw a tantrum. Then her hand was quick and fierce, and my buttocks stung from her displeasure.

You see, before I was two years old I had shown an understanding of music that made my mother's hair stand on end. If I hadn't become ill, my career would have been in music, as a pianist, or perhaps even a conductor. Music drops straight into my soul and takes the most shocking liberties with it. Wagner is for me what the Divine Arrow was for St Teresa, plunging in and out of her whole being with the heat of ecstasy.

My mother, as I said, had to work, and the only work she could find was as a poorly paid music teacher or governess for the children of her wealthier friends. She resented it, but had no choice, and even made herself put on a cheerful face for her employers so they would not believe she regretted her marriage. To make matters worse, her pampered charges were usually dull-witted and ill-behaved, quite unlike her own two darlings.

Her life had changed irrevocably, yet despite her new-found poverty she held on to the tatters of her past gentility with the ferocity of a panther. At the end of a wearying day it was in music that she found solace and refreshment. My earliest memories are of her at the piano, playing as Mabel and I drooled and cut our teeth and toddled about near her skirts. Every night when my father returned from the brewery she would sit us all down and play six pieces for us, 'so that we might hear good music instead of rubbish'. Like a good concertmaster she changed the programme nightly.

One day I *heard* the waltz music she was playing, and began to beat out the time with a little block. For Mother, it was as though I had suddenly been vouchsafed eyesight after blindness. She managed to restrain her excitement and began another piece, this one in a different tempo. Again I beat out the correct time with my block. Almost immediately I was swooped up, smothered with kisses, perched on the piano bench and given my first lesson. I soon learned how to pick out simple tunes.

Reading also came early. We could not afford lending libraries, so we read the books Mother had been given as a child (including the delightfully fearful story of Harriet). Mother also ransacked the library at Buckingham Road. What did we read? Primers, fairy tales, travel books, Dickens, Sir Walter Scott, sermons, poetry – we read, Mabel and I, everything we could get our hands on, not caring how ugly the bindings were, how cheap the paper, how debased the type. We were insatiable. We still are, only our tastes have changed.

My sister and I have been allies and conspirators ever since I can remember. Between us there are no secrets. We are as alike as twins, with the same intense mental sympathies womb-sharers are said to evince. We have had our jealousies, admittedly – we sometimes felt ourselves to be in competition with one another – but such temporary childish animosities soon passed, and of necessity we quickly learned the greater pleasures and safety in companionship and camaraderie.

I always feel inordinately proud and confident when Mabel is by my side in public, for she is now a strikingly handsome woman, and her presence is certain to excite a lively interest in both of us. We feel charmed when we are together – a couple – and I look forward so much to her visit here to St-Germain. She comes in a few days, having been touring America with a theatrical company. She is sailing from New York to Liverpool at this very moment.

Now we are both of us professional performers, pushed into the public eye by our adoring mother. Her later protestations against Mabel's acting career and mine as an artist fell on ears we had learned by then to deafen; in important matters, one should never listen to one's mother, for a mother's heart is an organ permanently swollen with misplaced concern. As for fathers, I begrudgingly tip my hat to Oscar, who once told me: 'Fathers should be neither seen nor heard; that is the only proper basis for family life.'

In her attempts to make money from our talents, my mother awakened our inner spirits. She could never have realized, of course, what a dangerous thing that is to do. Once your inner spirit has been awakened, and the flame begins to burn, the idea of an *ordinary* life becomes impossible.

There was never any money – I know this now, but did not then. There were days when my mother's sole meal was a penny bun and a glass of milk, but Mabel and I always had enough. Mother did everything she could to keep us ignorant of the poverty of our lives. We had toys – somehow; special little treats – somehow. But, young as I was, I sensed a gradual change in her: less vivacity; less laughter; a weariness and resentfulness she tried to disguise. She would sometimes rail against the dim-witted brats consigned to her care; they were ignorant and, worst of all, unmusical.

They did not then fight openly in front of us, my mother and father, but that something was dreadfully wrong between them became apparent soon enough. Once my father swung me up to his knee and put his face close to mine; I was frightened, for his breath smelled odd, and his manner was strangely reckless. He began to toss me into the air, calling me his little man, but I resisted him and cried out in fear. My mother ran over and wrenched me from his arms.

His demeanour changed at once. He looked at her, and then at me, clinging to her like a monkey, and his bloodshot eyes half-closed in what seemed to me to be disgust. Looking around, he saw Mabel – staring quietly at the scene – and he put out his hand. Mabel dutifully rose and went to him. His large hand closed around her tiny one. He lifted her up, shot another fearful glance at Mother and me, and left. Like some ogre exacting payment in a fairy tale, he took Mabel out into the night. From that time on it was as though a line had been drawn between us, and my father and I stood on opposite sides, unable to cross it.

Sometimes, tucked in our bed, Mabel and I would hear them through the walls, their voices like the bitter buzzings of wasps. Occasionally there were other noises, impossible to decipher – grunts and hushed cries, a rhythmic but unmusical grinding of bedsprings. What were they doing? Was he hurting her? She could still show rare moments of tenderness with him; more often, though, she was cold, distant, and no more than dutiful.

To cheer her up at night I would play on the piano; it was important that I play perfectly, with no missed notes, for her pleasure was greater then. Mabel would recite poems. We were her darlings, her solace.

On her free afternoons, if the weather was fine, she would wrap us up and take us for a walk along the Promenade, or to the pier, or in the gardens of Brighton Pavilion, whose queer turrets and minarets suggested an oriental fairy tale to me. She was always a rapid walker, and Mabel and I would nearly have to run to keep pace with her. We might hurry along to Buckingham Road, where tea would be waiting; or to visit Great-Aunt Pitt, who lived in Lower Rock Gardens. For my mother these were not always pleasurable visits, for these were houses of plenty, where she could not help but compare her own impoverishment with the relative luxury around her – luxury she had once enjoyed herself.

But she could show us off, her treasures. 'Mabel, recite your little poem for Aunt Pitt,' she would say, or: 'Mother, I want you to hear the charming new tune Aubrey has learned.' It was her way, I think, of preserving her pride. Then, knowing we were being scrutinized, Mabel and I would dutifully perform. By this time Mabel, too, could play the piano, so we were sometimes called upon to perform simple duets.

'But, my dear Ellen,' exclaimed one of her woman friends, a Mrs Sparks, who had joined us for tea one afternoon at Buckingham Road, 'the children are absolute prodigies! I wonder, my dear, would you allow them to show off their remarkable talents at a small gathering I have planned for next Wednesday evening?'

To this day I remember the bolt of fear that shot through me. I was not fond of strangers.

'Would you like that, Aubrey? Mabel?' asked Mrs Sparks, leaning down in a rustling mass of taffeta and peering at us through her lorgnette.

Mabel and I looked at one another.

My mother's voice sounded stiffer than usual. 'Tell Mrs Sparks you would be charmed to entertain her friends.'

Thus began my career as a musical prodigy. I should say *our* career, for Mabel and I always performed together. The evening at Mrs Sparks's inaugurated our entry into public life. Mabel was seven, and I was six.

Of course, Mother never realized the paralysing terror we both felt at being called upon to demonstrate our abilities in front of complete strangers. What would happen if we failed? Would we be punished?

'Performing?' My father was dumbfounded when he learned about it. The odd smell was on him, which generally meant he would erupt at some point into a passionate tirade or angry denunciation of his fellow-workers at the brewery. 'Are they to dance, then, like monkeys chained to an organ grinder? Jig about and tip their hats for the pennies of your friends?'

My mother remained cool. 'Mabel will recite a poem, and Aubrey will play a little tune on Mrs Sparks's very fine piano.'

'Shall Mabel and I play a duet?' I asked.

'Yes, darling, you shall play a duet.'

My father scooped Mabel into his arms. 'Do you want to recite a poem for the friends of Mrs Sparks?' he asked.

'I find it somewhat curious to hear you asking her what she *wants*.' My mother's voice was sharp. 'It's a question I've never heard you ask before. What we *want* we do not have. What we *want* is not an issue here.'

My father gripped Mabel by her shoulders. 'Do you want to stand in front of a group of gaping strangers and recite for them? For money?'

'The children want to do this,' said my mother. 'And, yes, we shall receive the charitable alms of Laetitia Sparks.' She was suddenly furious. 'Do you think I would stoop to this if there were any other way to survive? We would be in rags and on the streets begging if it were not for my parents and my work, and even that is not enough.'

My father released Mabel, who stood there, her green eyes large and terrified, afraid to move. My father looked at me and took a step in my direction. I wanted to dart away, to run to my mother, but I knew it would anger him.

His voice, when he spoke to me, had an edge of mockery in it. 'What will you play, Aubrey, on Mrs Sparks's fine piano?'

' "Fading Away"?' I whispered.

Was it a smile, as I hoped it would be, or was it a veiled sneer? 'Yes, that's what you should play,' my father said. ' "Fading Away." '

WRITE, DEAR FATHER Coubé, with the excellent spirits that always attend a favourable medical prognosis. Yesterday afternoon the highly esteemed Dr Lamarre came to examine me. It was the ulcer on my tongue which first prompted me to ask for him. Naturally, since his opinion is so highly regarded hereabouts, I took the opportunity to seek his opinion on my more serious trouble.

People who enjoy the full bloom of health can never know the nervous anxiety of the consumptive when a new doctor is called in. The body one struggles with day after day; the body that acts contrary to one's conscious will; the body that sings its own malevolent tune, its fever returning every afternoon like some diabolical leitmotif; the body one fears and despises because it stinks of premature corruption and decay – every time one exposes this secret pathetic body to the astute eyes of a doctor one risks hearing the final sentence of death: 'I'm sorry, there's nothing to be done.' So long as you don't know what, exactly, is happening, you can concoct miraculous cures for yourself; plan out a future; say to yourself: 'Tomorrow I shall definitely feel better.'

Imagine, then, my rush of joyous surprise when, after his percussive chest-tappings and inner soundings, the good doctor straightened himself, cleared his throat oracularly and said that, with care, *there was not the slightest doubt of my entire recovery*! Mountain air, he said, is definitely what I require, and went on to elaborate on the many cures effected by the elevated forest air here at St-Germain.

A consumptive actress, apparently given up as almost dead, insisted on coming here against the advice of her friends and family physician; she followed the cure advised by Dr Lamarre and was last seen, according to the doctor, dancing the bolero in a Parisian operetta based on the life of the Merovingian hero Chilperic. Similarly, a young dying lawyer, sent to Dr Lamarre by his despairing family, followed the doctor's special regimen and returned to his parents, wife and children a new man. His spasms of coughing had been so severe that his chest was weighted with damp bags of sand.

These are but two of the many recoveries Dr Lamarre has supervised and presided over here at St-Germain.

When I told him that I had spent some months at Bournemouth, he threw up his hands in utter horror. Nothing, he exclaimed, could have been worse for my particular case, unless it were the south of France. And there, dear Father, you have the contradictions of medicine and the frustrations attendant upon the consumptive patient: my English doctors recommended ozone-laden sea air, and said Menton would ultimately be the best place for the winter. Listening to their 'sound advice', I may have done myself real harm.

Dr Lamarre's cure is rather simple; but in that, I suppose, lies its miraculous efficacy. I am to rise every morning at four o'clock and take two hours' airing in the nearby Bois. At six I may return to the hotel to rest and sleep, but the promenades are to continue at my pleasure for the rest of the day. The forest air, strenuously inhaled during my peregrinations, will help cleanse my lungs. It is the *early-morning air* that is purest, according to Dr Lamarre; it becomes less beneficial as the day wears on, and on no account am I to be out of doors after five o'clock in the evening. I am then to retire as early as I possibly can.

Eager to begin the cure, I forced myself to rise this morning at the appointed hour, and slowly made my way through the deserted hotel. Mother had at first insisted upon accompanying me, but I forbade her to, adducing her recent sciatica attacks in Paris and her bouts of gastritis here at St-Germain. In truth, to take exercise at so early an hour is bad enough; to take it with one's limping constipated parent is pathetic.

How curious they are, these 'off-hours', when life hangs in a mysterious suspension. Being the only one awake in a world asleep, as though I were dreaming life itself, gave my mission a certain solemnity of purpose. And I was, in fact, a little relieved to be free of the burden of curious eyes which otherwise attend the enfeebled progress of an invalid.

Slowly, with the help of my silver-knobbed cane, I wheezed along the dark carpeted corridors of the hotel, envisioning the happy, robust, untroubled slumbers of the invisible inhabitants. From behind one door there came a sudden volley of high-pitched yapping, and the low grunting tones of a master calming his nervous dog. Light rustling footsteps behind another indicated an early riser, or perhaps a late-night reveller just returning. For two nights there has been a carnival set up on the far periphery of the wood, a charming setting for Grand Guignol and the *commedia dell'arte* – from my room I heard the gay noise and hectic laughter of the audiences, and had longed to be among them.

Then past the desk and the oily-skinned night porter, whose constant fight against sleep has given him a look of greasy preternatural alertness. This bald portly fellow, whose life rhythm is the obverse to that of most of the human race, guards against unregistered visitors and night-flitters (a night-flitter is not a nocturnal bird, Father, but one who sneaks out without paying his bill), thus ensuring the propriety of the establishment during its hours of darkness.

'Good morning, monsieur. Is there something I may do for you?' he asked, eyeing me up and down to make certain I had no luggage with me.

'Thank you, no. I am taking Dr Lamarre's cure, and shall be walking in the Bois for the next two hours.'

'Walking?' he said, blinking rapidly to express his surprise. 'Surely monsieur wishes an open landau for his airing?'

'Dr Lamarre insists that I walk,' I said, trying to sound confident and cheerful. I had seen the darkness outside the door and didn't relish it. I bucked myself up by remembering the nearly dead actress who was now dancing a bolero in Paris. 'I must walk.'

'Monsieur, we all must walk – but at four in the morning?'

There is no insolence like French insolence, but I ignored it. 'Perhaps you would be good enough to tell me – I have heard of a special shrine in the forest—'

'A shrine?' He rolled his eyes upwards. 'Ah, perhaps monsieur is thinking of the shrine to Notre-Dame des Anglais. Yes, it was once very popular with our English guests. Few people visit it now.'

'Can you tell me where it is?'

'Do you know the forest well, monsieur?'

'Unfortunately, no.'

'Then, you will never find it,' he said with a complacent smile.

'What is its general direction?' I asked.

He busied himself with some papers and wouldn't look at me. 'Walk straight to the centre of the forest, and there you will see a small clearing with benches. To one side is a path leading to the north. You pass a small lake, and come to a little hill. Climb the little hill—'

'I am exhausted already,' I joked nervously.

He threw me a quick humourless glance. '– and at the top you will see, in the distance, the shrine to Notre-Dame des Anglais.'

'Thank you.'

His voice, glinting with some horrid suggestion I could not decipher, stopped me just as I was about to step out. 'Did monsieur say that Dr *Lamarre* had suggested this . . . walking cure?'

'Yes. It is my understanding that several patients – dozens – hundreds, for all I know – have regained their health in this manner.'

'Of course.' Was it my imagination, or were his dark eyes glistening with mirth? 'But if some accident were to befall monsieur – deep in the Bois – how would we at the hotel know?'

'I shall be quite all right,' I said with determination.

'The carnival draws many strange types – gypsies – vagrants – do be careful, monsieur.'

I was cursing the entire race of hoteliers as I stepped outside. Except for the two blessed years when Mabel and I had our little house in Pimlico, my entire life has been spent at the mercy of hotel clerks and landladies, whose chief duty, it seems, is to make their paying guests uncomfortable. It took considerable fortitude for me to leave my bed at this unholy hour, and all my strength to get even this far. Now my head was racing with fearful portents, carefully planted there by the porter.

The Bois, which looks so charming in the sunlight, rose up before me like some dark mythological test of endurance. Why was I chosen for this hellish disease, which required pre-dawn regimens like this? Why? *Because my father had passed on the germ to me.* This central fact of my existence, as it always does when I am piqued or nervously susceptible, came back to fan my rage. Fuming, exhausted, I stood for a moment facing the new cure. How many cures have there been? Has a single one truly helped me?

The air was cool and sweet on my fever-flushed face, and I attempted a deep breath – half a breath, rather, for the Cough would instantly be upon me were I to inhale too deeply. Then I slowly made my way along the path into the dark wood.

There was no moon, but the stars stood out like sharp and brilliant grains in the velvety soil of the sky. It pained me to look at them, so many, so lovely, so unknowable. One can always adjust oneself to a human perspective in the daylight; at night, alone, one becomes a speck – perhaps an unseen speck at that. And then, in a fit of irritable perversity, I suddenly saw the stars as nothing beautiful at all: they were no more than teeming ripe tubercules eating away a black diseased lung.

It was darker in the wood. A canopy of young chestnut leaves hid the sky. A little wind agitated the flounced skirts of the pine trees, whose fragrance mingled with an indefinably sad odour of fallen leaves, damp fungi and vegetable decay. I crept along the gravel path, wheezing with the effort, sweat breaking out on my forehead.

Sometimes, Father, one's art is a premonition. Had I not recently drawn Ali Baba himself, the poor woodcutter, terrified in the woods by the sight of a band of murderous robbers? What easy prey I would be for an evil-minded vagrant! And ghosts. One never believes in them until one is alone in a strange place. One of my first published drawings was 'Hamlet Searching for the Ghost of His Father', in which I portrayed the youthful prince fearfully making his way through a dense wood after seeing an apparition of the dead king. Here, only half an hour from Paris, I could easily imagine an unhappy bewigged spirit of the *ancien régime*, a sour moan forever on his lips, condemned to creep through the old forest where once he'd casually raped and murdered someone.

A leafy rustling nearby struck sudden mindless terror into me. And at that instant I saw with unwonted clarity how fear dominates my entire life – fear on all fronts, but always tamped down by my conscious will. I always talked or 'reasoned' it away. Yet it took nothing more than a strange noise in the wood to make it spurt like a lanced boil.

I stopped. My heart was pounding. Silence. Little ghostly fogs and ribands of mist rose from the damp earth, twining among the tree trunks. The quiet was finally broken, and the rustling explained, by the querulous hoot of an owl.

'You are an idiot,' I said to myself, and moved on.

Finally, short of breath, I reached the clearing with its circular arrangement of benches. Here I meant to sit and rest before continuing on to the shrine of Notre-Dame des Anglais. But as I approached the benches I was startled to see a sleeping figure on one of them.

Strangely enough, this time I was not frightened; indeed, something drew me forward, as though I knew – somehow – what creature it was before me. He was clothed in a loose distinctive costume of white, and wore white beribboned dancing-slippers. His face, too, was white as a full moon. Before me slept none other than Pierrot himself.

How many times had I seen him on stage – in London, in Paris, in every place where the antics of the *commedia dell'arte* delighted the crowds? Pale, silent, enigmatic Pierrot, the clown of Bergamo, a delicate counterpoint to the coarse buffoonery around him. I loved Pierrot like a brother; I wept for his innocence, his poignant and elegant dignity. I drew him, over and over again, putting myself into his costume and his soul.

Evidently he had been performing at the carnival the night before. But what, then, brought him here, to the middle of the Bois, still dressed for the stage? Had he been hounded out of the company? Perhaps he'd crept into the forest to get away, for a short while, from the endless vulgarity of the audiences he played to. Or had he made an assignation with Columbina, waiting and waiting for her, only to become, yet again, the too-trusting fool jilted in love? And then there was the possibility that, being an *artiste*, he hadn't a franc, sou or penny for a bed. Lying there, his arms crossed against his chest, his face pale and tightly drawn, his lips rouged, utterly still, he slept the sleep of the dead.

No Madonna could have approached her sleeping son more tenderly and reverentially than I approached Pierrot sleeping on his bench. I thought of him as mine; he existed, there in the forest, for no eye other than my own – a vision of revelatory intent, a secret about to be revealed. My soul, seeing itself, throbbed in a sympathy so deep that it burned. There, stretched out on a bench in a strange forest, exhausted, alone, penniless, I saw myself. Yes, Father, before my very eyes, I lay there dead.

I wonder if it was my catch of breath, that moment before an involuntary sob, that woke him. I am not usually prey to outward expressions of emotion, and instantly I caught myself. But Pierrot opened one eye. It was clear, penetrating and almost instantly alert. He looked at me, bowed there before him as at a shrine, my body wasted, my spirit nearly broken, and he rose.

I thrill even to remember the unbroken fluidity of his movement, the sympathy it evoked in me, as though – had I only tried, *had I only believed* – I, too, could have risen with the same graceful ease. It seemed he floated. He stood before me, and his soul knew mine. And then he did dance, there in the clearing, in that moment before dawn, and he danced just for me.

His white flowing smock with the billowing sleeves and his outsized pantaloons rippled and draped themselves around his supple frame. He lifted a foot, and the ribands on his shoe fluttered above the grass like slender wings. He did not dance for joy, I think, but because movement was his tongue. He was speaking to me without the burden of words.

The vision did not last more than a few moments, I fancy, and yet for those moments I seemed to understand something beyond understanding. Pierrot, at the end of a pirouette, made a sweet deft bow and danced away, deeper into the woods, as though he were one of the shy old pagan deities – a spirit, a sprite – haunting the dark spaces of time. But for a moment I had known him, and he me.

The encounter left me dazzled and excited, as you may imagine. As the curtain of the sky began to lift, and a rind of nacreous light appeared along the horizon, I crunched my way back to the hotel. My footsteps were not nearly so light and nimble as Pierrot's, but they were not as heavy as they had been.

I'm certain now that, if I persevere, this cure will be successful.

Yet I most assuredly try your patience, good Father, with my descriptions of a reduced and at times pathetic daily life. The ordeal of illness is my only excuse: my days are measured around it. Let me pause and rest here for a moment, and then I shall resume my confession. It will be a relief even to go back to a time when I had all the fierce energy of a steam engine – which was, I remember now, my favourite toy.

Of all visible parts of me, it is my hands that are most beautiful. People often comment on them; if not, they stare. They are strong well-sinewed hands – tho' a bit thinner of late – with long tapered fingers, and I always make certain they are prominently featured in my photographs. 'Pianist's hands,' they are often called.

My hands have been my life, Father. In the deepest prison of illness, when all other functions were failing, my hands remained doggedly alive and working, as if they had a will independent from the rest of my ne'er-do-well body. A dancer may adore her metatarsals for the spring they give to her leap; for an artist, it is the metacarpals that provide the fundamental strength for the execution of his art. It is all in the hand and wrist.

I remember you once exclaimed: 'What fine hands those would make for praying!' There is no way you could have known that earlier that same day I had used my hands not for communications with God, but to simulate the smooth vaginal lips of Venus, the five-fingered goddess of love. Yes, Venus, too, resides in these palms.

I speak of my hands this way, Father, because were I sincerely and devoutly to repent of my past life and work, as you say I must before I can be received into the Church, I would have to forsake all that these marvellous flexible appendages have done for me, would I not? How could I betray them so? They remain clenched and grim in their current enforced retirement. What would they do in permanent exile?

I speak of my hands, too, because in casting my sights back over my life it is my hands that provide me with one of my first sensory memories – namely, my fingers darting over the keyboard of a piano.

Those are not unhappy memories, sitting beside Mother on the piano bench, watching her hands or, secretly, her hectically swinging ear-rings; listening to her, then trying things out for myself. Music gave her joy, and she used it to banish the exhausting frustrations of her life as a day governess, evening music teacher, and unhappy wife. I never failed to be amazed at the change that would come over her mood the moment she first struck the keys. She would begin by playing one dramatic chord, stop, but with her hands still on the keys, and then seemingly inhale the sound up through her arms and into her body; she would slowly close her eyes and lift her shoulders, and then begin to play. I have seen people react similarly to morphine, laudanum, ether and absinthe – the same tight anxious posture; the shot, gulp or inhalation of the drug; and then the small mysterious smile or bark of laughter as the substance whispers its secret to the imbiber.

Mother, with her iron wrists, was quite an accomplished musician, even studied with Dr Francis Wesley when she had half a crown to spare. Her fingers would skip and slide up and down the scale in breathtaking Mozartian arpeggios, pausing only to trill a perfect sixth; or she would gather herself up, contract her face, and fiercely play a sombre passage of Schumann. Once I asked her why she looked so strange every time she played a certain phrase.

'Because it is marked here *Mit tiefstem Gefühl*,' she explained, using her best and most incomprehensible German.

'What is *mit tiefstem Ge fool*?'

' "With deepest feeling." It explains just here, on the score, how the composer wants the phrase interpreted.'

'You mean like *con brio*?'

'Yes, darling, only a very different emotion.'

Oh, I knew emotion lay in the piano, a whole sobbing, joy-crazed, tragic, exultant world of it, for the more I played and listened the more glimpses of that world I had. I dimly began to understand how Mother reinterpreted the emotional circumstances of her life through music, writing on the piano not a letter of words but one of sound. I learned quickly – a fish in its element – and had no need of the endless repetitive exercises that formed a staple of Mother's life. My uncanny abilities even put a little dash of fright into her pride. She was afraid, I think, as all mothers are, that she had given birth to a superior being, and that her own abilities would be put to the test by mine.

I must confess, Father Coubé, that when Mother accuses me of being 'wilful' – her way of shaming me when I disobey her wishes – she is not entirely wrong. Even from those earliest days at the piano I enjoyed provoking her, and I had only to ignore her well-intentioned instructions to cause a little nervous trill to run down the keyboard of her spine.

'No, no,' she would say, trying to interrupt me in a certain passage, 'that is not to be played *vivace*.'

Ignoring her, I would play on. 'Yes, Mamma, it is.'

'It most definitely is *not*, Aubrey. The score is marked *adagio*.'

'Then, it is a mistake,' I would say, playing on, never stopping.

'A mistake! Do you now override the decisions of the composer himself?'

'If the composer is wrong, yes.' I didn't honestly believe this, of course, but I certainly couldn't allow my interpretation to be questioned. 'You would have to be a *tiefstem Ge fool* to play it that way.'

I could always tell from a certain bristling beside me what effect these childish perversities had on Mother. I knew, however, because she was about to make us perform in public for the first time, that she did not mean to punish me. If she did, I would simply refuse to play.

Yet there were those moments, too, when I knew I had been taken into the piano's confidence, and could make it sing. At such moments – they were rare moments only, but by far the most memorable of my infant years – I had a sense of dissolution into the instrument and the music, a sublime happiness that welled up from within, as if I were a clear sparkling spring releasing my flow in music. The moments came only when I was playing alone, when Mother was not by my side coaching and instructing me.

Like most people who are unmusical, my father regarded our music-making with a mixture of suspicion, boredom and jealousy. At night, when Mother bade us all be seated for her evening programme of six pieces, Mabel and I would sit rapt with expectancy and pleasure. To see one's mother performing with grace and intent is a keen pleasure for a child. For my poor father it meant something else entirely. I would look over to verify that he was appreciating Mother's performance as much as we, only to see his face grotesquely disfigured as he tried to stifle one gigantic yawn after another. At the end of a grinding day of loading vats of beer on to brewery carts, the sight of his wife's determined cultivation and enrichment of her children irked and shamed him at the same time.

It was he who gave me the toy steam engine, and a darling little engine it was. It suited a need for miniature worlds accessible to no one but myself – and Mabel. Where did it come from, I wonder, that childhood desire to create dark cosy little dens where we could escape from *them*? Mabel and I would crawl into various hiding-places created by draping rugs over low tables or two chairs pushed together. I would bring in my engine, Mabel her doll, and there, like some queer infant couple, we would intently play out strange little dramas of make-believe. The doll, Mabel insisted, was our child. I would go off 'to work' on my engine. The fantasy of it was delicious and utterly our own.

Perhaps we hid because when we were not in hiding Mother was coaching us for our début at Mrs Sparks's house. Naturally she was in an agony of nervous anticipation; true, it was a money-making scheme, and therefore vulgar, but Mother cloaked it with a Higher Significance. This was her chance to impress through her offspring; she was offering us up, in a manner of speaking, as her creations.

Mabel's musical talent was adequate, but not as developed as mine. Therefore I was to appear as a soloist on the piano, she as a reciter of poetry and prose, and together we would mangle a simple four-hand duet. I found it curious later on, when Mother continually tried to dissuade Mabel from her (to me, perfectly natural) plans for becoming an actress. 'You have neither the talent nor the temperament for a stage career!' Mother would cruelly insist, leaving Mabel in floods of tears. And yet all those early years she prodded Mabel to do nothing *but* act.

Mother did not teach acting – or the Expressions, as she called them – as well as she taught the piano. From somewhere, perhaps her nursery archives at Buckingham Road, she had acquired a hopelessly outdated text, translated from the German, which advertised itself as a 'Scientific Method for learning the Expressions used on Stage'. The book was filled with frightening engravings of faces registering everything from 'Admiration' to 'Simple Bodily Pain'. Poor Mabel had to study each engraving, with its labelled expression, and then mimic it. Mother would then compare Mabel's expression with that in the book:

'It's not quite right, dear,' she would say. 'See here, the lips are shown quite parted and curved downwards for the expression of Simple Bodily Pain.'

Mabel, utterly serious, would make the appropriate adjustment to her lineaments.

'That's much better, dear, but don't turn your lips *too* far downward or it becomes a vulgar cartoon. Now show me Admiration with Astonishment.'

Soon I could inwardly mimic, without changing my face, every one of the Expressions: Attention, Veneration, Admiration with Astonishment, Joy with Tranquillity, Laughter, Simple Bodily Pain, and Acute Pain. (These last two I have had considerable occasion to use in the past year.)

Mother would not allow us to look in the Expressions book on our own, and once we had rifled its pages in her absence we knew why: there were several expressions that Mother had quite deliberately ignored. One was Rapture, and the other was Desire. With a deliciously frightening certainty that we were surely committing a great sin, we quickly memorized the two forbidden Expressions on our own.

To this day Mabel and I burst into laughter at the memory of these Expressions she was forced to learn before she even knew what they meant. I simply have to shout, 'Veneration!' and she assumes the appropriate facial musculature, distorting it just enough to become hilarious. 'Rapture!' she will order me, and I will roll my eyes upward to heaven, clasp my hands to my breast, until both of us roll on the floor in laughter.

And then there was *The Pickwick Papers*. Mother had determined that excerpts from chapter 30 ('How the Pickwickians made and cultivated the Acquaintance of a couple of nice Young Men belonging to one of the Liberal Professions; how they disported themselves on the Ice; and how their first Visit came to a conclusion') would provide appropriately droll recitation material for the genteel audience at Mrs Sparks's. Thereupon Mabel was set to the task of memorization. Page after page of Dickens – that cockney Shakespeare – she learned by heart, with the result that to this day, whenever she is nervous, the dear will begin to murmur passages of the skating scene, using it as a Catholic uses rosary beads to invoke a tranquillizing novena.

For we were frightened, despite the show of bravado we put on for Mother. Mabel, less secure in her talent, given less attention because she was less talented, was terrified.

'Will there be many many people?' she would enquire pathetically, over and over again.

'There will be several,' Mother would answer. 'You will know some of them.'

'But how many will I *not* know?'

She has never conquered stage fright, my sister, despite any number of professional engagements. It is a most insidious fear, and I wonder they didn't engrave an Expression for it in the book. It plays upon one's personal confidence, teasing one to madness with visions of humiliation and defeat.

As the date for our début neared, a mysterious series of near catastrophes arose in quick succession, making Mother ever more nervously hysterical. One of her sisters became very ill with brain fever, and kept calling out in her delirium, 'Ellen, there's a snake, a snake!' – harking back, perhaps, to their childhood in India; Mabel, chasing a stray cat she had lured into 12 Buckingham Road, nearly fell into the wood fire, and only a quick douse of water from my grandmother prevented her from a fate similar to that of Harriet and the matches; while I complained of funny little aches and pains that would catch me at odd times and make me want to curl up and sleep for hours on Mother's lap.

We all knew that something was about to happen, that some new energy was going to be set loose; and that, like a caged beast, the energy was roaring with fear and impatience.

Finally the day arrived, and in our stiff new clothes, our hair brushed until our scalps almost bled, Mabel's decorated with a heavy bow, we – the two Prodigies – were led to Mrs Sparks's house in Regency Square. Mother kept up a constant patter, half-inspirational, half-admonitory:

'I know you will both perform beautifully and be a true credit to me. Remember, Mabel, not to pull at your hair or dress if you are afraid of forgetting a line; that will not help you; you have had plenty of time to learn it, and it is all there in your head. Aubrey, when you play "Fading Away", dear, strive for *pianissimo* in the final coda.'

As we stood waiting for the front door to be opened Mabel cried out: 'Mother, I've forgotten all the words!' She was hushed by a glance from Mother, and at that moment the door was opened by Mrs Sparks's butler. Mother quietly gave her name, and we were ushered into a smallish front hall. The voices and laughter of our audience wafted from the drawing-room. I looked over and saw sheer terror on Mabel's face.

'Mrs Beardsley!' Mrs Sparks, a perpetual squint in her eyes, rustled out in a patterned tea-gown and gave her hands to my mother. 'Everyone is *so* looking forward to the little concert we've planned. Now, do come in and have your tea. Bellows will take the children up to the nursery until we want them.'

Bellows, the butler, bent over and said softly: 'If Miss Beardsley and Master Beardsley will follow me?' It sounded wonderfully grown-up, and I was ready to go at once; but a half-choked sob sounded from Mabel's throat, and she ran to Mother.

'We shall be waiting for you in the drawing-room,' Mrs Sparks said to Mother, and rustled away.

Mother's voice was sharp. 'Mabel, what is this?'

'I can't,' Mabel whispered.

'You cannot what?'

'I can't remember the words.'

'Then, I suggest, dear, that you go up to the nursery and try to recall them.'

Mabel was nearly crying. 'But I can't!'

'Do you prefer the switch?' Mother hissed. 'I shan't use my hand, Mabel; I shall give you a sound thrashing with a birch.' She ignored Mabel's moan. 'Now, up to the nursery, both of you. You will be called presently. Remember to smile when you come in.' With that she nodded to Bellows and was gone.

A children's tea had been laid for us in the nursery, but Mabel couldn't touch the cakes. Her face betrayed the horrifying fear that possessed her. A small evil part of me was glad: she would do badly, and I would be showered with all the adulation. Mother would sing my praises, but Mabel would be thrashed. I stuffed a cake into my mouth and smiled.

And yet another part of me loved her, adored her, and wanted her to shine, wanted her to be admired. Young as I was, I knew the importance of *presentation*, and Mabel's fear-blotched face and scowling mouth were certain to displease the fashionable crowd waiting for us. She had nervously twiddled the big bow perched in her thick red hair so that it now hung crookedly, and instead of sitting down she hopped about from one foot to the other.

'Mabel, do you need to "go"?' I asked. She nodded. 'There.' I pointed, and she quickly darted over to relieve herself. As she sat on the chamberpot I smoothed her hair and set her bow straight.

'I can't remember any of it,' she whispered. 'Not a single word.'

'Of course you can.'

'I shall disgrace us, I know it, I know it.'

Mabel's hair has always enchanted me; at that age, seven as she then was, it was laced with shining golden strands which imparted a true radiance to the red curls. I kissed her head so that I could smell the clean kittenness of it and said: 'You're afraid. You can't be afraid.'

'I shall ruin everything. We shall never be asked back. People will laugh at me,' she insisted.

I stroked her hair slowly and said again: 'You mustn't be afraid.' Then a stroke of inspiration came on me. 'What do you wish for?' I asked.

This was a game we had invented one rainy afternoon in our tent house.

Mabel thought for a moment as she pulled up her drawers. 'I wish I was back at home, and this whole afternoon was over,' she said.

'What else do you wish?'

'I wish I knew all the words to all the poems and *The Pickwick Papers*.'

I made a magical sign over her head. 'Your wish has been granted, Miss Mabel Beardsley. You now know all the words and will be able to recite them perfectly.'

Bellows appeared in the doorway. 'Your presence is requested in the drawing-room. If you will follow me?'

We stood outside the drawing-room door, listening to Mrs Sparks speaking from within. Mabel clutched my hand as impressive phrases that seemed to have nothing to do with us – 'talented children', 'infant prodigies of verse and the keyboard' – were intoned. Bellows opened the drawing-room door. We stood for a moment looking in at the assembled crowd of well-dressed ladies, all of them staring intently, then I pulled Mabel's hand and we entered.

Two small chairs were placed near the piano, as Mother had said, so that one could sit while the other performed. The piano was a gorgeous Bechstein grand, quite a different kettle of fish from our parlour upright. Mother was seated inconspicuously to one side, as though she were no more than part of the audience, someone who had never seen us before.

The programme had been rehearsed dozens of times. Mabel was to start with a short poem by Wordsworth. Even my heart was thumping in anticipation. Mabel stared straight ahead without seeing. 'Your wish has been granted,' I whispered. And with that she gave a short nod, stepped forward and recited the poem, word-perfect, only her tightened voice betraying her fear. She did not acknowledge the sprinkle of applause, but turned quickly and sat down, her face crimson.

Now I solemnly made my way to the enormous piano and seated myself before its keyboard. The beauty of the instrument spoke to me. ' "Fading Away," ' I announced, and set my fingers on the keys. The sound was so rich, so plummy, so sonorous, that the piece seemed to play itself. All I did was listen.

Somehow we made it through that first afternoon, our début, without shaming ourselves or Mother. The duet was fairly dismal, but I made up for it with the other short bagatelles and nocturnes I played. When it was over, Mabel and I stood together and acknowledged the applause. Mabel curtsied. I bowed. Then we ran to Mother, whose hands squeezed our shoulders and pulled our ears as she fielded compliments and took orders for future performances.

'So charming, Mrs Beardsley! Such talent! I wonder if the children mightn't come to me for a small soirée?'

She was glowing and exultant afterwards, and bought us each a chocolate at Lindmayer's. We had earned a guinea, and Mother no doubt had visions of gold heaped at her feet. 'Miss Franklin says you have already an amazing technique, Aubrey,' she reported, 'and you know *she* is one of the best pianists in Brighton.' Now it was Mabel's turn for a compliment, but she never got one. 'Mabel, your posture left something to be desired, dear. A lady never slouches.'

Even Father, to whom the idea of our playing in public was detestable, was curious about the outcome. Mother informed him that we had another engagement in a week's time. 'Those present who know of such things said Aubrey is a true *Wunderkind*. If he continues, with proper instruction, he may be a virtuoso one day.'

I wasn't certain what 'virtuoso' meant – did it mean I would be particularly virtuous? – but I tucked away this bit of information. I was special. Something about me was extraordinary. I didn't feel particularly extraordinary – and yet, I must confess, I did feel somehow 'set off' from others. This may have been the result of our queer isolation. Mabel was my sole playmate, we were allowed no others; and our life of voracious reading, playing and reciting, and hiding in our playhouses did not give me much opportunity to gauge myself against other boys.

Our next recital, which took place one rainy evening, and for which the audience was more splendidly arrayed than in any engraving, was such a success that we were asked to perform again, and again. Word of our remarkable talents spread among the hostesses of Brighton, and soon Mother was accepting 'engagements' with the aplomb of a theatrical agent. The guinea we had earned at Mrs Sparks's eventually rose to two.

The money-making side of our talents was rarely discussed, however; perhaps because, when we worked, we out-earned Father. Once I saw a hostess press an envelope into Mother's hand before we left, understood that this was our payment, and always thereafter waited for this exchange with a certain formal expectation. Mother – irked beyond words for having to accept what was, after all, charity – always looked gratefully humble, and there was often some pretence of improvement in the encounter: the hostess might say, for instance, 'I hope this will allow your little boy to continue with his lessons.' The power of money was not lost on me. New books arrived, special toys, and there was even talk of a new piano.

Performing became a kind of artificial second-nature. I grew accustomed to people staring at me, and eventually quite liked it. Mabel, with her continuing stage fright, was never particularly enthusiastic until afterwards, by which time her blood would be coursing with the excitement of it all.

For it *was* exciting. It had a dream-like glamour. To enter strange houses, filled with fawning adults, to make music on all manner of fine pianos, to accept applause as my rightful due – I would not have changed it. I wonder now, Father, not only if these early years fostered in me a kind of creative singlemindedness, but also if they somehow contribute to the immense contempt for the public which sometimes overwhelms me.

I was still prey to odd fits of illness – queer little aches and chills that would blow over me like a March wind, and make me want to sleep for hours. One of these coincided with a summer fête at which Mabel and I were to perform, and I hid my symptoms from Mother so that I might play. I remember quite distinctly how life went on around me – how we prepared to go – and how everything seemed peculiarly sharpened, significant somehow, with the flushed energy of fever. I felt ennobled by my ability to perform despite sickness, and entertained lively if distorted fantasies about the crowd at the fête, and how I would impress them.

I managed my first piece, a little Chopin nocturne, without too much difficulty, but while Mabel was reciting the skating scene from *The Pickwick Papers* I felt myself slowly starting to spin. A bilious desire to vomit came over me as Mabel went on and on: ' "Mr Winkle struck wildly against him, and with a loud crash they both fell heavily down." ' The audience gave their customary titter, I rose as if to say something, and keeled over in a spectacular faint.

Dear Père Coubé, writing of that first introduction to the illness that would later make such a mockery of my life, I had to stop – for I was overcome with rage. I wanted to curse God, not praise Him. Yes, I must accept it; must, as you say, offer it up to God; must believe that it is a test and a sign from Him. Yet beyond those intellectual exercises – for thus they remain, so long as this bitter dust chokes my soul and makes prayer a sterile muttering – there is the daily reality of my abominable health to contend with: the tonics, tablets, baths, blisters, elixirs, the pre-dawn walks (or crawls, rather) in the Bois, the endless contradictory doctors, and the exhaustion of hope itself. That those who enjoy the miracle of a sound body can pretend to know what it is like to be constantly aware of death's pincers; that they can fatuously give advice when they have no idea of the willpower required to remain civil when one is mortally ill; *that they can pretend to know what it is like* infuriates me beyond measure.

I was but seven years old when the signs of consumption were first diagnosed. My body withstood this first assault upon itself, that initial siege, by erecting a barrier of fire. I burned and coughed within it. I could not eat, I could not rest, so long as the sirocco blew its hot breath into my flaming blood. My teeth chattered, I moaned, I tossed on a lake of flames, crying out in a voice that the wall of fire rendered into coughing or phlegmy gibberish.

I was taken to Buckingham Road and examined by my grandfather, who was more accustomed to battle wounds and malaria than he was to consumption. Cold vinegar compresses were laid on my burning head and limbs; I was laid in tubs of icy sea-water. I heard crying; I saw my parents seated anxiously beside the bed, my father holding my mother's hand. I wanted Mabel, for she was so often in the queer distortions that racked my fever-singed brain – Mabel, with her hair the colour of coals when they are glowing hottest.

One night I opened my eyes, wondering where I was. The fever had ceased its raging, though it still held me in a hot crisped swaddling. I had been dreaming of something exaggerated and grotesque, and the dream was somehow accompanied by the tunes I played on the piano – 'Fading Away' was one of them – only they were enormous tunes, expressive of an emotion terrifyingly new to me; they thundered and echoed until suddenly all was quiet, and that was when my eyes opened.

The light of a full moon filled the room like a white lunar virus, slowly dusting the furniture and objects into familiarity. But there was something unfamiliar in the room, something that I sensed before I saw. My eyes were drawn to a point on the wall which seemed to glow with some fine radiance, as though the roses in the wallpaper had been blown into full scented life.

There on the wall, dear Father, against the background of hot quivering roses, I saw a crucifix where no crucifix had ever hung. And nailed to the cross was Christ. His wounds dripped blood. His agony was eternal. He was in a garden of roses, yet for him the garden was as barren as Death. As I stared, struck dumb with terror and a kind of inexplicable rapture, the crucifix silently fell to the floor, and I dropped back into a cool stream of sleep. It was that night, I later discovered, that my fever finally broke.

I have told only one other person of that vision, Father, for seeing it seemed to mark me out for some special fate – and it is not a fate that I want or would choose for myself. It is, I suppose, a vision of reciprocal agony. It acted as a kind of brand, searing itself into my inner being. And, truth to tell, dear Père Coubé, I have attempted to rid myself of the burning scar it left in my soul. Yet would I be recalling it for you now, in these pages, if I did not think it bore some special relevance to my life?

The illness left me weak and chastened; and now, mulling over the circumstances of that first illness, I find it curious that it came upon me just at the time when I was beginning to excel at the piano. The illness took the piano away from me – oh, not instantly and entirely, but gradually, in increments. Later it snatched away my hopes for a theatrical career. Now it has – at least, temporarily – taken my drawing away. It has taken all things from me, everything I want, and eventually it will take my life itself. And you say I must offer up this grotesque subtraction of creative life to God, with thanksgiving! Seen in a certain dry hard light, Father, the self-abnegation of Christianity is utterly repugnant. Surely it is the individual Self in each of us that we should worship, not the absence of that Self.

However, I confess that I did enjoy my convalescence; and, when I was moved home, soon became quite accustomed to the attention it brought me. I lay enthroned in bed, the child as Pasha, half-lying, half-sitting, on soft feather pillows, wrapped in Mother's cool Chinese silk shawl. This shawl, fringed in black and with a faint ivory pattern woven into the white silk, was a luxurious relic of her past life; it lay hidden away most of the time and was brought out only for special celebrations. Mother was nearly always at my bedside, spooning meat broth into my mouth, or feeding me a sweet little cake, or sponging me with vinegar; I was allowed to sip port wine mixed with water; I was read to, fussed over; and drifted rather happily – especially after being given one of the nerve tonics prescribed by Grandfather – in that dreamy isolated world of invalidism I have since come to despise. Mabel was no longer allowed to sleep with me, however, and at night I often felt tiny and alone without her beside me.

Plenty of fresh air was prescribed, so it was not long before I was taken out for walks, and often it was my father who took me. He never said much – always there was that gulf between us – but he would take my hand in his or, if I were tired, hoist me on to his shoulders. On fine late-summer evenings we would traverse the Promenade several times, halting to watch the sun drop into the sea. I always wondered what he was thinking as he watched those fiery Brighton sunsets. Life seemed vast, sad and grandly mysterious at such moments. I wondered if he were disappointed in me because I was not one of the shouting, screaming, hoop-rolling boys flying past us on the Promenade, filled with blind masculine energy.

Perhaps he was guiltily recalling his own illness, now in remission, which he had passed on to me.

Walking beside him, my hand engulfed by his, which was rough and callused, or perched on his beefy shoulders, I revelled in his animal strength, gained from loading kegs of beer – the employment he hated and that was so beneath him.

I had grown quite accustomed to the pleasures of convalescence – indeed, could quite happily have continued the regime – when one morning my mother asked how I would like to attend school. A sharp fear of the unknown pierced me. School? Leave home?

'I have spoken to Miss Wise and Miss Barnett,' Mother said, 'and made arrangements for you at Hamilton Lodge.'

'I don't want to go to school!' I insisted, forcing a little cough for sympathy.

'You will learn all kinds of things there,' said Mother soothingly, probably secretly a little glad that I did not wish to leave the warm comforts of her care.

'I don't want to go!'

'Aubrey, I have made the arrangements. Hamilton Lodge is not far away – only eight miles, just over the Downs. It's a lovely school, and you will be quite happy there.'

'I shall hate it!' And, in truth, I already did. My lively imagination had concocted all manner of miseries and dreadful possibilities. Mostly, I suspect, I was afraid of the other children, who would bully and tease me and make my life miserable.

'Darling, it is something you *must* do. It is important for you just now to be in the country, high on the Downs where the air is healthy and invigorating. You will get nice and strong at Hamilton Lodge, and there will be other boys for you to play with.'

'What boys?'

'Boys from very nice families.'

'Will they be my age or older?' I asked.

'Both,' said Mother.

'Is there a piano?'

My question flustered her; she rose from the bed and began to busy herself in the room. 'There will be no more piano for you,' she said. 'At least, for a time.'

My wishes counted for nothing; a child's never do. Before the summer was over a dogcart was hired and Mother and I set out over the Downs to Hurstpierpoint. Mother, I remember, pulled out a pair of French Kislov gloves from somewhere; the tight leather, smelling faintly of eau-de-Cologne, stretched like a membrane across her bony hands and fingers. No doubt she wanted to look as smart as she had before her marriage. Those gloves, Father, introduced me to the same hidden sensuality as that of her silk shawl; only your countrymen, of course, know how to make gloves which must be fitted on to each finger like a miniature silk stocking.

I said goodbye to Father and Mabel, and we rattled off. It was one of my first long drives, and was exciting for that; but at the end of it I would be left by my mother at a strange new school. The cart rattled over the ancient chalky road worn across the Downs, and I sat holding on to Mother's mysteriously gloved hand, dividing my attention bertween that, the trotting rump and half-lifted tail of the horse, and the sight of the Downs and the sea, both of which seemed huge and mysteriously unfathomable under a billowing English sky.

Mother's hat cast a huge shadow as she leaned over the back of my head. 'You will learn to like it, darling,' she whispered.

'What if I don't?'

'You *must* learn.'

'All the other boys – will they tease me?'

'If they do, you need only tell Miss Wise or Miss Barnett.'

'I shan't see you, or Mabel, or Father again until the term is over.'

'It will go faster than the blink of an eye,' Mother assured me. 'And every week you will write us a letter, and every day I shall write to you.'

They were only words, and did nothing to relieve the sad hollow ache of my impending loneliness. I sat in a puddle of gloom and apprehension as we jerked and bumped our way on, roused only when the driver pointed his whip and said: 'Hamilton Lodge straight ahead, ma'am.'

LYSISTRATA.

THIS MORNING, FATHER, I woke sobbing and spurting from a dream which refuses to evaporate and continues to haunt my waking mind. I have done nothing wrong, yet the substance of the dream convinces some part of me that I have committed an actual soul-worrying transgression.

I thought I had left her, my prick-nagging Venus, back in England. I thought my final homage to her was the set of *Lysistrata* drawings; and that from henceforth, especially after so much

65

illness, she would leave me in peace. Then this dream appeared, forcing me to admit that the old queen still lurks in some piss-dank corner of my mind, threatening always, like an unwanted relative, to thrust herself into my notice.

There I lay, my night shirt soaked in sperm, coughing blood that always flecks some white surface, no matter how many handkerchiefs are at hand. The dream still had me in its fevered licentious grip, and I had to find a way to sponge away the outcome of my *rêve mouillé* before Mother noticed. I felt filthy, within and without; and of course it was four o'clock, and time for Dr Lamarre's regimen.

It is too much, I kept thinking, it is too much. I thought of the forest; of the distant tantalizing shrine to Our Lady, which I have yet to find; of the sharp-edged pain that slices through my lungs after too much exertion. I looked into the frothy pink ooze I had spat up; I remembered the dream, and thought of Mabel – the real Mabel, not the dream-slut who danced and enticed me into her arms – darling Mabel, who is on her way to us from America. And, dear Father, I began to howl. I did so quite silently, in good British fashion, but it was none the less a howl – of rage, of misery, of pain, of torment, of frustration, of the sheer unknowing that engulfs my life on all sides like a vast ocean. Am I allowed no certainties? Is there not one thing – just one – that I may claim as my own? I may not draw. I may not dream. I may not wake like the young man I am, with a healthy sprint and vigorous plans for my life; no, I must wake with a bloody cough, covered with my foul emissions, open my eyes on another day of grisly mortality, in which I have to wheeze for every breath I take – robbed of the very air that gives God's creatures their life. Does He hate me so much that he begrudges me even one deep breath?

I could not get up to begin my pre-dawn forest creepings; I could not, that is all. It has done nothing to help me so far, and I fancied that I actually felt worse for the damp air of the forest. Also, I have developed an unreasonable horror of the oily-skinned porter, who sits at the desk in a thin harsh glare of gaslight and seems to me like some ghastly Virgilian shade, speaking in riddles and guarding an entrance to the Underworld.

The forest before dawn has its adorable points, I grant you, but I am ill-equipped to appreciate any of them. Its only value is an aesthetic one: I notice details within different shades and gradations of darkness, and that is of some artistic interest. In terms of health, however, the cure has done nothing to rid me of the small haemorrhages that still come upon me at odd hours. I said the very same thing to Dr Lamarre when he came for his weekly inspection this afternoon.

'The forest air, Doctor, may be at its best between the early hours of four and six,' I said to him, 'but those also happen to be precisely the hours when my sleep is the soundest.'

He removed the lid from my chamberpot samples, drew back slightly at the sight, and then swirled the mixture at arm's length. 'For the cure to be successful, Monsieur Beardsley, the patient must, above all, not resist it.'

'Surely there's more health to be gained in two good hours of sleep than in these pre-dawn peregrinations?'

'It is the inhalation of the forest air at precisely those hours when it is freshest that acts as the central tonic for repairing the tissue of the lung,' the good doctor sternly reasserted.

'If it's repairing my lung, why am I still spitting blood?' I asked, not unreasonably I thought.

'These *crâchements* are relieving a long-settled congestion, Monsieur Beardsley; nothing could have been worse for your case than the damp sea air in Bournemouth – air which invites catarrh and respiratory ailments of all sorts. The blood-spittings are very good for you just now, so long as the forest air fills your lungs between four and six.'

'No, I think I shall give up the walks,' I said, with a thrill of insubordination.

That was when he sensed he might lose me as a patient; lose that pleasant jangle of francs which I put into his pocket every week. I've seen this transition with many doctors, and it never fails to amuse and disgust me. For all their purported care, money makes them care more. You keep a doctor, frankly, only so long as you can believe in him; if you begin doubting his wisdom, you are already looking for another doctor.

'I think, also,' I said, 'that I should be allowed wine. The ulcer on my tongue has now healed, and the milk here gives me wind.'

'Wine, I said, would be added to your diet within weeks.'

'And fish. I want fish and meat, and wine.'

'A glass of Vin Mariani as a digestive,' he bartered, 'might not be a bad idea, but only a glassful after the meal. Water to be drunk with the food.'

'I am not a monkey; I cannot subsist on milk and fruit. It was tried before, and it did nothing to help me. I am hungry for meat and fish; it is absurd to be denied French cooking when I am in France. And I want wine with my meals and Vin Mariani afterwards; and sweets, I want sweets. And most of all, Doctor, I want to sleep between four and six.'

Dr Lamarre is a small and rigidly precise man, much decorated, the darling of societies and institutions I have never heard of. His dress is admirably fastidious, and I often have the urge to look into his bag. Dr Lamarre never carries this bag himself; a young assistant does it for him. It appears to be filled with all manner of mysterious instruments – tools really – neatly stacked and coiled. Such medical arsenals fill me with absurd hope when I first see them; and then, increasingly, as their contents fail to do anything but scrutinize my decline, I begin to imagine how I might use those same instruments to torture the man who wields them.

'If the value of the cure lies in the forest air,' I went on, watching with delight as he began nervously to rub his hands together (doctors hate to listen, have you noticed?), 'why could I not simply open my window and inhale it while sleeping?'

'The organs are not sufficiently engaged while the body slumbers,' he said. 'In order fully to expel the poisons and ingest the salubrious benefits of the forest air, the patient must exert the diseased organs strenuously.'

'Doctor, I should love to be dancing a bolero on the stage, I should love to skip, hop and jump through the forest, but you seem not to understand – I cannot do so. My chest is so inflamed with pain when I return after the two hours that I am unable to move comfortably for the rest of the day.'

'That is a good sign,' he avowed.

'No, Doctor Lamarre, it is a bad sign. For the sufferer, it is a bad sign. And spitting blood – that, Doctor, is a bad sign, and it depresses me horribly.'

He turned away, avoiding my eyes, as he said: 'If you will not listen to me, Monsieur Beardsley, I doubt if I can do anything more for you.'

There! We were at the point of no return. He wanted me to submit unquestioningly to his medical authority, and I refused to do so. These moments with doctors – God knows I've lived through enough of them – must be similar to lovers' tiffs, the moment poised between reconciliation and final rupture until one or the other weakens and gives in.

'I would not be averse', Dr Lamarre said after a sufficiently thoughtful pause, 'to letting you sleep with the window open – provided the bed were moved closer to it.'

'That can be arranged,' I said, the shyly victorious lover.

'Vin Mariani as a digestive,' he insisted.

'And wine with meals.'

He ignored this, which amounted to acquiescence. 'I want you on the terrace at least twice a day, and at precisely ten o'clock every morning you are to be wheeled into the Bois for a two-hour airing.'

'In a chair?' He nodded. 'They do have a rather charming cart.'

'Chair or cart,' said Dr Lamarre wearily.

'And fish and meat,' I added.

'Provided you continue to eat fruit after each repast.'

'Of course.'

'I shall pay my respects to your mother before I leave,' he said, closing his case.

'Thank you, Doctor.'

When he left I knew it was over between us.

An invalid's relationship with his doctor – *doctors*, I should say – makes for an interesting study. One longs for the perfect doctor, just as one longs for the perfect wife or lover or even parent. One sinks into sentimental reveries: the perfect doctor; the one you can trust absolutely; the one who truly cares for you and is endlessly sympathetic to your wearying ailments; the one who will provide, at last, the relief you have been seeking.

Mr Raffalovich's personal physician, Dr Phillips, is such a one. When I was briefly under his care in London I knew a comfort which is difficult to explain in words. I've just written to Mr Raffalovich, in fact, to thank him for the gift he sent today, and mentioned that when Dr Phillips travels to the Continent, which he does frequently, going often to Paris, I would be grateful if he could examine me here in St-Germain. It is, after all, only a half-hour from St-Lazare, even if they seem like different universes. So high sits Dr Phillips in my esteem that I would even go to Paris for the consultation – no small homage, since even the simplest journey *aux chemins de fer* now induces in me distress like *mal de mer*. Meanwhile I have had the bed moved closer to the window, and can now, with my customary pinched bitterness, look out at the healthy ones taking their pleasure, running, strolling – all of them happily sucking up great lungfuls of beneficial forest air.

Must I call him Mr Raffalovich to you, who know him even better than I? Allow me the liberty of henceforth referring to him as André.

André's gift was a choice three-volume set of the sermons of Bourdaloue, published in 1840. I have dipped in here and there to extract a fiery phrase, a soothing thought, a sombre spiritual truth. But reading, dear Father, even the cadenced majesty of the Jesuit Bourdaloue, is difficult when one's mind is in such dreadful continual fret.

Part of it is that I long to draw again. Dozens of tantalizing ideas twirl on the roundabout of my thoughts. I had hoped Smithers would jump at the *Casanova* idea, but he is elusive; in Paris, before coming here, I began to plan out a series of drawings for Gautier's *Mademoiselle de Maupin*, even portrayed the lady in long lacy drawers to tantalize him, but that project does not advance, either; the two Ali Baba drawings are superb – poor Ali Baba frightened in the wood, and an obscenely fat, jewel-encrusted King of Thieves for the cover – yet that project hangs fire, too, and all because my publisher will not give me a definite undertaking.

I cannot pursue any project (once my health permits) unless I am *absolutely certain* that Smithers will publish it, and his dawdlings and prevarications are at times more than I can bear. I am under exclusive contract to him in return for a weekly salary, but his cheques continually arrive post-dated weeks in advance, or have such mysterious instructions attached about cashing them that I began to think his business must be in severe trouble. As it is, I must be discreet, even swear my patrons to secrecy, when special little private commissions come my way, lest Smithers find out about them and break our contract. Octave Uzanne has asked if I will design a *couverture* for his novel *Thémidore*, for the approval of his Paris publisher; and Herbert Pollitt, most generous and amusing of my private collectors, may be in the market for some new charming little obscenity. My circumstances being what they are, I would have no choice, Father, but to provide them with what they have asked for.

One dreams of the perfect publisher and patron in the same way one dreams of the perfect doctor, or lover, or parent. Smithers is hardly my ideal, but he did take me on when no one else would, for which I am grateful, and we have scraped by these last two years. It is dreadful, however, not to be able to trust someone completely, especially someone on whom one's livelihood depends; never to know when he is telling the truth and when lying to conceal the threat of bankruptcy. John Gray, André's companion, wrote to tell me that he had seen my drawing 'Venus between Terminal Gods' while strolling past Smithers's shop in the Royal Arcade; it was for sale, yet I had no idea it was in Smithers's possession; certainly he never mentioned it to me. One can only conclude that he will make a handsome profit on it and continue to post-date his cheques.

I know you will say that I should pray – and, believe me, dear Père Coubé, my hands are often clasped – but prayer does not solve any of my worldly problems: how to get on with my artistic work, how to trust my publisher, how to believe in my doctor, or convince my mother that we should remain in France, where she never feels quite well. How does one learn how to pray? How does one get beyond the endless bothers of every day and reach the Eternal? Beset as I am at every turn, it is at times difficult to believe in a merciful Providence who cares about my well-being.

Mother keeps to her room at meal-times, and maintains her diet of milk and Vichy water in the hope that her gastritis will be alleviated; but this evening I wheezed my way down to the dining-room to enjoy the superb cooking that Dr Lamarre no longer forbids me. Fresh trout, poached rabbit with a truffle sauce, and tiny carrots no bigger than a cherub's cock were among the delicacies; and one delicious glass of Sauternes and another of Château Latour 1865 put me in a more expansive mood than I have enjoyed of late. Dessert was a rich *crème caramel*, and after that I had coffee with a Vin Mariani to help my digestion.

Now that the season has officially begun, the Pavillon is filling up with visitors, some of whom are quite amusing; none, however, is English. Strange, the way one loathes one's countrymen at home, and misses them abroad. This perennial vagabondage in search of health can be frightfully lonely, but we have at last had the glad news that Mabel has landed at Liverpool, and will be joining us here as soon as she is able. Dear girl, I hope she is not too exhausted from her theatrical tour in America. I am so very excited at the prospect of seeing her again after long months of absence.

It must be the combination of coffee and the coco leaves in the Vin Mariani that has so wonderfully bolstered my spirits, dear Father; certainly I am less fretful than when I wrote earlier. One's mood most definitely flavours what one writes, and in resuming the narrative of my life I have no wish to review the sweeter and more innocent episodes of my childhood through the fog of adult apprehensions.

As I recall, I left the story just as the driver pointed with his whip to a sham-Gothic building atop a hill and said: 'Hamilton Lodge straight ahead, ma'am.'

Do you know the experience of fear, Father? The physiological symptoms which I have since come to know so well, but for entirely different reasons, swept over me as he spoke those simple words: the pumping heart, the clammy hands, the inability to draw a full satisfying breath. I clutched Mother's arm as we began the ascent.

My chief fear was meeting the other boys, whom I imagined to be mean-spirited and ill-behaved – the sort of boys who would cuff your ears and laugh, or knock your hat off and kick your bottom when you bent to pick it up. I had no experience of other children, except for Mabel, and the confinement accompanying my recent illness had increased my delicate tendencies so that I now had a dread of wild noise and activity. Then, too, it was to be my first separation from Mamma, Papa and Mabel.

Hamilton Lodge was run by Miss Wise and Miss Barnett, friends of my mother. We were greeted by the Rubensesque Miss Barnett, whose colour was generally as high as her spirits. How do some people manage to be so incorrigibly cheerful?

'Ellen!' she cried, waving her hands. 'Mrs Beardsley!' Then she caught sight of me, our eyes locked, and a smile like a crescent moon took possession of her face. 'Welcome to Hamilton Lodge, Aubrey!'

The sober Miss Wise now appeared, gravely shaking hands with my mother and asking after our journey.

'The day has been so *glorious*!' cried the inflamed Miss Barnett. She turned her attention to me. 'It must have been *very* refreshing to come bowling over the Downs on such a splendid day.'

All I could think to say was: 'We didn't bowl—'

'Did not,' corrected Mother.

'We did not bowl over the downs. We rattled.'

All three women found this charming, but Miss Barnett's appreciative shrieks were silenced by Miss Wise. I was often to see how Miss Barnett's enthusiasm and excitable nature were kept in check by nothing more than a raised eyebrow from Miss Wise.

Miss Wise's eyebrows were indeed impressive, jet-black and thick as caterpillars, so that when she raised one you felt it was a significant event. Where Miss Barnett was plump, bright and straining, Miss Wise was thin, sombre and reserved. Her complexion was dark, almost olive, while Miss Barnett's was soft and pink.

'We shall have a lovely tea, Mrs Beardsley, before you set off,' Miss Barnett said, ushering Mother into their private parlour. 'Miss Wise will show Aubrey about the place first, so that he may get to know the lie of the land.' The parlour door shut behind them, and I was left in the hallway with Miss Wise.

'First we shall visit the classroom,' said Miss Wise, starting off.

Without thinking I took her hand and felt it shrink a little. Her skin was dry and scaly, slightly reptilian. 'How old are you now, Aubrey?' she asked as we started up the stairs.'

'Seven.'

'Seven,' she murmured. 'Soon you will be almost grown-up.'

'Yes, ma'am.'

'There are other boys here who have been as ill as you have, did you know that?' I shook my head. 'They all come to Hamilton Lodge to regain their strength and to begin their lessons.' She went on to ask me if I could read, and at what level, and whether I knew any arithmetic. 'There will be plenty of fresh air for you here. Do you like games?'

'Some of them,' I said sullenly.

'Which games do you like?'

'Mabel and I play "I wish I had"—' And as soon as I had, I wished I hadn't, for inevitably she asked what sort of game it was. 'It's a wishing game,' I said.

'What do you wish for?'

'You wish for whatever you want but do not have.'

'Yes, I know that game,' Miss Wise said quietly, surprising me, for I had assumed that only Mabel and I, in the whole wide world, played the game.

Miss Wise fished out a bunch of keys and unlocked a door. A furious draught of air from within made it difficult for her to open it. Inside I saw several boys, all tucked in beds; the sash of the window had been raised as high as it could go, and white curtains billowed like flags on a standard.

'This is where you will sleep at night and rest every afternoon,' whispered Miss Wise, leading me past the sleeping boys to the window. The wind off the sea and the Downs was sporadic, but ferocious when it blew, and the high elevation of Hamilton Lodge only helped to conduct gale-force draughts into the room. I stood light-headed in the rush of fresh sweet air. The contours of the surrounding landscape, green treeless downs which led to the flat roll of the sea, stood out in clear sharp outline below us.

But I was more curious about the boys, for I guessed that most of them were only feigning sleep.

'You will meet the other boys after their rest hour,' whispered Miss Wise, ushering me out.

'Was that the classroom?' I asked.

'Why, no. I told you it was where you will sleep, and take your afternoon naps,' said Miss Wise. 'Why do you ask if it is the classroom?'

'Because you said that you would show me the classroom first.'

'Did I?' Her face registered a kind of alarm, which she quickly brought under control.

'Of course you did.'

She put a finger to her forehead and frowned. 'How odd of me to say one thing and do another.'

I shall spare you the details of bidding my mother farewell and settling in for a term at Hamilton Lodge. A huge void loomed about me those first few days, alleviated only by the maternal nature of Miss Barnett. I carried her umbrella when we went out for walks or on excursions; and I think I would have slept with that umbrella, had she permitted it — it gave me such a sense of comfort. Outdoor exercise was a prominent feature of the school, and every day we had a walk and several playground periods in which we were encouraged to inhale as strenuously as possible.

When I think of Hamilton Lodge, I think of wind. It must have been the windiest place in England. Miss Barnett positively worshipped the air there, and would constantly expand her enormous chest, exhorting us to do the same. Windows, whenever possible, were left open.

Miss Wise, who acted as our schoolmistress, was not quite so fond of the chilly zephyrs eternally chasing through the hallways and classroom of Hamilton Lodge, and always seemed to be irritably adjusting her shawls as a kind of rebuke. She was fond of closing or *lowering* the windows that Miss Barnett flung open.

To my surprise, I began to enjoy Hamilton Lodge. Many of the boys were even weaker than I, and would sit drowsing in their fevers as the winds roared around them. They were strange and fascinating, those sick boys with the deadly pallor in their cheeks and the faraway look in their eyes. Some of them would earnestly try to rouse themselves for a lively game of cock-on-the-hill in the playground, but would then lose their animal spirits and slink away. Beside these boys I was a veritable Atlas.

Others there were who seemed to enjoy such restless good health that the afternoon slumber periods were a torment for them. The moment the door was locked they would be out of bed getting into mischief, playing games, talking about the thrilling adventures they would have when they were older. (Some of them knew they would never be older.) There was little of the bullying or teasing I had so feared; indeed, the boys shared a kind of sympathy among themselves. None of us was older than nine, we had all been seriously ill, and I think we were all innocent, difficult as that might be to believe. We were still two or three years away from the torments of the awakening flesh. One boy, Hugh Saunders, I secretly hated and idolized, for I had heard him playing the piano with such effortless grace that I could only regard him as a rival.

I had supposed that I would be allowed to play the instrument myself, but was quickly disabused. Miss Barnett taught the piano, and she exhibited an uncharacteristic severity in musical matters. Mother had always allowed me to do as I pleased on the instrument; Miss Barnett insisted on strict formal discipline. There were endless repetitive scales to be mastered, horrible to one of my temperament. I had no interest in scales; technique irritated me; I wanted *expression*, and of that only my own.

'You have developed many bad habits,' Miss Barnett said, balancing a flat stick on the back of my poised hands. 'When your hands are held correctly on the keyboard, the sticks will not fall off.' With that she had me slowly play the C-major scale. The sticks fell to the floor and were replaced. 'Again.'

I managed to upset Miss Barnett's equanimity every time I sat down at the piano, and the effort of controlling her temper would bring a fierce red glow to her face. For the first time in my life someone was not only unsympathetic but also displeased with what I did, and my frantic attempts to correct my faults and gain Miss Barnett's praise only made my playing worse. 'No, no, no!' she would cry, rapping my knuckles. Even simple tunes were forbidden until I had mastered every odious scale and repetitive exercise she knew. Of course Mother was party to this; she wanted Miss Barnett to drill me mercilessly.

Meanwhile there were other pleasures. Every day we had pudding, and there were walks to the Chinese Gardens, which were a popular place for Temperance Fêtes. There, agitated women too genteel to shout would deliver interminable droning diatribes on the evils of liquor; but occasionally the spirit would move one of them, and her voice would rise to the very top of the pagoda, and the crowd would be infused with her passion. Men would then leap to the stage and take the Pledge never to drink again, and a revivalist spirit would twitter the limbs and souls of those assembled. I think Miss Barnett and Miss Wise brought us so often to Temperance Fêtes because there were also some compelling male preachers, certain to heat the ladies' blood. We boys were all encouraged to take the Pledge, and some did so, but even at seven I had the common sense to resist the pressures of a crowd.

When Myers' Great American Circus came to the Polo Grounds of Preston Park in Brighton, we were all herded off for the great event. There, for the first time, I saw ladies in tights, swinging from a trapeze or slowly wobbling across a high wire. After the examples of British womanhood moaning at the rostrum of Temperance, it was a glorious sight to see those strong unabashed American women doing their dangerous tricks in the air. It was the first time I had seen the natural outline of a woman's body, and it made me curious to see more. These Amazons were set off by American strongmen, and one figure in particular who, costumed as a savage warrior, made a tiger leap through flaming hoops and later performed acrobatics on the back of a cantering horse. To be so strong! So fearless! I imagined myself, whip in hand, shouting at a tiger while the audience gripped the benches in fright.

A drill master came to the school every Thursday to put us through some military paces on the lawn. This was a truly pathetic spectacle, Father. In ragged lines, the sweating, groaning boys of Hamilton Lodge would be forced to march in formation, left, right, quick march. Those boys stopping to cough, or gasp for a breath, were routinely humiliated by the drill master, who, I am certain, regarded us all as effete little snobs playing at illness. We hated the drills, yet when we were taken to see a parade of 20,000 Volunteers led by Prince Edward of Saxe-Weimar we wanted nothing more than to join their ranks.

At that time, Father, it was still the piano, and music, that called to me. I missed the tea-time recitals, and those special evenings when Mabel and I would enter strange candle- or gas-lit music-rooms hand-in-hand, bow and curtsy to the assemblage, and begin our performance. Now, because playing melodies was forbidden, I became restless – or, rather, my inborn creativity did – and sought some other outlet to gain relief. That, dear Father, is how I first began to draw, as a poultice for the inner fester that came from being denied the piano.

Those first scratchings and shadings with a coarse pencil; the sudden deft understanding that this was very difficult, but jolly good

77

fun; Miss Wise's scaly hand gently removing my pencil and showing me a technique for rendering foliage or grass – I remember those firstborn drawing sensations vividly, with a kind of gentle awe, now that the pencil, too, has been forbidden. Oh, my drawing work was not particularly fine, probably did not even show promise, but I was dreadfully proud of it. I copied or traced all the engravings from a big book called *British Cathedrals* – Durham, Ripon, York, Chester, Salisbury, Exeter, I drew them all. That was precision work, similar to exercises on the piano; and I needed something more original, more uniquely me, to offset it. So I began a long series of grotesque figures forming a kind of parade or frieze.

Where did they come from, these strange creatures? They were formed, in part, from my childish observations; but, though these were keen, I was never very skilled at or interested in literal likenesses. I would rearrange and exaggerate their features to amuse myself and to give imagination an airing.

I shan't go on about Hamilton Lodge, shan't recount how one day at the piano I made Miss Barnett so angry that she burst the bounds of her incorrigible good nature and beat me with a switch. Nor shall I tell you of the queer spells Miss Wise began to suffer, when she would nervously pluck at her hands, tearing away bits of the dry flaking flesh until her face would suddenly assume an expression of shocking misery, tears would rain down her gaunt cheeks, and she would run from the classroom stifling a cry. Was she ill? Was she mad? Was she spurned in love, or the only support of her entire family and thus doomed to a lifetime of drudgery among invalid boys? We would sit in stunned fearful silence until the oddly unperturbed Miss Barnett would enter to tell us with a smile that we were to continue our lessons under her tutelage.

My stay at Hamilton Lodge lasted for a year, ending in October 1880, and my moment of supreme triumph came when Hugh Saunders and I played a duet at the breaking-up party. Miss Barnett had by then acknowledged that I was capable of an entire tune, but continually told me about Hugh Saunders's excellence at the keyboard, his well-disciplined technique, and so on, *ad nauseam*. When we sat down to play for the other boys and their parents, Hugh was shaking with apprehension. Halfway through he lost his place entirely. It was an exquisite pleasure to smile sweetly at

Miss Barnett and continue the piece alone, having missed not a single note.

I was removed from Hamilton Lodge because Father had found work in another brewery, this one in London. London! You, who have spent your entire life in the sophisticated milieu of Paris, perhaps cannot imagine what London meant to a boy from Brighton. Oh, certainly Brighton never lacks its own dense crowds of three-and-sixpenny day-trippers, and the front there is always a-swarm with cockneys and invalids and peepshows and barrel organs. But London, Queen of Cities! Suddenly, after spending a year with a handful of under-vitalized boys atop the windy Downs, I was standing on a street-corner in London gazing dumbfounded at a dirty, ragged, shoeless boy, a boy my age, doing cartwheels in the street for the coppers of passers-by. Right there, amongst the crush of iron-clad carriage-wheels, omnibuses, and horses' hoofs, he capered and twirled, taunting Fate, a desperate look on his face.

'Aubrey? Aubrey!' Mother snatched my hand and pulled me away from this and a hundred other distractions. I gazed proudly up at her as we walked down the noisy London streets, pulled into the stream of rushing humanity. Like most provincial women, Mother felt livelier as soon as she set foot in England's greatest metropolis, eager to prove that she was no gawking novice. But London could still bring out the excited girl in her. 'Oh, look – how lovely!' she would gasp suddenly, pulling us over to stare for a moment at some richly laden shop-window. London's lively tumult and anonymous promise of gaiety worked on Mother's senses, no matter how decorous she thought she was.

I remember little of this period of my life, dear Father, except that it introduced me to sin. London, great and secretly wicked city that it is, could hardly have done otherwise.

We lived in lodgings somewhere – Clerkenwell or Holborn it may have been – in rooms that were not terribly cheerful, but which Mother tried to enliven with an assortment of artistic 'effects': draped shawls, Toby Jugs, framed lithographs, bits of colour here and there. But it was difficult to think of those rooms as home. Mother, I know, yearned for something better, but our reduced circumstances remained an ugly fact. What Father made at the brewery was certainly not going to allow us to buy a house in Belgravia.

As in Brighton, she found work as a private music mistress and day governess in the houses of those better off than we. Mother trod a very fine line between friend and employee in some of her positions – I can appreciate it all the more now that I have so often been in similar positions myself – and she used this delicate social skill to great advantage; it allowed her to recommend her own children to the households of the rich and the aristocratic, preferably both.

London, however, was evidently full of talented *Wunderkinder*, all of them vying for attention, and Mother came home day after day with the same forlorn but grimly determined outlook. Then, one day, she entered breathless with the news: 'You and Mabel are to perform at the house of Mrs Kemyss Betty in St James's Square, for the Duke and Duchess of X!' I feel compelled to conceal the identity of this notorious couple, Father Coubé, even though you are sworn never to reveal what you are told under the seal of the confessional. This confession comes by post, and is thus exposed to tampering of all kinds. Were I to reveal the true names of the Duke and Duchess of X attached to the appalling story which follows, they would most certainly haul me into court for libel, though every word I now recount to you is true.

The house in St James's Square was handsome and dignified, as you would expect. Mrs Betty, whose residence it was, was a friend or relation of one of those society women in Brighton for whom Mabel and I had performed in our recent heyday. In short, Mother didn't know Mrs Betty personally, and to this day I have not been able to tell her about the evils practised in St James's Square when the Duke and Duchess of X were in town. For Mother, the house was recommendation enough; the people within must be above reproach, for they were possessed both of money and position.

That Mrs Betty moved in very smart circles was apparent from the gleaming carriages pulling up at her door and disgorging gorgeously dressed men and women. It was a glimpse of the privileged at play, and as we approached I thought for some reason of that ragged boy doing cartwheels all day for the coins of people like these.

Inside all was light, noise, amusement, laughter. Women in low-cut dresses laughed and gossiped behind their fans, darting from one room to the next, while superbly attired rips and dandies stood ogling them. I think Mother had expected a sedate decorum; grave and important dignitaries discussing the Tory politics so dear to her heart. Certainly not this romp. There was evidently to be none of the ceremony we had come to expect from our other 'engagements', no separate room where Mabel and I might go to prepare ourselves beforehand; no formal introduction before a quiet audience. Our cloaks were taken, and we were immediately shown into an ante-room just off the entrance-hall, where we interrupted Mrs Kemyss Betty in low-pitched conversation with a one-eyed officer of the Dragoons. She disengaged herself when we were presented, the officer disappeared, and she stood for a moment looking us over. Mrs Betty's raven tresses gleamed against skin that shone like ivory; she was not young, but maturity did her no disservice. Her décolleté gown was of trimmed blue satin, its skirt quite full as was the fashion then. A tiny beribboned dog with bulging eyes and a pink quivering tongue occupied a permanent niche in her arm.

'Mrs Beardsley, how do you do? And how very kind of your children to fill in at such short notice.' Her voice was rich and low. 'The Duke and Duchess simply adore talented children and were too thrilled when they heard that yours were available.' Here her voice dropped. 'They lost their own, you know, in an accident too appalling to recount.'

'How dreadful,' said Mother.

'Unfortunately, the Duke is not quite well this evening, and has chosen to remain in his room. He would like to greet the children individually, however, when they have finished playing.'

'The children would be honoured to meet his Grace,' said Mother.

'He insisted that we should not call off the soirée on his account. The dear Duke is really one of the most selfless people I know.'

'And the Duchess?' prodded Mother.

'This is her birthday celebration,' said Mrs Betty. 'I'm certain we shall find her somewhere with a glass of champagne – or a young man – in her hand.'

Mother clutched our hands a little tighter than usual as we followed Mrs Betty and her tiny dog through a series of splendidly appointed rooms, all of them open for the obvious pleasure of her dozens of guests. Curious eyes followed our progress, voices murmured in speculation, and everywhere there was such a vision of rich stuffs that you could half-believe that all those barefoot children shivering outside in the streets, dancing, hawking matches, sweeping street-crossings, blacking shoes, begging, singing for a penny, were nothing but a grotesque mirage.

At last we were brought before a couch where the Duchess of X sat with a sheaf of hothouse lilies, holding her birthday court. The panoply of diamonds and emeralds sparkling on her high puckered bosom could not disguise the fact that she was definitely a queer-looking thing, with a capacious brow, receding chin, sharp little nose, and dark, darting, nervous eyes. When we were introduced I attempted to please her by saying: 'Happy birthday, madame.'

'At my age birthdays are never happy, my dear,' she said. 'Now, we have been told that you and your sister are quite a talented pair.'

'Yes, madame, we are,' I said. Mother started to reprove my effrontery, but the Duchess of X hushed her as if she were no better than a servant – which, in these circumstances, she was.

'If the boy is talented, let him say so,' she said. 'Now, will you play something for all these pretty people?'

'I bowed and went to the piano. 'A Nocturne by Chopin,' I announced. It was no good: the birthday guests would not be quiet, and obviously had no interest in my musical talents. I played as nobly as I could, hoping to impress, but only the Duchess applauded.

'That was excellent,' she said, and turned to Mabel. 'And what, my dear, is your speciality?'

'I recite . . . madame,' said Mabel.

'Will you recite something for me?' asked the Duchess.

Mabel launched at once into Tennyson's *The Princess*, which Mother had recently added to her repertoire:

> ' "Man for the field and woman for the hearth:
> Man for the sword and for the needle she:
> Man with the head and woman with the heart:
> Man to command and woman to obey . . ." '

I could see the hooded eyelids of the Duchess begin to droop after a few stanzas, and she kept herself awake by darting her dark strange eyes my way. I was suddenly very aware of those frosty orbs as they wandered over me, taking me in, coolly appraising me as might a bird of prey its next tender victim. There was nothing warm in those eyes, which seemed rather to be lit with self-serving cunning.

She has lost her children, and perhaps she will try to adopt Mabel and me, I thought nervously, full of unease as the Duchess continued to examine me before turning her attention back to Mabel.

'That was very splendid indeed,' she said, interrupting Mabel mid-line and motioning for me. When I went to her, she put two talon-like fingers to my mouth and popped in a peppermint sweet, then pressed into my hand a whole small bag of them. 'Will you go up now to greet the Duke? He has been much looking forward to it.' She motioned for a servant. 'Take the boy up to the Duke. You, my dear' – to Mabel – 'shall recite another pretty poem, and then go up yourself.'

Mabel was nervously piping away on another poem by Tennyson as I was led off by a well-starched maid.

> ' "But where is she, the bridal flower,
> That must be made a wife ere noon?
> She enters, glowing like the moon
> Of Eden in its bridal bower." '

The maid silently made her way to the stairs, looking neither to the right nor to the left as we passed through the increasingly raucous throng of merrymakers; there was a glimpse of a laden buffet-table, aching, one would have thought, with the weight of those hams and turkeys and joints; there was a knot of particularly animated drinkers around the punch-bowl; card-players of serious mien; couples dancing to music provided by a small orchestra; the maid – I wondered what her name was, and if she had any kind of life of her own – making her way through it all as though she were nothing more than a blinkered horse.

A pale, mustachioed face thrust itself into mine as we wended our way through the rooms, and a voice asked: 'Where are you off to, my lad?'

'I'm going to see the Duke.'

'The Duke? At your age? Did Brown send you from Curzon Street?'

'No, sir. I came with my mother and sister.'

He gave me a look of such astonishment that I thought perhaps I was mad. Didn't any of these people know that Mabel and I had been asked to perform here this evening? Already, you see, I was vain enough to consider myself noteworthy.

How the furnishings of those grand houses lured my eyes, Father; I could not help but compare this way of life to my own. I shall possess such a house one day, I thought, noting the oil paintings, the delicate crystal pendants twinkling on the chandeliers, the runner of Turkey carpet on the stairs. I shall own such a house, and we shall all live in it, and when I play the piano people will listen to me.

My childish reverie was cut short by the maid's sharp rapping on a door set far down a corridor on the first floor. The party noises from below were muffled, the light subdued, the hallway cold.

'One moment,' said a voice from within, and then: 'You may enter.'

'The boy, sir,' said the maid. She waited for her dismissal, curtsied, and disappeared.

A huge wood fire snapped and roared on the far side of the room, but there was otherwise no light. Seated in a leather wing-chair close by the flames was the Duke of X, wearing a dark dressing-gown. 'Come in, my boy,' he said, motioning for me to approach.

The Duke was then about sixty, but he was quite small and had a curiously boyish look, as though some youthful part of his soul was permanently immune from decay. For a bizarre moment I felt that I was confronting someone my own age, a boy trapped in the husk of an old man. His eyes were round and bright, his silvery hair abundant, and his smile and manner most welcoming. He didn't look at all ill.

'I must congratulate you on your playing,' he said. 'I paid keen attention, you know. Heard every note.' The room was utterly silent except for the dry chatter of the fire; not a sound from downstairs could be heard. How, then, did the Duke hear my brief nocturne? 'Few boys your age are so experienced on the keyboard,' he said. 'You are how old?'

'Eight . . . your Grace.'

'Come closer to the fire. It's warmer here.' He coaxed me to his side with an elfin smile. I now saw that he was sweating as profusely

84

as a Turk in his hammam, and his lineaments no longer looked quite so boyish. His face was covered with innumerable pits, perhaps from smallpox, and nervous anxiety seemed to have squeezed a large protuberance out between his eyebrows, where it shone in the dew of his sweating face like an incipient horn of pearl. 'Will you take a cordial with me?' he asked, pouring a thick green liquid into two tiny glasses on the table beside him. He handed one of the glasses to me, as if I were his equal.

Never before had I been offered anything more than port wine and water or a sip of Father's beer, and it seemed quite charming, the idea of sipping from this tiny glass, in the company of a duke.

'I think eight must be the very best age to be,' said the Duke. 'So full of wild animal spirits and endless curiosity. So rough-and-tumble with the other boys. Is that how it is with you?'

'Not exactly, sir.'

'No? Then, you must be that other sort of boy. There are two kinds, you know. The ones who explore from without, and the ones who explore from within.'

I sipped my cordial nervously; it was deliciously sweet and mingled harmoniously with the peppermint I was secretly sucking in the side of my mouth. With a nonchalant gesture the Duke reached his hand around to pat my bum and pull me up to his knee. His smile was puckish and secretive as his hand suddenly began to pluck and press persistently at the front of my trousers. I had no idea what he was trying to do; but then he undid my buttons, reached in, and began to diddle me.

Dear Father, I stood there like a paralysed idiot while the Duke, one hand in my trousers, fumbled open his robe and undid his own buttons. What particularly terrified me was his complete change of demeanour; his eyes, in particular, were at first frantic, pleading, pathetic – but as the moments passed they became boldly lascivious. Evidently no amount of sweat raining out from that pitted flesh could cool the insane fever now burning in his veins. That I was the object of his desire still had not occurred to me; it made no sense to what knowledge I had of life. I wanted to run from him, but I could not escape without pulling his hand away, and I was afraid to do so. He was a duke, after all.

The cordial splashed out of my glass and on to the Duke's trouser leg, whereupon he hastily snatched my free hand and pulled it towards his crotch. My clenched fingers brushed against his organ, very erect but very tiny, hardly bigger, it seemed, than a large acorn.

'Frig me, boy, frig me,' he whispered frantically, a horrid coy smile playing for a moment on his lips. Then, when I failed to understand his meaning, he extended his legs, held me by my wrist with one hand and did something to himself with his other. It made no sense to me at all.

And it was over so quickly. He let go of my wrist, pulled free a handkerchief and brought it to his groin, let out a gasp, a groan, and seemed to go into a galvanic seizure. Then, as rapidly as his demeanour had changed from old boy to satyr, it changed back again. He shot up, deftly wiped himself with the handkerchief and cast it into the fire, quickly rearranged his clothing, retied his robe, smoothed his hair and pulled the bell.

'You are a very good boy to come and visit me,' he said, tousling my hair. That was when I finally knew that I hated him, when he tousled my hair. My hair has never lent itself to tousling; until last November I wore it parted severely in the centre with a front fringe. 'I am going to give you half a crown,' he said, 'for your wonderful piano-playing. Would you like that?'

I said nothing. The cheapest people on the face of the earth are the rich. The Duke held out this paltry sum as though I should be thrilled to have it, but a sudden obstinacy kept me from extending my palm. I refused to look at the coin and stared instead at him.

'Take it,' he urged, trying to avoid my eyes.

I stared.

'Take it, or I shall give it to your sister instead.'

I stared.

He said, with a changed voice and a nervous smile: 'What do you want, a gold sovereign?'

I hadn't, until that moment. I nodded.

'A gold sovereign! My, you're a very expensive boy.' He turned his back and went to rummage somewhere beyond the glare of firelight. 'I don't think I've ever given any other boy a gold sovereign. But, then,' – turning back to me and dropping a surprisingly heavy coin into my hand – 'you are a very special boy. You know that, don't you?'

I studied the gold sovereign and nodded.

'You know how to keep a secret, don't you?' whispered the Duke, but his terror was betrayed just then by a rap on the door. He was no longer the young boy trapped in the body of an old man; in a revelatory instant I saw that the knowledge of sin was his, and that sin had the power to change a face. The little Duke suddenly looked quite aged, a sad, experienced roué. 'Give me your hand on it, and your word of honour,' he said quickly.

But I wouldn't touch him again, and backed away towards the door. 'Wait!' he hissed, then called for the maid – the same one – to enter, and instructed her to return me to my mother. I remember how he stared after me as I left, how hellish he looked in the ruddy firelight, and how puzzled and upset I felt by the entire encounter.

We passed a long mirror in the hallway, and I stopped to rearrange my hair. Whilst I was doing so, Mabel's reflection briefly appeared behind mine. There was a frightened look on her face. She was being led off, as were all children who came to perform there, to a private audience with the Duke of X.

I wanted to protect her, but I didn't know how; which made me feel like a coward. I turned round and shouted down the corridor, 'Mabel!' – catching her just as the maid was opening the door to show her in. The maid accompanying me said crossly: 'Do come along!' And from far down the corridor Mabel looked pleadingly at me before she was ushered in.

Sin, Father. The Duke could not resist a compulsion to do evil, and he did it with the full complicity of his wife, don't you think? Practised often, was it, like a sacrament for the devout? Or was it a special perversity reserved only for special occasions, such as the Duchess's birthday? Did she experience pleasure, too? Did he tell her about it afterwards, when her hair had been combed out and the servants had left them alone? Did she smile, ask for more detail, flatter him on his performance? Perhaps the whole thing had begun with a suggestion from her, a sympathetic understanding of his ways. A cosy domestic arrangement in any case, wouldn't you agree?

Such are my adult speculations on the matter. As a boy of eight, quite unaware of such possibilities, I knew only that something curious and rather unpleasant had happened to me, that some violation had occurred, and that I had a gold sovereign to show for the experience. I did not recognize it as evil, not then, only as somehow 'bad', and that only because the Duke had enjoined me not to tell of it. (And I have not done until now.)

It is astonishing, Father, the seductions practised by adults on children. My publisher Smithers is not very different: as a special treat for himself I have known him to pay upwards of £200 for the privilege of deflowering a young French virgin. And, when I read in the papers last year that W. T. Stead had established an agency for the adoption of orphans in London, even I half-fancied to adopt a nice little girl to satisfy my maternal, amatory and educational instincts. Who doesn't wish to stroke innocence?

The stain of our adult souls must begin somewhere, and for me it began with that secretive firelit encounter with the Duke of X. More than anything else it was an intellectual puzzle. What did it all mean? How was I involved in it?

Meanwhile, my parents had decided to move yet again. This time we were going to the spa town of Epsom, 'so you can get strong again', as Mother said, although the real reason was that London was too dear. She missed Brighton and her family, and Epsom was at least on the railway line there, and we could have better lodgings for less money. How I envy those children whose childhoods are spent in one place, and who develop an intimate familiarity with the sight of a church tower, or an ivy-clad wall, or a garden of wallflowers that comes up year after year. My life, dear Père Coubé, seems to have been spent packing and unpacking and packing once again.

Father kept his job in London and took the train in every morning and back every evening. We didn't see him much, and when he was around he was generally silent and full of a bitterness so deep that Mabel and I were afraid of him. He hardly spoke to Mother, nor she to him. Their lives – once so romantic, so full of promise – had been reduced to scratching along, denying themselves so that Mabel and I might at least have the advantages of the middle class over the lower. Mother continued to work, though her wages as a music mistress were wretchedly low and sporadic. I recall that Mabel and I gave one or two more recitals. And then Lady Henrietta Pelham entered our lives.

Lady Henrietta was a dear, and she helped to restore the aristocracy to favour in my mind. She was an old friend of the Surgeon-Major and Mrs Pitt, my Brighton grandparents – had known them in Burma, I believe; in any case, one day she came to visit us at our house in Ashley Road in Epsom.

Now, by that time, Father, the drawing demon had made his presence felt. When I wasn't reading, or playing the piano, I was drawing. It may sound absurd to anyone but an artist, but the materials began to enchant me – the paper and pencils and pen and ink and coloured chalks; the sound of them, the feel of them, the marvellous effects they produced singly and in combination. I drew very little from life; more often, I was copying. And when Lady Henrietta came in and saw me drawing at the table she approached to see what I was doing. To my everlasting shame, Father Coubé, I must confess that, yes, it was the drawings of Kate Greenaway that first inspired me and were responsible for my first drawing commission.

Do you know Kate Greenaway's work? It may seem dreadful now to the discerning eye, but something in it children can adore. The drawings are sweetly domestic, always cheerful, impossibly innocent and, of course, entirely false. Generally they are filled with small children dressed in Regency clothes and happily playing in lovely English gardens near charming English Cottages. Little stories, and rhyming moralities that pass as poems, accompany the drawings.

A child can enter such a picture; yes, take up residence in that world of tranquil happiness and not want to leave. I know I did. When Lady Henrietta bent over me, she saw my drawing of two little children struggling with oversized umbrellas in a rainstorm.

'What a charming picture,' said Lady Henrietta.

'The limbs are not right,' I said. 'I have such a difficult time with the limbs.'

'Practice will solve that problem,' said Lady Henrietta. She smelled of the violets pinned to her coat, and had a sweet kindly face. 'Mrs Beardsley,' she said, 'I have just hit upon a most charming idea.'

The idea was that I should supply a series of hand-drawn place-cards for a wedding in Scotland. I was to use Kate Greenaway's style. Of course I agreed, quite unaware that this was all a careful contrivance. Lady Henrietta came to visit because she knew from my grandparents that we were hard up. Rather than offer charity, she offered work; the work was of an artistic kind, and for it I should receive £30.

When Lady Henrietta left, Mother was a-quiver with such gratitude that her personal humiliation at being almost penniless was reawakened. She withdrew from Mabel and me, which was strange in itself, but becoming more frequent, and went to her room. We heard her muffled sobs and tried to guess at their reason. No one cried in the Kate Greenaway drawings. No one was ever afraid, or ill, or poor.

'I'm frightened when Mother cries,' said Mabel.

'You mustn't be frightened,' I said heroically.

But we had reason to be; for Mother was ill, and we were about to be sent to live with our old Great-Aunt Pitt in Lower Rock Gardens in Brighton. The thought of this, once we had been informed, wasn't just frightening; it was terrifying.

THANK YOU, DEAR Père Coubé, for your letter and very kind words of encouragement. I knew that you would understand this need of mine to unburden myself – to perform an autopsy on my soul, as it were; and someone so sympathetic and equable makes a difficult task a little easier.

Since I last wrote, I have prayed often – or, rather, tried to – and studied the catechism and book of devotions so kindly sent by André Raffalovich. He, as you must know, is now attached to

93

the Order of Oratorians, and writes most interesting accounts of Father Sebastian Bowden, Superior of the Order and evidently the best preacher at the Brompton Oratory.

You encourage me to omit nothing in my letters, dear Father, so I will admit to you now that I have been greatly depressed of late and cannot shake off a terrible mental oppression, no matter how I try. It began the very night that I went to the dining-room to sup on real food instead of the fruit-and-goat's-milk diet prescribed by that idiot Dr Lamarre.

How I enjoyed being in the public space of a restaurant again, with a lively scene all around to contemplate, instead of lurking in my room with an apple, a bunch of grapes, Mother, and that odious glass of goat's milk to choke down. And how I enjoyed my victory over Dr Lamarre! Nothing gives one a keener appetite than overriding medical counsel.

Then how I paid! That same night later found me with bulging eyes and gawping mouth, my stomach rent by violent convulsions, vomiting up my entire delicious meal; there it lay in the chamberpot, all that nourishment and fine subtle French taste, not even half-digested. The demon in my gut reached still deeper, fishing up what was left of the fruit. And then the final agony as, mouth stretched to the limit, the demon choked and squeezed out even the milk. A hideous sauce of green-black bile was the final garnish.

I lay there when it was over, grateful that it *was* over, gasping, trying to catch my breath, shivering and terrified. I was completely hollow; there was nothing left in me. Or so I thought, until the diarrhoea began its midnight flow.

Mother had come from the adjoining room when the retching began and silently helped me through the ordeal. Nothing disgusts her; she is unflinching in her duty; the noisome effluvia of my body, no matter how vile, she treats with imparital concern and tenderness. But how I wish she could for even a short while be relieved of the need to nurse me. My daily dying is all she has; it is her entire life, it has *shaped* her life and, my God, she must be tired of it by now.

A slight haemorrhage the next day added to my growing anxiety about the true state of my health, but still more hateful was the sense of disgust at myself and my life which began to grow in my mind. That same day I heard from Octave Uzanne that I shall not, after all, be designing the cover for his new book; the publisher had decided on someone else; so another opportunity to earn some money vanishes. If it were not for kind André's gifts of money, I don't know how we should manage.

Dear Père Coubé, surely you write with a certain disingenuousness when you ask me to explain more fully my current position as an artist. *I have no position.* I am no better than a pariah dog at which the public throws stones to keep it away from the front door. I am as one accursed, a Dutchman doomed to wander till he should find redemption in love. Why, you ask, do I subject myself to a publisher like Smithers, with his pornographic sidelines, disreputable connivings and financial uncertainties? I thought you knew the answer to that, Father. It is because no other publisher will touch my work. Did not Octave Uzanne's turn me down only yesterday?

I thought André, being a friend of yours, would have told you everything about the scandal that blackened my name for ever, destroyed my livelihood, and keeps me in eternal exile from all nice things and all nice people. Surely, Father, you know that I was the first victim of the Oscar Wilde débâcle? Mr Wilde destroyed me – were you not aware? Yes, because I had illustrated his ridiculous play *Salome*, because my art was linked to his name, because I knew Oscar and that whole crowd of green-carnationed butterflies fluttering about him, I was assumed to share his tastes. We were both Decadents, and therefore we were responsible for diverting English art and literature from its high-minded moral earnestness; our path was immoral, depraved, modern and, worst crime of all, suspiciously French. We were not considered good Englishmen, Oscar and I. Instead of sinking into the dull grey morass of English respectability, we rose to the top by flaunting our differences and our individualities. Nothing is better-guaranteed to enrage old John Bull, you know, than the sight of a successful man enjoying himself.

This, Father, is how we were perceived in the perennially blind public eye, as a demonic pair of inverted sympathies. Unlike Oscar Wilde, however, I was never tried. I was merely assumed guilty. Like Oscar, I was a sodomite – so they said (or whispered, rather) – and, because of it, must share in his public downfall. The very day Oscar's verdict was read out in court – two years' hard labour – I was dismissed from my job as art director of *The Yellow Book*, an advanced journal that I had helped to found, and from then on no 'respectable' publishers would touch me. Commissions dried up at once. With no salary, I could not afford the little house in Pimlico that I had bought for Mabel, Mother and myself. Everything that I had worked so hard to attain was lost overnight.

All because of Oscar Wilde, Father. I am sure that now you understand why I cannot forgive him. Quite simply, his reputation destroyed my livelihood. As well as having to endure this wretched illness, I now live on the precipice of complete pauperdom thanks to Oscar.

Let me not go on in this vein, for it fans angers yet unassuaged and perhaps unassuageable. Did I tell you that Mabel has written from London? She is looking for some theatre bookings, but will be here within a few days for a week's visit. I am beside myself with eagerness to see her again, and to hear of her American tour, filled as that undoubtedly was with curious incidents and people. I am hungry for talk with a sympathetic soul, and surely this depression will lift the moment she arrives.

Mabel writes that London is full of all the plans, parties and excitements attendant upon the Queen's Diamond Jubilee on 22 June. Imagine, Victoria, who came to the throne in 1847 at the age of eighteen, a few short years after the first steam railway, has now been sitting on it for fifty years! What changes she has lived through this last half-century! She has seen the institution, improvement or perfection of railways, steamships, telegraphs, the penny post, photography, gas lighting and now electricity; swiftness, speed, hurry characterize her century as it draws to a close; yet, throughout all the wonders heaped upon this era, the good lady of Buckingham Palace, Windsor Castle and Osborne House has remained dull, utterly respectable, thoroughly unimaginative. Our queen! whose fertility is surpassed only by Vienna's Marie-Thérèse; whose secluded black-craped mourning for her Prince Consort is the English equivalent of Andromache's wailing grief for Hector; whose phlegmatic qualities made popular once again a throne that had become a mockery of monarchy; whose empire has expanded tenfold, and whose subject peoples have increased twentyfold, to encompass more of the world and its riches than men ever dreamed possible. Queen

Vic *is* England now, at the end of the century, and at the end of her territorial supremacy and industrial greatness.

I say the end because France and Germany, as the papers here fondly point out, are quickly overtaking dear Britannia in industrial strength and capacity; they have newer ideas, developed from what they learned from us, and they are free of the smug complacency of the English, who believe there is only one way, the English way, God's way, a way that must never be altered because it is so inimitably *perfect* as it is. I say the end because, although the rebellions are only just beginning – in Egypt, India, and among the Boers of South Africa – they will surely spread. Ireland, that land of mystic patriots, is perpetually clamouring for Home Rule, and in its desperation will continue to agitate against our presence. England, dear Father, always sees itself as the colonized world's saviour, but the colonies do not exactly share that cosy view.

No, I am not a patriot. England has shown me her real face, and it is stern, forbidding, deformed by class, thoroughly unartistic, impeccably cruel. England will not have me; she has chased me from her shores, as she has chased every good poet or artist. Yet I love England, love London most of all, and never more than when I hear of some great event like the Queen's Diamond Jubilee. Then I long to be there, and be a part of the festivities and celebrations. I have suggested to Smithers that as a Jubilee tribute he present the Queen with a copy of our *Lysistrata*, so that she may have at least an inkling, before the century ends, of what modern British art is capable of. I am certain she would enjoy it – and her grandchildren, too.

But, rather than wander on among current events and the various sexual and intellectual speculations that give a slight *frisson* to my bedbound existence, let me continue the story of my life, for these confessions are just that, are they not? It occurred to me, dear Father, with a certain amount of irony – Jesuits, I know, do not believe in irony, but you do comprehend the term, do you not, and admit its existence in some men's lives? – that when I have finally flown the coop you will be the only man to know what I really was, and yet you will be unable, because of your vows, to reveal anything about me. To you, therefore, I can tell everything, need conceal nothing. I reveal to you what I cannot reveal to Mabel or Mother: for them I must always keep up at least a semblance of hope and good spirits. I must never fail in my duty as provider.

But to you, dear Father, I can unburden myself of this wearisome load. To you I can say, 'Sinning, for me, has always been a form of prayer,' and I think you will understand what I mean. If prayer is what puts us in touch with that ineffable Other, then I have prayed to sin. Through sin (I mean sexual sin, of course) I have entered areas of human existence closed to all respectable subjects of Victoria's empire. I have, through sin, escaped into a world beyond Duty, beyond Respectability, beyond Illness; in a way, I found myself, or part of my nature, through sinning, and am singularly grateful to it. Not yet having been baptized into your Church, I remain, according to your catechism, in a state of Original Sin; am therefore a direct descendant of those very first sinners, there in the first garden. Like them, my desire has been to eat the fruit of the Tree of Knowledge. I share the natural gluttony of Adam and Eve.

One could, if one were sufficiently dull, look at life through Aunt Pitt's eyes, and see a vision of stern and ceaseless moral duty, with hellfire crackling for those who shirk their tedious responsibilities or question their station in life. Living with Aunt Pitt, I came to know her version of existence quite well, and it is not one that suited me then, nor would it suit me very well now.

I was eleven, Mabel twelve, when Mother became so ill that she could no longer care for us, and we were sent to our Great-Aunt's house in Lower Rock Gardens in Brighton. We knew Aunt Pitt, of course, but had never dreamed we would one day end up prisoners in her household. She had the distinction of being a well-endowed Fund-owner and the leaseholder of her own house; she was quite comfortable with what she had, and could have lived happily, I think, on much less. But, to her way of thinking, God sat enthroned as a celestial director of the Bank of England; and, ever His handmaiden, she felt it her duty to remain shrewd and thrifty, on His behalf, in the management and dissemination of her income. She had never married; with a settled income of her own, she had never seen the need for a husband. Indeed, her views were remarkably progressive when it came to a woman's right to own property and dispose of it as she saw fit; she had even agitated on behalf of the Married Woman's Property Act, which finally became law in 1881.

Now, of course, I wonder if it hadn't been quite carefully planned beforehand by Mother that we should go to Aunt Pitt's and claim kin, as it were. Aunt Pitt was already old, and soon she would feel the need to draw up a will, and where would she find worthier legatees than in the talented but impoverished Beardsley children?

Because of her age and silvery-white hair, we wanted to think of her as a grandmother; but Aunt Pitt had none of the tenderness and intuition that can come from the daily rearing of children. Neither infant nor man had ever or would ever touch that stiff chaste breast of hers; Christ himself would have to beg. She had lived her life exactly as she pleased for many many years, and the thought of two lively children upsetting the Perfect Order she had created in her house must have struck a deep chord of panic. Her religion assured her that children were utterly depraved, could never be reprimanded too sternly or too often, and that perfect discipline was necessary if we were to be moulded into God-fearing adults.

Father took us there, and the four of us spent an uneasy quarter-hour in Aunt Pitt's spartan drawing-room. I believe she felt that uncomfortable furniture was somehow more Christian, for every piece she had was grotesquely unpleasant, and sitting on it became a kind of penance.

Aunt Pitt of the vinegary face and old-fashioned lace cap was sister to my grandfather, the Surgeon-Major — one of five sisters in fact, and one of three whose maidenhood remained intact into old age. She had not approved of my parents' marriage; which meant, I suppose, that she did not approve of the three of us sitting there in her drawing-room. My father was nervous and self-conscious under her intolerant gaze and kept rubbing his hands together.

'My niece is going *where* to convalesce?' Aunt Pitt asked, her interrogative tone implying displeasure no matter what the answer.

'To Margate, ma'am.'

'Margate has little to recommend it; its atmosphere is more carnival than spa, surely?'

'My wife likes it there.'

'If her intention is to get well, she would do better to go to Scarborough,' said Aunt Pitt. 'Of course, she is exhausted; any woman in her position would be.' She rang a charming little silver bell, and a moment later a maid appeared. 'Jones, bring the tea.'

Mabel and I sat nervously swinging our legs until Aunt Pitt targeted her sharp voice in our direction. 'In this house you will sit still!'

Do you know what a torture it is, Father, for children to sit still on uncomfortable chairs? And the naughty thoughts that go through their heads when they are commanded to do so?

'If my niece does not recover, what arrangements will be made for the children?' asked Aunt Pitt.

'Then . . . ma'am' – my father cleared his throat – 'then I will of course come to fetch them.'

'And how will *you* take care of them?' asked Aunt Pitt.

'They would have to work.'

'Their education would come to an end?'

'They would have to work, ma'am.'

Aunt Pitt allowed herself one piece of jewellery, a gold ring which she wore on the pointing finger of her left hand; in idle moments she would revolve the ring and rub the gold. She did this now, while Jones brought in our tea. Quite an ungenerous tea it was, no cakes or slabs of buttered bread or sandwiches of any kind; just weak Darjeeling and dry biscuits.

I had no appetite, for I had suddenly realized just how grave our situation was. It wasn't only that this place would be our home for some indefinite period of time, but the other horrifying possibility, one that struck me with the force of a thunderbolt: Mother might die, and then we would be in Father's care. If Mother died, we would be sent to work at once. Piano? Recitations? We would become no better than the thousands of wretched children labouring in factories and begging on the streets in every town and city in England. The thought was harrowing.

It was while in this morbidly affrighted state of mind that I first noticed Jones, Aunt Pitt's maid. She was calming somehow, her very presence a reassurance. Jones was a sweet-looking thing, from somewhere near the Cheddar Gorge, I later discovered, where all her family and friends had for years worked making cheese. Jones was the first one to leave Somerset. But the dairy maid in her was easy to detect; despite her starched uniform and apron, she remained a creature of barns, of sweet-smelling hay, of fresh curds and whey, and hot frothing milk squirting from swollen udders.

Jones was leaning over, setting out the tea things, when she looked up at me secretively and smiled. I swear, Father, it was like the first glance a shy girl gives to her lover. Her eyes were dark and fertile with promise, her hair black as raven's wings, and her skin had the look of fresh heavy cream. Two eager young breasts strained the bodice of her uniform.

Then we were stiffly saying goodbye to Father, who was returning to London.

It was his nervousness at being in Aunt Pitt's house, I suppose, that made it impossible for him to express any affection for us; or perhaps he was simply eager to be rid of the responsibilities we entailed. He hugged Mabel, but he shook my hand.

'You will be good children, I know,' he said. 'You will make yourselves useful to your Great Aunt, and obey her in all things.' And with that he was gone.

Aunt Pitt was an early riser, and she generally went to bed before the summer sun had fully set. As members of her household, we were expected to follow her regime. A scant breakfast appeared promptly at six in the morning, and if one missed it there was nothing to eat until noon. Aunt Pitt's cook was a daily woman, Mrs Lewis, whose soul was as devout as her cookery was bad. Fish was inevitably boiled to a rubbery glue, joints were dry and tough, fowl stringy and overcooked. Aunt Pitt had taken a strange liking to turnips, so Mrs Lewis always piled our plates with indigestible versions of that disgusting root. In all things, food included, Aunt Pitt's credo remained unyielding: the worse it was, the better it was for you. God, in her estimation, approved the endless discomforts man inflicted upon himself; the good Christian, despite a share in the Funds, used his imagination to think up ways to keep himself miserable.

One thing I do appreciate about Catholics, Father, is their understanding that God may be reached through the senses. Aunt Pitt seemed determined to obliterate all the sensual pleasant- ness of life in the belief that God would approve of her. But I ask you: which does God love more – a full-blooming tree, heavy with the experience of countless springs, or a dry stick?

Our first clashes with Aunt Pitt – Sarah, her name was; we called her Old Sarum – were sufficiently forbidding to let us know that she was quite serious about the Rules of her house. The problem was that we did not know what those Rules were until we broke them. Running was forbidden, reading for pleasure was forbidden, swinging one's legs on a chair was forbidden, touching things was forbidden, loud voices were forbidden, laughing was forbidden, music was forbidden, games of any kind were forbidden.

'Play', explained Aunt Sarah to our dismay, 'is an exertion of body or mind made to please ourselves, and not God. It is selfish, for it has no determined end.'

She felt it her duty to take us down a peg, thinking we had become unbearably affected because of our performing life. And that was true; we had performed together, Mabel and I, and shared the terrors and exhausting rigours that public performance demands of the nervous system. Probably we were affected; many say we still are. But let he who has not been through it try to tell *me* that one's character is not changed for ever by the act of performing. Now I stop to think of it, I have been performing my entire life; have always felt the need to please; have always masked the sad Pierrot of my temperament with an outer show of vivacious gaiety and malice. But no one can accuse Mabel and me of affectation who does not know how hard we have worked to make even a small name for ourselves in the artistic world. We have done so proudly, despite the Aunt Pitts of the world, and the Mothers, and the Fathers: we have the unique distinction of having created ourselves *for* ourselves.

Even under Aunt Pitt's watchful eyes, our lives, Mabel's and mine, were a kind of constantly evolving play, an assortment of queer mental games that would, at times, render us telepathic. These were a source of comfort, a way for us to express some of the fear and love in our hearts.

Oh, Father, why is it so difficult for adults to give sound guidance to their children? Above all else, a child wants love, from both parents equally; and not only when he does something correctly, but simply because he exists and is therefore worthy of love. The amount of love in our childish breasts was forever seeking expression, but now our mother was seriously ill, our father had left us, and to Aunt

Pitt we were a cold Christian duty. Is it any wonder, thrown together on our own resources as we were, that Mabel and I should become as close as we did?

In one way, I suppose, it was this troubled time that first led us to the path of Catholicism. My sister, as you know, with Miss Florence Gribbell acting as her sponsor, has recently been received into the Church. You are familiar with Miss Gribbell, are you not? She is the English woman who has acted as André Raffalovich's governess and housekeeper practically since his birth. Miss Gribbell is herself a convert – but who in André's house is not? First it was John Gray, who was followed by Miss Gribbell, after whom came André himself; and now, I'm told, André has converted his butler and has designs on his coachman. Surely the Pope would rejoice and believe the true faith to be making great headway in England if he could visit 72 South Audley Street, Mayfair.

Aunt Pitt was unpardonably Low Church, in the opinion of Mabel and me; for our religion, that past year, had taken a High Anglican turn. Mother, dissatisfied with St Nicholas of Smyrna, perhaps because it reminded her of her failed marriage, had taken to sermon-tasting, and discovered in the Church of the Annunciation of Our Lady a very satisfying repast. Aunt Pitt was suitably horrified when we told her we wished to attend services there.

'I shall not keep you from your worship,' she sputtered like a true Christian, 'but I do not approve of the Romish practices prevalent at the Annunciation. There is confession there, I believe, and Sunday service is called Mass?'

'Yes, Aunt Pitt,' Mabel said. 'But it's ever so lovely inside.'

'A church should be modest and plain, with as little decoration as possible to distract one from one's prayers.'

We said nothing, but were determined to press our religious demands – to the point of martyrdom if need be. In the end, Aunt Pitt offered further objections to our attending the Annunciation because it was in Washington Street on the far side of Brighton, but she could not in conscience actually ban us from Mass. Mabel and I, because it was a chance to be out and away from Lower Rock Gardens, began attending morning and evening services every Sunday and whenever else we could. That long, long walk up the old Brighton Downs to the very end of the chalk path, past the last of the market gardens, was our time for fanciful reverie; finally we would see the red-tiled spire of our beloved church high on the hill, and sometimes would even run there.

Yes, there was something slightly illicit about the Annunciation, which of course only added to its charm. Though it was very High Anglican, it reverberated with that quite peculiar and almost aristocratic sympathy one associates with English Roman Catholics. One felt almost an outlaw going there – an impression heightened by the situation of the church: it was built into a road of small brick and flint houses, and one entered directly from the street, without the hallowing prelude of a porch. The noticeboard outside had for me the glamour of a theatre bill; it listed all the mysterious ceremonies that took place within – nones, compline, confessions.

A sense of renegade superiority reigned within. The church was not old, but the steady chant of an ancient liturgy made it seem so. Architecturally it was eccentric, with a heavy wooden roof like an inverted ship's hull, and exposed beams and plastered walls that betrayed affinities with the Aesthetic Movement of the sixties and seventies. We loved it, I'm sure, for its beauty – or what we saw as beauty then. The Pre-Raphaelites had left the artistic stamp of their respectability in the east window, where a dusky blue panel of the Annunciation by Rossetti was flanked by a couple of Burne-Jones designs executed by William Morris. I would direct my gaze towards those panels with their lead outlines and stare until I seemed to merge myself with them. Father Chapman considered the windows as 'necessary luxuries', splendid examples of Art serving the greater glory of God.

Father George Chapman, now deceased, was the Annunciation's priest-in-charge, and there was some quality in him that drew people to the confessional like bees to honey. He was a tall gaunt man, who looked as though he were being consumed by his own spiritual fervour; his pale eyes had the feverish sparkle of a confirmed 'lunger', and one believed him to be party to those secrets whispered only between the dying man and his God.

Mabel and I longed to go to confession. It was too tantalizing, the sight of all those people entering a mysterious cupboard where the sins of the world were whispered, revealed and absolved. I'd watch, fascinated, as the sweetest-looking people in Brighton made their way to that dark closet of repentance. What had they done that was wrong? Why did they feel compelled to confess? I wonder if there may not be something in the determinedly bluff and unemotional English character that secretly craves the luxurious darkness of a confessional, and the voluptuous comfort that comes from admitting guilt and casting off an accumulated load of sin.

You may not have known, Father, that Brighton was the home of the Catholic Revival in England. Yes, in churches throughout the town the oath of Royal Supremacy was being questioned and gorgeous Eucharistic vestments flaunted. The more daring churches even adopted the Eastward Position. Low churches, such as Aunt Pitt attended, were appalled, indignant and intolerant of anything that even suggested that Scarlet Whore, Rome, with all her pomp and finery. The converts to Catholicism were called perverts. Fierce words and fulminations on the subject of Popery were hurled from many a pulpit. But there in the Annunciation we would sit, Mabel and I, for hours on end, morning and evening, intoxicated by the solemn mystical odour of frankincense, the chanted refrains of ancient Latin texts, the intricate rituals of the Mass, and Father Chapman himself, who was publicly dying.

Aunt Pitt, as I have already mentioned, did not permit reading unless it was edifying or instructional. Novels and poetry were incomprehensible to her; for us, they were life, and we were aghast to think that from now on we would be without them. Of course, she was perfectly furious when she discovered that I was hiding a novel that Father Chapman had given me to read, and I had a lot to do to convince her of the story's elevated moral tone. The book was called *Eric; or, Little by Little*; it is, I hope, a work with which you keep yourself unfamiliar. Thousands, perhaps hundreds of thousands, of British boys have had to read this drivel and pretend to learn from it. The book traces little Eric's moral progress – or decline, I should say – and would have us believe in the most simple-minded way that sin is always followed by retribution. Poor little Eric first gives in to temptation while he is at school. Soon he is using bad language and cribbing from the other boys; this state of affairs develops into lying and stealing, gambling, smoking, drinking, until finally and inevitably, little by little, Eric leads himself to an early grave. Aunt Pitt's quite unreasonable fear was that the book, despite Eric's deathbed renunciation of all his past ways, must be sensational and therefore sinful to read. In truth, Eric's sins, and those of his tempters, were presented in the dullest way imaginable; the author had obviously never read Baudelaire, who was closer to the truth when he wrote that vice is seductive and should be portrayed as seductive.

Aunt Pitt did allow us Green's *Short History of England* and a few other forlorn oddments of improving reading matter, but for the most part we were forced to rely upon our inner reserves of imagination; hence all the strange mental games between us. Worst of all was the complete absence of a piano. Music, like everything else, became an inaccessible luxury, and the only way to hear it was by going as often as possible to the Annunciation.

It was a strange year, that one spent with Aunt Pitt. It was a year of unusual apprehensions and almost supernatural emotions. Death, with its cataclysmic threat of loss and upheaval, lurked in the margins of our days. Would Mother die? Would Father Chapman die? Funeral processions took on a sinisterly personal aspect, and we would watch with a kind of stoic panic as the horses, their tall black plumes nodding in a horribly decorative acknowledgement of annihilation, plodded by carrying their load of death, followed by the black-craped mourners.

There was no *comfort* that year, except at the Annunciation. Aunt Pitt was too busy calculating her next penances to give any real thought to us. We were intruders, thrown upon her mercy, hopelessly corrupt. She read from the Bible, or made us do so, every morning and evening. The rest of the time, unless we were allowed to go outside, passed in a slow grey delirium of anxiety and boredom.

Jones, of course, was expected to see to our basic wants, and we warmed to her at once, but the poor girl was kept so busy by Aunt Pitt that we could only stare longingly at her as she dashed from one household duty to the next. She was not only Aunt Pitt's personal maid; she was also responsible for serving meals and all the housekeeping, in which capacity she acted as charwoman and scullery maid as well.

Occasionally I would catch a glimpse of her, sitting exhausted in a chair in the kitchen, her large red hands, flaming from strong soap and cold water, clasped demurely in her lap, her abundant chest heaving with an exhausted or dispirited sigh. Once she saw me peeping at her from around the doorway and gave a shriek, then began to laugh. What a lovely laugh she had. I longed to laugh with her, to cuddle up beside her and press my head to her bosom and laugh and laugh.

Jones's room was in the attic; and at night, after Aunt Pitt was in bed and snoring, I would sometimes creep up the stairs, my heart pounding, and position myself so as to peer under her door. There was a considerable gap, and I was sometimes rewarded with a heartwarming glimpse of her bare feet. That little attic room, Father, soon began to draw me to it. It was like a narcotic, calling the user back over and over again. I knew that what I was doing was somehow illicit, but I did not know why. I wanted Jones to love me, I suppose; or, rather, I wanted to be able to lavish my love upon her but had no direct way of doing so.

Through careful observation I soon learned the timetable of Jones's life at Lower Rock Gardens; knew where she was and what she was doing at all hours of the day. Slowly I became bolder. When she was out marketing, I would go up to the attic and peer through the keyhole. One day I finally screwed up the courage to open the door and enter her room.

It was a maid's room, small, plain, neat, conventual, cold in the winter and hot in the summer. Over a period of weeks I came to know every object in it. It became a holy cell, a place of illicit worship. Stroking the bedcover gave me an odd thrill; here was where Jones slept, where she laid her pretty head, where she dreamed. I even found two or three long black hairs and regarded them as treasure. My boldness increased to recklessness. The room, once forbidden, became a daily haunt. I opened Jones's drawers and gazed lovingly at her few mysterious underclothes, trying with all my might to imagine what she looked like under her flannel uniform and starched apron.

I was consumed with a mysterious love for Jones. There she would be, less than an inch away, serving one of Mrs Lewis's dreadful meals, and I could do none of the things I wanted to do: grabbing her lobster-red hands and kissing them, or pressing my cheek to her large, sweet, warm breasts. I could never express to her what she meant to me. Was it my imagination, or was there a secret sympathy and understanding between us? Every time those dark eyes of hers found mine, her small lips would pucker and her cheeks rise in what always looked to me like suppressed merriment.

I told none of this to Mabel, of course; but she, I think, sensing my mental absence, began to fear that she would lose my undivided allegiance. Jones was a rival, but Mabel also had a crush on her such as a younger sister feels for an older. The barriers of class thwarted Mabel's love for Jones as they thwarted mine. To spend time with one's maid was, after all, in Aunt Pitt's view, an unpardonable breach of decorum.

How difficult it is to put into words the quality of that year, the oppressive sense of waiting for something to happen, frightened by what it might be. Mother's illness haunted our waking and sleeping thoughts; frequently I would dream of losing some precious article, something whose loss made me desolate and inconsolable. Mabel developed a queer little stutter and was chided for it by Aunt Pitt, who regarded it as a deliberate provocation. When the stutter refused to vanish, Old Sarum began to devise appropriate punishments. Mabel was forbidden to speak until she could speak like a proper stutterless young lady; but since she never knew when, exactly, the stutter would appear she began to fear opening her mouth at all. It was humiliating for someone who had only a short while earlier recited Tennyson to a corrupt duchess.

I was considered precocious, and therefore dangerously liable to creative outbursts. Aunt Pitt harboured the utmost contempt for such selfish time-wasting tomfoolery. There was no keyboard to allow me to dream in music, and no paper to receive the shapes, patterns and characters of my imagination. Having a pencil was a subversive act, and once I procured one it gave me the greatest of pleasure to make tiny drawings in secret places on Aunt Pitt's walls.

One day I saw Jones carefully fold a parcel wrapping and put it in a drawer. Now I had a supply of paper; but because I was afraid to ask Jones for it I took to stealing it instead, one piece at a time. In the evening stillness of my room, in the forbidden light of one candle, I would cover the paper with scribblings of no particular distinction or merit, merely recording my fancies as they occurred. I drew crosses, chalices, objects associated with the Annunciation;

leering, hateful imp faces, as frightening as I could make them; rude insulting words addressed, I suppose, to Aunt Pitt.

While I was engaged in this clandestine activity one stormy night, my door was suddenly flung open and Mabel, her face awash with tears, ran in. She could never bear to be alone during storms; and this one, a gale blowing from the sea, was particularly frightening. Winds howled like tortured spirits around the house, and heavy rain beat furiously against the window-panes. The house creaked, moaned and rattled under the assault.

Mabel, barefoot in her nightgown, dived into my bed and pulled the covers over her head. I quickly shut the door and went to sit beside her. At once her arms reached out and pulled me under the blankets with her.

It was airless and toasty hot in the little nest we made for ourselves between the sheets. Mabel wrapped her arms around me and wept. She didn't have to tell me what she was weeping for. I knew. It was for everything, from the storm to her stutter, from our fear about Mother's death to the desperate boredom of our altered lives.

I sought to comfort her, Father; I swear that's all it was. But under my hands, taking solace from my caresses, was a quite different body from the one I had slept with as a child. It responded differently. Mabel had an incipient curve to her hips now, and her nipples thrust themselves out like swollen buds. She kissed me with what felt like real hunger, and pulled me closer, until something began to stir within me, some sympathetic restlessness and mutual desire for physical comfort. I had the foretaste of an urge stronger still, something dark and frantic and waiting for expression but not yet articulate within my body or consciousness. The moment passed, and we relaxed our straining bodies.

'What do you wish for?' I asked Mabel, stroking her hair. It was long, thick and violently red now, demanding attention wherever we went. My hair was still red, too; but instead of intensifying in colour, as Mabel's did, it was darkening into a tortoiseshell hue.

'Oh, I wish M-M-M-Mother was well and that we were with her,' Mabel said, valiantly mopping her eyes. 'What do you wish for?'

'I wish Old Sarum was dead.'

'Aubrey!' Mabel was shocked out of her grief.

'What do you wish for?'

Mabel thought for a moment. 'I wish we were all together again.'

'You already said that. What else do you wish for?'

'That's what I wish for the most,' said Mabel.

'There can be other wishes, too,' I said impatiently.

'What else do *you* wish for?'

'For a lovely grand piano in a big house – a castle – a palace—'

'Where?'

'In Paris, or Venice.'

'Paris . . . Venice,' Mabel whispered, tasting the words.

'Jones would be with us,' I said.

'And Mother and Father?'

'Yes. But it would be *our* house, yours and mine. We would have grand parties every night, and I would play the piano and you would do your recitations.'

'Could I be an actress?' Mabel asked.

'Later you could, when you were older. And I would be a concert pianist, and play with a whole orchestra.'

Mabel spied my piece of wrapping paper covered with drawings and shot me a nervous glance. 'What if Old Sarum found out?'

'She won't.'

'Where does the paper come from?'

'A drawer in the kitchen.'

'Does Jones give it to you?'

'No. I take it.'

'You steal it?' Mabel was aghast.

'It's only wrapping paper. It doesn't cost anything.'

Mabel reached out for the paper and began to study its crowd of designs and figures and rude words. She pointed to one particularly ugly imp face and began to giggle. 'It looks like Old Sarum.'

That hadn't occurred to me, but the idea led to convulsive laughter.

Among the many curious and bewildering events of that year spent with Aunt Pitt, it is the *physical* ones that linger most vividly in my memory. To this day I remember the puzzling, exciting sensation of feeling Mabel's tender young breasts under her cotton nightgown, and can still trace the slope and swell of her developing hips as they were that stormy night. Something of her as she was then, so vulnerable and so innocently devout and hopeful in the face of our circumstances, so childishly unaware of the power of sensual attraction, will always remain as a charming leaf in my album of memories.

My own body was changing as well, but on my frame there was, alas, no incipient voluptuousness. I remained thin as a rake, while my arms and legs shot out to disproportionately bony lengths. My clothes no longer fitted me; but that meant nothing to Aunt Pitt, who simply didn't see such things, and I was miserably aware every time I left the house that my trousers were now too short and too tight, that my too-small jacket was forcing my shoulders into a hunched stoop, and that my boots were pinching my growing feet unbearably. But physical discomfort of all kinds was the natural order of the day in Lower Rock Gardens. The only reason we weren't given hairshirts to wear, I'm certain, was that Aunt Pitt would have considered them too Roman.

What I find intriguing now, looking back on that year from the vantage-point of a relatively depraved maturity, is the extraordinary disparity between the unruffled surface of Aunt Pitt's pious, thrifty and efficiently run household and the deeper, darker, more dangerous currents that ran unexpressed, unacknowledged and unexplained through its prim, poky little rooms.

It seemed highly unlikely that Aunt Pitt, even in the antediluvian bloom of her youth, had ever been troubled by fevers of the Flesh; if she had, she no doubt remained in blissful ignorance of their source and methods of alleviation. Her attention had been directed away from corporeal matters for so long that her body had become nothing but a troublesome abstraction. But I burned that year with a growing impatience and curiosity about bodily matters. There, just on the other side of comprehension, an immense, mysterious, sexual firmament twinkled and teased. Mabel was part of it, I was part of it, and Jones was part of it.

Most of all, Jones.

Fresh from the incense, prayers and chanting of an aesthetic service at the Annunciation, positively glowing with piety and highmind-edness, I would return to Aunt Pitt's only to undergo a restless change of mood. I wouldn't know what to do with myself, since so much was forbidden, so I would sit with wandering mind until an image of some object in Jones's room – her Bible on the table, or her plain coarse bloomers resting in a drawer – would come to mind. The image would fill me with excitement. There was nothing for it but to plan out my next foray to that room in the attic.

I had by now discovered that she bathed on Saturday nights after household prayers. The ritual, which I would secretly observe, always pretending to be doing something else, involved her carrying a large tin bath up to her room, followed by the two meagre jugs of hot water she was allowed by Aunt Pitt. My view under her door, however, was most unsatisfactory, for the sides of the bath generally hid even her feet. Once, because of its placement, I did have a momentary glimpse of a strong milky-white thigh as she kneeled to pour water over herself, and I thought I should go mad from the glory of this vision, which haunted me for days and was rivalled in majesty only by Rossetti's panel of the spellbound Mary in the Annunciation.

My madness was such that finally I planned an all-out spying attack on Jones. I determined to look at her through the keyhole while she was bathing. A ruthless curiosity demanded that I see her naked.

Where did my stealth come from? Why did I know that silence and cunning were essential if I were to succeed with my plan? Yes, I had a sense of wrongdoing, of transgression, but I could not yet attach it intellectually to any fully comprehended dogma. That the body was sinful and disgusting, a lewd rubbish-tip of potential evil, had been the refrain of countless sermons; *Eric; or, Little by Little* reiterated the same theme. Yet all the injunctions and warnings counted for nothing in the face of my childish obsessive desire for Jones.

Oh, I was careful and quiet and appropriately mouse-like. On the chosen night, I waited until Jones had lugged up her jugs of hot water, then climbed the stairs and crouched in my usual place, gazing at the weird perspective of floorboards seen from eye-level. From within her room I could hear the soft rustling of clothing, then the delicate sound of pouring water. I made my move swiftly and surely, like a born criminal, and was the next moment gazing in through the keyhole with something akin to ecstasy. There, in full view, was Jones, utterly naked.

Venus herself, freshly hatched in her seashell, was never so ravishingly gorgeous as Jones, fresh from the Cheddar Gorge, standing nude in her tin bath. Dido of Carthage was a dolly-mop in comparison, Helen of Troy a dirty slattern. Cleopatra, Bathsheba, Delilah – none could hold a candle to the fiery beauty of my Jones.

It gave me exquisite pleasure to know that she was unaware of my eye, and was thus as natural as Eve. I think Jones must have loved her body, with all its ruddy country strength, for she caressed herself with great tenderness. She had unpinned her hair, which fell in thick ebony strands down her back. She shook it out, ran her hands through it, loosened it. She was Diana, quite – strong, beautifully proportioned, with slender thighs and a firm rump – only her breasts were fuller, more womanly than those I imagine the Huntress to possess. Those breasts, Father; I see them as clearly today as I did then, a boy of almost twelve. Their dark erect nipples looked ripe for sucking and made one long to be an infant again. They rose so charmingly each time Jones lifted an arm, swayed so drowsily when she leaned over. I stared entranced as she performed her ablutions, baptizing herself with a hum and a sponge. Then she turned, and I saw her frontally.

The dark patch of her pubis made no sense, even frightened me a little. What did it mean? It imbued Jones with a slightly dangerous and repellent glamour.

The humming stopped, and before I could register what was happening Jones had run from the tub and pulled open her bedroom door. There she was, no longer an image in a peephole, or a silent serving girl with a plateful of turnips, but a full-blooded, naked, furious woman.

She grabbed me by the hair and pulled me into the room. I was too terrified to cry out or struggle. 'You!' she hissed in fury. 'You! Always following me about with your eyes!'

'Jones . . .' I whimpered, for her grasp on my hair was painful.

She wrenched it even tighter. 'What do you hope to see?'

I was seeing it, Father – exactly what I hoped to see. Her warm naked flesh, still glistening from the water, was there before me. I made a blind lunge. Now she was startled, for I was desperately embracing her.

'No! No!' she whispered, starting to panic, trying to push me away.

'Jones, Jones, Jones.' I chanted her name as reverently and with as much feeling as I would the Kyrie Eleison at the Annunciation, all the while squeezing her body, moving my hands about so quickly she never knew where they would be next.

'I shall scream!' She wanted to slap me, but someone of her class could be dismissed for something as slight as a missed curtsy; if she struck me, she knew she'd lose her character.

'Jones,' I moaned, pressing my head to her breasts.

She gasped and pushed, and I landed painfully on my bottom, looking up at her with tears in my eyes. Jones was apparently shocked by what she'd done, for her features rose in instantaneous alarm and she let out a doleful 'Oh!'

I feigned a daze.

'Oh, Master!' Jones kneeled beside me in concern and penitence. 'I swear I did not mean to hurt you!'

Wisely, I remained silent.

She began to fuss over me, not knowing quite what to do. Her dark hair brushed against my face, soft and fragrant as an angel's wing, and those deliciously fresh breasts hung quivering before me.

'You should not have looked at me through the keyhole,' she insisted, but her tone quickly changed. 'You will not tell *her*, will you? Promise me you will not tell *her*.' Panic began to set in. 'I should lose my place and never find another.' Now she began to cry.

'Jones,' I whispered, 'I won't tell.'

'Promise?'

'Of course I promise.'

She smiled in relief. 'You must go now.'

Is there anything more thrilling, Father, than being dismissed by your lover? I crept away as quietly as I had come, my body flushed and alerted to a new and higher degree.

Thereafter Jones and I shared the torment and pleasure of a guilty secret. I smiled at her now, every time I could, and she furtively returned it. When Aunt Pitt bade me read our morning prayers, I pitched my voice in Jones's direction so that she would be impressed.

114

Jones avoided conversation, of course, not wanting to encourage any further passionate encounters; but one day she leaned over me to whisper, 'They're beautiful!'

She meant the small bouquet of flowers I had left at her door. That furtive acknowledgement of pleasure was the closest we ever came to a romantic understanding, and soon afterwards Jones disappeared from our lives for ever, sacked by Aunt Pitt for stealing food.

As for Mabel and me, Aunt Pitt had determined that we were to continue our education – at her expense. What supernatural agency intervened to make her loosen her purse-strings on our behalf, I shall never know. Gratitude, which we wanted to proffer in abundance, was severely eschewed.

'You may be Beardsleys in name,' the old dame asserted, 'but you shall be Pitts in upbringing and character.'

After several consultations with the Surgeon-Major, Aunt Pitt decided that I should go to Brighton Grammar School as a day boy, and Mabel to Miss Topp's establishment, a nearby girls' school.

Thus began four of the happiest years of my life.

NCE NEMESIS TAKES hold, Father, her grip is relentless. Imagine her as depicted in an old Dürer engraving, a hag with a sullen Sphinx-like face, lewd sour-looking breasts and long talons, one indescribably horrible foot resting triumphantly on the breast of an agonized man. I am that man. I'd like to knock the bitch down, or at least give her a decent manicure so her pinch isn't so mercilessly sharp. But the grip of Nemesis is the grip of death, of *rigor mortis*, and once embedded her talons cannot be prised loose.

What is this all about? you ask. It is about the absurd and malevolent complications that attend my every waking hour, and go on to torture my sleep. I want so desperately to believe that I am getting better, yet my strength is undermined by a most insidious fatigue. It is a little harder to suck in a full breath, so my filthy lungs must be dripping with moisture and rot. Dr Lamarre, whom I never trusted, I have dismissed outright. In desperation he told me that unless I underwent an immediate series of galvanic shock treatments, followed by the inhalation of medicated oxygen in his patented inhalation chamber, my left lung would disintegrate entirely. You can imagine the cost – and, of course, his stories of miraculous cures. Like a hundred other doctors I've seen, Dr Lamarre convinces me that the medical profession, despite its endless claims, knows absolutely nothing about phthisis, and improvises cures on this disease as musicians improvise musical themes.

My health fears are alleviated somewhat only by the imminent arrival of Dr Phillips, André's personal physician, who has a private practice in John Street, Mayfair. I think I have mentioned Dr Phillips to you before. It was he who, at André's expense, escorted Mother and me across the Channel and on to Paris last April. Now dear André has asked Dr Phillips, who was planning a trip to Paris, to call on us here at the Pavillon Louis XIV in St-Germain. He, I am certain, will be able to tell us what is or is not happening in my lungs, and the wisest course of recuperative action. Meanwhile, lost as I am in this fog of unknowing, I must attempt to remain optimistic and believe that my body is not in the irreversible state of mortal decay that appearances would suggest. In the mirror today I looked quite frightful, and could only stare at myself with a kind of forlorn contempt.

André's letter contained one other piece of news which has had the most undesirably disturbing effect on me. Oscar Wilde, he writes, has now been released from Reading Gaol after his two-year prison term. Although London is a perfect hive of speculation, no one has so far been able to discover Oscar's whereabouts. He evidently took a boat to Dieppe, and was there met by his two most ardent disciples, Bobbie Ross and Reggie Turner. André, loathing Mr Wilde as he does, is a perfect bloodhound when it comes to tracking him, but even André's permanently flared nostrils lost Oscar's scent in the sea air of Dieppe.

Where is he, then? Has he remained in Dieppe, or has he travelled on to Paris? Knowing Oscar's fatal weakness for the sins and sounds of big cities, Paris seems the likelier choice. I can easily imagine him, a magnificent ruin, haunting the cheaper bars and cafés of the Quartier, hunting out partners for dominoes, conversation (his own), and seduction, shunned for ever but at least tolerated by the French because the French love artists.

Paris is only a half-hour from St-Germain; and, the world being as tiny as it is, it seems possible, perhaps even likely, that we should run into one another again. Nemesis, always angling for an unpleasant encounter, for any excuse to make one regret one's past actions and associations, would undoubtedly arrange the meeting.

Truly, Father Coubé, any word about Oscar Wilde, I must tell you, agitates me dreadfully; the mere mention of his name makes me feel as though a huge shadow threatens to engulf me. To think that he is here on the Continent, perhaps even in the vicinity, can only increase my general anxiety. There is such a crushing load of guilt and recrimination between us that I fear to provoke any encounter at all; surely it must end in very sharp and very unkind words. And that he, the cause of it, should see me in my present state of physical and financial impoverishment is quite intolerable.

You know, of course, why André Raffalovich hates Oscar so much and devotes so much time to blackening his name? It is because they were once lovers, and former lovers can evidently forgive anyone except one another. Oscar, from all that I've heard, jilted poor little André and abused his literary efforts. André, whose hereditary temperament is thoroughly Russian despite his acquired veneer of Englishness, has a tendency to create blood-feuds and hunt down enemies with the vindictiveness of a betrayed tsarina. Dear André's animosity, when provoked, is something to behold!

The liaison between Oscar and André began just a few years ago, as André has probably already confessed to you; back in André's palmy days, before he converted to Catholicism and re-nounced all worldly and literary ambitions; yes, back when André wallowed in sin like a pig in mud. Did you know there was such a time in André's life, Father? That the inexcusably rich and generous

Marc-André Raffalovich whom you know, the devout Oratorian, he who will soon take the name Brother Sebastian (after his favourite saint, I wonder, or in emulation of Father Sebastian Bowden, the admired preacher at the Brompton Oratory?), a man who is ceaseless in his prayers and devotions, this very same man once painted his yacht black, named her *Iniquity*, and sailed the seven seas amidst an unending storm of orgies and cynical affairs? It is a remarkable testament to the power of the Church that he has been able to suppress his corrupt habits so successfully in so relatively brief a period of time.

In some ways, of course, André hasn't a humane bone in his body. That he loves his God passionately and serves Him faithfully, I have no doubt; it is what he feels for his fellow-man that I always wonder about. And, to speak frankly, has not the possibility at least presented itself to you that André's fervent embrace of Our Lord is in fact but a distorted substitute for the warmer, but forbidden, embrace of the saintly beauty John Gray? You knew, didn't you, dear Father, that André purchased Gray's affections once Oscar Wilde had done with him?

Of course, from the little that I or anyone else knows about him, it would seem that John Gray has always auctioned himself off, like a kind of *trésor précieuse*, to the highest bidder; his strong chiselled beauty is something his owner may then put on a shelf or mantelpiece to admire from many different angles. John Gray was never much of a sensualist, but he did succumb to Oscar Wilde's rampant carnality – everyone in London agrees on that point – and in return for being Oscar's private prick-tickler he was able to attain a measure of literary fame and notoriety that would have otherwise forever eluded him.

That John Gray found God just at the time André found John Gray has always seemed to me to be providential for all parties concerned – except, perhaps, for André. Having taken a vow of celibacy, Gray can rebuff André's invert tendencies in all good conscience, and thus help to keep André on his road to Rome.

André's first encounter with Oscar was in America, of all places. Having been strongly encouraged to leave his father's house in Paris at the tender age of eighteen, André had the money and the leisure to travel about and decide where he might settle. In 1882 he happened to be in America, visiting various cities on the eastern seaboard – Boston, Philadelphia, New York – when he noticed a poster proclaiming a lecture by Mr Oscar Wilde on 'The English Renaissance' and immediately booked a seat.

Oscar Wilde's American lecture tour was a phenomenal success, as you may know, and had been planned to achieve publicity both for himself and for the opening of Gilbert and Sullivan's opera *Patience*, which mocked the same Aesthetic Movement that Oscar was then espousing. The Americans had never seen anything quite like Oscar; André, the Russian-French anglophile, certainly hadn't. How could he not have been mesmerized in the face of such superb flamboyance? Audiences sat speechless in wonder as Oscar, six foot four and long-haired, strode on to the stage wearing the cloak of a cavalier and whipped it off to reveal a dark purple sack coat, black velvet knee-breeches, black hose, and patent-leather shoes with bright silver buckles. He spoke in a languid paradoxical manner on what he called the English Renaissance, claiming that some sort of movement afoot in England actually mirrored the Renaissance of Italy (the period of my beloved Mantegna!), and was evidently persuasive enough to settle André's mind for him: soon after, André emigrated to England, a land of high literary culture *if* you can worm your way into the right artistic set.

Nor did he ever forget Oscar Wilde. How could he? Oscar was back in England and still flaunting himself. Once settled in London, André wanted above all to establish himself as a writer, and began to host the lavish and tireless rounds of entertainment that eventually led to Oscar's quip, 'Poor André. He came to London to found a salon, and has succeeded only in opening a saloon.' Oscar allowed himself to be wined and dined by André, of course – like any celebrity he cannot resist the offer of a free meal – and the other guests were always interesting or amusing, even if André was not: Oscar could meet his old Oxford hero Walter Pater for luncheon at André's, or have an amiable chat with Henry James or George Moore, both of whom were guests; he could eat well, and drink better; but he was undeniably rude in the face of André's desperate hospitality.

One day Oscar, along with several of his green-carnationed disciples, had been invited by André to luncheon. The guests came in a single group but were kept unaccountably waiting at the front door for several minutes in the middle of a downpour. When André's butler finally opened the door, Oscar swept past him into the hallway, snapped his fingers and said: 'Waiter, a table for six *at once!*' Impeccably correct André was horrified when the story got back to him.

André's clumsy social gaffes and frequent *faux pas* – none of which he was aware of at the time – were eagerly seized upon by Oscar and made into embarrassingly memorable lines which sniggered their way through the very literary and artistic set that André most wanted to impress. Yet there seemed to be something in Oscar's cruel, witty, dismissive malice that provoked André to ever greater shows of admiration. André has the *maladie du cœur* I have noticed in several inverted natures: a secret desire for belittlement and debasement. André, perhaps like most of us, is most eager for what he cannot have. Imagine, then, his thrill, his injection of rapture, when one day he was alone with Oscar, and heard from those flabby and so frequently abusive lips the seductive words: 'You know, Mr Raffalovich, I believe that you could give me a new thrill. You have just the right measure of romance and cynicism.'

André's cynicism at the time was more an affectation than a soul-sore reality; later it became quite horribly real – a crisis in fact – but at that time he was still relatively fresh, and had been gently bewildered in love only a few times.

Poor André! So lilliputian in stature and so hopelessly ugly. You knew, of course, that André's own mother, seeing him for the first time, gave a horrified cry and screamed for someone to take away the ugly dwarf that had been substituted for her baby; she never wanted to see it again. The peculiar Miss Gribbell was then hired to bring him up. His father, André once told me, regarded him with the utmost contempt, and André had always been afraid of him. In short, he craved physical comfort as we all do; and was denied it throughout his entire life, as we all are.

My own sex madness bewilders me, but sometimes I wonder if those of us who suffer from this erotic erethism crave not the fevered clawings of a lover but the warm caress of an understanding parent. I think André did. And huge Oscar, being older, and well known, and invitingly seductive, promised to provide *entrée* to a whole new world of sensual awareness. He was irresistible to someone who longed to be held.

If you ask me, it was Oscar who instigated André's eventual crisis of cynicism. André provided Oscar with the *nouvelle frisson* Oscar was continually seeking; his very ugliness perhaps added a grotesque spice to Oscar's Dorian ideals. The lion and the runt kitten. They were seen together at openings and first nights, and André basked in what he perceived to be Oscar's undying affection. He returned Oscar's kisses with the ardour of a young woman in love, and did everything Oscar said without question, shameless in his frantic desire to be loved deeply; he was fully initiated by his enormous lover into those secrets bequeathed by Plato and the Greeks directly to the British public schools.

One evening, after they had enjoyed a bit of brown, André drove Oscar back to his house in Tite Street. As his cosy little brougham made its way down the foggy London streets, carrying him and his lover, André indulged himself in the romantic reverie that overtakes every young man in love. I wish this carriage ride could last for ever, he thought. His tongue tingled pleasurably from its contact with the tobacco caught in the crevices of Oscar's mouth; as a kind of romantic homage, he liked to fish there, between Oscar's black protruding teeth, with the very tip of his tongue.

Oscar had been somewhat subdued that evening. His usual voluble flow of conversation was much diminished, and even in the moment of ejaculation, when he was usually at his wildest, he had remained obdurately self-contained. 'You know, my dear,' he said to André now, as the carriage turned into the Brompton Road, 'you and I, we must be most careful of the people we are seen with.'

'Careful?' said André.

'Yes. I am so conspicuous, you see, and you are not *le premier venu*.'

There followed a horrid scene as André came to the realization that the affair was irretrievably over, and there was nothing he could do about it. He tried everything — weeping, pleading, coaxing, offering presents of enormous value. He tried recrimination, reproach, abuse. Nothing worked. Oscar remained coldly civilized through it all. Emotional endings bored him. By the time the carriage reached Chelsea Embankment, André, always known for his excitable temperament, was contemplating a dramatic leap into the Thames.

'Good night,' Oscar said when the carriage rolled up to 16 Tite Street. 'Thank you for the ride.' A moment later he entered the house where his wife and two sons were waiting for him.

Wounded, jealous, betrayed, abandoned, André had to endure one final humiliation at the hands of his ex-lover: this one public, and perhaps the most unpardonable of all. He was accused by Oscar of misusing the English language, and treating the word *tuberose* as though it were trisyllabic.

Tuberose and Meadowsweet, Father, was the title of the book of poems André had just published, his second volume in fact, and Oscar reviewed it in the *Pall Mall Gazette*. André kept the review, of course, to torment himself, and showed it to me once.

Oscar was rather too kind, I thought, and it was apparent he was trying to give André as much of a puff as he was able in good conscience to do. But there were other phrases in the review that incensed poor André. At one point Oscar called André's verses 'unhealthy' and said they brought with them 'the heavy odours of the hothouse'. And then came the remark that *tuberose* was, in fact, disyllabic.

Now André, like any writer who has abandoned his native tongue to work in another, is keenly aware of his adopted language. He cannot bear to be incorrect, and he was certain that the word was *tu-be-rose*, just as Shelley had used it. He wrote off to the editor of the *Gazette*, citing Shelley's example, and hoping to provoke a public apology from Oscar. What he received instead was a return example from Oscar, also culled from Shelley, in which the word was unmistakably *tube-rose*. From that moment on, André nursed only the deepest of hatreds for his former lover. Never underestimate the power of a syllable, dear Père Coubé, when it comes to making an enemy!

Yes, André's hatred for Oscar Wilde must be seen as a fundamental element in his character. It is an active hatred, you see; it seeks release in action just as the other emotions do, only the action is poisoned by the emotion itself.

André's attacks are never physical, of course. Being a gentleman, he fights his one-sided duels in print. I say one-sided because Oscar,

I am sure, has never been more than momentarily annoyed by André's impotent thrusts. The first fruit in this now ceaseless harvest of malice and malevolence was published by André in 1890 after the appearance of Oscar's *The Picture of Dorian Gray*. It was called *A Willing Exile*, and in it André attempted to stab Oscar and Constance Wilde by portraying them as Cyprian and Daisy Brome, hinting broadly that Cyprian Brome's cult of male beauty was in fact based not on intellectual ideals but on physical ones. Daisy Brome, like Constance Wilde, was more bewildered than distressed when her husband began to spend hour after hour discussing current fashions with his male friends.

Then, you must know of André's pamphlet published in France just after Oscar's downfall in '95? *L'Affaire Oscar Wilde*, it was called, and I believe it was the first piece to be written about the whole scandalous mess of the trial. It sold relatively well here in France; but, then, of course André wrote it for a French audience. In it, our dear saintly André was assiduous in his malicious cross-hatching of Oscar's character and temperament (and that, of course, weakened the document's value as social history). I felt that the tract betrayed some guilty apprehensions of its own, but didn't say so to André, of course.

If I didn't hate Oscar on my own account, and for my own reasons, these persistent doses of André's venom might sway me, or any jury, to do so. But alas! there is one final factor in the equation that tends to render André's Oscar-baiting void. Oscar, you see, is the artist André will never be. André cannot make fashions, he can only follow them. He is the smaller man. Oscar, hideous and flamboyant and irritating as he is, has the flame of genius to compensate for his countless inadequacies. André, except for his money, the celibate John Gray and his prayers, has nothing; he possesses a slight talent, but no great gift, and part of his rage with Oscar must surely stem from his frustrating awareness of this galling fact.

How comforting it is, Father, to be able to say some of these things to you. My position with André is such a delicate one that I dare not provoke him with my private speculations. The cultivation of a patron is a most difficult and delicate series of negotiations, and follows a strict etiquette in that the artist seeking the patronage never abuses his patron — at least, not to his face.

Truly, I am grateful for André's generosity. You must not think otherwise. I fawn a little, when I must, and tease a little, when I can, and I see all of André's many good qualities with clear-sighted gratitude. None of this can prevent me from observing his life, his habits and his household from my own peculiar vantage-point.

André, I am certain of it, feels that a large part of our incipient *brotherhood* stems from our mutual loathing for Oscar Wilde. In a way, it was Oscar who brought us together; or, rather, it was the havoc that Oscar wrought in my own life two years ago that brought us together. If I were ever to receive Oscar Wilde – socially, I mean – and word of it got back to André, he would, in all likelihood, see me as a traitor and tear up any cheque with my name on it.

You must remember, Father, that I am penniless, and very ill, and have a family to support. This disease sucks up every spare penny by way of local doctors, medicines, travel necessities, hotel bills. Dying has become far too expensive in the late nineteenth century. And, were it not for André, I and my mother should most likely be inmates of Spitalfields Workhouse, rather than the pampered invalids we are here at St-Germain. God knows Smithers's cheques won't pay any bills. Every one of them now carries nearly inscrutable instructions for cashing at some far distant date.

This, the hag Nemesis reminds me, is my reward for throwing in my lot with a pornographer.

Mother has just entered with a telegraph from Mabel, who arrives at St-Germain tomorrow. Darling Mabel, here in my arms at last! She is the one blessing in an otherwise cursed life, and on her account I must do my utmost to appear strong and untroubled in the general catastrophe of my situation.

It has been only nine years, Father, since I left Brighton Grammar School, but in that time I have received an education for which no amount of classroom theorizing could ever have prepared me. This is not to belittle Brighton Grammar School, or to suggest that my education there was deficient in any manner. It was, rather, the best education I could ever have received, for it allowed a generous freeedom to my creative temperament and introduced me to the existence of worlds previously undreamed of.

How sweet those four brief years, when Nemesis hadn't yet seized upon me, and my future hadn't become a perennially cloudy crystal ball. My health was relatively stable then; whole terms went by when a low fever was the only indication of the pestilence slowly brewing in my blood. The fever became a part of my life, physical and creative, during those four years at Brighton Grammar School, only it was a benign force then – or seemed to be – a flush that gave a shimmery heroic tingle to all my artistic efforts.

You can imagine how my imagination flowered after the desert of Aunt Pitt's. Books, at last, and a piano! Paper and pencils! I was twelve, and started my career as a day boy, horribly embarrassed by the short trousers I was forced to wear. The trousers seemed to get shorter every day, and my charmless stick-legs longed to be covered and out of view. I certainly was not an Adonis when I showed up on my first day. Confronted by the curious and sometimes openly malicious stares of several dozens of strange boys, I remained self-conscious and shy that whole first term.

Mother's sciatica forced her to remain in bed, and Father continued to work in London, so I had to adapt myself to new circumstances without the benefit of any parental guidance. I should have liked some. I dreamed at that time of having a strong loving father whom I could talk to, question, respect and look up to; a father – albeit one who met my own impossibly exacting specifications – was what I wanted most.

I was different, you see. I preferred Virgil's *Eclogues* to the *Sporting Gazette*; Plato's unillustrated *Symposium* to the *Oarsman's Companion*, with its steel-plate portraits of famous rowers; Balzac's magnificent *Illusions perdues* in lieu of the *Football Annual*. Playing, so far as I was concerned, meant Chopin, at the piano, and not French and English or Tom Tiddler's Ground in the field. Mother, and my delicate health, and even Father Chapman's sermons at the Annunciation, had been responsible for instilling in me an appetite for culture quite at odds with the rough games and athletic aspirations that formed the meaning of life for most of the Brighton boys.

In English boys' schools, you know, games are used as a preventive for indecency; a way to counterattack all those deliciously evil little habits that creep up on the idle, inspire hands to forbidden pleasures and lead, inevitably, to irreversible physical deterioration. Mr Marshall, the leonine headmaster, summed up the institution's philosophy in his opening talk.

'In this school', he thundered, 'you are expected to imbibe a love for manly tastes and pursuits; an active, enduring, persevering spirit; a true contempt for effeminacy and indulgence and torpid idleness. The more sickly and morbid elements of character will be purged out of you if you adhere to the discipline this school seeks to foster.'

The boys in BGS, according to Mr Marshall, were going through a phase of life called the Magnetic Age. 'A perilous sensual period is before you,' he warned 'when the animal appetites most need control and transmutation. And, to this end, healthy physical energies must act to dispel unhealthy ones. The body, let us never forget, is a temple. Physical health is its adornment, lust its desecration.'

No amount of lecturing, hectoring, doomsaying, speechifying, good Christian oratory, sculling or cricket, however, can dull the sensual appetites of twelve-to-sixteen-year-old schoolboys. All the pent-up energies of youth, all the secret, savage, forlorn reveries they entertain, all the promptings and sensations of the newly awakened body point the way to buggery and onanism. By segregating boys from girls at this coarse crucial age of discovery and habituation, English schools perpetuate the very thing English society most abhors. Where, after all, do you suppose Oscar Wilde first tasted the dangerous spice that led to his eventual sex-madness? It was, I am certain, at Portora Royal School; and if not there, then at Trinity College, Dublin, or Oxford's Magdalen College. Wherever men gather without the daily society of women, there will flourish inversion and what André calls unisexuality.

Something in me was vaguely aware of this dark undercurrent of vice stalking the dormitories of Brighton Grammar School, and contributing to the array of cockstands in the classroom, but as a day boy I was spared further knowledge of its habits and camouflage. It was only when I entered as a full boarder wearing an Eton suit that carnality raised, as it were, its big, ugly, unmistakably fascinating head.

If a newcomer was good-looking, he was given a female name by the older boys and immediately appropriated as someone's 'bitch'; unless, that is, he decided to remain unattached, in which case he generally became known as a public prostitute. It was hearing the word 'bitch' that gave me my first jolt of awareness that there might be dangerous shoals ahead. A 'bitch' was any boy who gave himself up to a lover, and amazing it was to watch the pathetic transformation of some boys over the course of a year, from rosy-cheeked angels to flaming-arsed strumpets. Oh, the cruelty of those loves, and the strange, constant, breathtaking dramas they provided in the backdrop of one's days! Yet one simply accepted the oddity of it all and never dreamed of telling; it was a world so darkly and directly antithetical to the one publicly espoused as ideal by Mr Marshall that one thrilled a bit to be in on it. Certainly a familiarity with its by-laws and byways helped me later on, in London, when I was introduced into Bobbie Ross's circle of public-school Uranians.

Of course, it took me some time to comprehend how it all worked. Luckily I wasn't considered handsome enough to be sought after as a 'bitch', and I certainly had no intention of becoming a public whore, so I was pretty much left alone. Actually, I was something of a muff at first. Occasionally I was mocked for the way I looked – 'Weasel', I was called – but I was never taunted and abused the way Scotson-Clark was; he, poor boy, was known as *notissima fossa*, and it positively ruined Latin for him.

I first noticed him, or he me, during one of Mr Marshall's inspirational morning talks. 'A good, wholesomely cultivated mind and body,' Mr Marshall was heroically intoning, 'disciplined to obedience, self-restraint, and the sterner duties of chivalry, should be the distinguishing mark of our middle-class youth . . .'

Scotson-Clark's only distinguishing mark was his painfully erect cock. He was seated next to me, and I noticed that his hands, apparently resting in his lap, were in fact secretly rubbing and pinching his crotch. He seemed to be in a kind of fidgety torment; contradictory emotions flew across his lineaments, and his breathing became deep and rapid. At one point he suddenly turned and looked at me; and I, afraid that I had been caught out seeing something I wasn't supposed to, quickly turned away.

He caught up with me on the way to Mr King's science class. 'You're Beardsley, aren't you?' I nodded, still afraid, but he said: 'I heard you playing the piano.'

I never played in public at Brighton Grammar School. If I had an odd quarter-hour to spare, and no one was in the day room, I liked to sit and compose little repetitive chords and melodies from my own imagination, or perhaps play a Chopin nocturne or barcarolle; but if anyone entered I would leave the keyboard immediately and go to sit with a book instead. Without Mother's need for me to perform, and because the school had no music master, daily practice became irrelevant.

'You play very well,' said Scotson-Clark. He had fair hair and a pimply troubled face – a face that wanted to break out into laughter, but was prevented from doing so by some heavy load of private travail. His Christian name was Frederick. 'Do you like art?' he asked. Again I nodded. 'Do you like to draw?' he whispered, as though it were a sin.

'I draw quite a lot,' I said.

'I've seen you drawing,' he said. 'I like to draw as well.'

I felt an incipient spark of camaraderie. 'I was thinking of taking some of my work to Mr Godfrey, so he could criticize it for me.'

'May I see some of your work?'

An older boy, Frank Simpson, hissed as he passed by: 'Get your fat bum into Latin class, *notissima fossa*.'

Scotson-Clark stiffened with what looked like terror. 'Simpson the Simian,' he said in a weak wavering voice. I could see that he wanted to cry.

'Why do they call you that – "the infamous trench"?'

'Because they hate me,' he said. 'I do what they want, and then they hate me for it.'

My friendship with Fred Scotson-Clark was a bit illicit; I liked him, but he was tainted somehow, like an overripe cheese, and I was coward enough not to want to risk the smell that attends the pariah *and* the pariah's friends. Fred was a dear soul really; and that he was a bit strange made sense once you knew something of his background. He was the son of the Reverend Frederick Scotson-Clark, who was an organist and composer of church music. As a choirboy in his father's church, Fred had been repeatedly buggered by the choirmaster; when his treble broke, he was discarded for a boy with a higher voice.

My other close friend at BGS was Charley Cochran, or C. B. Cochran, Theatrical Management, as he now styles himself. It was one of life's more pleasant surprises when Charley Cochran turned out to be the manager of the acting troupe with which Mabel recently toured America.

He was always mad for the theatre, and I liked him because he had the reputation of a troublemaker. The headmaster at his last school in Eastbourne had asked for Charley to be removed, although he'd done nothing more serious than climb over the wall and go to town to see the Guy Fawkes celebration. Charley was always escaping; the discipline of school was a dull torture for someone who craved the freedom and excitement of the theatre.

Feeling deliciously bad about it, I began to sneak out to the theatre with Charley. These excursions became elaborate adventures, for we often had no money and had to sell the few possessions we owned in order to buy tickets. Ah, I remember it so well – the stealth one had to use, the cunning and nerves of steel required to risk one's entire school career for nothing more than a dangerous lark.

But the theatre – once inside, who cared what we had done to get there? The theatre welcomed us as it welcomes everyone with the sixpence for standing-room.

Mostly we went to Mrs Nye Chart's Brighton Theatre, where a succession of sensational melodramas shared the boards with other touring acts.

The lure of the theatre, Father – have you ever felt it? It's far more than the spectacle on stage that draws one back again and again; it's the atmosphere, the endless mixture of people, the decorations, the moments of mystery and speculation, as when a gentleman in evening dress leans over to light a cigarette from the gas-jet below his box and you see the character of his face sharply illumined for the tick of a second, or you espy a lady suddenly opening her fan and masking her face with it as she leans back to whisper to a friend or lover. What the Aunt Pitts of the world will never understand is that the theatre unites people, however briefly, and that through shared emotional excitement, guided by the actors on stage, an audience experiences catharsis, trite or otherwise. I wonder if Mabel will ever be given the chance to take on a truly great role, and command an audience from behind the footlights?

Charley would inevitably be filled with a great rush of energy every time we stole through the dark Brighton streets on our way back to the school. He would laugh and chatter, box with himself, play shadow games. Often he wanted to prolong our adventures, and would suggest that we walk along the front or duck down under the old chain pier, that decayed relic of Regency Brighton, where penniless lovers now staged their ancient versions of love to the gentle slap of the waves.

One night when the moon dropped her light like pale coins between the slats of the old pier, I followed Charley down there. A rank sea smell pervaded the place, and the giant pillars were alive with black marine encrustations; monstrous ropes of kelp and tangled coils of seaweed, spat up by the sea, rotted on the shingle. I had never played there as a boy, so the area held for me that night all the charm and terror of the unknown.

'Know how to feel good, Beardsley?' Charley asked suddenly.

I was puzzled by his question and could only repeat: 'Good?'

'I know how. Shall I show you?'

'Yes, please.'

'It has to do with this,' Charley said, unbuttoning his trousers and exposing his cock. 'If you rub it back and forth, it makes you feel good.'

'How?'

'I don't know how,' Charley said impatiently. 'It simply does, that's all.'

That night began a new part of my sexual education, Father. Charley called it 'frigging yourself'; it was, of course, that oldest of sins, attributed in the Bible to Onan, who by spilling his seed in the infertile sand ignored the biological impeachment of a woman's ripe cunt. There are few ripe cunts about for thirteen-year-old boys, dear Father (and none for bedridden twenty-four-year-olds, either), so one's hand quickly becomes adept at providing one's own pleasure. Just as Charley avowed, it made me feel good. My body gave a shudder, and expelled a terrific energy – still dry then – from between my stiffened legs. Charley treated it all as a kind of secret sport, and would frig himself at any opportunity in a variety of splendidly comical poses. He it was who showed me the various strokes, fingerholds and leverages that can turn mere self-love into a courtesan's art.

In one, which he called the Spider's Stroke, the cock was held and frigged between the index and second fingers, while the little finger moved down to agitate the balls teasingly and the thumb rubbed the head; another, dubbed Palm of Venus, involved a cupped hand performing a rapid *glissando agitato* on the tender underside only; a third, Ploughman's Lunch, made use of both hands, the pego held between like the bacon in a labourer's sandwich. Thrusting his bum forward, Charley would goad himself on to athletic feats of spunk-spurting. 'Ooh, yes, ma'am, see thar how she blows!' he could cry out huskily as wave after salty wave of spunk shot from the bright pink head of his poker.

Every boy is initiated into the rites of masturbation, Father; it is a long and time-honoured tradition that males share, and provides a rare example of men helping and encouraging one another rather than attempting to oust someone from the pack or blackening his eye. Is this why so many fearful injunctions are placed on the activity, and why it is a confessable vice? To you I do confess that since that night under old Brighton pier I have been a confirmed onanist. If I were to estimate the number of times? Roughly 30,000, I should say.

I did try to stop. Over and over, after each episode, I would vow never to sully myself again, and then succumb again the next day, sometimes with Charley, oftener alone, in bed. I was never free from guilt; perhaps it was even the guilt that made it so desirable. For here was I, practising the very same 'solitary vice' so endlessly warned about and preached against; the most sordid sin in that enormous catalogue compiled by Mr Marshall; the bad habit that undermined one's moral and physical health and led inevitably to insanity and disease, including tuberculosis.

It made me wonder about my father. Was it because he had done this, and his father before him, that the debilitating habit and its diseased aftermath now echoed in my blood?

One night, using the Spider's Stroke in bed, I had a sudden clear memory of the Duke of X before a roaring fire using the very same technique with one hand while he used the other to fiddle with my childish member. I was amazed and affronted. Did this create some disagreeable bond between us? And every time I practised the Palm of Venus an image of Jones, naked and angry, would fall unwarranted into my fantasies; or, stranger yet, one of Mabel in my bed the night of the great storm.

That was my secret life, Father. It is the secret life of nearly all boys, and has been, I suspect, since the Ancients first delineated and named the constellations.

One person there was at BGS to whom I shall always be grateful: Mr King, my housemaster and the science master of the school. He called me in one day and said as I stood before him: 'Are you Aubrey Beardsley, the boy who drew these caricatures of the masters?' Spread out on his desk was a sheaf of sketches that had been confiscated by the history master.

'Yes, sir.'

Mr King carefully scrutinized me. He was young compared with most of the other masters, and it was rumoured that he began each day by exercising with Indian clubs. He looked honest and enthusiastic, as fine a specimen of English manhood as Mr Marshall could ever hope us to emulate; with eyes the colour of Windermere on a bright clear day, a ruddy complexion, and hair the colour of Welsh slate. Lots of lonely boys like Scotson-Clark had crushes on him, I know that for a fact, and envisioned him as a sort of all-round ideal figure, almost god-like. Mr King was himself a product of Brighton Grammar School, and an excellent recommendation for what was good about the place; but he had also seen a bit of the world and kept his wits alive, unlike the older masters.

'The other boys call you Weasel,' he said. 'Why is that?'

'I suppose it may be the way I look, sir.'

'Hm. You have been heard lecturing the other boys on Shakespeare's plays—'

'Yes, sir,' I broke in excitedly, 'I love Shakespeare.' That year I had enthusiastically started to read every word the Bard set on paper, and occasionally Charley and I saw a bad touring production of *As You Like It* or *Hamlet* at Mrs Nye Chart's Brighton Theatre. The language of Shakespeare and other Elizabethan English playwrights appealed to me in the way the piano once had.

'Be that as it may, I have here your classification exams,' said Mr King drily, 'and *they* indicate that, whatever you may know of the comedies, tragedies and histories of Shakespeare, you do *not* know the multiplication tables.'

Oh, I was pert, something in me wanting to goad him on. 'I find multiplication tables entirely unnecessary, sir.'

He raised his head higher. 'Oh, do you?'

'As long as one can count money – and has enough of it to count – what does it matter if one knows the multiplication tables or not?'

He sat poised between laughter and the sterner demeanour demanded by authority. 'Mr Killingsworth would not agree with you,' he said, referring to the school's ancient mathematics master.

'Sir,' I ventured, 'I have been put in classes with babies. None of the boys have read as much as I have. All they think of is cricket.'

'You avoid the playing-fields, Beardsley?'

'My health does not allow me the pleasure of sport,' I said grandiloquently. 'I prefer reading anyway.'

'What are you reading now – beyond your classroom assignments, I mean?'

'Congreve and Wycherley. Charley Cochran and I are—'

'Charley Cochran?' Mr King pounced on the name with such alacrity that my heart pattered. Did he know of our secret vice? 'He's the boy from Eastbourne, isn't he? A year ahead of you?'

'Really, sir, he's more like a year behind. Except for theatrical—' I came to a halt, again afraid of revealing too much.

'Yes?'

'Charley knows heaps about the theatre, that's all.'

'You enjoy the theatre, Beardsley?'

'I adore it above all else.'

'Then, why don't you give a Shakespearian recital?' Mr King suggested.

I stood bathed in the sudden delirious idea of standing on a stage and reciting the bloodier speeches of Shakespeare. 'No one told me that I might, sir.'

'I shall help you to prepare it. And why not try lightning sketches on the blackboard with chalk, or on paper with coloured chalks? Lightning sketches that catch the essence of a personality instead of distorting it. Instead of giving annoyance to your victims by these innumerable sketches, use your talents to amuse and instruct without giving offence.'

I was most impressed by his offer of guidance. 'Yes, sir.'

'And since you are so keen on reading, Beardsley, you may use my personal library—'

'Any volume I wish, sir?'

'You have a quick mind. I would like to help guide and direct it so that as you grow older it will flow in a properly wholesome direction.'

'Thank you, sir.'

'You may count on me as a friend,' said Mr King.

What a godsend certain people are at crucial moments in one's life, Father! Without Mr King's influence – without his *friendship*, for such it was that he offered me – my years at Brighton Grammar School would have been dull indeed. What did he see in me, I wonder now, that made him take me under his wing the way he did? Some people seem to have a natural selfless instinct to guide and instruct; help to mould character without strangling it; draw from an endless fund of patience and goodwill. Mr King was such a one. He served me well; and in my darker moments I cannot help picturing him as disgusted with what I have made of my life and my talents. He, for his part, had only one vice that I knew of: he loved to write rhyming couplets.

Of course, what I could never have known was that Mr A. W. King, he of the science classroom, pointing with a stick to a wallchart containing all the known elements, he of the arcane formulae and dizzyingly precise theories, was in fact as stage-struck as Charley and I. Circumstances had not allowed him to pursue what he felt to be his true calling, so he became a devoted amateur and began to infect even the cricket-loving brutes of BGS with his love of theatre and theatrical entertainments.

I quickly became Mr King's favourite, and under his sponsorship, as it were, had less need to fear the insults and charges of effeminacy that would otherwise have been my daily lot (as they were the daily scourge of poor Scotson-Clark). Do you know what it is to be encouraged, Father, rather than undermined? What boy seeks anything more? I sometimes even believe that if I had confided in Mr King about my insatiable onanistic practices he would have helped me then to overcome them.

Between us, Mr King and I eventually became almost solely responsible for the Entertainments, weekly and annual, of Brighton Grammar School. You cannot imagine the fervour with which I threw myself into the tasks set by Mr King.

From the beginning he encouraged my drawing, even when that third-rate failure Mr Earp urged me to remove myself from his painting class for want of talent. Mr King, and Mr Payne, my form and classics master and Mr King's closest friend on the staff, would pore over my innumerable sketches – rough little things mostly done in brown or violet ink that allowed me to exercise a bit of feeble humour (I have always found caricature to be irresistible) – and pronounce on them as though they were important works by a famous artist. At the time I was madly enthusiastic for Fred Barnard and his drawings of Henry Irving, and would copy these drawings as I had earlier copied Kate Greenaway. I drew in small; often the figures were tiny, as though I wanted to preserve some mysterious miniature world of childhood that I carried about in my imagination. It was Mr King who first suggested that I should draw up the programmes for our Entertainments, to be decorated around the margins any way I desired.

Not only that, there were sets to paint, and costumes to create from the oddments at hand. It had the thrill of a treasure hunt really – assembling all the elements, putting everything together so that it would enhance the performance. I quite understand the desire to lead the nerve-racking life of an impresario that eventually took Charley to America: it is endless hard work, but endless fun as well.

And, moreover, I became a performer again, this time not on the piano but on the stage. Our first school entertainment was an educational discussion between the former rulers of England and their courtiers. Henry II, Bishop Langton, Oliver Cromwell – all these power-mad men were introduced by the goddess Minerva, whose part I played to perfection. I had wheedled one of the matron's nightdresses, procured a long yellow wig, and could barely hold my head steady in its heavy Roman helmet. Arm upraised, clutching a paper-tipped sword, I sententiously orated in the dullest of Mr King's rhyming couplets.

Mr King used to take me for long walks so that we could plan the weekly Entertainments and my own contributions. He would stride faster and faster until I had almost to run to keep pace with him. Sometimes I could keep up; sometimes I would start to cough and have to sit, light-headed, on the grass until my wind returned. Mr King was tenderly solicitous at such moments, sitting patiently beside me until I had recovered sufficiently to go on, but always I would see his foot tapping or his knee jiggling up and down as he kept up his own rapid internal pace.

Our 'Weeklies' could be anything from a farce to comic songs to serious recitations, and were enjoyed in part because they offset the perpetual gravity of Mr Marshall's moral discourses. Given a poem or part to learn, I would take myself down to the old chain pier, book or play under my arm, and there, like an adolescent Lear, recite my lines to the howling winds and storm-racked heavens in the loudest voice I could muster. I derived a queer thrill from leaving behind the me I knew and assembling with impunity a new character; and when the time came to perform I realized that I was good at it because of my experience with audiences as a pianist. *I was a performer*, and no longer because I had to be but because I wanted to be. This seemed an astounding revelation at the time.

There I stood in front of all those boys – the very boys who made Scotson-Clark's life such a miserable torment, and who liked nothing better than to kick and bruise one another in games of football; who bullied, buggered, swore, stole, poached, drank, and practised the solitary vice – there I stood before them, *holding their attention* as I declaimed 'Mary's Ghost', 'The Spitalfields Weaver', or Thomas Hood's *Eugene Aram*; hearing their laughter when I played Victor in the farce *Ici On Parle Français*; bowing to their applause. I wanted it to go on for ever.

My grandfather, the old Surgeon-Major, died during my time at Brighton Grammar School. He had been taken by a sudden whim to visit London, my grandmother told us; no one could stop him, and off he went, only to drop dead in a Bloomsbury hotel. Did he know that Death awaited him? Was that the summons, the unstoppable 'whim' he had to satisfy? I am so curious always to know

how one knows when one's time is up. One does, of course; there is
an unmistakable foreknowledge of the event that obliterates the
trivial concerns of daily life, and forces one to a final reckoning of
all earthly accounts. The family tried not to be shocked when they
discovered the apparently successful Surgeon-Major had left behind
a legacy of less than £150. 'Hardly enough for a decent funeral
nowadays,' Aunt Pitt complained.

Mabel all this while was a boarder at Miss Topp's establishment
at 7 Alexandra Villas, a few minutes' walk from the Surgeon-Major's
house in Buckingham Road. Aunt Pitt paid Mabel's school fees, just
as she paid mine, and we would spend our holidays with Old Sarum
and the dwarfish farm-girl she had hired to replace Jones. On Sundays
I was allowed to attend services at the Annunciation, but Mabel was
not: none of the other girls at Miss Topp's attended such a high
church, and of course Mabel couldn't go such a distance unchaperoned. Eventually we hit upon a plan whereby I, the honourable
brother, would go to pick Mabel up at Miss Topp's, escort her to
the Annunciation and return her to 7 Alexandra Villas afterwards.

Her school was not as lively and stimulating as mine. 'The girls
can be quite jolly,' Mabel said, 'but they don't like to *think*.' She
was appalled at the idea that, given a brain, a woman should not
use it. My sister was beginning to realize how intelligent she really
was. Under the special tutelage of Miss Callow, who held advanced
views on nearly every subject, Mabel was blossoming intellectually.
This Miss Callow would often be anxiously waiting for Mabel when
I returned her from the Sunday service. She was a thin, intense young
woman who wore spectacles and later died of consumption; and she
treated Mabel as a special friend and confidante, in much the same
way that Mr King treated me. Mabel, of course, would never stop
talking about her.

'Miss Callow says that women should very definitely be given the
vote,' she said one Sunday. 'She says it's shocking that a country like
England, calling itself civilized, should deny full citizenship to half
its population.'

'Is Miss Callow a suffragette?'

'She is not allowed to be. Miss Topp does not allow the teachers
to hold or express political opinions.'

'But Miss Callow expresses them to you,' I pointed out.

139

'Yes,' Mabel whispered ardently, 'but only in private, you see. Then we talk about everything. She tells me everything she knows. Miss Callow is the sweetest friend I've ever had.' She must have seen a look of displeasure cross my face, for she quickly took my hand and kissed it. 'After you, of course.'

Our holidays together were as merry as circumstances allowed. We saw Mother and Father briefly, and perceived that there was a terrible strain between them. What was it? They were like strangers to one another, and almost strangers to us. Mother wore the grey strained look of ill-health. Mostly they would question us about school, and praise Aunt Pitt's generosity. 'A good education will allow you to find and hold a decent job, something above *mere labour*,' Mother would say to me, looking at Father with a sad little smile on her face.

There was no further prodding of the prodigies. Whatever we had done as children was evidently worthless now, in the light of adult practicality. It seemed treacherous of Mother to withdraw her encouragement of our artistic endeavours, which previously she had not only encouraged but also lived on. Father, of course, bore the daily sting of failure, and failures are never encouraging; it gets in the way of their jealousy. Thus, for Mabel and me it soon became apparent that a new load of responsibilities lay ahead; *they* had plans for *us*; again, we were potential wage-earners.

Oh, just for once to be free of this incessant need to make money! To swim in the freedom of creativity alone, unhindered by considerations of production and payment! Commerce determines our every move nowadays; perhaps even determines the direction of our thinking. No age surely has ever been as tainted and greedy as this Victorian age of ours, which attaches a price-tag to everything and everyone.

But Mabel and I, despite the grim prospect of having one day to take jobs, managed to keep our creative instincts alive. In the mid-eighties Havelock Ellis, who had not yet become a sex chronicler, was editing and bringing out a new series called the Mermaid Dramatists; and Mabel and I began to act out, quietly, in low voices so that Aunt Pitt would not hear us, the plays of John Ford, Congreve, Wycherley and Christopher Marlowe. The sex of the role never mattered to us; if anything, we enjoyed slipping off the masks we had to wear in our respective schools and for our parents and for Aunt Pitt. As Pope wrote in *The Rape of the Lock*, 'For spirits, freed from mortal laws, with ease/Assume what sexes and what shapes they please.' My sister and I were not free from mortal laws – on the contrary, we were the prisoners of them – but for a few hours anyway we could assume other sexes and shapes, and dream that remarkable futures awaited us.

THIS MORNING, FATHER, after a dreadful night of pain and depression, I was sitting shakily in a chair in my room, my face lathered, the old barber with his impeccable moustache and doughy flesh prattling on about the healthful effects of well-cooked veal as he scraped away my whiskers.

'Il ferait du bon veau, Monsieur Beardsley, vous l'avez bien saigne,' he said, quoting an old French proverb of the butchery trade and waving the razor in his hand for emphasis. Satisfied that he had made his point, he pursed his lips and redirected his attention to the long bony ridge that makes my jaw a perfect Matterhorn. French barbers, of course, like French ladies' maids, are the most delicately skilled interpreters of human physiognomy; and the old violet-scented hands of Monsieur Vella, because they are the only hands that touch me these days, almost make me weep with pleasure and gratitude.

The razor made a smooth trajectory down my jawbone, and I sat drowsily waiting for the next stroke, when a pair of hands suddenly covered my eyes from behind.

'What do you wish for?' a low musical voice asked.

'I wish that my sister Mabel were standing behind me,' I said, my heart racing. 'What do you wish for?'

'I wish that my brother Aubrey were seated before me.'

We burst into tears, and Mabel got shaving lather on her face and gloves as we embraced and kissed. Then Mother entered, her eyes brimming, and stood for a moment looking at her reunited offspring. The three of us, together again! Our hearts were too full to do anything but drink in the realization of happiness. Monsieur Vella took a respectful step away and stood beaming in our glow.

Mother's voice was tremulous with emotion as she said: 'Mabel dear, do let Aubrey complete his toilette. He has not had a good night, I'm afraid.'

Concern instantly flashed into Mabel's expression, and a little stutter of fear, too, and I cursed Mother for reminding us all so immediately of my disintegration: the reason, after all, why we are here and not in London, the reason why Mabel must travel across the Channel to see us, the reason why every meeting becomes so intolerably heartsore, because it may be the last.

'Yes, in a moment,' Mabel said, 'but there is something that cannot wait.' From the pocket of her travelling-cloak she extracted a folded paper, opened it, and began to read. ' "A Book of Fifty Drawings by Aubrey Beardsley. Demy quarto, bound in scarlet cloth extra, with cover design by Mr Beardsley. Edition of five hundred copies printed on Imitation Japanese Vellum, ten shillings six pence per copy; fifty copies printed on Imperial Japanese Vellum, two pounds two shillings net per copy." '

'Mabel,' I whispered. She silenced me with a glance, and continued to read.

' "This Album of Drawings will comprise, in addition to several hitherto unpublished designs, a selection by Mr Beardsley of his most important published work ('Morte D'Arthur', 'Salome', 'Rape of the Lock', 'Yellow Book', 'Savoy', etc.) The volume will be of additional interest to the Artist's many admirers from the fact that the plates will in most cases be reproduced from the original drawings, with due regard to their size and technique, thus preserving many delicate features which have been to a great extent lost by the treatment the drawings received on their first publication. The frontispiece is a reproduction of the latest photograph of Mr Beardsley." '

'It's finally advertised,' I said.

'Mr Smithers says it will be published in August at the latest.'

'August.' I knew now that I simply must not die before then.

'Come, dear, let us see to your unpacking,' said Mother.

Mabel, never taking her bright green eyes from my half-shaven face, handed me the advertisement, gave me a kiss of triumph and left with Mother. And I, galvanized with so much pleasure that I momentarily forgot my pain, sat back with such a broad smile that Monsieur Vella said he could not continue while my face was so 'joyeux'.

' "You are an enclosed garden, my sister, my bride," ' I whispered to her late that night, when Mother was finally asleep and we two were alone in my room, ' "an enclosed garden, a fountain sealed." '

' "Let my lover come to his garden and eat its choice fruits," ' whispered Mabel, stroking my lips.

' "I have come to my garden, my sister, my bride; I gather the myrrh and my spices, I eat my honey and my sweetmeats, I drink my wine and my milk." *Especially* my milk.' I turned my face away, afraid of my own arousal.

'He sounds like an idiot!' Mabel said. She had caught my meaning at once and knew I was referring to Dr Lamarre. I had of course told her the whole story of my prescribed walks in the forest before dawn, the milk and fruit diet, the utter worthlessness of it and perhaps all 'cures'. 'Dr Phillips will be here in a day or two,' Mabel said, 'and then we shall know what to do.'

'The most fearful depression comes over me at times, and I feel so powerless against it. The most awful sense of . . . nullity.'

Mabel got up from the bed, where she had been resting beside me. 'I never know what or how much I should tell you, Aubrey.'

'What do you mean?'

'Oh, one hears of different cures, things that sound impossible but – who knows? – may help.'

'What sort of cure? I thought I'd tried all of them: milk, wine, fruit, roast beef, activity, inactivity, sea air, mountain air, cold air, warm air, sunlight, water, arsenic, creosote, vinegar, copper salts . . .'

As I ranted on about doctors and 'cures', Mabel wandered about the room claiming my possessions with a stroke of her finger or a glance from her eye. She picked up a volume of Bourdaloue's sermons bound in calf, a gift inscribed from André, and flirted me a brief, bemused, wonderfully knowing look. Frowningly she examined a framed photograph of herself taken last year when she played Mrs Maydew in *The Queen's Proctor* at the Royalty Theatre, and another of Richard Wagner, that god of composers, and a third of ugly little André. How beautifully she moved, how robust and sturdy, even though she was haunted by fatigue. In Mabel's face and constitution I see myself, a little jealously, as I might have been had not this disease decided to use me as its feeding-trough. She had let me unpin and take her hair down for the night, let me stroke it, play with it, bury my hands and face in its thick pungent abundance.

'When I was touring in America, one of our engagements was in Chicago.' My sister was now worldly enough to pronounce it 'Shi-kaw-go', as the Americans evidently do. 'And while we were there I heard of a place called the Healthotorium.' She paused, nervously clasping her hands.

'Yes?'

'Oh, it sounds so queer, but who knows what will help? The theory at the Healthotorium is that since all human beings once walked on four legs, health can be restored by a course of walking on one's knees and one's knuckles.'

I burst into laughter at the notion of creeping about the floors of some enormous American institution on all fours; a hilarious vision of its stairways and corridors, all crowded not with people walking, but with people *crawling*, overtook me; the fever will often seize upon some bizarre notion like this and stretch it into a brief and absurd internal visual dementia.

Mabel, the dear, began to laugh, too, and larkingly got down on all fours.

'Good evening, Mr Beardsley,' I said. 'Are you enjoying your stay at our Healthotorium?'

'Yes, Doctor, quite,' Mabel said, 'but there's one thing I simply cannot work out.'

'What is that, Mr Beardsley?'

'Well, Doctor, how do you do your business in this position?'

We laughed until we wept, one of those painfully delicious laughs that wrench your deepest parts and leave you sated with pleasure. But my pleasure turned to sudden alarm as I heard a smothered whistle in my left lung, and I stopped laughing as quickly as I could lest the Cough begin.

Mabel came again to take my hand and sit beside me. 'There are other places, too,' she said. 'Other new methods.'

'They might as well revert to the old methods,' I said bitterly, 'back to leeches and bleeding and cupping.'

'Yes, really it's intolerable,' Mabel said, rubbing the back of my hand with her thumbs. The sensation of tender loving flesh against mine undammed me, Father, made me expel a gust of bitterness that lay rotting in the deepest, most stinking parts of me. 'I'm certain there will be a cure now – any day,' Mabel said. With a sweet glance, she smiled and started softly to hum as she rubbed her palm up and down my forearm. Mabel – here with me, touching the barren desert of my body and turning it to oasis.

'Do you remember seven years ago, when Koch announced his cure for tuberculosis in Berlin?' I asked. (When you are dying of a disease, Father, you follow news of it the way some of us used to follow our careers.) 'Lymph, he called it.'

'Lymph?'

'It was some sort of clear brown liquid – a kind of beef consommé, I suppose – that he injected into the back, right between the shoulderblades.'

147

Mabel took a deep breath and shuddered.

'The injection, he said, was always followed by a severe reaction, even worse coughing and spitting; but that gradually, after you'd been through the worst agony of it, when you thought you couldn't take any more, your fever would suddenly drop and your lungs begin to mend. So of course half of Europe – my half, the desperate half that has this vile disease – immediately booked passage to Berlin. There were so many that you couldn't find a hotel room in the entire city. People simply poured into Berlin; so many and so ill that they died on the trains, on the way to their final cure. Which was no cure at all. Which didn't work the way Koch said it would. The way none of them works.'

'You mustn't be so pessimistic.' Mabel laid her cheek against mine. Her skin, so sweetpea-soft, still fresh as a baby's, but already showing a light dry tracery of worry-lines around her eyes. Poor thing! She had, I know, many worries, but hadn't yet confided any of them to me. I plunged my hand into the cool depths of her hair, lifted it, and let it fall like tickling rain upon my face, a strand at a time. Mabel sighed.

'The Shadow always hovering near,' I murmured. 'That against which will is powerless.'

'Dr Phillips will know the best thing to do. You like him, don't you?'

'He is a good doctor, and his services are gratis – that is recommendation enough.' This piece of sarcasm was misleading, for I was in fact making Dr Phillips into my new medical Messiah.

'How thin you've become,' Mabel said anxiously. 'Are you eating enough?'

'The old adage among lungers, my darling, is to eat once for yourself, once for the germs, and once to gain weight. Yes, I eat; I have absolutely no appetite, but I eat; I force myself; I gorge.' What I didn't add, of course, was that whatever I ate my body refused to accept, so vomiting had become as great a pastime for me as it was for the ancient Romans.

Her hand was cool as mist on the desert of my forehead. 'Do you want to sleep now?' she whispered.

I grabbed her wrist. 'No. No, I want to be with you. I want you to tell me everything you've been doing, and everyone you've been seeing, and all the gossip from London. I'm so frightfully cut off here – I want to hear what is happening in the real world.'

Mabel tiptoed into the adjoining chamber, which she was sharing with Mother, to extract a cigarette from her carefully hidden store and to make certain that our progenitrix was soundly asleep. The sweet pungent smell of Egyptian tobacco teased my nostrils as Mabel sat cross-legged on the bed, a smoking odalisque. Over a pair of Zoave-style breeches she wore a threadbare but still flamboyant silken wrapper painted in broad strokes of green and blue, the fabric as soft as sin. I was in my favourite yellow robe and red oriental slippers with turned-up toes.

'Most of the gossip is about Oscar, of course,' Mabel said. 'Where is he? Who is he with? Is he with Bosie Douglas?'

'André scouted him as far as Dieppe,' I said.

'I do have some rather sensational information about Oscar's whereabouts on the day he was released from prison.' Mabel's voice deepened in the manner of a Pythian oracle, and she half-closed her eyes as she began to puff more heavily on her cigarette. 'Where do you think he went?'

'I have no idea, but it was probably the only day in Oscar's life when he *wasn't* looking for publicity. How shamed he must have felt.'

'I know where he went,' Mabel said, poised for her bit of drama. 'From the prison yard – but by a different gate, so he wouldn't have to face the hordes of reporters – in a cab to Stewart Headlam's house. He hid there until he could take the steamer to Dieppe. And do you know who went to visit him there, at seven o'clock in the morning?' Another pause, for dramatic effect. 'Ada Leverson, my dear.'

'She's a remarkable woman,' I said. And obviously she had confronted her worst fears, for Ada Leverson had once confessed to me, whispering behind her fan: 'I am not afraid of death, Mr Beardsley, but I am terrified of scandal.' This same woman, Father, had sheltered Oscar between his trials, and she once did something rather remarkable for me as well, but I had never told that story to Mabel. 'Remarkable,' I murmured.

'Well, you know how close she and Oscar have always been. Practically lovers. She adored his mind and all of that, but she also loved the way he laughed at things. She said he healed people with laughter.'

'Yes, Oscar laughed at a great many things once. I wonder what he finds amusing now?' I could feel the Oscar-poison seeping into my veins, Father, as Mabel spoke of him, and had to refrain myself from spitting out insults.

'Do you remember that portrait of Oscar that hung over his mantelpiece in Tite Street?' Mabel said. 'The one by Harper Pennington?'

'Yes, very flattering as I recall.'

Mabel blew out an excited mouthful of smoke and leaned forward confidentially. 'Ada, my dear, bought that portrait at Oscar's bankruptcy sale and had it draped in black crape the entire time he was in prison.'

I already knew that, Father, for I had secretly visited Ada Leverson myself, in that horrible June of 1895 when Oscar was tried and sentenced to prison and my own life fell apart in the wake of those events. I didn't want Mabel to know of this episode, however, for it would ruin her pleasure in telling me what she thought were state secrets.

'But no one knows where the Tetrarch Oscar is now?' I asked.

'No, it's all been very secret. Ada did say she was particularly looking forward to Dieppe this August, and hinted it was because Oscar would be there.'

'She would let herself be seen in public with him?'

'One does all sorts of mad things in Dieppe, my dear – things one would never dream of doing in England.'

'I can attest to the truth of that observation.'

'I know you can,' said Mabel, spicing her voice with an arch theatrical emphasis.

'You're seeing a great deal of Ada?'

'She's been adorably good to me. We went to the theatre nearly every night – not that there's anything worth seeing. Ada always has a box, you know. And she does know a great many people.'

'Any who can help you?'

'Perhaps.' Her manner was charmingly evasive. 'I *have* made the acquaintance now of Bernie Beere.' She meant, dear Father, Mrs Bernard Beere, an actress notoriously fond of *travesti* roles.

'You've been seeing a great deal of our Russian prince André as well, haven't you?' I couldn't help but ask. I hunger to be in on the intrigues of London life, you see, and must live it all through Mabel. 'He mentions you in nearly all his letters.'

'What a kind man André is!' Mabel said with a peculiar emphasis. 'I feel very close to all of them, really – André, and Mr Gray, and Miss Gribbell.'

'I'm sure the Grib takes an extra-special interest in you now that you are numbered among the True Believers.'

Mabel fished out a small but surprisingly heavy crucifix on a long chain deep between her breasts. The object was still warm as milk and I studied it intently. 'The Grib gave me this the day I was baptized.'

'Are those tiny rubies?'

'Four of them. They represent the blood of Christ's wounds.'

And, indeed, I saw now that there was a brilliant speck of deep vermilion red in the palms of the crucified Christ's hands, one in His side, and another in His crossed feet. His blood had turned to precious stones.

'She's also just given me a lovely evening gown,' Mabel said. 'It couldn't have been hers; it's like nothing she would wear.'

'Perhaps it was one of André's,' I said.

'Naughty!' She sparkled with momentary delight, but then became somber. 'Aubrey, the most frightful complication has arisen. Sometimes recently it has been difficult for me to go to South Audley Street.'

I braced myself for the worst. Nemesis, I was certain, was standing behind a curtain that was just about to go up. Whatever was left in my life to ruin would now be ruined; the abyss would open to reveal fathomless depths.

'The Grib, you see, seems to think that André and I—' She was suddenly adorably shy, and turned very red.

'That André and you what?'

'Well, that we should . . . marry.'

This was too hilarious and absurd to be true! 'And what will John Gray be at the wedding?' I said tartly. 'The priest, the best man, or the bridesmaid?'

'She is hopelessly blind to all of that,' Mabel said.

'Who does she think John Gray is?'

'He is André's best and dearest friend.'

'Yes, I suppose friendship could explain why André would pluck Gray out of a tiny flat in the Temple and buy a house for him in Park Lane.'

'Aubrey, you know what the Grib is like. She is completely innocent about the darker matters of the heart.'

'This woman is an acute observer of life, I must say. She acts as mother to André for his entire life and never once suspected him of travelling regularly to Sodom?'

'She is his mother, my dear, because she is paid quite handsomely be so. And, like most mothers, she doesn't see her child as he really is, but as she imagines him to be. She thinks André is shy and unsure of himself with women because his real mother is such a beast. Did you meet Madame Raffalovich when you were in Paris?'

'No, I was too ill,' I lied.

'The Grib wants André to marry and have children. Enter Miss Mabel Beardsley.'

'Mysteriously unmarried.'

'An actress perennially searching for theatrical work. Or perhaps,' she sighed, 'not an actress at all.' This is and always has been her one stumbling-block in life, Father: she doubts her own abilities. Our darling mother, asleep in the next room, had to countenance mine, finally, only because I proved that I could earn a steady income through its exercise; how much less excusable the desire to be an actress, a profession which will never be 'nice enough' for Mother, and pays well only if one becomes an established celebrity on the order of Sarah Bernhardt, or Réjane, or Duse, or Mrs Patrick Campbell, or Ellen Terry. Is there anything more disheartening and dispiriting than to hear one's heartfelt desires constantly abused as 'unrealistic' or 'impossible'? But that is what my sister has been exposed to since she decided to abandon teaching and concentrate on a theatrical career.

'You mustn't stop trying, ever,' I said to her.

'Oh, Aubrey, I never dreamed it would all be so difficult.' Finally I saw those tears I loved so much because they confided her entire heart to me. Finally I could hold her as she liked to be held, her body, close to mine, suffused with the deep shuddering sobs of unexpressed fears and emotion. Finally I could be all things to her – a sacred trinity in one person: father, brother, husband.

The weather here at St-Germain has been too charmingly hot for words, Father, and early each morning Mabel wheels me in a chair across the terrace with its panoramic view of Paris, through the gardens and a little way into the forest. Twenty-four years old and already confined to an invalid's chair! We go early because it is cooler, and because I cannot bear the curious stares and whispers that would accompany our progress later in the day.

I sit, mentally alert and physically enfeebled, as Mabel pushes the chair through a blooming wealth of nature, of organisms effortlessly pouring forth their vitality and beauty. 'White roses!' she exclaims, stopping to pull the perfumed heart of one to her nose. 'Do you remember, Aubrey, how we tried to grow roses in the back of a hundred and fourteen?'

She means Cambridge Street, in Pimlico, our one and only home; and the moment I think of it – with happiness – I am forced to remember how we lost it, how we lost everything, that summer of 1895, two short years ago. The Oscar-poison rises like gall in my throat. But I am determined to savour every moment with Mabel, and to control or overcome my darker thoughts, so that she won't be burdened with knowledge of my terrors about money and the true nature of my health, or my thousand other apprehensions.

'Let me smell!' I say, and rise with her help to stand light-headed and swooning over the rose bush. Each rosebud is a gathering flame that ignites into a full-petalled fire; there are thousands of them on dozens of rose bushes, all happily feeding on the rot of manure, gaining extra health and beauty from the assimilation of rich ordure. Is it not the same with the sinner who repents, Father? The deeper his roots have delved into life's filth and mire, the richer and more beautiful his soul is when at last he decides to step free of the muck and bask in the light of Christ.

The roses remind me of a completely modern picture of the Annunciation I once drew and published in *The Yellow Book*: a naked Mary and a handsomely mustachioed supernatural messenger wearing winged boots and skirts of embroidered flame stand in a bower of burning white roses, the messenger whispering the Great Secret to Mary from behind his hand. (My fellow-editor, Harland, feared charges of sacrilege would arise if I called the drawing 'The Annunciation' and persuaded me to change its title to 'The Mysterious Rose Garden'.)

'The sinner who returns from sinning rejoices God more than the man who has never sinned,' I say, easing myself back into the chair. 'Do you know why?'

'No, why?' Mabel crouches beside me, droplets of sweat collecting already on her top lip. She is wearing an ornate tailor-made costume of pink and green vivogne, with leg-of-mutton sleeves and a skirt gored with back pleats, the whole ensemble topped off by a pretty but over-trimmed hat. She has such rare opportunities to buy clothing, my darling penniless sister, that when she does she gorges on bright colours and spectacular trimmings, like a child on sweets. Her object, always, is to make people notice her; her self is perpetually 'for hire', as it were. This was once my goal as well, so I cannot disparage the desire – in startling times one goes for a startling 'effect' – but the pariah *malade* that is now Aubrey Beardsley, while loathing solitude, of necessity seeks it: people are such ghouls when they come face to face with a public dying that I don't like to encourage their natural morbidity by putting myself too often on display.

'Because', I say, 'the great sinner has tested himself fully in the world; he has done his very best, and his very worst; he has tasted sin, even enjoyed it, and he gives it up only because he knows just how enjoyable it is.'

'And God loves him for it,' Mabel whispers fervently. She quickly unfastens the crucifix given her by Miss Florence Truscott Gribbell, worn nun-like on her bosom, and presses it into my hand. 'Since I was received, Aubrey, my spiritual worries are at an end. That one part of me, at least, is at peace.'

'I cannot take this from you,' I say, adding flippantly as I hand it back to her: 'You may need to pawn it some day.'

'This I shall never pawn,' Mabel says seriously, kissing it.

She pushes me on. A smell of hot coffee and bread from the dining-room of the Pavillon; a gathering heat that draws out fragrance and sounds: overhead, a high-arching canopy of birdsong. 'It's difficult to think of the endless rush of London in this lovely place,' Mabel says quietly.

'Give me the rush of London,' I say. 'I'd rather die of overwork in the foul air of the city than live amongst the scented boredoms of the country.'

'London,' Mabel sighs. 'Racing about from one interview to the next, from one possibility to the next, trying on new sensations as though they were new hats. Did I tell you the new rage, my dear? Strawberries soaked in ether! Everything must be new, new, new — only if it is new can they call it *fin de siècle*; and how tired I am of hearing that phrase attached to everything from morphia addiction to the way a room is done up, until it has no meaning at all.'

'People have to call it something, I suppose. It needs a name, this queer end-of-the-century sensation.'

'Do you suppose people feel it at the end of every century? That it produces almost a kind of . . . madness?'

'Waiting for the end of anything is difficult, that's all. It's always terrifying to see the last grains of sand dropping from the hourglass—'

'Has it been beastly with Mother?' Mabel asks.

'For her, yes. I know that she would rather be in England.'

'She would rather be with you, in a place that will make you well.'

'I wish I could tell her to go. I wish with all my heart that I did not have such need of her. But I cannot manage yet by myself.'

'If only I could stay,' Mabel says, pushing me along the gravel paths, sweating with the exertion on this hot dry day in June.

There is not enough money, and she knows it. She is trying to eke out her own living in that most nebulous of worlds, the theatre, rather than ask for a regular sum from me. I could not give it if she asked, and she knows that as well. The idea of marrying André, though perfectly absurd, crosses her mind now and then: a *mariage blanc*, of course, based not on love but on social and financial necessity; an adorably *fin de siècle* solution to the problem of their respective reputations, André's being considered too womanish, Mabel's too mannish, and both of them far too unmarried. What André calls unisexuals or Uranians, and Krafft-Ebing calls Urnings, and the rest of the world calls inverts, sodomites and buggers, are quite fond of my sister. Who wouldn't be? She is splendid to look at, she enjoys a good improper story in both the telling and the hearing, and occasionally she likes to masquerade as a man. Her conversion to Catholicism could only be an added inducement, one would think, for André to propose.

But it is the Grib, and the Grib only, who entertains this notion, and has hinted of its desirability to her spiritual god-daughter. Prince André remains, I am certain, blissfully unaware of their fantastic female notions, his cock turned ever upward in fervent prayer at the side of John Gray.

My sister! If she only knew how I worry about her; that my nights are filled with febrile visions of catastrophes lying in wait. For she, after all, my darling sister, will be left behind when I am coffined and dropped into Mother Earth; she will continue, alone, without me, without the protection of a brother or a husband or a father.

We enter the cool shade of the forest, comment on the charming effects of the sunlight piercing through the leaves, the vast echoing quiet of it, quite a cathedral of nature. Somewhere in this forest, perennially unfound, gathering moss in a quiet woodland glade, is the elusive shrine to Notre-Dame des Anglais; by now I almost prefer to imagine it, visited by shy deer and carolling birds, rather than actually to see it.

And then a sense of wonderment overtakes me; a sudden delicious sweetness that has to do simply with being alive for these precious few days with Mabel rises in a sudden sap – it feels, Father, like the stirrings of my soul, that which I have prayed for, as though, having watered my soul with prayer, I have been rewarded with an outpouring of spiritual verdure. And it is all the sweeter, I suppose, because it must end in such a short time.

Mabel pushes me along to a bench, where she seats herself, garlanded with her heavy trimmings. We begin to talk of Smithers, and my forthcoming *Book of Fifty Drawings*. Late last year, Father, just before Mabel went off to America on her tour, and when I was so ill that I could hear the gravediggers murmuring impatiently outside my door, Smithers hit upon the idea of issuing an album of my drawings, a book that would show the best representative samples of everything I had done from *Morte D'Arthur* to *The Savoy*. He proposed to publish it in just the luxurious fashion I like best, with a new design by me stamped in gold upon a royally red cloth cover and a recent photograph as frontispiece. Aymer Vallance was commandeered to provide an iconography.

This project gave me the will to go on living. Mabel and I decided what should be included; and she, darling girl, went round to half the publishers in London to secure the drawings and the permissions needed to publish them. It was to be an album, you see, to show people the whole range of my style and talent; and as we assembled the drawings I emotionally relived my entire artistic career. Subscriptions for the de luxe edition, I had imagined, would pour in.

But they didn't; or Smithers ran out of money; became evasive anyhow; the publication date was postponed; all the usual problems one encounters with a Smithers were encountered; and only now do I know with any certainty – based on the claims of an advertisement – that the book will be out in August.

'I don't even know where I'll be in August,' I say to Mabel as we sit in the dry pine-scented air of the forest.

'We must wait and see what Dr Phillips says.'

'I only know I shan't be here. This was a mistake. Dr Lamarre was a mistake.'

'Imagine it, Aubrey – a book of your drawings.'

'It's only taken a lifetime.'

'And Mr Smithers says that, if this one is successful, there will be a second book of fifty drawings.'

Successful! The tantalizing possibility of recovering my lost fortunes twinkles before me – but for one thing: Smithers. Can one trust him, ever, completely? 'What did his office look like?' I begin to interrogate Mabel about her visit on my behalf to Smithers's offices in the Royal Arcade.

'One must be on these publishers like a hawk, at all times; and really, Mabel, one *cannot* do business with them by post. It's so loathsome having always to underline things in a letter for special emphasis: *Send money at once*, for instance.'

'Has he been honouring his contract with you?' Mabel asks. 'I told him he must. I was quite bold. "Twelve pounds a week, Mr Smithers," I said, "that was the arrangement. If its terms are not met, my brother must be considered free to look for another publisher." '

'The cheques come, but oftener than not they are for five pounds and cannot be cashed. He post-dates them, that is the problem. Oh, damn it all!' I reach for her hands; she gives them to me. 'Ask me what I wish for.'

'What do you wish for?'

'I wish I had another publisher, one who was rich and honourable.'

'Let them see this book in August, let them just see it, and then they will come crawling to you,' Mabel prophesies. 'You know I will do all I can for you in London.'

'I can count on you to administer a sound thrashing to Smithers once a week?'

'As ready with my birch whip as Mrs Termagant Flaybum.'

She then delicately asks what I am thinking of drawing next.

'I must settle something definitely with Smithers before I begin.'

'*Mademoiselle de Maupin?*'

'The few drawings I did are adorable, but I think the project is too much for Smithers to take on. If he were serious about it, he would have hired a translator by now.'

'They couldn't ban *Mademoiselle de Maupin* as obscene, could they?' Mabel asks quite astutely. This, I believe, is one of the reasons why the project hangs fire: Smithers, when it comes to the English translation and illustration of this great literary work, is afraid of prosecution. Meanwhile, and paradoxically, he churns out those obscene stories and photographs of happy and tireless couplings that would instantly put him in prison were they ever discovered.

'Of course,' I hint, 'I am always turning possibilities around in my mind.'

Mabel quizzes me with a raised eyebrow. 'Such as . . . ?'

'Such as – that man who was a fox. The work of one of our greatest English dramatists.'

'Elizabethan? Jacobean? Restoration?'

'Jacobean. A man who worships earthly treasure, who builds shrines to the glory of gold, and who is pitilessly unmasked in the end.'

'Volpone,' Mabel guesses with a smile.

'Kiss me,' I am about to say, when Mabel kisses me.

*　　*　　*

The orchestra is playing 'Amoureuse' as we enter the dining-room of the Pavillon Louis XIV, Mother, Mabel and I. Heads turn in our direction, then bow close to whisper and speculate. Mabel's gown is devoured by the curious ladies of the hotel, most of them so startled by its modern cut and brilliant colour scheme that they don't know whether to wince in pain or gasp with pleasure.

I must describe this dress to you, Father, this *ensemble*, for it is the most extraordinary creation and makes one want to be a beautiful woman simply for the experience of wearing it! This garment worn tonight by my sister, this bewilderingly unlikely gift from the modest Virgin Mother, Miss Gribbell, indirectly comes to usurp and dominate our last evening together. No male clothing could ever excite so much passion and opprobrium.

The décolletage is so low that the bodice, as Mother acidly commented upon first seeing it, hangs on Mabel's shoulders by nothing less than a miracle. A broad gleaming swathe of Mabel's naked pink and white flesh – the colour of a haemorrhage mixed with heavy cream – is thus exposed down to the ripe swelling of her breasts. A scarlet choker garnished with a soft outer scallop of yellow chiffon serves to draw still greater attention to this delectable portion of my sister's anatomy; but the rubied crucifix rests right there in the snowy midpoint of desire, a discouragement to the meek and an incitement to the pagans amongst us. Mother felt such a crucifix should not be worn openly, as adornment, but Mabel, flush with the confidence of a neophyte, insisted that by displaying Christ's precious symbol on the white velvet of her breast she was but showing her deepest reverence for the One who had recently flooded her heart with such happiness; yes, it was a love-token of sorts. And it was a gift from Miss Gribbell, she reminded Mother, as was the gown that made Mother's eyes start out of her head when she first saw it. Mother, you see, is now quite bewildered; she strongly wants to disapprove but cannot, quite, because the gift came from a noble benefactress whom she has met and reveres as the mother of André, our potential saviour.

The fabric of the gown is yellow silk draped with scarlet chiffon; with the train there are about eighteen feet of material around the hem; enormous double-puffed sleeves of deep wine-coloured velvet gather just above the elbows and then become a transparent yellow gauze that flows down to tie itself in adoring ribbons at her wrists. The rise and foldings of Mabel's Titian-coloured hair against this ensemble leave one breathless and irritated at the spectacular vision of herself that she has managed to create.

Mother wears her one 'good' evening dress, the ponderous corded silk with white lace trimmings, and her old fringed Chinese silk shawl, the same one I was wrapped in as a sick child. Its complicated ivory-on-white patterning always seems about to reveal the curious secret of its overall design, but never does.

And I, Father, am in evening dress myself, a spectral vision of the successful man I was just two years ago, when I dashed and darted and tarted my way around the dinner-party and soirée circuit of London, Paris and Dieppe. My evening dress, I am only too well aware, now hangs on me; I have lost weight, *against doctor's orders*. But, as Mabel has the new secret confidence of her religion, I have the new secret confidence of my new doctor – or, rather, of my long consultation earlier in the afternoon with Dr Phillips. What he told me was reason enough to make me want to dress up on this, our last night together before Mabel returns to London, to fill my clothes with spirit, if not with corporeal bulk. I slipped into my patent-leather pumps with the ease of Cinderella, and with the vulgar finesse of a performer in a music-hall flipped my silver-knobbed Malacca cane into the air and caught it again. Mabel had filched the slender bud of a white rose for my buttonhole. No Bath chair tonight! Tonight I *walk* into the dining-room of the Pavillon Louis XIV with my beautiful sister and purse-lipped mother, just as the orchestra is playing 'Amoureuse'.

'If Miss Gribbell could have known the interest her generous gift would provoke,' Mother cannot stop herself saying, *sotto voce*, as Mabel silences the rattle of cutlery and the three of us stand in a tight mesh of curious gazes, 'I wonder if she would not have offered another in its place?'

Mabel remains deaf to Mother's persistent innuendoes; she stands with the cool haughty pride of a Society Beauty expecting immediate attention and reverence and bestows a tiny but special smile on the *maître d'hôtel* as he flashes through the jungle of diners towards us. Mabel, without a penny to spare, commands the attention of the entire room. I am suffused with pride that she has learned this much, for it is a difficult accomplishment, to be penniless and confidently amazing at the same time; and I wonder – never having seen her act professionally – if she is as good on stage as she is off it.

The *maître d'hôtel* bids us follow him, and Mabel bends with a gracious, almost flippant nonchalance to gather the train of her gown over her arm as we make our way through the staring, ruminating crowd, Mabel on one arm, Mother on the other, propping me up between them.

Our progression through the dining-room is quite slow because of me. Plenty of time for people to examine us closely as we pass by. 'Stop for a moment,' I gasp, as a spasm of undefined pain shoots from my hip socket down into my leg. More horribly, I can feel the incipient lung tremors which herald the Cough, and I pull out my handkerchief just as it strikes.

Sheer willpower, Father. I somehow manage to stop it, but not before noticing several diners whipping out handkerchiefs to cover their averted faces. I am a peripatetic pool of germs, you see; a walking plague; an upright contagion; can evidently infect infant, octogenarian, or young bride by expelling invisible droplets of my rotten inner stew in their direction. Now I am aware, too, of a sudden rise of fever, of that inner fire which steadily consumes me from within, that hungry tongue of flame which inspires visions as it sears and scrapes the flesh from my organs; the cross upon which I am eternally hung, I think, fixing my flushed gaze on Mabel's rubied crucifix.

'Perhaps, Aubrey, we should dine in our rooms,' Mother says, ever fearful of the public eye.

'No, we dine in our rooms nearly every evening and tonight we shall have a celebration,' I insist as, blissfully, Mother and Mabel drop me into a chair at our table. 'Oh, this is charming,' I say, motioning for the *sommelier* and ordering a bottle of Veuve Cliquot. 'Look, we can see the lights of Paris in the distance.'

'Rather a good orchestra,' Mabel says. 'Don't you think so, Mother?'

'I think the English are better musicians than the French,' Mother says.

'Back to London tomorrow,' I say gaily as the wine is delivered, tasted, poured out.

'Aubrey, the expense,' says Mother. 'And should you have wine?'

'We should all have wine, Mother.' I lift my glass. 'To Mabel, and to her success in London.'

Mabel smiles. Mother is silent but raises her glass.

'Have you a definite engagement?' Mother asks Mabel.

'Yes, Mother, I told you – I have a part in a new play at the Criterion in July.'

'What is it called?' I coax.

'*Four Little Girls.*'

'And are you one of the four little girls?' Mother asks.

'No, Mother, I told you – I play the part of one of the girls' sisters.'

'What is her character?' Mother asks.

Mabel is silent for a moment; she smiles, wondering if evasion would be better; takes a sip of wine. 'A tart,' she says finally.

Mother cannot understand our laughter. 'A tart?' she says.

'Yes, Mother, a London tart.'

'What kind of a role is that?' Mother asks, stiffening, pulling her shawl tighter.

'A bad one mostly,' says Mabel.

'And you believe that playing such a character will help to further your stage career?'

'It's in the West End,' Mabel says, smiling at me, covering my hand with her own. 'People will at least see me.'

'Yes, and think what?' Mother asks.

'Mother, please don't be depressing about it,' Mabel says. 'It is not a good part. It is badly written, as all of them are, but it is a part and it is in the West End.'

'You are paid?' Mother asks.

'Fifteen bob a week,' Mabel says.

'Fifteen bob a week,' Mother contemptuously repeats. 'And you will be able to live on fifteen shillings a week in London?'

'I shall be doing walk-ons for Mr Tree as well,' Mabel says.

'You mustn't exhaust your nerves by taking on too much,' I counsel.

'It seems to be that she will have to take on far more than *tart* roles and occasional walk-ons for Mr Tree if she hopes to live in London on her earnings from the *theatre*.'

'Mother, it will lead to other parts,' Mabel insists.

Mother is merciless. 'You gave up a headmistress-ship at the Polytechnic, a position that paid some forty pounds a year and carried with it the honour of respectability, in order to play-act for fifteen shillings a week while Aubrey and I are forced to count our pennies and pray for the continued assistance of Mr Raffalovich in order to stay alive. That is what I call selfish. That is what I call foolish and irresponsible.'

Mabel has turned crimson all over; the crucifix now rests on pink velvet; she is disconcerted, but maintains a composure that I find heartbreaking and admirable at the same time. 'Mother,' she says quietly, 'we will never be in accord on this subject, so I suggest that we talk of other things.'

'If you were a great actress, Mabel,' Mother goes on, determined to fire every bullet in her arsenal, 'one could forgive and even support your theatrical endeavours. The fact remains, however, that you are not a great actress, and you never will be. I have seen you on stage, and you do not cut a very remarkable figure; you have neither the talent nor the temperament of a great thespian; you have neither the artistic genius nor the determination of your brother, though you like to think you have both, and the best and wisest course of action for you is either teaching or marriage.'

Mabel's bowed head, the determined contraction of her mouth and the flare of her nostrils betray her struggle for composure. She drops one hand to her lap and with the other grasps the embosomed crucifix. Silently she turns to look out of the dining-room window at the distant sparkle of Paris.

Mother is silent as well, her gaze stony. No doubt she believes that she acts as she does out of love and concern, but love does not seek to punish, does it, Father? If I were Mabel, I would question, just as she does, the whole concept of love; advocate, as she secretly does, Free Love; arrive through personal experience, as she has, at a philosophy compounded of the New Woman principles of active engagement tempered by a classical Aurelian detachment.

Luckily our waiter comes just then with the jellied soup, breaking the bitter spell that has paralysed all of us. The very sight of the soup, excellent though I am certain it is, reminds me of my inner effluvia and makes me bilious; my stomach groans and churns; I pour more wine for Mabel and myself.

Mabel, the actress, turns to me with a pleasant smile. 'You've told us practically nothing of your consultation with Dr Phillips, Aubrey.'

'To Dr Phillips,' I say, sipping the wine which has already gone to my head. 'A wise and respectable English physician who listened to the resident oracle of my chest cavity and pronounced' – Mother and Mabel are hanging on my every word – 'that I am still quite curable.' A sudden giddiness lifts me high above the dull plane of pain and despair where I am pinned most days and nights; I begin to laugh. 'Dr Phillips, dear Dr Phillips, found my right lung in fair working order; the left, he said, is weaker than it was when I saw him last, but recovery is still quite possible. I have every reason to expect a few years more, perhaps even a long life. And, as you suspected, Mother, he found my liver to be considerably enlarged, which explains my lack of vitality and my depression.'

'And what are we to do now?' Mother asks, as she always asks. She has been fretting all day because I would not allow her to be present at the examination. Generally she is in the room with me; but today I had prepared myself for the final sentence of death, and I wanted to be alone when it was pronounced.

'Have you ever heard of an artificial pneumothorax?' I ask. They haven't. 'It's an Italian method devised to induce the infected lung to rest. Nitrogen is injected between the ribs into the chest cavity, and that causes the ailing lung to collapse.' Mabel winces. 'The bad lung is thus rendered temporarily inactive, and is gradually healed – a kind of internal rest cure.'

'And the other lung remains active?' Mother asks.

'Yes it maintains all the work of respiration. The procedure, Dr Phillips said, may be a useful one for me at this point.'

'Must we go to Italy, then?' Mother tremulously asks.

'No, he wants me to consult a Dr Prendergast in Paris before anything is decided. In fact, Dr Phillips thinks it would be a good idea to spend the remainder of the summer in Paris . . .'

I can tell that what sounded like good news to me is troubling to Mabel and Mother. I wish to celebrate – Dr Phillips said I can still be cured! I may yet go on to live a long life! – and despite my fever and giddiness, perhaps because of it, I wish suddenly with all my heart to find the shrine of Notre-Dame des Anglais, to kneel there, Father, and give my thanks.

'Nitrogen,' Mabel says. 'Does the collapsed lung eventually recover, then, and start to work again?'

'Evidently,' I say.

The strains of 'Valse bleu' now fill the dining-room. I wish I could dance! I have never danced in my life. And would not Mabel and I, whirling about a dance-floor, make us the cynosure of all eyes? Love for her, for my dear darling struggling penniless sister, floods my being; hurts me with its sweetness and sorrow; makes me want to laugh and cry simultaneously. I have never known the full intimate depths of love – love that is pain, love that is mystery, love that is waiting and arrival – for any woman but her. And tomorrow she leaves me. We cannot know when, or in what circumstances, we shall meet again. Can one ever hope to communicate the passionate intensity of *un grand amour fraternel*, Father, without rendering it vulgar, sentimental or obscene?

And now, Father, she is gone. We held one another, gazed deep into each other's eyes, shared our very souls. 'You know I will come the moment—' Mabel was unable to finish; I could only nod.

The wise old hands of Monsieur Vella are once again my only comfort. 'If you will permit me to say so, Monsieur Beardsley, your sister is a very beautiful woman,' he said this morning.

'She is, isn't she?'

Mabel! It is all I can do not to cry out. I want to fill the air with lamentation, like one of Giotto's angels hovering in anguish near the Cross, only I want to curse God instead of weep for Him. Does He not curse me? As bare and lonely as Golgotha, my life now, again, without her.

It all has meaning, you say. What exactly is the meaning of suffering? What is the meaning of loneliness, of illness, of poverty, of constant fear? Why are some of us singled out for a crushing load of ill-health, penury and social punishment, while others – equally vain but far less talented, stupid even, and mean-spirited – are given enormous incomes, robust constitutions, the means to gratify their every whim?

Mother has been unusually quiet today; the silence of a guilty conscience, I hope. She accompanied Mabel to the station, where no doubt she refused to apologize for her intolerable behaviour last evening but tried in some other clumsy way to tell her daughter that she loved her. Mother disgusts me at times. Today I am punishing her, and she knows it, and she knows why: when she attacks Mabel, she attacks me. All I need do is remain silent and turn my face to the wall when she enters my chamber – she knows then that she has angered and displeased me, and becomes remorseful and stupidly penitent.

I cannot bear to think of Mabel, alone, on her way back to the grind and grime of London; to incessant disappointing interviews in the offices of theatrical management companies; returning exhausted to a dingy room in a third-rate lodging-house; counting out her pennies in the hopes that she has enough to buy a bun and a glass of milk; forced to be humbly grateful to the Grib for a new gown or hat. She has at least the impending excitement of a West End play to look forward to, and the increased attention and emoluments it may bring; but, as I have, she has chosen the most difficult life imaginable: the life of the creative spirit over the life of numbing drudgery. Unless she is very very lucky, or very very brilliant – and I fear that without me she is neither – my sister is doomed to a life of penury and a daily menu of disappointment. It is the sort of life that can quickly wear one down, and take its toll on one's health.

But who was it who always encouraged her in the face of resistance from herself and others (like Mother)? Who is it, then, who is more than ever responsible for what ultimately becomes of her? I am.

Let me not continue in this vein, Father. Let me rather continue to examine the earlier facts of my life, confess to you everything that I have done in my twenty-four years of earthly existence, so that my spirit may be cleansed and ready for baptism. Now that Mabel has set the precedent, my own moment of spiritual reckoning cannot be far behind.

IVEN THE DRUDGERY of adulthood they must face upon leaving school, is it any wonder, Father, that men cling to their memories of those times with such fondness? I am no different.

You have guessed by now, good Father, that science never appealed to me as art and theatre did. I suspect that it was the same for Mr King, for he became quite different when he stopped explaining the scientific laws of the universe and enthusiastically embarked on the costumes, text or programme for our weekly Entertainment.

He was something of a father and an older brother in one, and I shall always be grateful to him for keeping me in manageable conceit with myself by taking me out on special walks and allowing me to come to his rooms, where we would have long delightful talks. I would toast our bread; he would make good strong tea. He talked to me frankly, encouragingly, without the condescension, censure and sanctimonious lecturing of the other masters. In this way I grew more confident of the gifts I had.

Unlike Aunt Pitt, Mr King loved to play, and actually encouraged it; it was a part of his own temperament, and so perhaps he knew the dangers that result when Imagination is stifled or castigated: how it may then go underground, burrow into a dark hole like a hissing cornered animal, gather a rank and unwholesome strength there in the stinking sunless depths and reappear in some new and stunted guise.

It happened that eventually, under the direction of Mr King, we formed a special set there at Brighton Grammar School – I, Charley Cochran, Fred Scotson-Clark and a few other boys. For the most part we were intellectually or constitutionally disinclined to athletics; but, given a co-operative creative task with our weekly theatrical Entertainments, we worked tirelessly and with the vitality of a cricket team to ensure its successful outcome.

It was there, at BGS, that I began to turn the material of my life – such as it was – into the material of my art. Allowed to play, I became conversant with aspects of my character that might otherwise never have surfaced. Once encouraged, for instance, I became an indefatigable performer: my weekly theatrical coups were the talk of the school. Once I even recited the entire skating scene from *The Pickwick Papers*, and had the deliciously odd experience of imagining myself as Mabel while performing it; I used the same gestures and dramatic emphases she had used when Mother was dragging us about as prodigies.

I did not then distinguish one branch of art as more important for me, personally, than any other: all of them gave me intense pleasure. From Mr King I developed a fearless aptitude for versifying, and published nine quatrains in the school magazine. Acting imbued me with a sense of power and otherworldliness; its rewards were immediately and most gratifyingly apparent in the cheers, laughter and applause of the other boys. And drawing – that art for which my name has since become renowned and reviled – drawing teased out my inner humour, my talent for satire. I comically illustrated the revered *Aeneid*, and signed my name to it in Latin as Beardslius de Brighthelmstoniensis; was forever scratching out humourous little sketches which I then gave away because the other boys seemed to like them; and finally, as an assignment from Mr King, turned my hand to the illustration of Robert Browning's poem 'The Pied Piper of Hamelin'. How proud I was of my rats! This was published to great acclaim in the school journal, and made me realize for the first time the hideous discrepancies that exist between fine linework and its mechanical reproduction.

All the while, you understand, I was perfecting that private repertoire of masturbatory techniques shown to me by Charley Cochran under the old chain pier – perennially terrified that Matron would find tell-tale stains on my sheets and inform Mr Marshall, or Mr King, or my parents. Didn't they know of my guilt simply by looking at me? Yet no matter how great my fear of exposure and expulsion, my certainty that I was grievously offending God and undermining my own physical and moral health – I could not stop. I would not. The feeling was too delightful to end it voluntarily! And my cock, you see, once hard, refused to wither. Poking, prodding, rubbing – nothing helped. I remained hard for weeks on end; would practise the sin of Onan two or even three times a day; frigged myself as vigorously and with as much ritualistic fervour as a Spanish *penitente* flagellating himself.

Believe me, dear Father Coubé, I was not alone in the practice of the solitary vice; one heard the experienced saliva-slicked smackings of a dozen other 'young sirs' every night along with the nocturnal squeals and muffled cries of those 'bitches' and 'whores' being taken by the older boys. Was it any different, I would wonder, my mind wandering to historical precedent, from what went on in the barracks of lonely soldiers sent from Rome to England fifteen hundred years earlier? Without women, what could men do?

What is it, Father, that fuels this incessant sexual fire in us? What is it that burns down every barrier religion and society can erect,

171

and blinds us to everything but the satisfaction of our carnal desires? If we take the Darwinian view, I suppose it is the old rutting animal that, beneath the veneer of polite society, still sniffs and prowls in our blood. You yourself, so unabashedly celibate, would advance a theological claim and say that human venery springs from the Devil.

All I know is that in the cold comfortless darkness of the dormitory I would see my friend Scotson-Clark sneak off to the bed of Frank Simpson, his daylight tormentor, and could only wonder at this strange discrepancy between public and pubic; that gulf of hypocrisy that seems always to lie between what one says and what one does.

Many scenes stand out in my memory of Brighton Grammar School, but one in particular had a subtle influence on me that only now am I fully able to appreciate. One evening in his rooms Mr King conducted an experiment which, he said, was aesthetic rather than strictly scientific. He set out on a table, rather like a Dutch still life, two candlesticks, a bowl of fruit, a decanter of sherry, some bunched fabric and two small cut-glass goblets. The room and the objects on the table were illuminated by the harsh glare of electric light, recently installed and regarded by all of us as something of a modern miracle.

Mr King first asked me to do nothing more than look carefully at the objects around me. 'Pay attention to the shadows and textures,' he said. I looked, but saw nothing unusual. He then switched off the glaring electric light, turned up the gas-jets over the mantelpiece, and again told me simply to look at the objects on the table and in the room. 'Do they appear different to you in this light?' he asked; but when I began to speak he silenced me by saying quietly: 'Just look, Beardsley, just look.' So again I looked, more bewildered with each passing moment.

After a few minutes he turned off the gas. The room became very dark. I heard the scrape of a Swan Vesta, saw the flare of its small clear flame, watched as Mr King touched the wicks of the two candles. A lovely warm glow spread over the table, picking out the silken nuance of the fabric, inveigling the prisms of the cut glass to sparkle, deepening the mellow glow of the sherry, darting into the ripe contours of the fruit.

'Do these objects look different to you in candlelight than they did with the light from gas or electricity pouring over them?' he asked.

'Yes, sir.'

'How do they look different to you, Beardsley?'

'They look . . . more alive. More . . . mysterious.'

'More beautiful?'

'Yes, sir.'

'That is all I want you to remember,' he said, and the experiment was over.

So was my time at Brighton Grammar School. My parents informed me that I would be withdrawn at the end of Michaelmas term in 1888, and begin working as a clerk on New Year's Day 1889. This scheme had been planned for some time. We were all to live together again, in London, and Mabel and I were expected to contribute the lion's share of the familial expenses.

There was no reason in the world, Father, for me to assume that my fate would be any different from that of the other boys. And yet I was mortified. I wanted something more than a clerkship; I wanted to go on with school, wanted to make something of myself based on my true talents. I went to Mr King and, to my everlasting shame, broke down and sobbed in front of him. His voice was gentle as he put a hand on my shoulder.

'We must all work, Beardsley. The world has been set up that way. We must labour, and try not to curse our lot.'

'But I do curse my lot!' I cried. 'To work as a clerk!'

'Is such work beneath you?' asked Mr King.

'I look upon it with contempt.'

'And, if the world were ideal, what would be your place in it?'

'I would be an actor!' I said, for the public part of me desired this more than anything. 'Or an artist! Or a writer!' These solitary occupations held an almost equal charm.

'You would continue to do what gives you pleasure now.'

'Is that not right?' Sixteen-year-olds are easily bewildered. 'God gave me these gifts, and so I serve God by using them.'

For a moment Mr King looked as though he had been inspired to begin one of his rhyming couplets; his blue eyes flashed, and with clenched fist he began to tap on his mouth, knocking on the door of his Muse. 'I will not pretend with you, Beardsley,' he said. 'What you say is true. You have been blessed with an extraordinarily creative mind. Yet often God gives us these gifts not as a blessing, but as an extra burden.'

'The burden is not the gift,' I insisted, 'it is being unable to use it.'

'That is it exactly, and no seasoned philosopher could have put it better. The burden is in having the gift but being unable to use it in the daily commerce of existence. It is a burden I have come to know quite well in my own life.' He kneeled beside me, his manner hearty and tender at once, and I wished with my whole being that he was my father. 'But listen to me, Beardsley. If you have faith – and if the gift is great enough – you will continue to use it; it will never desert you. It will give you the comfort of expression when your spirit most needs it.'

'Cold comfort,' I said sullenly.

'There is another side to this,' said Mr King, going now to stand at the window; a thin monotonous rain had been steadily falling for days, keeping him from the long rapid walks that he claimed always put him to rights with himself and inspired his rhymes. 'When God gives us something, it is often because something else has been taken away.' He turned, his arms crossed, to look at me.

'What do you mean?'

'I shall always be frank with you, Beardsley. I mean your health.'

I had forgotten illness, except for the low current of fever that came on as predictably as the tea-time ritual of lighting the gas-jets on a winter's afternoon. As it slowly and steadily rose, my pulse and my imagination would keep pace with it, become flushed and hectic. But I spoke of this to no one, and did not regard it as anything out of the ordinary.

'You must husband your resources,' Mr King said. 'And you must guard against taking on too much. You are at an age when you think you are capable of everything and anything; but I want to caution you: your constitution may not be able to withstand too great a strain. Great gifts, when they are exposed to the public arena, strain one to the very limit. And when they are a partial result of illness they may easily be led astray – become unwholesome in their expression rather than noble—'

'But how shall I ever use my gifts at all if I am condemned to a clerkship for the rest of my life?'

'Use them for your own pleasure,' said Mr King. 'Cultivate them, but do so privately, not with the aim of impressing any public. The growth of artistry is inseparable from the growth of the soul.'

He spoke wisely, but from the viewpoint of one already creatively vanquished by the dreary facts of practical life. Failure, I have found, is often the father of philosophy. And, from my vantage-point of sixteen years, his words, kind and well meant as they were, offered nothing but verification of the eternal capitulations practised by adults faced with the eternal need for money.

My final public appearance as an actor was in Brighton's Dome, before an audience of almost 3,000 people. The previous year, 1887, Mr King had written an original script to celebrate Queen Victoria's Golden Jubilee, and we repeated this so that I could again play the Spirit of Progress and review the whole of English history for the Queen. Scotson-Clark, about to be apprenticed to a Brighton wine merchant, was unusually impressive in the unlikely role of the Virgin Queen Elizabeth at the time of the Spanish Armada; and Charley Cochran, planning to emigrate to America, was an appropriately dashing Sir Walter Ralegh. Our boyhoods would expire – we all knew it – with this final school production, and we acted our last parts with all the vitality that Mr King's leaden rhyming couplets would allow. I shall never forget the sound of that applause: 6,000 hands clapping their approval. A few years later it would be a very different story indeed.

So there we were in London, in Pimlico, rehearsing how to be a family again. It was very difficult, for the parental reins had slackened during our school years, and now were being pulled tight once more. Mabel was always far more obedient than I, more willing to bow her head to the supreme authority of our ridiculous paterfamilias.

Poor Mabel! Under Miss Callow's intense and unremitting tutelage, she had been placed fifth in all England in Cambridge University's 'local' examinations, and had in consequence been offered a scholarship to Newnham College. But was she allowed to do this, to bring academic distinction to the House of Beardsley? She was not. Father thought that higher education for women was 'unnatural', and so, like me, Mabel was forced to become a wage-earner, and sent to work as a teacher at the Polytechnic School for Girls in Langham Place.

And I? Oh, I was marked with the sign of Clerk, and expected to take my place with a million other of that miserable species toiling in the dimly lit warrens of London. I was expected to hand my £70 a year over to my beloved parents in exchange for room, board and a negligible sum of pocket money. At first I did this without complaining, but it festered, and a long-hidden resentment towards my father began to cause me great turmoil. Much of the time I avoided him; when he entered a room I would leave. There was nothing in him for me to admire. School, he muttered, had done nothing but give me 'airs': the same notion of exalted rank he had enjoyed before his downfall, and which he could not bear to see refracted in his son. Like most men, my father wanted no one to be happy, for he was not happy himself.

The trouble was, Mabel and I were positive ginger pops of creative enthusiasm. Our brains wre just coming alive; they wanted to be fed; they were hungry for stimulation, and not only of an intellectual kind. I was accustomed to weekly theatrical Entertainments; indeed, these were the *raison d'être* of existence, so far as I was concerned.

Thus began our seasons of elaborate Home Theatricals, when we finally turned the dark cocooned tents of our childhood make-believe inside-out and created a makeshift public stage where we could present our new selves to a tiny audience of two. Our parents had no idea that these theatricals were revelations of what we considered to be our 'true' personalities.

That December of 1888, just before our new lives as wage-earners began, Mabel and I went to the theatre as often as we could. We'd arrive in the West End hours before curtain-time in order to get standing-room. How happy we were then! London was a ceaseless joy, an unending marvel, an eternal spectacle! Every plodding inch of a simple penny ride on the omnibus – along Grosvenor Road and Millbank, up Whitehall, past the Houses of Parliament, and on to Charing Cross – provided a year's worth of education and entertainment. From Westminster or Blackfriars Bridge, vast panoramas of the Empire's mightiest city – now *our* city – would open up before us, as detailed and compelling as any Doré print. There was a queerly ennobling sense of belonging to something greater than oneself while remaining deliciously anonymous within the uproar of its huge maw.

And then the London theatres, so grand, so grimy, so plentiful, so crowded. Mabel, of course, had not had the opportunity for play-going that I had had with Charley Cochran; in her entire seventeen years she had seen little more than a holiday pantomime or two. True, we had read and acted our way from the Elizabethans through the Restoration; but now, at last, together, we were seeing some of the plays we had only imagined.

Exponents of the Higher Drama, modern playwrights like Ibsen, were just then beginning to be seen (and hated, of course, by the theatrical standard-bearers) in England. (*Ghosts*, which I saw a few months later, was called a moral cesspool; but it spoke quite directly to my experience and sensibilities, unlike most of the modern English claptrap.) Counting out our pennies, Mabel and I generally confined ourselves to the classics. Henry Irving as Macbeth stands out as a personification of Genius, an actor so perfectly wedded to his role that you believed every word he spoke and could imagine no other speaking it. Ellen Terry played Lady Macbeth – badly, I thought, but Mabel disagreed.

My sister came out of the theatre with a dreamy exalted look on her face, and said: 'At last I know what I really want: to be as good an actress as Ellen Terry.' Ellen Terry, with her green eyes and flame-coloured tresses, inciting her husband to murder, going mad with guilt, had blown the final dangerous spark of theatrical ambition on to Mabel's tinder; from now on my sister wanted only to be an actress.

The Guardian Fire and Life Insurance office in Lombard Street in the City – an eternity has passed since I sat on my clerk's stool there, scratching figures and inscribing policies in the company ledger-books. Each dip of the pen was a dull torture, my workday an endless recording of unforeseen misfortunes resolved into figures.

Praise God, Father, that you are not an artist, and do not have to endure what an artist must. This debased late-nineteenth-century world of facts and figures, of financial formulae, of method over miracle, and cold-blooded calculation over the warmth of spontaneity – it is not an easy world for artists to reverence (unless, that is, you are a grotesquely successful Royal Academician like Frith, who now commands a fee of nearly five thousand guineas for a picture and its engraving copyright).

It took me a good two hours to get to the office, and another two to get back – more, if I decided to wander along the streets and alleyways of the city. Dark ancient London at night in the sporadic flare of gaslight came to hold a strange and overwhelming fascination for me. Odd sights would suddenly appear, curious scenes emerge, strange characters pass me by with hurried step.

Once, just a minute's walk north of St Paul's, I stumbled, quite by accident, across the hellish scene and stench of an underground slaughterhouse. Sheep, crying in terror, were hurled into a pit so that their legs would break; a moment later they were knifed and flayed by the men working below, whose bodies and clothes were soaked and spattered with blood and viscera. The walls of the place, which I could see through a ground-level window, were coated with a thick layer of putrefying blood and fat, and it was all I could do to stumble away and retch my disbelief into the gutter.

Hideous slums, the infamous 'rookeries', where the very idea of fire or life insurance was preposterous, where the inhabitants stared hopelessly into the sunken face of starvation, were crowded in everywhere. Hidden behind the most prosperous streets and neigh-bourhoods, where the obsequious proprietors of exclusive shops would bustle out to wait on the luxurious chariots of the wealthy, were other streets and other neighbourhoods. In these places I furtively observed a life that I had never known existed. How could such wealth live side-by-side with such utter squalor? What did Empire mean, if this was its result at home?

A *frisson* of danger would run through me as I penetrated deeper into the unknown streets, deeper into London's maze, deeper into the knowledge of evil. It soon became apparent that the very heart of upper-class London, that area between the Strand and Regent Street, encompassing Soho, St James's and Whitehall, that most exclusive quadrant of our dear British Empire, was in fact nothing more than a walking whorehouse. Men, women, children: everyone was openly for sale.

The strange thing about it was not that it existed, but that it was never talked about, never written about, and never shown in modern pictures. It did not conform to the Official Version of English Life as seen on the walls of the Royal Academy, and so it was ignored as the material of art. Yet there it was, not so far from the sacred portals of the RA itself: filthy, glamorous, lewd, pestilential, flea-bitten, pox-ridden, utterly criminal; an unseen obscene London that set my pulse hammering and my cock throbbing in nervous sympathetic excitement.

Those teeming London pavements, filled with their sweet, stinking, garish assortment of human characters, all going about the business of making money and spending it – all of us living in what Shelley called 'the dream of life'! Those filthy streets, churned to mud by the incessant crush of omnibuses, drays, cabriolets, broughams, landaus, hansom cabs, fire wagons, funeral carriages; whose crossings were swept by wretched ragged children; whose edges were so variously crowded with men wearing shiny top-hats and costermongers hawking their wares; with rich elegant women unable to dress themselves without a servant's help sweeping past shivering penniless flower-girls; where clergymen encased in starch and broadcloth rubbed shoulders with ruffians wearing moleskin waistcoats! How I loved the stew of London!

My eyes would meet other eyes – those of a smiling child-minx, no more than ten, yet powdered and rouged like a seasoned whore – 'Wanting a bit of company, sir?'; those of a drunken gap-toothed harridan, whispering that she'd lift her skirts in a nearby alley for a glass of gin; those of a half-starved seamstress, whose feverish orbs hopelessly cried out, 'Save me!'; those of a clever unscrupulous maid, searching restlessly for a male conspirator.

I looked, but never bought, storing up memories to fuel my nocturnal cock-chafings. Yes, there in Pimlico, too, urged on by my friend the Fever, surrounded by my family, I continued my copious outpouring of seed; visions of whores and pretty girls from the halls danced in my head as I pounded my insatiable organ to the spurting froth of its inevitable conclusion.

Are they incompatible, Father, those silken erotic reveries of youth and a deeply felt love of God? Sometimes I wonder if they are not, perhaps, merely different flowers growing from the same stem. For ecstasy, but of a spiritual sort, also played a part in my new London life.

We chose St Barnabas as our church in Pimlico, not because of its convenience, but because it was the most ritualistic and fashionable Anglo-Catholic church in the metropolis. St Barnabas, where the ethereal tones of ancient Gregorian chants were heard through a fragrant cloud of incense, provided Mother with a tie to Brighton in the person of the Reverend Alfred Gurney, a former curate at one of her favourite churches there.

I suspect Mother was a little bit in love with Alfred Gurney, the vicar of St Barnabas, but who could blame her? He had a long cleft beard, tender blue eyes, and was immensely rich. He was a man of strong and sudden contrasts, a scholar in church ritual who wore riding breeches under his cassock so that he could take a quick canter in the park whenever the mood struck. He was a spiritualist, an occasional poet, a collector of drawings, and a music-lover who could describe a Wagner concert conducted by Richter with the kind of enthusiastic passion that women found irresistible. He also had the great grace to include us – Mother, Mabel and me – as guests at his sumptuous Sunday luncheon-parties. The Reverend Alfred Gurney's luncheons were far more inspiring, I must say, than his sermons.

These feasts were held in the Clergy House next door to the church after the late service, and provided us with our first entrée into London society. The other guests, all relatives or artistic friends of Mr Gurney, might include his brother Willie, his sister-in-law, his niece, the textile Halifaxes, the Reverend Gerald Sampson and his younger brother Julian, an art dilettante. Since these were all potential patrons, I began to carry with me a portfolio of my latest drawings.

One afternoon the talk at the luncheon-table turned to Rossetti, a collection of whose drawings Mr Gurney owned and proudly displayed on his walls. In years gone by, the Reverend had come to know the Pre-Raphaelite artist and his poetic sister; and that afternoon he began to tell us stories of Rossetti's last hours – how Rossetti's lifelong fear of being alone, for instance, was exacerbated in his final illness to the point where he would keep a friend with him all through the night, begging him not to leave until dawn, when finally he would be able to sleep; and how even in his last days, unable to rise from his couch, he would feebly stretch out his brush and touch a canvas with it. The luncheon guests reverentially murmured 'How beautiful!' to every anecdote, but my secret response was quite different. None of it sounded the least bit beautiful to me; awful, rather, pathetic and terrifying. Where healthy people get the idea that death is beautiful and ennobling, I shall never know.

Afterwards Julian Sampson sidled up to me and asked if I would show him the contents of my portfolio. 'With pleasure,' I said, and we found a spot some way off from the others.

Recently I heard rumours that Julian Sampson has fallen prey to one of the many devilish cults that seem to be springing up, as the century wanes, like fetid fungi on the trunk of a decaying tree; even then, eight years ago, he evinced a fascinated interest in a *sub rosa* world that one could only whisper about at Gurneyesque luncheon-parties. A middle-sized man of great elegance, Julian would have been remarkably good-looking were it not for the slightly degenerate Hanoverian cast to his features. The pampered son of a rich colonel and the grandson of the Comte de Méric de St-Martin, his life had been dedicated to useless pleasures of all sorts. He had studied art, and occasionally wrote on the subject, so I was honoured when he directed his gaze at my drawings.

Thanks to Mr Gurney's collection of Rossettis, my drawings at that time showed signs of incipient Pre-Raphaelitism, and were mostly concerned with beatific subjects – at least, those drawings that I brought with me to the Clergy House. Other subjects, such as the courtesan Manon Lescaut, and the adulteress Emma Bovary, culled from my secret reading, never accompanied me.

'You have a clever hand,' said Julian, as he examined my various celestial beings strumming lutes and bearing lilies. 'I wonder . . .' He pursed his lips thoughtfully. 'I wonder if you would be interested in a small commission from me – to do a drawing – but not of any heavenly creature.' He laughed softly at some private joke. 'Heavens, no, not heavenly – classical, rather.'

'I would certainly like the opportunity to try,' I said. 'What subject do you have in mind?'

181

Julian looked quickly to the right and left and spoke in a lowered voice. 'I should like a drawing of Hermaphroditus.'

Good God, it is difficult to believe now that I was so utterly ignorant. Julian must have seen my bewilderment, for he said: 'You are unfamiliar with the subject?' When I nodded, he paused for a moment, perhaps wondering if he should withdraw his offer.

'I can draw anything,' I said quickly, noting his hesitation.

'In the Vatican Museum,' he said, his voice low, 'in a room off to one side of the main gallery, I first encountered Hermaphroditus – asleep. A pagan creation, the child of Hermes and Aphrodite – one of those creatures accepted and understood by the idolatrous Ancients, but quite deliberately ignored by our own petty moralistic age.'

'Hermaphroditus was a god?' I asked.

'In some places, yes. The form of worship was quite curious. A statue of the god would be set up in a clearing on a night when the moon was exactly half-full, and the worshippers – men and women both – would exchange their clothing – the men would dress as women, the women as men.'

I was so shocked to hear such a thing, Father, right there in the Clergy House, that a kind of nervous giggling yelp escaped my lips. The other luncheon guests looked curiously towards us; both Julian and I returned enormously sweet smiles and bent closer over my portfolio.

'A kind of bacchanalia', Julian went on, 'would transport the worshippers into a frenzy as, for that one night in the year, they assumed the characteristics of the other sex. The most virile of men would become mincing ladies, and demure maidens would stride about slashing people with whips.'

'I've never heard of such a thing!'

Julian smiled. What a deliciously corrupt smile it was. 'Do you think we get the full story of life from listening to sermons in church and lectures in school? Do you think that we, politely gathered here in November of 1889, are allowed the full range of expression that was permitted to the ancient world? Christianity wiped out a whole world, my boy, and an entire method of understanding human nature. Hermaphroditus, you see, was the personification of an ancient desire and an ancient physical paradox – the desire of one sex to be another, or to be both at the same time.'

By now my mouth was dry. Oh, how fatal knowledge can be!

'Hermaphroditus represented a third sex, neither male nor female, but with the attributes of both.'

'How can that be?' I asked.

'That', said Julian; 'is what you, as an aspiring artist, must discover. If, that is, you are truly interested in pursuing this subject.'

I said that I was.

'Then, may I suggest that you read – or reread – *The Symposium*. Aristophanes' speech – the most memorable one – begins with his discussion of a third sex, and leads to a definition of perfect love. And, to help you visually, I shall send you my photograph of the Hermaphrodite sleeping in its dark chamber in the Vatican.'

I had the sense that I was sealing a pact with him without fully understanding its terms or personal implications, yet the very idea of trying to create such a creature – half-man, half-woman – was intoxicating; a most curious problem to solve.

'Good afternoon, Mr Sampson,' said my mother, approaching us with a vaguely suspicious smile. 'Has Aubrey been showing you his charming drawings?'

'Indeed, he has,' said Julian, and I heard a tincture of secret mockery in his voice – a mockery, I hasten to point out, that I quite enjoyed. 'In fact, I was thinking of purchasing one.'

I had been a clerk at Guardian Fire and Life for less than a year when I again became aware of the disease lurking in my lungs. It made itself known just as the dark wet fogs of winter were settling in over London – its symptoms a short dry cough, a febrile lightheadedness, a growing sense of displacement from the rest of the world.

I could not afford to stay at home and continued to make my long daily treks to and from the office, often in the half-tranced state that accompanies serious illness. Every second of the day was a struggle to remain active and alert, for I wanted no one to know that I was becoming enfeebled. It frightened me to admit it to myself.

Late one morning, as I was sitting hunched over a ledger, my heart suddenly began to hammer out a message of terrible urgency and I found myself unable to draw a full breath. My gasping lungs contracted to a tight stinging ball of pain. I began to cough; the cough led to violent choking; and just as I thought I was about to suffocate a lava-hot stream of blood, phlegm and bile burned its way up my throat and spewed itself on to the ledger-page I had been copying. As my colleagues looked on in helpless embarrassed alarm, I dramatically threw up my arms and collapsed in front of them.

That was the year when Death called on me a second time, leaving his *carte de visite*.

That was the year my lifelong career as a consulter of physicians began. Then, and for several years thereafter, my doctor was the distinguished Symes Thompson of pulmonary disease fame, whose consulting-room was in Cavendish Square. At that time, Dr Thompson made no mention of my lungs; it was my heart, he said, that was endangered. Work was out of the question; indeed, he wondered how I had managed as long as I had. Complete bed rest was required.

There followed the tedious months of illness – an invalid at seventeen! And the worry of it all, for without my wages the family could not make ends meet. Drawing was out of the question; I had the desire, but not the vitality. All I could do was read and work up fanciful sickbed schemes for making money. Perhaps I could write, and earn a few shillings that way? My dream of a career in the theatre or the concert-hall was quite shattered; I would never have the stamina.

Mostly I lay restlessly dreaming with fever; it would overtake me in a great hot wave, pull me under, suck me into a burning sea of delusion. The patterns in the wallpaper and carpet would twitter and shift to reveal hidden faces and figures; hideous creatures would appear, my chaste Rossettian angels transmogrified into perverse hermaphroditic demons; thoughts and words and images and memories would spin like a whirlwind of fiery leaves in my head, and in my delirium I would imagine myself sketching them at lightning speed, a Paganini of the pen.

Schenck's Pulmonic Syrup, prescribed by Dr Thompson, helped to stifle the pain but did nothing to stop the haemorrhages that punctuated my days and nights. Each time I saw my own blood I was terrified anew. I did not want to die! It was too monstrous – to die without ever becoming a man, to die without having lived!

And all because of my father, because he had passed the hot unholy germ from his blood to mine. This agony because of him, a man I had come to loathe!

Then slowly – oh, so slowly – I began to recover. One can measure the return of health, Father, by the re-emergence of the will. One day an inner voice cries out, 'Fight back!' and one does. A vision of the future, of something beyond the numbing daily horizon of pain, stirs and stretches. Many of my now numberless doctors have counselled acquiescence and passivity in the face of this disease; one is exhorted to accept it as one's inevitable lot, life on a diminished scale, the glass half-full instead of half-empty, all that rot. I would rather burn myself to a crisp and die active than lie putrefying in my steaming puddle of corruption.

Mother is right, you know – I *am* wilful. It is through my will alone that I have managed to conquer my tiny piece of artistic immortality. I set my mind to a task, and do not rest until I have achieved success. When I had more strength I determined on writing a short story; I called it 'The Story of a Confession Album', and sold it to *Tit-Bits* for a guinea. What did it matter if it shared a page with a story about Billingsgate fish-market? It was a sign that I was again alive, working, and that a life outside of the sickroom was possible.

I also wanted to write a clever three-act play – dreaming of being a playwright earning a hundred or two a week from a successful West End run – and even began a kind of manic farce which I called, appropriately, 'A Race for Wealth'. Unfortunately, it didn't race beyond the brilliant first act. I did, however, complete a farcical playlet which Mr King staged for the Brighton Old Boys Association, of which I was now a member; it was to be Mr King's last Brighton Grammar School Entertainment before taking up a new teaching position at the Blackburn Technical Institute.

Do you know how sweet fresh air tastes to an invalid, Father? Do you know the giddiness of stepping outside into the world's deliciously mad rush after months of solitary confinement? There I was, creeping slowly down the street on the arm of Mabel or Mother, a babe of eighteen learning how to walk again. Out on a London street, even a dull street in Pimlico, I would sometimes be so overcome with the glory of Life that I would break into delighted laughter.

But peering into the dreadful honesty of a looking-glass I could see that the illness had permanently altered my physiognomy. Fever had fried away all my superfluous flesh, and my face had been sharply engraved by the burin of pain. My skin was sallow, yellowish, and my dull chestnut-coloured hair fell in two lank folds from my centre parting. My body was twisted into a permanent stoop; never again would I be quite able to straighten my spine. A walking-stick was required; my third leg, I called it. And yet, however altered that face in the cheval-glass, it was still mine – I lived on; and more than ever I was determined to vanquish death and anonymity (which are, after all, one and the same thing).

My colleagues at the insurance office didn't know quite what to make of me when I returned, and they seemed even duller than before. They were polite; I was polite. But now I would stare down at those sheets of ledger-paper, all that fresh lovely paper condemned to be buried under numbers, and imagine drawings there instead. Imagination, given such free fiery rein during my months of sickness, was now forced into hiding during office hours, and it did not appreciate obscurity. The paper and the pen, there at my fingertips, but forced into prosaic servitude! I couldn't help myself; little secret drawings would appear, unbidden, like the fantastical creatures that crowd the margins of medieval manuscripts. Sometimes they were obscene – erect cocks and naked breasts; sometimes caricatures or quick profiles of the other clerks. Every night I stole a sheet or two of the paper so that I could continue to draw at home.

One hot afternoon in July 1891, six summers ago, Mabel and I stood nervously at the door of The Grange, Edward Burne-Jones's house in North End Lane. We had heard at one of the Gurney luncheon-parties that the great artist opened his studio to interested visitors on Sunday afternoons, and from the moment that bit of intelligence dropped into my ears I had resolved to go there.

Worshippers standing at the threshold of a hallowed shrine must know the nervous apprehension I felt. Behind those portals lived and worked the man whom I then considered to be the greatest living artist in Europe, the god whose stained-glass window designs had preoccupied me years ago at the Church of the Annunciation. And now I wanted him to pronounce on my work and tell me if I had talent enough to pursue an artistic career. To this end I had assembled a portfolio of my best and latest drawings to show him. I needed advice and help, neither of which I could expect from my revered pater.

The door opened, and an impassive butler listened as Mabel explained our desire to see the studio and meet Mr Burne-Jones. Unnerved by that stony face, the poor darling lost her polite reserve and carried on about our simple mission as though she were giving a dramatic recital.

'Mr Burne-Jones discontinued the practice of admitting visitors to his studio several years ago,' the butler said when she had finished.

Mabel's voice grew shrill. 'But my brother is an artist, and he so much wanted to see the pictures.'

'You may write for an appointment, if you wish. Good day.' The door closed.

Mabel turned to me, her tender green eyes moist with emotion, and pressed my hand. For a moment I was in that odd suspension of hope that has not yet understood defeat. 'Knock again,' I said, shifting my portfolio to my other arm.

'Let's find a place for tea,' said Mabel quietly, turning me away.

We set off, disconsolate, stepping from the cool shade of the porch into the hot gritty glare of London. How petty and meaningless the world appeared. I swore under my breath. And, as if in answer, a voice behind us said: 'Pray, come back!' We turned, and there, standing on the porch, beckoning us to return, was Burne-Jones himself. 'I couldn't think of letting you go away without seeing the pictures, after your journey on a hot day like this.'

It was the sight of Mabel's red-gold hair flashing in the sunlight that got us in, I am certain. All through that hot consecrated afternoon I saw Burne-Jones staring at it with the love of an artist for a colour he has yet to describe in paint.

He graciously escorted us into his house and took us to his studio, where he showed and explained everything. My starving eyes darted about, taking quick impressions of the room and its contents. An artist's studio, after all, is a material reflection of his soul. Several large canvases, some finished, others in various states of completion, hung on the walls or were neatly propped up on the floor. Didn't I see 'The Arming of Perseus' that afternoon, and 'King Cophetua and the Slave Girl'? There were several easels, and a raised modelling-platform, works by other artists, queer treasures and mementoes, busts and clay figures, all the odd paraphernalia that artists collect to fuel their imaginations. The studio was flooded with light, quite hot, and exuded an intoxicating scent of paint, varnish, and stale tobacco smoke.

'My brother and I recently went to see Mr Leyland's collection,' Mabel prompted.

'Yes, and your pictures, sir, formed the best part of it.'

'You would be wise not to let Mr Whistler hear you say that.' Burne-Jones fended off further flattery by adding: 'My poor pictures hang with some very distinguished company there.'

'The picture of "Merlin and Vivien" I found especially interesting,' I said. 'Two magicians, each working to avert the other's magic.'

Burne-Jones studied us with his pale candid eyes. 'You two are brother and sister?'

'I am Aubrey Beardsley, and this is my sister, Mabel.'

'You will excuse me for saying so, but the pair of you make a most curious study in contrasts. Are you students of art?'

His question was directed to us both, but it was I who took up the gambit. 'I hope to study art, sir.'

'What do you do now?'

'Clerk,' I murmured.

'Eh?' The artist was losing his hearing.

'At present I am employed as a clerk by the Guardian Fire and Life Insurance Association.'

'And you, Miss Beardsley?'

I had to snatch all the attention before he was caught in the magical lure of Mabel's hair. 'My sister is a teacher at the Polytechnic for Girls in Langham Place.'

'A teacher, are you?'

Before he could pursue further questions with Mabel I boldly laid down my portfolio and said: 'By chance, sir, I happen to have some of my most recent drawings with me. I wonder if you would look at them and give me your candid opinion as to their merit.'

With Mabel's most charming smile as an added inducement, Burne-Jones nodded his consent. I studied his expression as he opened the portfolio and saw the first drawings. They were, of course, my best, and were meant to show dramatic characters in a surrounding tumult of action. If I were ever to paint great historical canvases such as the ones now hanging around me, they would be based on these drawings. One was 'Saint Veronica on the Evening of Good Friday', another 'Dante at the Court of Don Grande della Scala'.

The old artist said nothing as he assessed my drawings. I kept thinking he might give something away, flick his hooded eyes upward in amused exasperation, or step backward in amazement, but there was nothing but his pure concentrated gaze. 'Notre dame de la lune', 'Dante designing an angel', 'Insomnia', 'Post Mortem' – all the designs that crowded nightly into my imagination, waiting to be released by the magic of paper and ink, exposed to the judgement of the greatest artist in Europe.

'There is *no* doubt whatsoever about your gift,' he said finally, keeping his eyes on my portfolio and pulling out certain drawings for re-examination. 'One day you will most assuredly paint very great and beautiful pictures.'

A choir from heaven sang, and I was baptized in the name of Art.

'These drawings are full of thought, poetry and imagination. Nature has apparently given you every gift which is necessary to become a great artist. Yet to be truthful, young man, I seldom or never advise anyone to take up art as a profession – it is too infernally difficult, and one generally finds oneself lacking not only butter for one's bread, but also the bread itself. Life for most serious artists is a permanently empty larder.'

'But there is the ecstasy of the work itself,' I interpolated. 'Surely that must be the first guide for an artist?'

'Ecstasy?' Now I heard a glint of hard-edged scepticism in his otherwise kind voice. 'My dear boy, mysticism generally leads to one of two things – madness or martyrdom, neither of which is particularly conducive to art; and ecstasy – that losing of one's self in the Other – should never be considered a substitute for worldly

189

wisdom.' He paused to look again at my St Veronica. 'Here before me are some remarkably promising specimens of a youthful talent that, with proper training, could blossom handsomely. And though, as I started to say, I rarely advise anyone to take up art as a profession' – here our eyes met – 'in your case I can do nothing else.'

A solemnity hangs over that moment. Yes, it was that afternoon that determined my course in life; it was Burne-Jones's endorsement of my talent that gave me the courage to persevere in the face of endless obstacles; there, in that studio, my crucible was forged.

Only, of course, I didn't see it that way then. Youth sees only the triumph of the moment and nothing of the long defeat of the years.

Now, as I lie here in St-Germain, nearly penniless, ill to the point of exhaustion, an exile from my country, forbidden to draw, my name an aspersion, casting my mind back over past events, that afternoon at Burne-Jones's haunts me for another reason. I wish that I could end the reminiscence there, in Burne-Jones's studio, but to do so would be to overlook the other introduction that changed my life. Both of these on the same day, and in the same place – what a fateful juxtaposition!

With assurances that he would immediately begin to search out an appropriate art school for me, Burne-Jones escorted us through the house and into the lush fragrance of his garden. Dense tangles of climbing roses spread a heavy scent through the hot still air, peaches were ripening on the wall, and bees were drunkenly humming in the blue-pink blur of the lavender. We had been invited to tea.

Mrs Burne-Jones came up to us at once, and listened with great attention as her husband extolled my talents. 'I must congratulate you, Mr Beardsley,' she said when he had finished. 'My husband is a very severe critic.'

'Two hours' daily study at a good art school will be quite sufficient for you,' the artist went on. 'Study hard. You have plenty of time before you.'

'Of course,' I said.

'I myself did not begin to study till I was twenty-three. You must come and see me often, and always bring your drawings with you.'

'I will,' I promised. It was all I could do to keep myself from kneeling at his feet.

'Design as much as you can, for you will find your early sketches to be of immense service to you later on. Every one of the drawings you have shown me would make a beautiful painting.'

His enthusiasm had naturally made me an object of considerable curiosity, and Mabel and I were now led around the dappled confines of the garden to meet the Burne-Joneses' other guests.

When I first saw him, he was standing and holding forth beside a small statue of an ancient garden deity – a prickless Priapus – using it as one uses a lectern on stage. A small knot of tea-drinkers stood about him in expectation of pleasure, half-smiling before he finished a sentence. His voice was mellow, plummy, ripe, and he used his hands a great deal for additional emphasis. '. . . because all excess,' he was saying to his audience, finishing up an anecdote, 'as well as all renunciation, brings its own punishment.' Appreciative murmurs from the tea-drinkers, and then, from him: 'Who is the young portfolio'd genius you have in tow today, Edward?'

Burne-Jones introduced us. O fatal moment! Why did I not see Nemesis, hiding there in a dark corner of the garden, heavily draped, head bowed, talons hidden, a horrid smile on her lips? I was too blinded by personal auguries of success; I saw around me, in that crowd, nothing but confirmation of my brilliant future as an artist.

'Mr Aubrey Beardsley, Mr Oscar Wilde.'

We shook hands.

Oscar was far more civilized then, keeping his grosser indulgences a secret within a small circle of adoring young men. He was happier; not the haunted, frightened, tragic figure he became at the time of the trials. Large in both stature and girth, he was not yet corpulent; and his protuberant teeth hadn't then turned quite so rotten and black. I must confess that I loved him a little at first sight, as one loves a theatrical figure, someone who has lived through vast experiences – and survived.

That was Oscar's year, 1891; his *anus mirabilis*, if you will forgive a bad pun. *The Picture of Dorian Gray* had been published the year before in *Lippincott's*, where Mabel and I had read it with terror and admiration. Never before had an English novel openly hinted at so many forbidden topics, or hidden so much corruption in such a polished style. Its impact on us had been considerable; it made us want to sin elegantly and epigrammatically.

Just three months earlier, *Dorian Gray* had been published again – this time in book form – unleashing a renewed storm of critical protest. By now all of London knew that W. H. Smith & Co. had called the novel 'filthy' and refused to stock it on their shelves. People read it clandestinely, furtively, on the omnibus, in the Underground, alone in their rooms, when the children were asleep. In short, *Dorian Gray* had suffered the fate of every anathematized book: it had become scandalously successful, and especially amongst the young.

Someone now made mention of *Dorian Gray*, and Constance Wilde, Oscar's wife, emitted what to my ears sounded like an annoyed sigh. 'Since Oscar wrote that novel, no one will speak to us,' she said.

'My dear Constance,' said Mrs Burne-Jones, 'it hardly matters since Oscar does all the talking anyway.'

Mabel and I joined in the laughter, as did Oscar. I then caught his attention by asking for his personal thoughts on the controversy surrounding *Dorian Gray*.

'Well, any attempt to extend the subject-matter of art is extremely distasteful to the public,' he said, 'and yet the vitality and progress of art depend in a large measure on the continual extension of just that – the subject-matter. And there, as our host would no doubt agree, you have the dilemma of the modern artist in England – a creature who must have the courage to expose the truth of his private imagination to an unimaginative public. Once he has done so, of course, he is immediately regarded as untruthful and unwholesome. In the end, however, it is always the public, and not the artist, that is shameless and immoral.' He extracted a cigarette from a silver case and lit it with a curiously dainty flair. 'To the true artist, of course, virtue and vice are of equal value as material for art. In France and elsewhere on the Continent this has been understood for some time; it is only here, in England, that Mrs Grundy retains her post as Guardian of Public Morals and interferes with free expression.'

Later, as the other guests strolled through the garden, examining the roses and exclaiming over the scent of the lavender, I had him to myself for a few moments. Yes, Father, I wanted to make an impression on him; hoped for further intercourse; saw Oscar as the aspiring always see their heroes, not as a mortal man with throbbing bunions and insomniacal money worries but as a genius who has triumphed over his foes and feasted with the gods. He was exquisitely dressed, almost to the point of over-refinement, and as polished as the Queen's doorknob; and it is impossible to convey the charm, playfulness and witty erudition which made his conversation so fascinating. He played the role of Lord Henry Wotton to perfection.

'The public, of course, can be wonderfully tolerant,' he said in response to some feeble remark of my own. 'It will often forgive everything except genius.' And then he startled me by asking: 'Are you a genius, Mr Beardsley?'

'My father doesn't think so—'

'Fathers should be neither seen nor heard,' he said. 'That is the only proper basis of family life.'

It gave me a curious thrill to hear this heresy; and looking out into the garden where Oscar's two sons were playing I could only wonder what kind of a father he was to them. 'I quite agree,' I said.

'You see, to be an artist, you must first be a personality. It is personalities, not principles, that move the age. And personality, Mr Beardsley, even though it destroy itself, should be the final work of art. Art is the medium of personality.'

'Yes – definitely – personality—'

'Personality is the full expression of one's inner temperament, which is why anything so unusual as personality is considered dangerous here in England. England strangles spontaneity because it considers anything beyond the dreary mechanical worship of facts and figures to be wicked. But what is each of us here for, if not to realize our nature to perfection? Every impulse that we strive to strangle broods in the mind and poisons us.'

He said he was going off to Paris soon, and began to rhapsodize about that city. 'Of course England doesn't know what an artist is. France is the source of all the arts, as I am sure you know, and we go there, every one of us, like rag-pickers with baskets on our backs, to pick up the things that come our way. One learns in France to appreciate not only art; one learns to appreciate life, to look upon life as an incomparable gift. You've been to Paris, of course?'

I smiled dumbly and shook my head.

'Perhaps you shall accompany me to Paris one day. You do speak French, don't you?'

'I read it better than I speak it,' I admitted.

'French, of course, is essential to our *fin de siècle* temperament. Without French, one can hardly be a *décadent*,' He used the French pronunciation, and pursed his lips to keep from smiling. 'That, you know, is what I am called now – *décadent*.' He dropped his cigarette to the gravel and immediately withdrew another, lighting it and then offering it to me. It was a curious gesture, and frightened and fascinated me at once.

Mabel joined us at this point, and I introduced her. She paid homage by saying simply: 'I adore your work, Mr Wilde.'

'An acquaintance that begins with a compliment is sure to develop into a real friendship,' Oscar said, smiling genially as he extracted his watch. 'Dear me, we must be going. I'm dining tonight at Solferino's with a delightful young poet named John Gray. Can we drop you somewhere?'

'Oh, that's not—' Mabel began.

'Very kind of you,' I broke in. 'We should be most grateful.'

While Oscar went off to collect his wife and children, Mabel and I found Burne-Jones. 'Thank you, sir,' I said, shaking his hand. 'You have done me a great honour today, and I shan't forget it.'

A few minutes later we were installed in the Wildes' carriage, the first private carriage I had been in since coming to London, and moving out into the late-afternoon crush of traffic. I sat between Oscar and Mabel; Constance and the two boys were opposite. How different the world looked from this privileged, upholstered vantage-point; how deliciously cosy. One was shut off from the stink and glare of the July streets, and the pain, disorder and unending misery of life that one saw there. The two boys, Cyril and Vyvyan, babbled with delight as the carriage passed an old man with a monkey on his shoulder, playing a barrel organ.

'Will you be accompanying Mr Wilde to Paris?' I asked Constance.

She looked startled for a moment, unprepared. 'To Paris?' Obviously she had no idea that he was going.

'My wife has too many family duties to attend to here in London,' said Oscar.

He was an enormous presence beside me; I could feel the splay of his giant thighs with each jolt of the carriage. 'Are you now writing another novel?' I asked, determined to keep the conversation moving.

'No, I think I am finished with novels and prose-writing for the present.'

'Oscar has two volumes of stories that will be published later this year,' said Constance, 'and a book of critical essays as well. Is that not right, Oscar?'

It was soon apparent that she bored him unutterably; that husband and wife were, despite their tandem public appearances, complete strangers to one another. It was Constance's income, I know now, that provided them with luxuries like the carriage; Oscar's earnings as a writer were negligible before his success, the following year, with *Lady Windermere's Fan*. She adored; he ignored.

'Papa's written a book of fairy stories,' Vyvyan proudly exclaimed.

'We know all of Papa's stories before they are in books,' Cyril added.

Oscar smiled indulgently at his sons, those two little boys whose lives just four years later would be turned into a nameless tragedy. 'But Papa is now thinking of writing a play – in French,' he said, adding with a chuckle, 'and it will make Papa an Academician.'

'A rich Academician, I hope,' said Constance.

'What is the subject of the play?' Mabel asked.

Oscar was silent for a moment, leading one to expect a brilliant epigram or paradox. All he said, however, was, 'Salome. Daughter of Herodias. Princess of Judaea. She who danced for the Tetrarch and demanded the head of John the Baptist as her reward.'

We were all silent as the carriage picked up speed and moved quickly down Sloane Street towards Chelsea. And now – yes, I was sure of it – even when it was not moved there by a jolt of the carriage, Oscar's thigh remained firmly pressed to mine.

DREAMED I WAS walking in the woods, Father, with an energy and eager stride that seemed to presage actual flying. At any moment I felt I might simply rise into the air. Imagine my elation! I was on my way to Paris, but first had to visit the shrine of Notre-Dame des Anglais.

A shadow grazed the forest floor beside me, appearing and disappearing as I strode onward. I knew I had to ignore it, but the shadow grew larger, more persistent, and I was afraid to look behind me, fearful of acknowledging it.

197

But I did look up. I had to, even though fear made my head as heavy as lead; I groaned with the effort. And there, above me . . . Oh, Father! An enormous black bird, not quite a vulture, not exactly a raven, but malevolent, evil, its eyes, glittering with hunger, fixed on me. I tried to escape, but my body grew heavier with each step as that terrifying shadow descended from the heavens and began to engulf me.

I woke in a panic, exhausted, my lungs creaking, my sheets soaked with sweat, and I cursed, Father, I cursed the Creator of all things who is the Destroyer of all things. I longed for peace, for one day of health, one night of dreamless sleep, one moment of freedom from this filthy disease. Mother came in, as she always does, just as dawn was breaking and the birds were mindlessly twittering in the Bois. Dear Mother, who has constantly been at my side these past three years, helping me to die . . . And I cursed her, too. I could not help myself: when the black mood is upon me, anyone with even a modicum of health can inspire my rancour.

I told her that we should begin packing; we were going to Paris as Dr Phillips had suggested. Knowing perfectly well how much Mother loathes Paris, I watched for hidden signs of mutiny – a twitch in her cheek, a deep involuntary sigh – but there was none. Since Dr Phillips is English his advice carries weight with her. Of course she is terrified, as I am, that the artificial pneumothorax will kill me; but, good English people that we are, we do not discuss such trifling matters.

'It will be easier to find students of English in Paris,' was all she said. Whenever she can, in order to supplement our income, Mother flattens the vowels and takes the pucker out of the mouths of French anglophiles.

Most of my life, Father, as you must have guessed by now, has been spent packing and unpacking; the full baggage of my existence, my entire home, now consists of eleven trunks – at least six of them filled with books and drawing materials – and one mother. The great irony, of course, is that, for all this incessant flitting about, travel has become an absolute horror for me. So much so that a simple half-hour train-ride from St-Germain to Paris fills me with nervous dread. Still, we cannot remain here, and if Dr Prendergast recommends artificial pneumothorax the operation will have to be carried out in Paris.

André has most charmingly suggested that a little change at the seaside might be beneficial post-Paris (perhaps post-operation), and today sent a cheque to cover the costs. His promise of further help leaves me too grateful for words. At present, he, John Gray and Miss Gribbell are installed at André's country house near Weybridge, enjoying the fine summer weather. Did you know that John Gray, like St Sebastian, is an archer? Yes, those few hours that he is not writing or praying he spends shooting arrows at a target set up on the lawn. André, pretending to read, watches from the shade of a garden pavilion, perhaps wishing that the arrows were love-shafts intended for him; and the ingenuous Miss Gribbell, an avid plant-collector, devotes her time to compiling a list of the local flora of Surrey. Every morning the three of them attend Mass, and offer up prayers on my behalf, and I desperately want to believe that God hears them. (Does He, Father? If He does, why does He send dark birds of death to torment me?) Mabel has been invited to join the Holy Family in Weybridge, but does not know when her hectic schedule and empty pockets will permit her to leave London. Poor dear, I am certain she could use a few good meals.

It will be at least three days before all our arrangements have been confirmed and we actually set off for Paris, and I mean to make use of the time by writing to you. Dear Père Coubé, I could never have anticipated the strange comfort I receive from telling you the story of my life. It taxes me to the limit, putting all these words on paper, scratching away deep into the night, reliving scenes that candidly reveal my life as an artist and lion of society; but the exhaustion is a delicious one, for it is the exhaustion that comes from unburdening one's soul, freeing it from the weight of sin and memory so that it may be filled with new light and grace. Confession by post – the night school of repentance.

By the time we meet again in Paris, Father, you will know me as no man has ever known me, and you will baptize me with holy water which will at last extinguish the inner fire that has raged through my flesh and burned the footprints of the Devil into my soul.

*   *   *

Inevitably, now that we are about to return there, I find myself thinking back to my very first trip to Paris. It was June 1892; I was twenty years old, and half-delirious with excitement. That trip, Father, marked a clear turning-point in my life as an artist. How circumstances have changed in five short years!

Nearly a year elapsed between my initial meeting with Burne-Jones and that first excursion to Paris – a year spent in hard disciplined work. Burne-Jones's encouragement fuelled my determination to succeed as an artist; like an Etruscan diviner he had peered into my artistic entrails and seen favourable omens. That dear old man, now Sir Edward, his canvases filled with sexless, creatures from Arthurian legend and old myths, afraid like everyone of his generation to show an honest cock and balls, or an enticing pair of breasts! Made dishonest by the times he lives in; a superb designer, yes, and a brilliant colourist; but lacking the hot startling breath that is necessary to pump life into his creations. Impeccable, correct, inoffensive, and utterly dead – his work has all the attributes necessary for an artistic knighthood. A dear, nevertheless.

In five years I've grown far far away from the aesthetics of the Pre-Raphaelite Brotherhood, but they did provide me with my first training-ground, and to Sir Edward Burne-Jones I shall always remain humbly grateful. Some while ago, during my *Morte D'Arthur* days, I sent him my drawing of Siegfried, which he hung in a place of honour in his drawing-room. I like to imagine it there among his other artistic treasures; Siegfried has a home even if his creator does not.

After investigating various schools, as he promised he would, Burne-Jones recommended two: the Royal College of Art in South Kensington and the Westminster School of Art, which was more Impressionist in outlook and training. His endorsement, of course, assured my entrance to either, perhaps with a scholarship.

But my fanciful dreams of throwing up my job and becoming an art student were not shared by my parents and resulted in some pretty rows, I can tell you. The very idea incensed my father to such a degree that he was continually threatening violence. Burne-Jones? Who was he, and what did it matter what he said about my ridiculous drawings? Was I a man or not? Was I going to shoulder some of the financial responsibility for our charming home life or was I not? Look at Mabel – did I ever hear her complaining about her lot? No, she went off to teach every day, returned exhausted, and handed over her wages like the dutiful daughter she was. While I, with my easy job in the insurance office at seventy pounds a year, had the audacity, the perversity to consider throwing it over for something as uselessly effeminate as art school! He would throttle me if I brought up the subject again. Didn't I have the brains to realize that my illness had used up every spare shilling we possessed? Thus spake the failed gentlemen, upon whose shoulders I once rode; and I confess that I wished him dead and out of our lives.

Mother, often ill these days, still wedded to her sciatica, was oddly acquiescent in his presence; sickness had taken away much of her spirit, and her old fiery antipathy towards him had been further doused by hearing too many of Mr Gurney's sermons on the dutiful obedient wife; she now harped on the theme of practicality and health. She commiserated with me in private, but claimed to be powerless to do anything to help. Could I not relegate my love of art and my desire to be an artist to some secondary shelf in my life, make it a hobby instead of a career? She knew how talented I was – by then I had sold several pious drawings to Mr Gurney and his circle – indeed, she thought I was a genius – but £70 a year was not to be sneezed at.

Their own dreams of happiness had been stifled, so of course they felt it their parental obligation to stifle mine and call it wisdom.

Every English artist learns, to his dismay, that there is no real Bohemia in London; but somehow, then, I had the notion that there was, and could not wait to throw over my boring job and be a part of it. Meanwhile there was art to look at, and look at it I did.

Something had happened to me, Father, after that long breakdown of my health; perhaps even as a result of it. I became concentrated; moved swiftly – or so it seemed – into a new and deeper phase of intellectual and artistic development. Unable to dissipate itself through physical exertion, all the nervous energy and vitality of young manhood went straight to my head, as it were, and suffused my brain with a keen power of observation and assimilation. I can explain it only by saying that my eyes felt hungry all the time, and that they devoured what they saw.

Every piece of art I looked at had the glow of revelation, as though it existed only to impart its secrets to me. I seemed to *understand* in a new way. The British Museum, the National Gallery – I burrowed through them room by room, object by object, canvas by canvas, sketching everything I saw, from golden Byzantine madonnas with infants sucking at their stiff detached breasts to black-figured satyrs dancing with hard-cocked joy across the curve of a kylix. Most revelatory of all were the Mantegnas at Hampton Court. The huge canvases forming the series called 'The Triumph of Caesar' had inspired Burne-Jones for years, and they worked their wonders on me as well. Every cloven hoof in my *œuvre* of grotesques stems from my study of Mantegna; just as Mantegna's grotesques were themselves prompted by the Renaissance discovery of ancient Roman frescoes covered with monsters they called *grotteschi* (because they were found buried in subterranean grottoes) – fanciful pagan creatures (like Julian Sampson's Hermaphroditus) whose existence had been deliberately suppressed for centuries by the Christians.

Thus, you see, Father, the eternal triumph of style; how one artist can speak to another through all recorded time; and how the official subject-matter of art – the art that is allowed to be seen – is determined by the ruling powers. The irony is not lost on me: the same Church I am now seeking to join had proscribed whole areas of human expression – the very areas that have, in the past, most fascinated and inspired me. Surely you can understand my quandary; the difficulty I have in renouncing work I consider to be part of myself, and part of humanity, even though the Church and the Royal Academy would never recognize it? I cannot bring myself to call it evil.

When old Aunt Pitt died, leaving me a legacy of £500, I rejoiced as if it were a sign from Heaven. That tough old bird had evidently repented of her dour outlook and wanted me to enjoy life as she never had. Five hundred pounds – all I needed to set myself up! But the money, I discovered, was entailed until I reached my majority (I often wondered if I would); and even when it came into my possession, my darling parents informed me, it was not to be thought of as mine alone, to do with as I wished. How selfish could I be?

No, the money was, like everything else, to go into the common pot, to be used by all of us. With that money we could buy a house and never again have to look for lodgings or deal with nasty landladies.

Without Mabel's encouragement and my own stubborn wilfulness I should never have been able to persevere. But I did. I clung to my dream despite every obstacle thrown in my path. Scotson-Clark, now clerking for a wine merchant in Brighton and writing cantatas in his spare time, was another secret ally; and so was Mr King, although he, too, counselled prudence and suggested that I keep my job and begin to look for illustrating work from publishers.

Finally a compromise was reached with my parents and I began to take night classes in drawing at the Westminster School of Art. Fred Brown, a member of the New English Art Club and fresh from a long sojourn in Paris, was the instructor. He took to me at once.

I had imagined working in a studio like that of Burne-Jones, flooded with natural light; but these were night classes, so we drew to the hiss of gas-jets. Fruit, flowers, draperies (at which I excelled), clothed models and, at last, nude models.

We all tried very hard not to be excited at the prospect of seeing a naked woman; before the model appeared, Mr Brown tried to prepare us by eulogizing the human body and going on to speak of its mass, density, curvature, planes. My cock at full mast, I was expecting a dainty young Venus, blushing with a nacreous virginity, but there appeared instead a wall-eyed hag who had obviously just come from stirring a cauldron on the blasted heath – with massive sagging breasts, thick legs bursting with veins, an enormous dimpled *derrière*, and rolls of fat that hung down over her hips. Her feet were small and dirty. We stared, appalled and a little frightened, as she lumbered up to the modelling-platform and assumed the pose requested by Mr Brown; as the gas-jets hissed, we sketched her form divine. I thought of her later, when I was drawing Messalina.

Anyone who truly wishes to understand my best work, Father, must realize that I draw from my imagination and not from life. My figures are carefully worked out *styles*; individuals, yes, but also parts of an intricate overall design, and often verging on the grotesque or on caricature. This is my penchant, my signature, my Mannerist temperament. Academicians like Sir Luke Fildes may spend years searching for authenticity – indeed, before he painted everyone's favourite, 'The Doctor', old Sir Luke had a complete replica of the interior of a fisherman's cottage built in his studio! – but my art is, in a way, a race against time and a comment on it. I haven't, like Frith, two years to spend on a single panoramic canvas of Derby Day or Ramsgate Sands. Even my choice of materials – pen and ink instead of oils – stems from a precocious knowledge of my mortality. How could I, feeble worm that I am, often barely able to stand unaided, muster the time and the tremendous resources needed for the virile snobberies of oil painting?

Better to master what one can while one can, so black and white is my world, pen and ink my materials, and outline – clear, beautiful, revealing – my greatest strength. I never intended my work to be seen on the hallowed green velvet walls of the Grosvenor Gallery or some other exhibition-hall; I draw with reproduction in mind, and aim for quick startling effects within the confines I have chosen.

Pre-Raphaelitism, as you know, sprang up as an objection to the industrialized production of identical objects, which were thought to kill the soul; it was my ultimate heresy to design pictures with just such mechanical reproduction in mind. I say that the artist must use such technology as exists to convey his vision; he must use the times he lives in, even if his work harks back to earlier models.

As for the human body – it is my belief that the artist reproduces versions of his own physical nature, his own inner psychic structure, his own knowledge of life. Art comes first from within; what we are, or believe ourselves to be, is what our art exposes. And my body, Father, is something I have for a long time loathed or tried to ignore; withered, wasted, worthless, at times no more than an envelope of fiery pain and the container for a disgusting disease, this impossible flesh of mine corresponds to the impossible flesh of my creations.

Which is not to imply that I learned nothing from the life drawing classes of Fred Brown. Before one can remodel a body, one must know its raw form. Mabel helped me, too, by posing nude when our parents were away. Now there was an adorable grace and beauty! At twenty-one she was tall and agreeably plump, with high firm snowy breasts capped by most delightfully rosy aureoles around the nipples. 'Let me unpin your hair,' I would say, and she would smile and walk naked to where I sat with my sketchpad, kneeling in front of me, shivering a little perhaps. Then down would fall that heavy fiery Celtic cascade, and she would look up, a different person, a woman ready for the abandon of love, an Isolde with lips still wet from the love potion. We still had our private world, and could retreat there with no more than the shared glance of an eye.

Mabel, to our parents' bewilderment, had no suitors. She claimed to have no need or desire for one. There were, of course, no male teachers at the Polytechnic, and the men who gathered at the Reverend Mr Gurney's Sunday luncheons were either married or, like Julian Sampson, inclined towards permanent bachelorhood. Where, then, was she to meet this hypothetical husband? And did she even want to?

With another teacher, Netta Syrett, she had formed a mutually passionate attachment not unlike the one with Miss Callow in Brighton. In Mabel's eyes, Netta could do no wrong; she felt as stifled as Mabel did and, just as Mabel dreamed of going on stage, the clever Miss Syrett hoped to escape her dreary lot as a teacher of shopkeepers' daughters by writing sensational novels.

The ripe naked virgin before me, whose soft contours I stroked and caressed on paper, exhibited all the charms and quandaries of the New Woman of the Nineties. She was keen for Experience, but had no means of finding any. Leading morning prayers at the Polytechnic was the only way she had to practice her stage deportment and diction. Mabel had seen and shared the battles I'd gone through to get into night school, and shrank from the idea of asking the revered parents to support her dream of going on the stage. She was delightful in our home theatricals, deliciously droll as she sang 'Quite English' or 'The Little Stowaway', and acted a virile Faust to my frail Margaret. But she wanted more, just as I did; she wanted to pluck and eat the luscious fruit of the Tree of Knowledge.

The frantic hum and hurry of London had gone to our heads like some intoxicating dram, making us want to drink still deeper. What is life for, if not that? Together we haunted the theatres, music-halls, bookshops and, over and over again, the British Museum, National Gallery and South Kensington Museum, where for sixpence I would buy photographs of the artistic treasures of Italy. Around us rose the sweet rough singsong din of the city: girls off Holborn crying on hot August mornings, 'Buy my sweet blooming lavender!'; ragged newspaper boys with their hoarse shouts of 'Ixtree Speshall!'; men calling out, 'Old chairs and baskets to mend!' How could anyone not love London, in all its infinite variety and grimy splendour? This was the great laboratory, where ambitious men were the scientists and success the elixir they sought to formulate.

Late at night, curtains drawn, I would shut myself up in my room and draw by the light of two candles. This came to be a kind of ritual, regular as Mass and just as holy. My drawings were still much influenced by Burne-Jones and Mantegna: enormously complicated pseudo-medieval processions of interlocking figures with one historical personage as focal point. I also continued to experiment with other subjects culled from my reading and my fancy. When the fever came on, as it generally did, I would lose myself to time and surroundings; all that mattered was the drawing in front of me. I would draw until my eyes burned, and then I would lie in bed in a state of nervous mind-racing exhaustion.

Before Mr King took up his new duties at Blackburn Technical Institute, he made a brief trip to London, and I met him after work one evening at the Covent Garden Hotel to show him my expanding portfolio of drawings. It was a hot airless night; my eyes ached, and I was suffering from dyspepsia, but I excitedly told him of my visit to Burne-Jones, showed him the great artist's most recent letter to me, and described my classes with Fred Brown. I needed to please him, for his opinion meant more to me than anyone else's.

'You look fatigued,' he said, putting a hand on my arm. 'Your eyes are quite red and swollen. Are you getting enough rest, Beardsley?'

'Look at my new drawings,' I said impatiently, handing him my portfolio. 'I think you'll see great improvement.'

Mr King was indeed astonished by what he saw, and astonished me in turn by saying that he would try to find buyers for my work. 'What do you call this one?' he asked, removing the best of my recent drawings.

' "Hamlet Patris Manem Sequiter." '

' "Hamlet Following the Ghost of His Father." ' Mr King studied it for a long while. The drawing showed the young Danish prince wending his way through a frightening wood, wrapped in what looked like a winding-sheet. It occurs to me now that I have been drawing figures lost in a dark wood since my breakdown in '91; now I am dreaming them as well.

'He fears becoming a ghost like his father,' I explained, 'and he fears seeing it, but he must find the ghost none the less.'

'He fears death,' said Mr King.

'Yes, because he is still so young.'

Mr King's blue eyes were as frank and sympathetic as ever. 'How much would you ask for a drawing like this?'

'I have no idea. Ten shillings?'

'It would be wise for me to have a copy of Burne-Jones's letter to you. I can use that as an endorsement.'

Yes, it was beginning. Fate was shifting slightly, acknowledging my existence. And, though Mr King was never able to find a buyer for my Hamlet, he did something else with it that was even better.

On Christmas morning 1891, a copy of *The Bee*, the magazine of Blackburn Technical Institute, arrived in the post. Within its pages was a lithograph, beautifully reproduced in sanguine, of my drawing. Mr King had published a note by himself with the picture, prophesying that one Aubrey V. Beardsley was 'destined to fill a large space in the domain of art when the twentieth century dawns'.

Well, it now seems unlikely that Aubrey V. Beardsley will fill any space at all in the twentieth century, except for a grave-space, but at the time I was overjoyed and scarcely knew whether I should purchase for myself a laurel wreath and order a statue to be erected immediately in Westminster Abbey, or whether I should bust myself.

On a blustery St Valentine's Day in 1892 I nervously made my way, portfolio in hand, to the rooms of Aymer Vallance, whither I had been invited for 'Coffee and Cigarettes'. I had dressed with special care, but each passing reflection in the glass of a shop window reminded me how gaunt I had become. Strangers, seeing me for the first time, must inevitably conjecture on my state of health, or lack of it. It made me self-conscious to a degree.

Mr Vallance had appeared in my life just after Christmas – a gift, as it were, from Father Chapman of the Annunciation in Brighton.

Father Chapman, with that worldly outlook that makes High Church people so attractive, thought Aymer Vallance might be able to help me in my artistic career, and to that end had inveigled the poor man to call on me in Pimlico.

Aymer, an antiquarian and a designer, was well connected in the London art world – indeed, for two years he had been an associate of William Morris at the Kelmscott Press. Twice my age, nearly forty, and unmarried, his long ascetic face, lean frame, bald head and fastidious priest-like air seemed a natural consequence of his passion for ecclesiastical architecture and decoration.

We had spent an afternoon – this stranger and I – going through the drawings in my portfolio. Aymer's voice was almost reverential when he said, looking up from my drawing of Shelley's *Cenci*, 'Yes, you are indeed an artist – you must live by it.'

'What? And give up making out insurance policies in Lombard Street?' I said sarcastically. 'Impossible.' For so it seemed that day, after another recent row with my father – utterly impossible.

You could have knocked me over with a peacock feather when Aymer said: 'We must see about getting you a commission from William Morris. Would you be interested?'

Would I! Morris, a hero of mine since I'd read his book *The Earthly Paradise*, was planning to publish a Kelmscott Press edition of Meyerhold's novel *Sidonia the Sorceress*, and Aymer suggested that I draw a sample frontispiece for the book, which he would show to the great man. This, of course, I did, and soon thereafter found myself standing reverentially in front of the bearded old Pre-Raphaelite himself as he examined my picture – and quickly dismissed it.

'The face is not half pretty enough,' Morris said impassively, handing back my sorceress. 'I can see that you do have a talent for draperies, however, and I would suggest that you cultivate it.'

Rage and humiliation strangled any possible utterance, and a queer self-consuming fury took possession of me. A talent for draperies! I was a genius! Once outside, as Aymer looked on in horror, I tore my sorceress to pieces and watched with bitter satisfaction as the wind sucked her up and scattered her down the dark rainy street. If she was not good enough for William Morris, no one should have her.

'Beardsley, it is not the end of the world!' Aymer exclaimed.

But I was in the mood for black, solemn, magical vows. 'I shall never again regard William Morris with anything but contempt,' I said.

Now, on St Valentine's Day, Aymer's next round of useful introductions was about to take place, and I was to meet, among others, a young art critic named Robert Ross. He, I was told, skated effortlessly among the rich, fashionable and influential; was a close friend of Oscar Wilde; recognized and promoted talent with a rare largess of spirit and a bewildering lack of self-interest. All of this, as I later learned, was true: Bobbie lived for others, and inspired friendship to a degree hitherto unknown in the British Isles.

What I did not know was that a secret vice, an unmentionable sexual predilection that tortured their cocks and their consciences, was shared by Bobbie, Aymer and most of the men in their intimate circle.

Aymer's rooms were intimidatingly exquisite, reflecting the tastes and interests of their sacerdotally inclined occupant. The walls were distempered with rich muted colours against which a collection of prints and antique treasures stood out in marvellous relief. There were old engravings of French and British cathedrals – some of them the very ones I had copied as a boy; a polychromed torso of St Sebastian with an arrow through his neck and an upturned, understandably agonized face; a curious stone baptismal font with Norman dog-toothed lines geometrically incised into its base; a small marble madonna with a queer remote smile; and, most remarkable of all, a painted wooden panel of four male saints, all of whom were depicted in the midst of their monstrous martyrdoms – being flayed, stoned, decapitated and boiled.

From this cheerful group portrait of times gone by, I turned to examine the young men of today. Smart, well groomed, refined, every one of them; social creatures all, nuanced, graceful, well educated; with high Piccadilly collars, butterfly ties, delicately coloured waistcoats, exquisite buttonholes. A low buzz of conversation and laughter filled the room; thin china coffee-cups delicately clicked against thin china saucers; a blue haze of cigarette smoke swirled about the smiling madonna and the agonized Roman martyr. It was impossible to imagine pain amidst such civilized grace.

Aymer escorted me about and provided introductions. I smiled under the severe weight of scrutiny. Who was I? What was I, a consumptive clerk, doing here amongst such robust well-heeled university-educated beauty? My appearance shocked them, I was certain of it. And then a voice within me said: 'You have the talent that men such as these can only study and admire. Do not be afraid.'

'That's Mr Ross over there,' Aymer murmured, indicating a small elfin-looking man earnestly engaged in conversation across the room. 'He's with MacColl, another art critic, and More Adey, who has just translated an Ibsen play.'

The three men continued to talk as we approached them.

'She was not known as "la Dame de Beauté" because of her good looks, my dear,' MacColl was saying to Ross, 'but rather because Charles gave her an estate known as Beauté-sur-Marne.'

Their eyes, severely attuned to fashion and male beauty, quickly darted over me, dissecting my jacket, collar, foulard, boots.

'We were just talking of Agnés Sorel,' said Mr Ross. His eyes were kind, tender and a little sad.

'Oh, yes, Charles II's mistress,' I said.

'You know French history?' he asked.

'I know the history of French mistresses.'

They laughed, and I with them.

'Mr Ross, Mr MacColl, Mr Adey, I would like you to meet Mr Aubrey Beardsley,' said Aymer. 'He's brought some quite remarkable drawings with him, and I wonder if you'd care to look at them. His work has been admired by Burne-Jones himself.'

Showing my drawings wasn't so different, really, from performing on the piano as a child; I had the talent, I had the audience – all that remained was to convince a group of strangers that I warranted their admiration and further support. I untied the ribbons of my leather portfolio and opened its covers. They looked. If they had any knowledge of art, they made comments; if not, they criticized. It was a routine at which I would soon excel – even begin to enjoy.

Bobbie Ross became one of my earliest patrons, and tried that very day to buy my drawing called 'The Triumph of St Joan of Arc'. Bobbie was a devout Roman Catholic – a Pagan-Catholic really – and St Joan one of his favourite saints; he'd never forgiven the

Dauphin for handing her over to the English, 'who delight and excel', he said, 'at inflicting punishments.'

Bobbie was himself a victim of English persecution. He came from a distinguished Canadian family, but had been sent to England at an early age with his mother and sisters to be educated. At Cambridge, though a dutiful oarsman, he was subjected to such merciless ragging that he became prostrate with nervous hysteria and anxiety. One night he was hoisted from his rooms and hurled into a fountain by his inhuman tormentors; and became so ill as a result that he left the hallowed confines of the University, never to return.

As the months passed and we grew more intimate, I often wondered if Bobbie were not, at times, actually seeking out the very persecution he most feared and abhorred. There was a saintly quality to him, to be sure; but do not the gentlest of saints paradoxically anticipate or even ask for the cruellest of martyrdoms?

I told Bobbie that I could not sell him the original St Joan because it was promised to someone else – namely Frederick Evans, of the Jones & Evans Bookshop in Queen Street off Cheapside. I could, I assured him, draw another version of the same; and, since my work was improving hourly, the new St Joan would be even better than this one. He agreed, and we settled on what I said was my standard price, thirty shillings.

Frederick Evans must here be added to my list of stepping-stones, for it was through him that I was to receive my first major commission from Dent to illustrate the *Morte D'Arthur* – the work that made my name in England.

All the time I worked at the Guardian Fire and Life Insurance offices I made a habit of using my lunch hour to explore the streets, shops and especially the bookshops of the surrounding area. Initially I was drawn into Jones & Evans because of the Japanese prints displayed in the windows.

These were something new to me, and beckoned to my ravenous imagination at once. As I sought my own style, I was highly susceptible to all kinds of influence, particularly those expressing the familiar world in startling unfamiliar ways. The tired conventions of English artwork, anecdotal and suffocatingly literal, appealed to me less and less; for all of its so-called 'realism', it hardly seemed to reflect 'reality' at all.

'They are called *ukiyo-e*,' said Fred Evans, noticing my interest in the Japanese prints. He was a small, rather ugly man; as vivacious as a spaniel, and with something of that breed's nervous excitability, especially in matters of art and music; his bookstore, full of unexpected treasures, was a perfect haven for habituated browsers like myself, for one was never pressed to buy anything. Fred, I often thought, should have been a teacher, for he loved to impart knowledge. '*Ukiyo-e* is a Buddhist phrase that describes the transitory nature of life,' he said. 'It means "pictures of the fleeting world".'

I stared, transfixed, at the snarling cross-eyed mask-faces of Kabuki actors, the identically benign tea-house beauties, the charming scenes of everyday household life. Dainty figures I assumed to be women were often, in fact, men; for, as Fred pointed out, all female roles in Kabuki were played by male actors. These characters of the fleeting world, often no more than heads, hands and feet protruding from gorgeous robes, were all perfectly natural within the severe stylized boundaries of their world; they loved the cherry blossoms in the spring, snow on the mountains, walking beside the sea. The lines were smooth, assured and superb.

'Now have a look at these,' Evans said, pulling out another stack of prints. 'You will notice they are different – done about a hundred years ago, just as the eighteenth century was changing to the nineteenth.'

They were indeed different: the postures of the characters more provocative and deliberate, more elegant and technically assured, and yet withal more grotesque. They penetrated to the very depths of my soul.

'Through most of the eighteenth century everything in Japanese society was new and interesting to its artists,' Fred said as I leafed through the prints. 'But by the 1790s a kind of exhaustion evidently set in, and you have this strange transitional period where things are no longer settled and certain and secure. The last decade of that century, if its art is any indication, was marked by anxiety, fear and resignation; and the artists no longer lapsed into convention, but into caricature.' He tapped a stubby little finger on a print of a courtesan with an impossibly elongated body. 'They became more wilful, less gently witty – lost a little of their humanity.'

212

'They must have felt that the fleeting world was fleeting even faster. Don't we feel the same thing in our Nineties?'

'Are you an artist?' Fred Evans asked.

'I draw a little.'

'Bring in some specimens of your work. I might hang some examples in the window.'

I did, and he did. Besides letting me barter some of those early drawings for books, Fred Evans reproduced them as platinotypes and tried to interest other collectors. His own artistic proclivity was for photography, and several times he used me as a model; my face, he said, was as compelling as any Holbein. The poses were quite candid and perfectly extraordinary: in one I simply sat at a table with my hands propped up on either side of my face; for another he had me crane my head forward and captured me in profile, like a gargoyle. My beakish nose was shown off to wonderful advantage. I wonder what has happened to those photographs, taken in '91 and '92 – those photographs of a young artist in a transitory world?

In April and May of 1892, as the lilacs wafted their dense lovesick perfume through the Park, and the plane trees grew thick with leaves, and all of sprawling London felt the green, giddy, quickened pace of spring, I worked with the ferocious concentration that attends the discovery of a new style. Call it possession, if you like, or even madness. Nothing mattered except to get my new vision on paper, to fix and hold it secure.

Where did it come from? It came from within. It was everything I had seen, studied, sketched, pondered, envied – all the myriad influences that had been simmering in the mysterious alchemy of my temperament and waiting for the one spark that could ignite and transform them into something entirely new.

When this happens to an artist, Father, when he finally stumbles on to his own path, and a new vision appears before him, burning open the inner eye of imagination, he must be willing to forsake everything – *everything* – to follow it. If he falters or hesitates, he is not worthy of being called an artist. The rewards? Generally there are none, for the stronger the internal vision, the greater the likelihood that, when seen, it will excite the wrath of the Philistines, who understand nothing of art and do whatever they can to prevent its advancement.

I write with the bitter lessons of experience behind me. At the time, I was simply lost in the white heat of my imagination. My routine was quite simple: at nine in the evening, after a full day at the office, I would sit down at my table and draw. Remembering Mr King's simple experiment with light, I always worked to the soft flickering accompaniment of two tapers; they softened reality, invoked reverie, released fancy. A low fever, my hot inner flame, helped to tease fantastic shapes and figures from the shadows. Night after night, without a deliberate intellectual conception, I would simply put my pencil or pen to paper and begin to draw whatever came to me.

Gradually, from a web of lines and a pool of black ink, queer but compelling beings began to emerge and greet me. Strange hermaphroditic creatures appeared, some costumed as Pierrots, others in modern dress. The formal linear style of Japan met and coupled with Western realism, producing fantastic hybrids whose blurred sexual characteristics and curious postures betokened a new world entirely of my own creation. I was well aware that nothing like this had ever been seen in England.

A furious energy possessed me; the days in the office passed in a restless dream; all that mattered was to return nightly to my new world, refine it, explore it further. At last I could call myself an artist! I used my new method autobiographically, drawing myself as a Pierrot hunched over a ledger-book, 'Le Débris d'un poète' lettered above. I trusted my instinct for the grotesque, for symmetrical patterns in black and white, and for the importance of line to convey my vision.

With my annual holiday approaching, I now conceived of a scheme to take my new drawings to Paris – wafted in that direction by my growing egotism and self-assurance. How could anyone consider himself an artist who had not been to Paris? Burne-Jones provided me with important letters of introduction to the venerated Puvis de

Chavannes, President of the Salon des Beaux-Arts, and a young English artist named William Rothenstein. My parents, of course, were incensed that I should want to go to uninhibited Paris when there were so many dreary towns one could safely visit in England, but I stood my ground and made my third-class train and steamer bookings at Thomas Cook's in Ludgate Circus.

One evening before I left I called on Bobbie Ross to drop off the St Joan drawing and ask for hotel recommendations. Bobbie had been to Paris many times, and knew the city, as he put it, with the calculating thoroughness of a streetwalker.

He was living then in Church Street, in just the kind of bachelor rooms that I have always envied; rooms filled with art and curiosities and a delicious air of refined self-sufficient freedom. To be out on my own, away from the cramped confines of rooms shared with my family – I dreamed of such liberty! What was to prevent Bobbie from picking up a whore on the Strand late one night and bringing her here to complete their transaction? Nothing. A thousand such intoxicating daydreams beset me when I thought of living in rooms of my own.

My host was in evening dress when I arrived, for he had a dinner engagement in an hour's time with Oscar Wilde and John Gray. 'Do you know Gray?' Bobby asked. 'He writes poems. Quite remarkably beautiful.'

'His poems?'

'His person,' Bobbie said, adding: 'His poems, too, of course.'

Although I hid my uneasiness, the flippant tone of his answer troubled some sensitive nerve in me – why, I could not say. Bobbie was one of those rare individuals with whom one felt immediately intimate; the endless veils of social convention could be dropped with him at once; and he had a worldliness and a wealth of experience that a semi-invalid could only envy. But what sort of experiences had they been? My innocence at the time, Father, despite all I had seen and learned at Brighton Grammar School, was still remarkable.

'He's been Oscar's favourite for quite some time,' Bobbie said, offering me a cigarette. He lit one himself and in a curious fish-like manner gulped the smoke into his mouth. 'Oh, blast the tea! Won't you have something stronger? A pick-me-up of brandy would be good.' He filled two tumblers as a dragon's stream of smoke poured from his nostrils. I was highly impressed.

Framed photographs were everywhere: Bobbie's family and his endless stream of friends. I never knew anyone who gave so much kind attention to so many people; his social obligations were positively daunting. I saw a photograph of Oscar Wilde among the collection, and was pulled back in memory to that afternoon in Burne-Jones's garden, a year earlier, and the carriage ride afterwards when I had felt certain that Oscar Wilde's knee was deliberately touching mine. What had that meant? Oscar was much in the papers that year because his play, *Lady Windermere's Fan*, had been a great popular success.

Invitations and *cartes de visite* lay scattered across half of Bobbie's writing-table, and loose sheets of foolscap filled with his rapid scrawling handwriting covered the other half – these were the pieces on art history and criticism that he wrote for various papers.

'Of course, a man like Gray is always somebody's favourite,' he said, draining his tumbler in a single stupefying gulp. 'People who look like Greek gods and speak passable French generally are.' Immediately he poured himself another.

Before an hour had passed, I was to know a great deal about John Gray; more, perhaps, than he likes to recall; even more, perhaps, than André, who keeps him now. In the early nineties John Gray was one of the most talked about young men in fashionable London – and no one was in a better position to talk about him than Bobbie, especially when he had been drinking brandy.

John Gray's background was even humbler than my own, for his father was a carpenter employed in the London dockyards, and on his mother's side there was said to be gypsy blood. Gray was the eldest of nine children and left school at thirteen to labour in the Woolwich arsenal. But he was precocious and determined and remarkably good-looking, and taught himself to play the violin, draw, paint, and to read and speak French. Eventually he was able to leave the arsenal and move on to a position in the General Post Office, and from there to the post of librarian in the Foreign Office. His singleminded determination to better himself meant cultivating a cultivated manner and cultivated friends – of whom Oscar Wilde was, at that time, the best-known and the most influential.

Earlier that year the *Star* had published a front-page story identifying John Gray as the original of Oscar's Dorian. Gray, though he sued for libel, was suddenly wafted aloft in the delicious hot air of publicity. People knew who he was, but not what he was. If he was a 'poet', where were his poems? The influential Oscar set about remedying that situation by underwriting the costs of Gray's first volume of poetry. John Lane and Elkin Mathews of The Bodley Head had agreed to publish. It was to be called *Silverpoints*, after that delicate silvery-grey art form.

Bobbie continued to drink and smoke as he talked of John Gray and Oscar Wilde, who were evidently his two dearest friends in the world. But, as he drank, the whites of his eyes changed to red, and the shadowy circles underneath turned as dark as bruises. His fey sprightly elfishness now verged on a sort of obscene gnomishness. He became animated, and uninhibited in a way I had never encountered before, with a daring and amusing cut to his tongue.

'So you are going to Paris!' he exclaimed. 'Paris, most sacred of cities, the world's *atelier*. This is your first trip? You must go one evening to the Rat Mort! You will find it the most deliciously *outré* club in the city. Go very late – after eleven – and you will see sights that will positively enrage your senses.'

'What sort of sights?'

'My dear Beardsley, are you a virgin?'

The question stupefied me. 'My dear Ross—' I flustered.

'Bobbie!' His small, grinning, elf-like face held an expectant expression. 'Well?'

'I've never been asked such a question.'

'One can't tell with you,' Bobbie said. 'You look as though you know everything. More Adey was quite astounded by your familiarity with Balzac and Molière, you know, and all of us were amazed by your knowledge of music. We all liked you, Beardsley, and I hope that you will consider us your friends.'

'That I shall do with pleasure.'

'Pleasure', Bobbie said, 'is the key. You do know that? And pleasure is what you will find in Paris – an understanding of the senses – all the senses. An appreciation for the sensual complexity of modern man, and modern women. Go to the Rat Mort after eleven, Beardsley, and you will see the French vampires at play.'

'Do they bite visitors?'

'Only one another.'

He shocked me, Father, and I must confess that I loved it.

'And go to the Vaudeville to see Madame Réjane, for she is the Parisienne incarnate. Whatever role Réjane plays absorbs the attention of all of Paris. She carries the very soul of Paris with her.'

'I should like to see Sarah Bernhardt.'

'The Divine Sarah? Why, one day you'll be able to see that old serpent of the Nile here in London, in Oscar's new play *Salome*! But enough of Paris and actresses,' Bobbie said, rubbing his hands. '*Now* I want to see my St Joan. You do have her with you?'

Without a word, delighted by his anticipation, I fetched and opened my portfolio. 'Ah!' His was the cry of the connoisseur whose taste has been satisfied. He took the drawing closer to a lamp, squinting at it through his drink-sodden eyes. 'What a fine line you have, Beardsley. Most impressive.'

'It's the best thing I've done in that style.'

'Do you have other styles as well?'

I gestured to my new drawings in the portfolio. Bobbie was seized with interest and began to examine them. 'I've never seen such perverse little creatures!'

'You must be a virgin, Bobbie.'

He laughed and was about to reply when the room began to shake. Someone was pounding at the door.

'Who on earth——?'

From without an agonized voice cried: 'Bobbie! Bobbie! For God's sake, open the door!'

'John Gray's voice,' he said, hurrying to the vestibule. As he opened the door, a young man literally fell into the room and crouched for a moment on the rug, overcome by hysterical weeping. It was an extraordinary sight: I had never in my life seen an Englishman cry.

'Gray!' said Bobbie, trying to hoist him up. 'Gray, what is the matter?'

John Gray was evidently beautiful in repose; in his current state he looked like the tormented heroine of a melodrama. His face was soaked with tears, his golden locks dishevelled, his evening dress crumpled. He looked up at Bobbie and moaned: 'Oscar has dropped me!'

'What? Gray, get a grip, old boy. Come and take a brandy.'

'You knew about this, Bobbie – I know you did. Oscar tells you everything.' Now, for the first time, John Gray saw me. He started, turned away, then flung himself into a chair and covered his face with his hands, shuddering with the weight of his emotion.

'Gray, this is Aubrey Beardsley,' Bobbie said, handing the distraught young man a brandy. 'The young artist – you remember, I told you about him. Here you are; now, drink up like a good boy and pull yourself together.' It was the kind of scene Bobbie would play over and over again in the next few years. He was the one you went to when the Furies were snapping at your coat-tails; it never occurred to you that they might be snapping at Bobbie's as well.

'I was just leaving, Bobbie,' I said, gathering up my portfolio.

'Yes – er – in the circumstances—'

'I shall write you from Paris.'

John Gray moaned and hurled himself into another contorted position in the chair.

'Did I give you the name of a hotel? No? Try the Hôtel de Portugal et l'Univers in the rue Croix des Petits Champs.' He saw me to the door, but kept looking back anxiously at John Gray. 'And do not forget the Rat Mort.'

'After eleven,' I said.

'I look forward to seeing you upon your return. Good night, Beardsley. I shall send you a cheque for St Joan tomorrow.'

When the door closed, I put my ear to it. That was how I learned that Oscar Wilde and John Gray had been lovers. The knowledge of a new world dawned on me. Certain things fell into place, like the design of a drawing.

John Gray, for all his laborious wailing, seemed to be more worried about the fate of *Silverpoints* than he was about losing Oscar's company. His voice turned peevish and malicious as he described the young poet – a new one – who had replaced him in Oscar's affections. 'He's a lord, and he flatters Oscar's vanity. You know him, do you not? A young lord! Just what Oscar has always wanted. Bobbie, what am I to do? What am I to do?'

I crept away and walked home in the soft velvety languor of an

English spring. The streets were full of mating couples, their eyes drowsy with love, and looking at them I wondered when my time would come, and with whom.

Paris. The ecstasy of early summer. One year earlier there had been anarchist riots in the streets; while I was there in '92 a series of bombings destroyed the homes of the officials involved in the trials; the modern Babylon was beset by turbulence and bloodshed – and I loved that lurking sense of danger and intrigue. The quickened pace, the elegant boulevards, the luxurious boutiques. Charvet, *the* haberdashery in Place Vendôme; Goutel's scent shop, where I purchased a small flagon of Mystères de Paris for Mabel; Cassegrain, the stationers; Sennelier, the art suppliers on quai Voltaire – I adored every commercial inch of Paris.

Paris, Paris: the city of Pierrot, the city of decadence, where souls went nightly searching for pleasure – and found it. Streets, shop-fronts, ordinary human faces – all were transfigured by the magic of artificial light. Even the smells – sudden, sharp, rank – betokened a richer class of shit than we produced in England.

I presented my letter of introduction from Burne-Jones at the studio of the revered Pierre Puvis de Chavannes and was cordially received by him. There I stood going through my portfolio of drawings with none other than the president of the Salon des Beaux-Arts, he whose murals graced the Pantheon! Another painter was there, and Monsieur introduced me to him a 'un jeune artiste anglais qui a fait ces choses étonnantes'. I fairly floated back to the hotel after this accolade. I was recognized as a young English artist who did amazing things!

The annual Salon of the Champs de Mars is, of course, the art event of the Paris season, and I went several times to study the paintings and the public that viewed them. Hardly the atmosphere of the annual show at the Royal Academy, I can tell you. Gorgeous, sensual pictures by such veterans as Renoir and Degas hung alongside those of aspiring unknowns; dozens of beauties – some of them instantly recognizable as the models on the canvases – paraded through the crowded rooms wearing the most extraordinary gowns;

and people clambered on to tables and chairs to see celebrities like Zola pass through. Unlike the English, the French were not afraid to show off their enthusiasm and excitement. The true Bohemian gaiety everywhere around me was too delicious; but it made the solitary visitor a little *triste* as well. One always wants to share an exciting atmosphere with a lover. I wished Mabel were with me.

I strolled in the sunshine, and through the long cool galleries of the Louvre. I sat outside cafés, drinking sweet strong coffee, sketching like any artist, writing letters, catching an eye or two, learning how to flirt without blushing or regard for sex.

When I asked William Rothenstein why he chose to live in Paris he said: 'Because of the light, of course. And then poverty is easier to bear here.'

'And the wine is finer, and the poetry better,' I said.

William pursed his lips. 'I never drink wine, and as for poetry I still prefer Milton to Verlaine and Baudelaire.' He was the most obsessively neat man I've ever known, and could not bear flamboyance or disarray of any kind; perhaps it was this very fear of impending chaos, itself a kind of hope for the same, that kept him in wild unpredictable Paris.

Rothenstein affected the dress and airs of a dandy, but nothing could displace his essentially pinched and moralistic temperament. His dark, round Hebraic face, abetted by the small spectacles he wore, registered an almost constant expression of disapproval. And yet he knew everyone, and moved in the most advanced circles. Yes, William carried all the signs of the future Academician even then, a fellow my age, an artist, with a studio in Montmartre (and a family supporting him, despite his claims of poverty) and he didn't even have a mistress! I was appalled.

As you know by now, Father, sexual matters have always fascinated me, even when the subject is a lack of sex, and that was definitely the case with William. I suppose, like all of us before we are initiated, he was afraid of it, and of his own desires. I know he had sampled Paris nightlife, for he took me out to raucous Bohemian cabarets in his neighbourhood: the Chat Noir and the Moulin Rouge, frequented by that brilliant dwarf Toulouse-Lautrec, where Yvette Guilbert rasped out her gay naughty songs. But in the midst of this surrounding hilarity William sat stiff and suspicious, a true Englishman in his armour.

One wall of the Chat Noir, Father, is covered with an extraordinary painting by the cartoonist Willette, a work called 'Lord, Have Mercy'. It draws me back every time I am in Paris, no matter how ill I am. Probably you don't know it. The figures are all Pierrots and Pierrettes winding their way down the slopes of Montmartre to the Seine. At the top of the picture they appear gay, youthful and fresh, but as they descend, glasses in hand, they grow old and begin to wear the pitiful look of those who have lost their hopes and illusions. Finally, at the bottom, quite horribly, they fall one by one into a black ditch, driven there by sickness, suicide, depravity and insanity.

William couldn't understand my raptures over this work. 'It only goes to show you that Bohemia as a way of life is quite untenable,' he said primly.

I had been drinking wine – far more than I had ever had in my life – and it loosened my daring. 'Do you know of a place called the Rat Mort, Mr Rothenstein?'

Good God, he was shocked! 'I have of course heard of it.'

'Would you care to accompany me there?'

'I think that would be unwise. And I think it would be unwise for you, Mr Beardsley, as well.'

'In two days' time I return to dreary London, and a dreary office on Lombard Street, and I'm damned if I won't see everything in Paris there is to see while I can see it!'

'If it is the damned that you are seeking, Mr Beardsley, you will be in very good company at the Rat Mort.' He rose and put out his hand. 'I shall expect you for tea tomorrow, then, at five?'

I went on alone, pulse hammering, weak in the knees, down narrow passages, past whores and murderers, until I found the place. It was tiny, dark, and utterly charming in its own Bohemian way. This, the infamous Rat Mort where my senses were to be enraged? The gentle young man who took my order, the smiling older chap at the piano, the other gentlemen and ladies seated at tables and around the bar, they all grazed on me with their curious eyes. I smiled and drank and waited for the shameless spectacle – whatever it was – to begin.

A couple was dancing and there was something odd about the

man. What was it? He was beautifully dressed, his evening clothes cut in the latest French style, with turned-back black velvet lapels. His hips were wider than a man's, perhaps, and his face softer. That was it – he looked terribly effeminate. When he and the woman parted, I saw that even a stiff shirt-front could not hide the evidence of two large breasts. And then at last it all fell into place, and I laughed with drunken delight and raised my glass to Paris!

Mabel was a study as she slowly turned the pages of the book. She kept drawing her face up in a kind of amazed alarm and bursting into nervous laughter; occasionally she would frown and examine something with microscopic intensity and a murmured, 'How perfectly extraordinary!'

I had brought the book back from Paris, hidden amongst dozens of others picked up in my walks along the quays. This one was quite special. It was a bound collection of Japanese prints called *The Book of Love*, and each print was devoted to some form of erotic pleasure.

'What on earth are they doing?' Mabel said, peering at another print. Her tone became exasperated: 'Really, this one is too impossible.'

And how did I come by this delicious specimen of *Shunga*, or 'spring drawing', as it is called? It was a gift from none other than the fastidious William Rothenstein.

It had been given to him – one wonders by whom – and William, as an artist, could not bring himself to destroy it, even though he considered it gross. 'It is a debased form of art,' he said, 'and concerned with only one aspect of the human condition – the most tiresome aspect at that.'

Feigning composure in the presence of such tantalizing matter was difficult, but I did not want William to think me an eroto-maniac, so I turned the pages with an imperturbable equanimity, like a guest politely turning the pages of an album. 'Regardless of the content, Mr Rothenstein, one can always learn a secret or two from the Japanese. Their lines are quite beautiful.'

'You may take the book if it interests you,' said William. 'I shall be glad to be rid of it.'

'And I should be delighted to have it.'

Mabel turned a page, let out a small cry, and covered her face with her hands. 'Aubrey!' She pushed the book in my direction. On a moonlit terrace in the springtime, a young Japanese prince with a grotesquely enormous cock was vigorously pleasuring a dainty lady wearing stockings and sandals.

'You will notice, Mabel, that they are both smiling,' I said.

The next page was the one I was most eager for her to see. Two moon-faced ladies, their hair intricately bound and lanced with sticks, enjoyed a secret romantic interlude on a mat. Just outside, the men of the household toiled in a rocky garden.

Mabel said nothing, but she stared harder than I have ever seen her stare before or since. 'Tell me again about that place called the Rat Mort,' she said.

 **XI**

NOTHER BAD NIGHT, Father. I begin to sound like a barking dog; my cough is my voice. Disintegration continues unabated; lung turning to porridge; night fevers; a major haemorrhage is near, I can feel it. Blind animal fear; the panicking urge to gnaw one's foot off in order to escape the truth of the trap. Today I asked Mother to buy me a rosary so that I might stupefy myself with prayer.

Dr Phillips was so reassuring when he said that with proper treatment a full recovery was still possible. Perhaps he was lying. They often lie to comfort you. Or to disguise the fact that they know nothing at all about the disease, and can therefore do nothing to help you. André may have told him to lie, to spare me unnecessary pain. I can trust no one; that much is apparent.

After all these years of illness I must still fight rage. How dare this happen to me! I am afraid that if I stop raging my will to live will leave me.

Be resigned and trust in the will of God – those were your words, Father. Sentimental drivel! How can I trust in God if it is He who is doing this to me? Why should I? Is this an example of His perfect wisdom? I must not let myself believe that I am being punished this severely for my few meagre transgressions – and yet I do, dear God, I do.

I could endure so much were it not for the despair that comes flapping into my room at night like a great black bird and, heedless of my terror, proceeds to peck and gorge on my very soul.

Around me, half-packed trunks, symbols of my racing rootless existence.

Writing this to you is my only way of forgetting fear.

How different it was when I returned from that first trip to Paris. Then I was confident and self-assured, I can tell you. Of course I was still tethered to the insurance office, but now at least I knew I had to chuck it. The trouble was, I could not give up the job until I earned enough as an artist to warrant it. The torrent of abuse that came down on my head from my father when I even suggested the possibility made that quite clear.

He was in the same position as I was – loathing his daily work, but having no alternative if his family were not to starve. The brewery was expanding, and there was talk of sending him to a better job outside London. He wanted to go, I could tell, but Mabel and I worked in London and could not leave. Mother, I think, wanted him to go as well, tho' she never actually said so. But, faced with the prospect of leaving us and going to live alone, the tyrant balked.

I knew I was a disappointment to him, and that the very sight of me was an annoyance. What father wants a frail artistic son? Our shared disease stared him in the face every time he glanced in my direction, reminding him of what he had to look forward to, and what his corrupt seed had produced. My artistic gifts he regarded with contempt; somehow they signified unmanliness to him, an effeminacy of misdirected purpose. I gathered from what he said that he considered me 'spoiled' and 'pampered' by Mother; and that his greatest disappointment in life was that he would never have a hearty healthy son to support him in his old age.

I had little ways of letting him know how ridiculous I thought he was. Bow to the revered paterfamilias? Kneel to the most highly esteemed British patriarch, who incorporates in his person all moral authority and higher wisdom? Bah! If you want the naked truth, Père Coubé, it was men like my father who sentenced Oscar to prison, and ensured that I was severely punished for knowing him. Fathers are the ones who construct the gaols out of their own hypocritical self-righteousness.

'Where are you off to tonight?' he would ask if he saw me preparing to go out.

'To the opera.'

'The opera!' He looked to my mother for support, but she avoided his eyes. 'Tonight it's not the theatre, or a music-hall, or an art class, it's the opera. I suppose Mabel thinks she is going to the opera as well?'

'Yes, Father,' Mabel said. 'It's a Wagner night. They're doing *Tannhäuser*. Aubrey has the score.'

Now his simmering anger would start to build in an impotent attempt to belittle or intimidate us. 'Oh, he has the score, has he? So he can follow along, I suppose, because he is such a musical genius. How much does such a score cost, I should like to know?'

'Not much.'

'How much is not much?'

'A couple of bob. Hurry, Mabel, or we shall be late.'

'Since it is raining. I suppose you will ride to the opera in a cab,' Father said.

'Even if we did, it would be paid for with my money.' I knew perfectly well the effect this would have on him, but was unable to resist the goad.

'Get high and mighty with me and you'll feel the back of my hand right enough!' our former gentleman would threaten. 'Spending all that money in Paris – it's criminal, that's what it is!'

And so it would develop, becoming a tirade about my utter disregard for money, or our flighty inability to remain at home in the warm happy bosom of family life, or one of the hundred other trifling matters that so easily ruffled the dark calm of his miserable daily existence.

None of it mattered once the overture began. That was the year, 1892, when I first heard *Tannhäuser* and *Tristan und Isolde*, and knew myself to be in the presence of genius. Those stories, fused to that music, moved me in a way that mere life never could. I felt rapture in my crooked spinal column, bliss in my fevered heart. Tannhäuser, the knight who seeks redemption from the voluptuous arms of Venus only to be spurned by the Church for loving her; Tristan and Isolde, enemies doomed by fate to fall passionately in love – they were never far from my imagination after that. As I followed the glorious rise and swell of the music, Mabel, seated beside me, acted unconsciously as my Venus, my Isolde. Does it sound perverse to say that I could understand the plight of Tannhäuser and Tristan, prisoners of desire both, only through the intense love I felt for my sister? Were it not for Mabel, dear Father, *les grandes passions amoureuses* would always remain an abstract intellectual puzzle to me. She is, and always will be, the naked numinous figurehead guiding the prow of my ship to port.

It was also about this time, the autumn of 1892, that Fate entered Jones & Evans Bookshop in Queen Street and waited, patient sorceress that she is, for the proper alignment of stars, moons, planets and people. I had become quite fond of Fred Evans by then: we had come to an amicable agreement by which I sometimes traded him pictures for books; and he would often make platinotypes of my work to hang for sale on the walls. I had come to feel that the bookshop was my own little gallery, and looked in nearly every day during my lunch hour.

Fred knew many publishers, the esteemed J. M. Dent among them. Together they had planned Dent's Temple Shakespeare series, and before undertaking any new publishing project Dent would always discuss it with Fred. Like most publishers, Dent was eager to spot a trend and make money from it, and it was William Morris's arty and popular Kelmscott Press books that he had his eyes on now; the public adored their medieval appearance, and the fact that the artwork was printed from hand-carved wooden blocks added to their romantic allure.

Dent told Fred that he was thinking of publishing Malory's *Morte D'Arthur* in a de luxe edition, but could not find an artist who understood the Kelmscott style well enough to copy it. Dent, you see, wanted Morris-looking work, but he did not want to pay a Morris-sized fee.

Now, who do you think just happened to enter the bookshop at the very moment Fred Evans was showing J. M. Dent a drawing of the Virgin Mary by a twenty-year-old artist named Aubrey Beardsley?

It all happened with the swift sweet fatality of a dream. Fred called me over to meet Dent, and explained that the publisher was looking for someone to illustrate *Morte D'Arthur* in a William Morris manner. The job would entail several full-page drawings, as well as hundreds of chapter headings and ornaments – but none was to be reproduced using the laborious hand-carved methods of the Kelmscott Press. No, a cheaper and more modern method of line-block photo-mechanical reproduction was to be employed: the illustrations would only have the *look* of being hand-carved; technology had rendered that old process obsolete. Dent's book would be issued in instalments starting in about a year's time. Did I think I could do the job?

How delicious it was to imagine myself a rival of the great Pre-Raphaelite William Morris, he who had dismissed my picture of Sidonia the Sorceress as not pretty enough! Now he would see that I had far more than a meagre talent for draperies; I would show him such astonishing work that he would regret not discovering me before Dent.

'Yes, I can do the job,' I said. It's as simple as that, Father, once your fate has been spun. You need only say yes and the quest begins.

Dent sucked meditatively on the hairs of his long brindled moustache and peered down at me through his spectacles. He was a man who combined in his person the cunning energetic hurry of a successful lord of business with the wise authority of a tribal elder:

a beard of epic proportions flowed nearly to his waist, giving him the look of a biblical patriarch; and his suit, tho' modern and well made, was as crumpled as if he'd slept in it.

'I like your pictures, Mr Beardsley,' he said in a low and surprisingly sonorous voice, 'but before we talk further I must ask for a specimen drawing that pertains to the *Morte D'Arthur*. If it is appropriate, we can then begin to discuss terms.'

I told him he would have the drawing in a fortnight.

When Dent left I turned to Fred in a veritable daze. That queer solemn feeling that overtakes one at moments one knows to be important had descended upon me, as it had at Burne-Jones's studio; I can describe it only as a sense that one has slipped into the warm secretive fold of one's own deepest desires; at such moments fate seems unusually welcoming, benevolent even, and humility the only appropriate response. 'It's too good a chance,' I murmured. 'I'm sure I shan't be equal to it.'

'Of course you will,' said Fred.

'I am not worthy,' I said.

'Do the drawing for Dent before you pass judgement on yourself.'

Two deep chimes from St Paul's brought me to my senses. 'I must get back to the office!' I cried, pumping Fred's hand before racing back to my stack of insurance policies in Lombard Street.

I began Dent's drawing that very night, impelled on a veritable gale of inspiration. For my subject I chose the highest and most sublime moment in all *Le Morte D'Arthur*, the achieving of the Sangreal. In my picture, two knights, after a long and arduous quest, receive a sacred vision of the Holy Grail from a tall, feathery, epicene angel. All is solemn reverence and deep spiritual communion. To this medieval Morrisy-looking business I added a modern landscape entirely my own, utilizing my new discoveries of line, distortion and perspective from Japanese prints. I invented monstrous growths of barbed vine and hybridized thistle lilies springing from a viscous black lake to symbolize the poisonous earthly snares the knights had overcome, and counterpointed this evil garden with the distant view of a serene kingdom on a hill.

Mr Dent was aproproately speechless when I presented him with the picture, and awarded me then and there a commission to illustrate the entire *Morte D'Arthur* for a fee of £250. I was exultant!

I wanted to yank his beard for sheer joy! I was certain that I had achieved my own Sangreal, and that the soft feathery rustlings I heard in the air around me were the wings of my angel. I could never have known, Father, that the sound was an excited poisonous hiss emanating from the flowers in my garden of evil.

The people at Guardian Fire and Life seemed quite relieved when I handed in my resignation; I had never fitted in there, and never would; and, of course, after witnessing my one dramatic collapse they were always afraid that I would drop dead in front of them, which is never good for morale.

Mabel had been encouraging me to chuck the Guardian; she said I must devote myself entirely to my art – a view with which I naturally concurred. Over and over again we had taken our case to Mother, who, sensing the loss of what little financial security she had, became ever more desperate in her attempts to quell the mutiny.

'Your health!' she would squawk. 'You will never manage to stand up to working all hours of the day and night, when publishers want designs in a hurry. Try to think *practically*, Aubrey.'

'Mother, I shall be the practical one,' Mabel would insist. 'My teaching at the Polytechnic is certain to lead to an appointment as headmistress. I shall support us. But Aubrey must be free to draw and look for artistic work. His pictures are beginning to attract attention now.'

'Your father will never agree.' It always came back to this.

'That's only because he can't earn enough to support us,' I would point out, 'and never has.'

Money, money, money. How it rules our lives! The situation with Father was made even more galling because, although Mabel and I between us earned more than he did, his was the final authority in all domestic matters. Thus, the only way I could actually leave the Guardian office was to do it secretly and inform the revered parents afterwards.

I shan't go into the thrilling hearthside scenes that followed this decision of mine; let me just say that a positively Greek fury raged in Pimlico, and resulted finally in the overthrow of our hated tyrant. Since, as he rightly pointed out, we evidently had no need of him or his counsel, he would take the new job and move away from

London. From henceforth Mabel and I were the sole providers for the family; and Mother, in effect, became our child.

By February of '93 I was so inundated with work that I stopped sleeping. There was time enough to sleep when I was dead, and there were the usual reasons to believe that I wouldn't make it through another year, yet alone to the end of the century. (That has always been my one desire, Father – to kick this old exhausted century out on its arse, and welcome in a fresh new one.)

Aymer Vallance and Bobbie Ross had been working assiduously on my behalf for a year by then, and the fruits of their combined efforts were ripening fast. Already I had a modest reputation, one that was sure to grow once the *Morte* was published, and a miraculously expanding purse. I purchased a handsome leather portfolio for my drawings and lugged it to every at-home, Sunday luncheon, soirée and afternoon tea-party Bobbie and Aymer could arrange, spreading its pages like an ambitious whore her legs for every important person in artistic London. As a result, there were now more patrons trying to buy drawings than I had drawings to sell.

Speed and versatility were my hallmarks – fortunately, since I quickly become bored. For the *Pall Mall Budget* I now provided sketches, caricatures, portraits and cartoons. I was given free tickets to plays, concerts, operas, and exhibitions for all kinds; and for ten pounds a week had simply to record my impressions of the performers, composers or artists who were that night entertaining, boring or infuriating London. Then there was my *Morte* work.

After a brilliant start, and scores of intricate complicated drawings, I felt my interest in the project starting to sag rather badly. Was there ever a work more long-winded than the *Morte D'Arthur*? I had to maintain the Kelmscott style, but all that sanctified factitious Morris-medievalism began to bore me unutterably. Drawing after drawing, sometimes as many as four a day – how could one ever hope to find something new to say? It kept me from developing my own style. My one consolation – besides the fee, of course – was that William Morris was now a bona-fide enemy. In the mistaken belief that Morris might reconsider me for a commission, Aymer had shown him a sample drawing from the *Morte*; Morris, sensing a rival, let out a jealous howl and accused me of copying his style. The truth of the matter was that his work had grown old and stale, while mine was fresh and original; he saw that but could not bear to acknowledge it.

To stimulate my creativity and provide me with a temporary reprieve from the *Morte*, Dent had given me other work besides. For an exquisite little three-volume series of *Bons Mots* and a charming fee of £100, I was allowed to draw whatever I fancied, only in miniature. Here was a test of pure virtuosic imagination! Using the finest of lines, sometimes no more than three or four for a drawing, I created a veritable bestiary of grotesques: queer stunted creatures with deformed bodies or no bodies at all; angry skeletons wearing fashionable gowns accompanied embryos in evening dress; abortionists, devils, pirates, sad Pierrots, smiling dancers, hermaphroditic monsters – sometimes even I wondered what part of my imagination they sprang from.

Aymer, when he first saw them, was horrified. All his refined liturgical tastes were somehow threatened – 'mocked', as he said – by the revelation of this other diseased universe. 'These creatures are damned,' he said, noticeably wincing at the abortionist. Aymer fussed continually about 'bad influences' on my work and, I think, wanted to redeem me and set me on the path to artistic righteousness by curbing my natural talent for the grotesque.

'I think they're rather pretty,' I would say to annoy him. 'They make me want to laugh.'

'They make me want to pray,' said Aymer. Yet I noticed that, for all the seeming revulsion they caused, he could not stop examining them. 'One knows of such things only in one's nightmares.'

'Or in one's wet dreams.'

Raising an eyebrow, he let out an unexpectedly arch '*Hardly*'. But it was the same when he examined my *Morte* work: the exquisite suffocating tangles of flora and fauna I invented for the borders of the pictures, because they were not drawn from the life, and were therefore 'unrecognizable', sent Aymer's overtaxed brain plummeting to the foulest bogs of hell for some kind of artistic explanation. His own ethereal imagination was generally preoccupied with nothing more exciting than the architectural details of the old churches he loved to haunt, and the seraphic choirboys who sang in them.

Bobbie, on the other hand, was charmed and titillated by my circus of grotesques. 'Too delightful!' he exclaimed. 'Quite uncanny, verging on the fescennine. Profane Roman *grotteschi* remade as modern images in the style of the Japanesque, isn't that the idea?'

Bobbie loved introducing me to useful people, and afterwards I would report to his great satisfaction on my rising fortunes: a new commission to illustrate Lucian's *True History*, a quick job for *St Paul's Magazine*, a good notice in *Livre et l'image*, the impending article on my work that was to appear in the inaugural April issue of *The Studio*. We met frequently, drank tea and lunched or supped together. Bobbie took me to those pitifully few restaurants and taverns that pass for Bohemia in London: the Crown in Shaftesbury Street, the Café Royal, Jimmy's, Aux Gourmets, the Thalia – places where burgeoning decadents could find decent food, inexpensive wine, and an atmosphere as seductive as rotten meat to a fly.

It was through Bobbie, in fact, that I first came into possession of a copy of a new play by Oscar Wilde, written in French and published in Paris and London in February of '93. It was called *Salome*.

Everyone knew *about* the play, but few had yet read it, and no one had ever *seen* it. That was because the year before, in June of '92, the Lord Chamberlain had banned *Salome* from the English stage. That summer Sarah Bernhardt had agreed to produce it and play the depraved teenage princess: she had had a disastrous London season and was desperate to recoup her reputation and revenues. The production of *Salome* was by all accounts (mine are mostly gleaned from Bobbie) to be perfectly sensational. Bernhardt was going to powder her hair blue, wear a heavily bejewelled headdress, a golden Cleopatra-ish gown, and dance the Dance of the Seven Veils herself; the night sky over Judaea was to be tinted purple, the floor of the palace ebony to reflect the Divine One's dove-like feet, and braziers of scented incense were to burn on stage, Oscar having suggested a different perfume for each emotion. It was a decadent's dream come true. Aymer Vallance, who often helped people with the furnishing and decoration of their houses, often in a style surprisingly advanced and un-Morrisian, clasped his hands together and gasped in ecstasy when he heard of the proposed colour scheme.

Two weeks into rehearsal, Piggott, the licenser of plays, refused to grant *Salome* a licence on the absurd grounds that it introduced biblical characters on stage. Saint-Saëns' *Samson and Dalilah*, Massenet's *Hérodiade*, Racine's *Athalie* – none of these masterpieces could be performed in England; surely an exception was not going to be made for precious little *Salome*! Most distressing of all was the fact that, almost to a man, every leading figure in London's theatrical world stood behind the Lord Chamberlain's decision, George Bernard Shaw being the one exception.

Oscar interpreted the ruling as a direct attack on himself and was furious. He threatened to leave England for ever and take out residency papers in France – a move that brought jeers to the eyes of old John Bull. The newspapers, provided with the perfect excuse to be unkind to Oscar, were merciless with their lampoons, caricatures and mocking poems. If the decadent aesthete Oscar left England for France, they gleefully pointed out, he would be obliged to perform service in the French army, and the very idea of Oscar in uniform spawned further gibes (there is no compulsory military service in England, Father).

Thus the poor Divine Sarah, instead of dancing in golden triumph, was forced to drag her veils back to Paris; and *Salome*, because of an archaic law, became one more victim of English prudery and official meddling.

Oscar had gone ahead and had the play published in its French version and, undaunted, was now going to have it translated into English as well. 'He wants an English version to shock those readers who are unfamiliar with French,' Bobbie excitedly informed me, adding, 'And I have spoken to him of having it *illustrated*.'

I took the hint and read *Salome* at once, finding it both corrupt and amusing. So this was the story that could never appear on our hidebound English stage! Oscar had indeed stretched the boundaries beyond anything known in this century.

My French was good enough to render a translation – the job I really wanted – but I decided to make a sensational picture instead. The scene I chose to draw was, of course, the most shocking one in the play, Salome holding aloft the dripping severed head of

John the Baptist and proclaiming: 'I have kissed thy mouth, Jokanaan – I have kissed thy mouth!' The result was nothing less than sensational, and I made sure of the picture's inclusion in the April *Studio*, which was to act as my official début to the English public. Oscar was certain to notice and be flattered.

Through Bobbie, Oscar and I had met socially again, but always in such large gatherings that intimacy was impossible. At the time, I was only one of many ambitious young men orbiting around the planet Oscar, sighted by him like some distant moon but not singled out for special rays of his attention. Those, in any case, were reserved exclusively for the pale lunar flesh and cheese-coloured hair of that dreadful Bosie Douglas.

I did find it annoying that wherever Oscar went he made the sun reflect back on himself alone. Everyone else was eclipsed by his huge presence. He would take the centre of a carpet like a stage the moment he entered; the guests would deferentially stand back around its margins; Oscar would begin to talk.

Yes, Oscar was captivating as he wittily extolled the joys of a sybaritic life, but his endlessly brilliant talk also isolated him as surely as if he wore an impenetrable mask. In his presence one could only compete and lose, for he was tyrannical when it came to sharing the stage.

With the exception of a few clergy and club men – and the journalists, of course – people still adored Oscar, and none more than little Bobbie Ross with his receding hairline and grinning, melancholy face. I had no idea then that Bobbie, too, had been one of Oscar's boys – the very first, as it later transpired: the student who seduced and tutored his master in the geography of forbidden sins. Unlike André, or John Gray, however, Bobbie remained fiercely loyal to Oscar, acting as occasional mistress. Now that John Gray was out and Bosie Douglas was in, Bobbie had also become inseparable from the latter; and since Bosie's propensity to drink was even greater than Bobbie's it made for a very wild pairing indeed. Oscar, whose own passions grew purpler by the glass, called Bobbie 'our Scotch friend' or 'St Robbie' and maintained the sweetest affection for him.

Dear Bobbie had quickly befriended Mabel and Mother, charming both of them with his gallantry and his selfless concern for our welfare. Mother, poor darling, envisioned him as the perfect suitor for Mabel, and was alternately coy and grateful in his presence. It was interesting to observe how much and how quickly she had changed since her husband's departure. Long-suppressed sparks of gaiety would now occasionally burst into flame, and in a way that surprised Mabel and me she sometimes became almost vivacious. Now and then, when she could forget the pain of her sciatica, she would even go to the piano and play a little waltz or popular street-tune.

But of course the impeccably correct public Bobbie who presented himself to Mother and Mabel was quite different from the incorrigibly debased private Bobbie I came to know and love. Men are one thing when they are with women, and something else entirely when they are with other men. With women, propriety is maintained and polite convention honoured; with men, especially men of like temperament, the satyr twitches his tail and impropriety reigns. The public Bobbie was an adorable saint; the private Bobbie was endlessly finding ways to confirm his hopeless sense of damnation.

The problem was – what else? – boys. Dear Bobbie seemed to look upon his sodomitical tendencies as a desperate social obligation; and his name, as a result, was well known to Inspector West of Vine Street. He had narrowly escaped arrest on more than one occasion; and, had it not been for his family connections, might have found himself in gaol before Oscar.

Yes, our Bobbie was well known to the bobbies, and like them had his own regular 'beat' in and around Piccadilly and the notorious edges of Green Park. There, slouched in the glare of a gaslight, or idling near the piss-rank stalls of a public urinal, he would find those *louche* young men – stablehands, telegraph clerks, unemployed valets – whose services he required. Seeing small, well-dressed, half-drunk Bobbie, they would leer, wink, murmur propositions, pout their lips, raise an eyebrow – and he would excitedly make his selection for that night's pleasures, all the while terrified that his choice might suddenly turn on him, beat him, rob him, blackmail him. He who was so tender never expected tenderness in return, poor man; rather, he sought a Dionysian unloosing of restraint, oblivion from the polite sanctity that otherwise ruled his life.

Bobbie, like many sexually inverted men I have known, longed

239

to throw off the burden of secrecy and stealth such a life requires. The Church which he dearly loved condemned his acts as mortal sins, and in the eyes of the law, which in all other ways he respected, he was nothing more than a low criminal. On a sensitive and generous nature like Bobbie's, these injunctions carried double weight, burdening him with a guilt that drink and boys could only exacerbate.

But he could not stop himself. Like me with the sin of masturbation, he simply could not halt his actions. He flew from one confessional to the next, kneeling in the dark and pouring out his offences to one impassive silhouette after another, grateful for absolution, promising God he would never sin again. And then, as the blanket of night slipped over London, and the lamps were lit, and the brandy-glass was filled, the old insatiable urge would overpower him and, helpless in its grip, he would be out on the pavements.

Fortune continued to rain down on me that glorious spring of 1893. In April several of my pictures were featured in the inaugural number of *The Studio* (whose cover I had also designed) together with an article by Joseph Pennell called 'Aubrey Beardsley: A New Illustrator'. One simply cannot, Father, these days, overlook the tremendous importance of publicity in establishing (or ruining) a career. Oscar was right, you know, when he said it was personalities, not principles, that rule the age; my work in *The Studio*, including the picture of Salome kissing the head of John the Baptist, now excited the interest of other artists and even made complete strangers curious to know me.

Joseph Pennell, whose *Studio* article so severely flattered me, was a tall, handsome, silver-haired American artist and critic from Philadelphia who had settled in London with his wife Elizabeth. I met him through Bobbie Ross. Pennell was a superb etcher, a lithographer of views rather than an oil painter, and he impulsively offered to teach me all there was to know about modern reproduction techniques. What kind generous souls are the Americans! Mabel and I began to attend the Pennells' Thursday at-homes in

240

Buckingham Street where there was always an interesting sprinkling of artistic and literary guests. The well-known illustrators Phil May and Walter Crane were friends of the Pennells, as were Whistler and Walter Sickert. Pennell had a wise, calm, fatherly quality that my own nature readily responded to: with my staggering accumulation of work I was often like a nervous horse in need of petting.

The Pennells were intimates of another American couple, Henry and Aline Harland. In a year's time Henry Harland would be my fellow-editor at *The Yellow Book*, but when I first met him we were both suppressing coughs in the consulting-room of Dr Symes Thompson. Harland, like me, was consumptive, tho' his case was not nearly so severe as mine.

He was a bit of a fraud, Harland was, but I liked him then. He had published novels in America under the improbable name of Sidney Luska until, armed with introductions from a rich grandfather, he came with Aline to London in 1889 to fulfil his literary and cultural aspirations. By the time we met in Dr Symes Thompson's consulting-room, Harland had managed to acquire not only a British accent and a spuriously genteel European background, but also friends like Henry James, Edmund Gosse, H. Rider Haggard and Thomas Hardy. He and Aline were at home on Sunday evenings to a delicious crowd that verged on the Bohemian.

Is there anything sweeter than one's first burst of social and artistic success? The skies over London were raining money and influential friends. There was no office to report to at 9.30 every morning, and no grumbling father to deal with at 6.30 every evening. For the first time in my life I could go to order a new top-hat from Hatch, and present my meagre figure to the fashionable tailor Doré to be fitted for several new suits.

'Shall I pad the shoulders and upper arms for you, sir?' Monsieur Doré asked frankly, taking hawk-eyed note of my stooped spindly frame.

'Is it much done?' I asked.

'Oh, yes. Nowadays most gentlemen realize the value of shape and silhouette in creating a favourable impression. Many gentlemen are wearing padding and corsets this season.'

'But . . . the young ladies,' I said, 'do they like it?'

'Oh, yes. The ladies are quite fond of it. It makes them feel closer to a man when they know he is padded.'

'Very well. Pad.'

I needed evening clothes now, and patent-leather evening pumps. The only thing I didn't require was a coat, and that was because the fever kept me as warm as a chestnut on top of an oven.

Another delicious surprise came when Fred Brown, my former art teacher at Westminster, asked me to exhibit at the New English Art Club that spring. The NEAC, Father, was founded as a protest, an exhibiting alternative to the Royal Academy; the old duffer critics generally ignored or deplored the NEAC's spring show, but those with any modern interest in modern art knew it was important. I exhibited one rather severe black and white work (I chose a Japanesque picture called 'La Femme incomprise') beside an impressionistic oil painting of the Mogul music-hall by Walter Sickert. (Poor Sickert has now left England for good, I understand, having realized that the British public will never understand and accept his work, which is considered 'too French'.)

The thrill of dashing about town with friends, entering into the spontaneity of an at-home, sitting in an old tavern to discuss art and books, or enjoying the boisterous atmosphere of the music-halls, where Marie Lloyd might be cheekily singing 'There Was I Standing at the Church' – these comradely activities were new delights for me, and I revelled in them. I lacked only one thing: a woman to love.

Yes, I loved Mabel – adored her, and was proud of her beauty and intelligence. She often accompanied me to the Pennells' or to the Harlands' in Cromwell Road. But I wanted something more, something that Mabel could never give me – at least, not without the horrified censure of the world. Other men had wives, or mistresses, to share their beds and their bodies. When would I? I longed to have a beautiful mistress like Sickert's Bessie Bellwood, a singer who flashed him bold glances that bespoke a private language of physical adoration. I wanted to prise a strong, scented charmer from my neck, pat her on the rump, and tell her to go and wait for me in my rooms, as I had once seen Fred Brown do at the Crown. I wanted desperately to penetrate the mysteries of the female sex, to be bluff and hearty and bold with them, instead of merely polite.

The longer I was deprived, the more convinced I became that my physical appearance must be far worse than the reflection I was accustomed to seeing in the looking-glass. Perhaps I actually repelled women? Perhaps the padding of my jackets made them snigger? A hundred times a day some blazing erotic fantasy worthy of Laclos would flash into my thoughts only to fade miserably as I imagined myself naked beside my phantasmal Helen. There I would be, larval white, with stooped shoulders, stick-thin limbs, the shallow pestilential breath of a consumptive, and a raging cockstand – more a sexual demon than a strong virile lover.

Mabel sensed my restlessness and, I think, knew its cause. She became wifely, greeting me at the door no matter what hour I came in, asking if I wanted anything, if she could do anything for me. And then, Father, I would have to turn brusquely away to stop myself from taking her in my arms. For Mabel did love me, more than anyone ever has, unequivocally, body and soul, and we both knew that if we were not careful we could slip into the passionate love Siegmund shared with his sister Sieglinde. That possibility always hovered near, tormenting us both.

There was another concern as well: my seed. No matter how modest my dreams of eventually marrying and raising a family, they were nipped in the bud by the hereditary nature of my disease. I could not in good faith bring another doomed child into the world, to suffer as I suffered, to die in the springtime of life. It would be too cruel. And then, of course, there was the abiding question: how long did I have?

So, like Bobbie, I took to prowling the streets late at night, teasing myself with the sight of nocturnal dollymops and park doxies, those ladies of frayed hem and snake-like tongue who prowl Piccadilly from Green Park to Charing Cross. A sovereign would get the youngest and most beautiful among them; ten shillings one as appetizing as I could ever want. Nor was I without offers, some of them shockingly depraved. All one had to do was choose, and then go off to any one of a dozen nearby accommodation-houses where one could rent a dirty bed.

Still, no matter how Priapic my desires, my fastidiousness became alarmed at the thought of dirt and disease. Thus, because I could not bring myself to act, the imagining of sexual delights became even greater.

All day long now I was forced to draw to keep up with my growing commitments. I would toss for an hour or two, sleep for an hour or two, then rise to embark on my work for that day. No more mystic candles to light my boyish altar of art and ambition. Now that I was a success, my vital energy had risen tenfold, and my temperature with it. I drew and burned.

In May of that year I made my second trip to Paris for the New Salon *vernissage*, but this time round I was in the company of Joseph and Elizabeth Pennell. Scores of other young English artists were making the same migratory crossing, but I dare say I was the only one who had had an article written about him, and so much work that I had to carry it with me.

Paris welcomed us with its sweetest springtime breath. The chestnut trees were aflame with thick flowery candles, and the air rising up from the Seine was cool and delicious; little tables with white or checked cloths had been set out on the pavements, and everywhere one looked some charming nook or vista enchanted the eye. 'Paris!' I cried as our fly set off for the Hôtel de Portugal et de l'Univers.

I was longing to impress the Pennells with my knowledge of the city, and did so at every opportunity. To me they were an enchanted couple, both so handsome, so healthy, and so obviously delighted to be in one another's company in Paris. Like me, they responded instantly and joyously to the heady charms of French culture. It was poignant to watch their secret little looks as they came upon moments of their past – a corner of the Tuileries near the boat-pond where the old lovebirds had once sat as honeymooners, or the Sainte-Chappelle, its medieval glass glowing in a mystic fever of red and blue. On the Pont Neuf, where we stood admiring the Louvre, I saw Mrs Pennell's hand reach for her husband's and clasp it tightly; their eyes met; he could not kiss her lips because of her hat, all brim and veil, so he kissed her hand.

'We must climb to the top of Notre-Dame!' Elizabeth cried, her dark eyes flashing with excitement. 'Can you, Mr Beardsley?'

'Of course!'

We did, and at the end of it I felt I deserved a view of the Holy Grail. While the Pennells, twenty years older than I, dashed gaily out on to the parapets, hardly winded, I stood with pounding heart and burning lungs, blinded by the dazzle of the sunlight and my own temerity in making the climb. Stepping out among the tourists and the gargoyles was an exultant experience, let me tell you. Behold Aubrey Beardsley on top of the world! Behold Paris spread out all around in panoramic splendour!

Most of the artists wore tails and a top-hat to the *vernissage*, but with Doré's help I had devised an exquisite grey harmony for my entrance: coat, waistcoat, trousers, all were grey. I wore grey suede gloves, a soft grey felt hat, and knotted my grey silk tie wide and loose in the French style. Plenty of heads turned, believe me. From Madeleine Gély's I purchased a slim gold-capped walking-stick which completed my ensemble to perfection.

We were there to look at pictures, and gawk at the celebrities (Zola passed by not ten feet from where I stood), but we also made time for excursions to see the palaces and gardens of Versailles and Saint-Cloud. When you are among Bohemians (and good wine), Father, restraint gives way to spontaneity and sheer *joie de vivre*. Ecstasy was in the air. Life away from London became a feast, full of talk, games, nonsense and easy affection. While Mr Pennell dashed up to the top of Notre-Dame to sketch the views, Mrs Pennell and I rummaged for treasures amongst the bric-à-brac of *brocanteurs* and stared in the windows of one gorgeous *épicerie fine* after another.

One Saturday evening Mr Pennell and I went to the Opéra to hear *Tristan*; and afterwards, with the weight of that music still hanging in my soul, and a new drawing of the Wagnerian audience shaping itself in my brain, we crossed over to the Café de la Paix. There, at one of the choicest tables, sat a friend of Mr Pennell, the acid-tongued artist James MacNeil Whistler. He removed his pince-nez the moment he spotted us, and turned away with what looked to me like disdain, but Mr Pennell insisted on introducing me.

Whistler was known as a dandy, of course, but he was at an age when too high a regard for fashion can make a formerly smart man look foppish and ridiculous. One long white curl trod a dainty pathway through his thicket of frizzed grey hair, and his face was falling like some moulded dessert left too long in the kitchen. Vanity and unhappiness mingled in his person: his past few years of prodigious success could evidently never make up for the lifetime of neglect he had previously suffered; he was pinched and vain, suspicious of everyone, and determined to hold on to his throne, now that he had it, by verbally guillotining everyone around him.

He only nodded when Mr Pennell made the introduction. There was no invitation to join him.

'Mr Beardsley is making quite a name for himself as an illustrator,' Mr Pennell said.

'I should say, rather, that *you* are making quite a name for him as an illustrator,' Whistler replied, in what sounded like an accusation. 'It was you, Pennell, who wrote him up in *The Studio*.'

'You've seen his work, then, Jimmy. You know how extraordinarily original it is.'

'I know only that it is covered with hairs,' said Whistler, and then turned sharply to me and said: 'You are the hairiest young man I have ever met.' He was referring to my penchant just then for adding short bristly pen strokes to the heads and bodies of my Japanesque grotesques. Someone distracted him, and I quickly told Pennell that I was exhausted and had to leave. Whistler was too engrossed with his new guests to bid me good evening.

It was the first unpleasant encounter I'd had during the entire trip, and I couldn't help brooding about what amounted to a snub. People would hear of it, and my fragilely established name would be shattered by the ensuing mockery. The next day, however, Pennell told me that Whistler had said I might come along to his new flat on the rue du Bac. I agreed, but with a queer sense of foreboding. Some trap was being laid, I was certain of it.

Whistler had recently married a rather fat middle-aged woman named Beatrix Godwin. The old Greek saying that happiness is only reached through suffering did not, I think, apply to the new Mrs Whistler. Sheer stupidity kept her quite jolly, and of course it was her buxom animal spirits that old Whistler needed to give spice to his tired blood and to keep him youthful.

As Mrs Whistler chugged among her guests, hooting like a Thames steamer, old James MacNeil, his face screwed up to hold his pince-nez, buzzed waspishly in a corner. I was not made to feel at ease among the older masculine crowd that surrounded him, and was left to wander about unmoored and adrift. Artists do love exquisite things, and Whistler's flat was filled with them. Most exquisite of all, of course, were his paintings, those supremely romantic Nocturnes as he called them. The oils showed a breath-taking mastery of form and colour; no wonder Whistler was known for his inability to part with his own work – he was in love with it himself.

As I moved about examining each painting, I could feel the jealous enlarged eye of the Master following me behind the pince-nez. What did he really think of my work? I wondered. Our visions and methods for achieving them were so antithetical. Yet I must confess that, apart from Mantegna and Burne-Jones, Whistler provided one of the strongest visual influences on my own emerging style. Ever since I'd seen that magnificent Peacock Room in the Leyland house, and understood his own manipulation of Japanese motifs, I had been in awe of him; his pictographic 'Butterfly' signature I regarded as sublime; and once I'd even spent a week's salary on a small etching he'd done in the seventies.

Whistler loved to show off the small beautiful garden of his Paris flat, and ritualistically led his guests there in groups of three or four. I was left until the very last, and then it was not the Master but his fat Romneyesque wife who asked me to join the others for an al fresco tea. 'You are Mr Harry Beardsley, are you not?' she asked.

'No, I am Aubrey Beardsley.'

'How peculiar. I am certain that my husband said "Harry". Yes, "Find that Harry Beardsley," he said, "and show him to the garden."'

She was blind to the clever insult that was so apparent to me, and looked befuddled when I said I must leave at once. I did not betray humiliation or fury, and merely took my leave with a mental vow to avenge myself.

After a week the Pennells returned to London and I was left to my own devices. Oh, Father, what would I not give for a wife like Elizabeth Pennell, a steady constant companion, sympathetic to the needs and emotions of an artist; a woman whose charms are enriched by age, and whose ardour for her husband glows so strongly that he would never think of betraying her. Lovesick, I wandered about Paris thinking of her, and of Mabel, and wondering if I would ever meet

247

a woman whom I could love unequivocally – or, rather, one who could love me.

Bobbie Ross, always eager to encourage my longed-for debauchery, had provided me with the names and addresses of several *maisons closes* where the inmates were girls rather than boys; and now, as the pearly grey dusk of Paris deepened into night, I found myself wandering in their vicinity. The rue Vendôme was filled with gay women of every description, from the haughtiest to the naughtiest, from the fattest to the thinnest, parading through the harsh veils of gaslight on the street or pressed back against dark crumbling walls. As I passed, these costermongers of the flesh called out their delightfully filthy specialities in sweet hoarse voices, making my cock rise and stand as painfully erect as a palace guard. It was not from lack of interest, Father, that I feigned aloofness, but from a kind of bewildered panic: there were too many choices. Any one of those women could have ensnared me for ever. I felt more comfortable at the Rat Mort, where the ladies were perfect gentlemen and oblivious to my charms.

One night I betook myself to the Chat Noir simply to sit and be fascinated by the whirl of sights around me, nothing more. As the evening wore on, and the wine kept flowing, and the smoke and the talk grew equally dense, all around me men gave in to the desperate hilarity born of mortal despair. Soon it would be 1900! We were approaching the end of our century and, as with anything that ends, we all wanted to know what, if anything, lay beyond its oblivion. I then saw the horrible truth of Willette's painting of the Pierrots and Pierrettes falling into the black ditch one by one: that was the fate of everyone here, only some of us would reach the ditch sooner than the others – my shallow breathing was a reminder of that.

A glimpse of uncannily familiar red-gold hair startled me out of my melancholy reverie, and I nearly upset my wine-glass as I whirled to get a better look. No, it wasn't Mabel – but it was her hair, that same coppery blaze, and worn in a very similar manner. With palpitating heart, I raised my glass to its possessor; she smiled; I motioned for her to join me; she did.

Yvette was young, but harboured few romantic illusions about life. An orphan, she'd been raised in a convent in Brittany – did not that explain the fair Celtic features and tresses the colour of molten ore? – and then was sent out at thirteen to work on a farm. The farmer's wife beat her, the farmer raped her, and finally she ran away, covering the entire distance to Paris on foot, sleeping in fields, stealing eggs and apples to stay alive.

In Paris she found work as a seamstress but was dismissed when it was discovered that she was pregnant. She prayed for guidance, but there was no answer. Finally, in desperation, she took to the streets. From convent to the drunken world of the sub-demi-mondaine: the tale is old and unbearably commonplace. It was apparent that already, at fifteen, she liked her dram, and who could blame her?

'What are you doing?' she asked.

'Drawing.'

She peered at my sketchpad and then searched the Chat Noir for my subject. 'Who is it?'

'An artist named Whistler.'

'You must hate him very much.'

'Why do you say that?'

'It is not a very nice picture.'

'Shall I draw you?'

'Not if I am to look like that!' She put her small, slightly sticky hand on mine. 'Your hand is trembling. Are you ill?'

'There's nothing wrong with me,' I said, lightheaded from the soft pressure of her fingers.

Oh God, Father, that sweet tender soul, already so abused by life, making its way among the cynical roués of Paris – I wanted to protect her from them, save her; but I wanted, at the same time, knowing what she was, to tear away the bodice of her frock and plunge my mouth to suck on her soft little nipples, and lift her skirt so that my raging cock could gain entry to her hot treasure-filled cave.

'I live nearby,' she whispered, her husky tone suddenly that of an experienced slut. Her hand grazed my thigh. 'Would Monsieur care to accompany me there?'

Without a word, not daring to think, I lurched up from the table. Yvette had the foresight to down the remaining drops of wine from my glass.

I was drunker than I had ever been, but instead of filling my heart with a buoyant devil-may-care joy the wine had a depressing effect. My lungs ached and wheezed from the inhalation of stale smoke; my guts fretted and roiled sluggishly from days of heavy French food. When I belched or farted, the smell emanating from my body was thick and sour. Yvette, chattering away as she guided me up and down the dark ancient passageways and rank narrow alleys of Montmartre, was the happy sort of drunk who finds, after a glass or two, that life in all its infinitesimally prosaic details is really worth talking about.

Finally, after an interminable climb, we reached the tiny garret where she lodged. A baby with the croup cried and coughed miserably in a corner, and Yvette went to it with a cluck of her tongue, lifting it from a pile of rags. 'Hush now, be quiet, we have a visitor,' she whispered. With experienced hand, still holding the baby, she lit a candle and poured out a spoonful of dark liquid which she fed to the wailing infant. 'Here, drink this and you'll go right to sleep.'

'You leave the baby here alone?'

'What else am I do do – carry her with me?' She was undressing now with a brusque matter-of-factness that implied I was not to be her only lover that night; and I found myself wondering how many other cocks – cocks of what shapes and sizes and colours? – had preceded mine.

When she was naked, she came and put her arms around me, then drew my mouth to hers. A naked girl in my arms! I thought I should go mad from the excitement that coursed through my body. I remembered Mabel at this same age, with this same flaming hair but such complete innocence; I remembered Jones, Aunt Pitt's servant, whom I had adored and tried to ravish without knowing how; and now here was Yvette, in my arms, offering her warm flesh to me as though I were a pasha – a girl who wanted me, or at least appeared to.

She gazed into my eyes with promise and squeezed my arms once – then again – perhaps a little amazed that they were so thin – and smiled, showing a mouthful of bright crooked teeth. Her maquillage, the kohl around her eyes, the painted lips and chalky powder flaking from the down on her cheeks made her face resemble a strange little mask. 'Put your clothes there,' she said, indicating a chair, and then went to lie on the bed. After a few phlegmy gasps and burbles, the child lay silently on its bed of rags.

And what did I do, Father? I looked at that picture of desire, those tender blue-veined breasts, swollen with milk, the delicious curve of the thighs that cradled the little nest of hair and moisture – and I began, suddenly, to cough. At first I thought it was controllable, and tried to suck in my chest and stomach, but out it spewed. With this spasm came an involuntary image of my body rotting from within. My head began to throb painfully, from the excess wine, I suppose, and as I sat down to take hold of myself, I saw the infant on its bundle of rags staring at me with dilated and terrible eyes. Those eyes were warning me, begging me not to bring another like it into the world: from germ to germ, the flesh of mankind procreates in a stew of its own corruption. My desire evaporated on the spot.

When the coughing wouldn't stop, Yvette sat up on the bed and began to gnaw on her lips, then pulled on a dirty wrapper and stood beside me. 'Is it the English disease?' she asked. That, Father, is what the French think the English have given to the world: Shakespeare and consumption. I could only nod, and hope that a vomiting attack was not on its way.

'I must go,' I rasped. 'How much—?'

Yvette shook her head, and maternally stroked the back of my skull. I took that sweet sticky little hand and put it to my burning cheek, then kissed it just as I'd seen Joseph Pennell kiss his wife's. This was as close to marriage as I would ever get! I left more money than I should have, and made my way back to the hotel, no more than a shadow in a shadowy world.

When I returned to London it was to the great good news – or so I thought then – that the publisher John Lane had commissioned me to illustrate the translation of Oscar Wilde's play *Salome*.

XII

SALOME! CRUEL VIRGIN temptress of the cruel virgin Baptist, you who craved the chaste impossibility of his holy flesh, and danced in vengeance so that you could claim the grim reward of his dripping severed head; Salome, incarnation of carnal rage, proud princess of Judaea, daughter of purple-blooded Herodias, stepdaughter of the Tetrarch Herod, how I wish you had never danced for me! You destroy all who see you, all who imagine you, all who want you.

Yet what inspired joy my hand felt,

Salome, as you and your family emerged in all your thwarted, bloated, sexual fury. You were a wholly new vision for me – far looser, freer, more Japanesque, than the dense medieval *brochage* I was forced to embroider for the *Morte D'Arthur*. I *understood* you, my dear Princess; heard the low warbling of the pipes and the plangent twang of the plucked strings as you danced on the cold marble floors of the palace, discarding your transparent veils one by one, until at last you stood panting and naked before Herod – he who desired you as you desired the Baptist, and ordered your death just as you ordered Jokanaan's. What a bitter lesson, Salome, that we inevitably destroy what we love the most!

My plan had worked with the smoothness of a well-laid magic spell, Father. When Oscar saw my drawing of Salome in *The Studio* he immediately sent me a copy of the French edition of the play, inscribed: 'For Aubrey: for the only artist who, besides myself, knows what the dance of the seven veils is, and can see that invisible dance. Oscar.' Of course I was flattered, and of course I let it be known that I was interested in illustrating the English version.

Although I had literally hundreds of drawings still to do for *Morte D'Arthur*, the first instalment of that interminable epic had been published by Dent in June, a much-heralded event in literary and artistic circles, and John Lane of The Bodley Head, Oscar's publisher, was quick to realize that my name was now saleable. It was he who made the offer: ten drawings and a frontispiece for *Salome*, the fee to be fifty guineas, and all drawings to be the property of the publisher. Of course I accepted. I would have crowed like a cock had I been able to muster enough wind.

Every illustrator in London was vying for the plum of the *Salome* commission; but I, not yet twenty-one, had it dropped into my lap. I was chosen over all the others. Dear God, how I secretly gloated! From henceforth my name would be allied with that of the great Oscar Wilde, and the profitable possibilities springing from that association must be endless. Little did I know, Father, that Nemesis was backstage, lurking in the wings, patiently waiting to drop the curtain on my triumph.

How could I have known? The gods were showering me with bounty. When news of the *Salome* commission became public, other publishers began to dance like moths around my flame. Once I had charged ten shillings for a picture; now I demanded five guineas. Offers poured in, some from the same publishers who had once eyed my work with dismissive incomprehension. Now that I had a family to support I kept the money end of my art keenly in view.

On a wet windy Saturday morning in the summer of 1893, Mother, Mabel and I stood under the dripping portico of a small house in Cambridge Street in Pimlico. The address was 114. Mabel held the latchkey in her trembling hand.

'I am so stupidly nervous!' she said, holding on to her hat so the wind would not blow it away and trying at the same time to fit the key in the lock. 'Aubrey, you do it.'

'No, you are the leaseholder,' I said. 'The house is in your name, so you should be the first to open the door.'

'Hurry, dear, or we shall get even more drenched,' said Mother. 'I should hate us to catch a chill.'

Mabel leaned over, carefully fitted the key into the lock, turned it, stood up with a deep breath and, as if she were afraid of what might be behind the portal, slowly pushed open the door. We stood speechless with excitement and emotion, peering into the tiny entrance-hall of our new home.

'Come along,' said Mother, briskly shaking out her umbrella and stepping inside, 'we have so much to do.'

Mabel and I remained outside for a moment. 'What do you wish for, Mabel?' I asked her.

She looked at me with tears in her eyes. 'For this,' she whispered tenderly. 'For a home of our own, after all these years. What do you wish for?'

'I wish I had a wife who was as beautiful, tender and sympathetic as my beautiful, tender and sympathetic sister.'

She started slightly, and the colour rose in her cheeks. 'Then . . . you wish your wife were your sister,' she said, her eyes gleaming.

'Or . . . my sister my wife.'

'Oh, darling,' she said, her voice a low impassioned throb. 'Oh, darling.'

We joined hands and crossed the threshold just as a wedding party emerged from St Gabriel's across the street and the church bells began to peal in damp celebration.

It was remarkably unremarkable, the house, identical to every other house in our bit of Cambridge Street, but it was *ours*. We had purchased it with Mabel's inheritance from Aunt Pitt, the surety of my own inheritance, which I was to receive in August, my earnings from Dent and Lane, and Mabel's wages from the Polytechnic. Though she jibbed at the idea, I thought it better to have Mabel designated as the official householder because of my health; if I died, there would be fewer legal encumbrances for her to deal with.

Together we had purchased our own home in London – you cannot imagine our pride in this achievement, Father! No longer would we have to answer to stingy landladies, shiver in damp underheated lodgings, live on tiptoe and plan our lives around those of other tenants. At last we were free to live as we pleased!

Mother was as thrilled as we were, and immediately became our bustling busy housekeeper, humming arias from oratorios as she arranged flowers, planned meals, sewed, did the shopping, poured out tea and sternly supervised the Irish charwoman. Sometimes at night, when I was working in my studio, I would hear the subdued strains of Chopin or Liszt from the piano, and know that Mother was happy again after many years of suppressed anguish. I hoped that I would always be able to make her happy. In some strange way I felt it was my duty; I had nothing else to offer her except my death.

Those familiar keyboard phrases seeping through the floorboards coaxed out stifled dreams of my own as well, induced a melancholy reverie, took me back to those times not so many years earlier when I had hoped to be a virtuoso of the piano, or a great conductor, and have music flow through me and pour out of my hands. What a great thunder I would have made, what intense and furious emotions I would have revealed – stronger than anything I could ever put on paper! The disease had eroded those dreams, but still I dreamed them. I had already drawn myself, ill, hands useless at my side, confronting 'Les Revenants de Musique'; now I drew another great man of music felled by consumption, Carl Maria von Weber.

Mabel and I planned out the general decorating scheme of our new home with the help of Aymer Vallance. Aymer's private tastes might lean towards the archaic and liturgical, but he could be surprisingly modern when it came to other people's houses. His years with William Morris had taught him a great deal about wall colours, furniture and fabrics, and he was happiest when he could be flamboyant on someone else's behalf. I was, in any event, eager to repay some of the enormous personal debt I had incurred from Aymer's professional introductions.

'Orange and black,' he murmured, like a medium picking up vibrations, as we sat discussing plans for my studio room. Once pronounced, the idea seized him and he leaped up. 'Yes! Walls distempered orange, doors and skirtings black . . . a *green* carpet . . . too heavenly! . . . and chairs and chaise-longue upholstered in white and blue. I can see it all!'

'And framed prints on the walls,' I said.

'Of course. Some lovely engravings, perhaps – things with strong clear lines – architectural renderings?'

'No, these,' I said, handing him the Japanese *Book of Love*. 'They will go beautifully with your brilliant colour scheme.'

Aymer looked through the book with studied calm, his dilated nostrils the only indication that he was repressing emotion. I wanted to shock him, Father; it gave me a curious tittering pleasure to be the source of erotic revelation, to show others the contorted postures and inflamed organs that lay at the heart of their own and all mankind's secret desires.

'Impossible, surely,' Aymer said, handing the book back to me with priestly imperturbability.

'Why impossible? This is my house, my studio – why should I not surround myself with what gives me pleasure?'

'Your sister, Miss Beardsley, and your mother, should they see—'

'My sister finds the prints as charming as I do, and my mother's opinion in artistic matters does not concern me. I see nothing wrong with the prints; they merely acknowledge an aspect of life that hypocritical respectability deems unworthy of artistic reproduction. *All* of life should be shown, Aymer; art has a higher mission than merely to provide stupid people with the sentimental rubbish they wish to see.'

'That may be true, but human depravity can be rendered less

graphically.' He plucked at his collar and nervously twisted his neck within its stiff confines. 'Vice should be depicted only if it is to act as a moral deterrent.'

'Depravity? Vice? My dear Aymer, these are simple facts of life; they are responsible *for* life! Pray, show me the depravity in any of these prints. Each and every one of them is rendered with the utmost delicacy, understanding and joy.'

'Sin is never beautiful, Beardsley,' he said tersely.

'On the contrary, it can be remarkably exquisite, and requires a palette of the greatest strength and delicacy to do it justice – a palette no English artist has the courage to mix.'

'I shall leave these grotesque prints in your hands,' Aymer said, 'and beg you not to associate my name with their exhibition in this room.'

Aymer was protecting himself by dissociation even then, worried, as everyone is eternally worried, about his reputation. Despite this little contretemps, we adopted his suggestions and thereby transformed 114 Cambridge Street from a prim little spinster into a modern woman of the world. How beautiful we made it, our little house in Pimlico! Mother, excessively fond of her Toby jugs and ugly unartistic clutter, was rather startled by some of our choices, but was in no position to object; she had her own room and was free to embellish it in her own style. We were after an elegant Bohemianism, Mabel and I, a house that would impress and be uncommonly comfortable at the same time. It was to be our personal theatre, a place for us to perform our new lives! With the smell of fresh paint still lingering in the rooms, we decided that we would be 'at home' on Thursday afternoons, and began to invite all those friends who had offered us hospitality.

Teaching at the Polytechnic was grinding Mabel's robustly generous spirit into mud and cinders; I could see it quite clearly. She felt temperamentally unsuited for her work and cheated out of her youth. Restless, her bosom occasionally rent by heartbreaking sighs, she wandered about the house declaiming scenes from plays and dreaming of success on the stage. Mother of course would have none of it, and fiercely remonstrated with her on the 'unsuitability' of her aspirations. My sister, however, refused to relinquish them. Little did she suspect, in the midst of her Polytechnic depressions, that in a year's time she would be touring England in a play by Oscar Wilde.

Mabel has always loved animals, even though her little childhood pets always perished in her care: goldfish, lovebirds, white mice – no matter how assiduous she was in tending them, they would inevitably be discovered one morning floating motionless on top of the water or stiffly curled in a corner of their cage. She needed *something* to receive the lavish daily brunt of her exiled affections, and now that we had a house it was possible for her to have the kitten she had always wanted.

Nip was glossy black except for his white boots; an adorable thing, quite tiny when she found him, who loved nothing more than to be carried about in a home-made sling affixed to her hip. She would go about her household duties with Nip's little black head and absinthe-coloured eyes peeping out sprite-like from his safe haven. As Nip grew older, Mabel's body remained his home territory, and she allowed him to take the most frightful liberties with her. The cat would ride on her shoulder, sleep in her hair, knead her stomach, play with her ear-rings. It became her runty spirit familiar.

Mabel also had the idea that we should plant roses to liven up the dim little back garden of the house. We none of us knew the first thing about gardening, which may explain why Mabel's admirable experiment was such a cankerous failure. Day after day she would rush out to examine her rose bushes, scratching about in the sour sooty grit they were planted in.

'Has anything appeared?' Mother would ask.

'I think I saw a bit of new green on one of them,' Mabel would report.

But, in fact, they were all dying, and within a month the rose bushes were black thorny skeletons.

The troubling fact that there were no men on her horizon seemed – at least, on the surface – not to bother Mabel in the slightest. She and Mother argued incessantly and intricately about the advantages (Mother) and disadvantages (Mabel) of marriage, as if the connubial state were some kind of military campaign. 'Things are different now for women!' Mabel would cry in the heat of battle. 'We have higher aspirations than merely to be the slave of some man! We seek freedom and independence!'

'Then, you seek loneliness,' Mother would counter.

'Why is a woman without a husband always assumed to be lonely? Aunt Pitt never married, and she seemed quite content.'

'Your Great-Aunt Pitt had a large private income; if she had not, she would have married.'

'And been unhappy, just as you were unhappy when Father was with us. How can you defend marriage this way when your own was such a failure?'

'How dare you speak to me like that! And what, may I ask, will you do when you wish to have children?'

'I shall hire a man of sound mind and sound body to provide me with some.'

'Mabel! I will not tolerate such perversity in this house, even in jest!'

On it would go, the question of marriage, round and round, unending, unanswerable, in the end more a matter of temperament and luck in finding the right person, surely (Mabel's view), than some conscious duty (Mother's). I would listen to their heated feminine arguments with the detachment that comes from knowing one will never be a player in the game. Yet even I, looking up from my endless *Morte* drawings with stinging eyes and an aching neck, my fingertips stained black from Chinese ink, restless and exhausted at once, staring out of my window into the dark possibilities of a London night, would find myself idly dreaming of a soft hand stroking away my weariness, a gentle voice bidding me put away my work and come to bed, an inviting pair of breasts, a white ripe belly, and a fragrant breath blowing hot in my ears as we tilled the fertile soil of our bodies to create a new life. Such ordinary sanctified tenderness would never be mine, so I would go to stare bitterly at the copulating princes and the smiling courtesans from the *Book of Love*, and imagine myself a participant in flagrant orgies, drowned in a lustful sea of flesh.

Or I would go to Mabel's room, near her bed-time, and unpin her hair as she sat, Nip curled in her lap, at her mirrored dressing-table. Those thick silken locks were like cool fire in my hands, and I would brush them with the reverence a disciple shows his saint. Her creamy complexion, so quick to chafe or burn, was sprinkled with the palest of freckles no matter how well protected she was from the sun; well-formed brows and thick lashes glowed with the same red fire as her hair, and provided appropriate adornment for the deep green treasury of her eyes; her bust was high and firm, and her figure increasingly willowy.

What a distasteful contrast my own visage provided. I was like some crooked toadish refraction she might glimpse with horror in a distorting glass, a monstrous abortion sloughed off from her own flesh, a malformed vision of her worst fears. But she loved me. Dear God, she loved me as no one ever had and never will. And I loved her – *loved* her, Father, with a ferocity that agitated the deepest fibres of my being and made me pray to the Devil that she would never meet another man – or woman – who would take her away from me.

Oscar was too great a celebrity to attend our modest Thursday at-homes, and was in any case spending that spring and summer at Goring with Lord Alfred Douglas, but we were not otherwise lacking in interesting guests. Bobbie Ross and Aymer Vallance came often, and so did Mabel's close friend and fellow-teacher from the Polytechnic, the would-be novelist Netta Syrett, whose small unhappy eyes flamed with jealousy every time Mabel left her to speak with another guest. Henry and Aline Harland, Joseph and Elizabeth Pennell, and Julian Sampson all showed up, and a growing number of new friends and introductions now made their appearance in our lives: Max Beerbohm, Billy Rothenstein, just back from Paris, Count Stenbock, and the artists Charles Ricketts and Charles Shannon. On Thursday afternoons the little drawing-room of number 114 was crowded and lively; Mabel and I passed round plates of biscuits while Mother, her face beaming with pleasure and importance, simultaneously poured out and boasted of her darling son's latest artistic triumphs.

'Ah, Mr Ricketts,' I overheard her saying, 'another cup?'

'Yes, please, Mrs Beardsley.'

'I like my tea to be nice and strong, don't you? Milk? Sugar? There you are. You've heard, Mr Ricketts, that Aubrey has been commissioned by Mr Lane to illustrate Oscar Wilde's *Salome*?'

Of course Ricketts had heard; he was my chief competition! He had been illustrating Oscar's works for years, and his cover designs for *The Sphinx* were in production at the time of this conversation. Like every other artist, he had hoped for the *Salome* commission himself, perhaps even expected it, but unlike the other losers he had had the magnanimity to praise my preliminary drawings instead of abusing them. I wanted to throttle Mother, but she prattled on blissfully while Ricketts smiled and stroked his sharp dark beard as though he were honing it to a point.

Mother knew of course that the Van Dyck-handsome Charles Ricketts – artist, illustrator, book designer and stage designer – shared a large house, The Vale, off the King's Road in Chelsea with the reserved, fair-haired and boyish-looking Charles Shannon. It would never have occurred to her, however, that 'the two Charlies', as I called them, shared a bed as well. Certainly they were the happiest and most connubial of all the unisexual men I have known. Together, in 1889, they had published the first number of an advanced literary magazine, *The Dial* (they were the first to publish a French-inspired poem by John Gray, which led to Gray's intro-duction to Oscar), and their spirited Saturday at-homes, which Mabel and I sometimes attended, often did not end until early Sunday morning, when everyone would gather in the kitchen while Shannon cooked omelettes and Ricketts made coffee for their exhausted talk-happy guests. I had met Oscar at more than one such gathering there earlier in the year; like London's other literary and artistic Uranians, he seemed to feel quite at home at The Vale, and was less flamboyant there than at those other places where he felt duty-bound to make an extravagant impression.

It was at The Vale that I first began to hear talk, as yet guarded and ill-defined, of what the Uranians called 'the new Culture' or 'the Cause'. Some of them dared to dream of a new society in which Arcadian liaisons would be not merely tolerated, but openly accepted; secret books, magazines like *The Chameleon* and *The Spirit Lamp*, and slim well-thumbed pamphlets passed surreptitiously from hand to hand; there was endless discussion of Plato and the Greeks, of Edward Carpenter's lecture on 'Homogenic Love', of Walt Whitman's poetic definition of 'adhesiveness' and Sir Richard Burton's theory that inversion flourished in the Sotadic zones of the globe, between latitudes 43° and 30°. Mabel was most intrigued to hear about Eonists, a term Havelock Ellis took from the Chevalier d'Éon to describe women who liked to masquerade as men (he might just as well have called them Maupinists, since Gautier's *Mademoiselle de Maupin* occupies the same territory).

I found this secret society intriguing, for it had nothing to do with conventional morals and, like the Freemasons or Knights of Malta, was a font of curious lore with its own rich clandestine history unknown to outsiders. I was neither afraid of it not repelled by it. Its practitioners – at least, those I met at The Vale – were for the most part talented, learned, amusing and charming; at the very least they were extraordinarily good-looking. How could one not be sympathetic knowing the lifelong stigmata of depression and loneliness they were forced to bear because of their 'unsuitable emotions': thanks to the Labouchère Amendment of 1885, which they contemptuously referred to as the 'Blackmailer's Charter', any one of them could be sent to prison for acting on his desires – even in the privacy of his own rooms. And how could one not laugh at the exaggerations and affectations of their anecdotes and stories, their rapier-sharp ripostes burnished in the heat of pain but sharpened on the sweet blade of malice? What is more, they accepted me, treating me as one of them, and I found with them that I could be freer and less guarded in my expression than with any other group or person.

It was through the two Charlies, too, that Billy Rothenstein made his reappearance in my life. John Lane, Oscar's publisher, had commissioned Billy to do a series of engravings of Oxford characters, on the strength of which Billy had packed up his Paris studio, bade adieu to his Parisian friends and returned to England. Oscar, to Billy's initial pride and subsequent embarrassment, sought out his friendship (perhaps hoping to be included in the book of portraits), and took him round to The Vale. There, Billy later told me, he heard the two Charlies talking so enthusiastically about my work that he decided he must renew my acquaintance. He was learning how to make his own lithographs and sorely in need of a London studio just then, so I offered him half my worktable. From then on, every time he was in London, Billy would work on one end of my table and I at the other. Art is generally so crushingly solitary an occupation that it was good fun to have company for a change. That curious, disapproving puritanical streak in Billy surfaced again when he saw what use I had made of the prints in the *Book of Love*. He would studiously avoid looking at them every time he came into my studio.

Billy in turn introduced me to that charming embryon Max Beerbohm, whom Billy had met at oxford whilst engaged on preliminary work for his series of Oxford characters. Tiny, gentle, dandiacal Max, a character if ever there was one, was to be included in Billy's portrait gallery. Max had decided to exercise the prerogative of a fourth-year Oxford man and spend his last term in London.

These two, Billy and Max, became my closest friends that summer and autumn of 1893 and remained so for two years; we became, in fact, an inseparable trio. They have deserted me now that I am in disgrace, but for a time I enjoyed the forthright happiness and intimacy that only male camaraderie can provide.

We were all born in the same year, 1872, Max in fact being only seventy-two hours younger than I. We were all bright, ambitious, curious about life, eager to make an impression on the world. Billy, the bespectacled portraitist, was more cautious than either Max or I, more physically robust, certainly far less 'showy', and ultimately in danger, I felt, of becoming conventional. Max and I, on the other hand, revelled in the mysteries of style and paradox; masks, maquillage and all things artificial appealed to our natures; we could not resist caricature; we mocked hypocrisy and cherished the flagrant absurdities of life. Yet, in the end, for all their talk of modernity, I couldn't help feeling that Billy and Max were timid in its artistic expression, held back by a reticence that I did not share.

In the beginning, Father, the Word was made flesh, and the flesh was Oscar, and we all three stood in awe of that temple of wit whose fame was growing hourly. We were ripe for influence, precocious nursery boys playing at being men of the world; and Oscar, we thought, embodied a universe of experience, a perfected way of life, a studied pose that was both glamorous and useful to the modern artist. Oscar commanded the kind of public attention we hoped for one day. We did not want to recognize, then, that our public temple was privately degenerating into a house of ill-fame; we watched it happen with closed eyes, silently, afraid to arouse the ire of the god, who was, in any case, undergoing a fiery metamorphosis that put him far beyond any mortal interventions.

Three sexually unmatriculated virgins, Billy, Max and I, all of us courted in one way or another by the overwhelming Oscar, and none of us quite certain at what point friendship and admiration were expected to give way to something else, or if they ever were. Certainly we were not in *love* with Oscar, the way Bobbie still was, and certainly we were soon aware that Oscar's preferred cuisine was not *haute* but *basse*, mid-adolescent, a little dirty under the fingernails and generally sent round on approval from the kitchens of Alfred Taylor of Little College Street. I knew Oscar wouldn't eat me, yet I always felt a curious and annoying sublimation of personality in his presence, a subtle sense of menace, as though I were a small feeble organism being eyed by a larger and hungrier one. Oscar expected fawning adulation – Max laughingly called him 'The Divinity' – but by that time, Father, so did I. I loathed his condescension and the sense of inequality between us and was determined to change it.

To do so required not only artistic brilliance, which Oscar knew I had (and which had stunned him when he saw my *Salome* drawings), but also an arsenal of wit and enough self-confidence to deploy it in public. At first I was unequal to the task, and could only listen with chagrined annoyance as Oscar scattered his *bons mots* with licentious abandon and fought his conversational duels with the likes of Frank Harris. One night, for instance, Harris invited Oscar, me, Max, Billy and Bobbie to a dinner-party at the Café Royal; we were a captive if not captivated audience as Frank, with his usual virile arrogance, declaimed endlessly on his brilliant successes among the aristocracy. Oscar felled him with a simple well-timed, 'Yes, dear Frank, you have dined in every fashionable house in London – *once*.' How could one not be impressed?

It was in August of that year, just a few days before my twenty-first birthday, that Oscar invited me to share his box at the final performance of *A Woman of No Importance* at the Haymarket, a social coup that suited my rapidly advancing reputation. We were to dine at Willis's, and go on to the theatre from there. Bobbie Ross and, to my annoyance, Lord Alfred Douglas were the other guests.

'Bosie' Douglas I have always found to be uncommonly un-pleasant, a youth damned by the violent hereditary madness of the Queensberry line and for that reason not to be trusted. Vain, utterly spoiled, lacking the internal gravity of talent or purpose, he would be nothing without his title. Given everything, he gives nothing in return. If crossed, he becomes cunning and malicious.

Bosie was by then the fatal flaw in Oscar's life, the blind spot in his vision, the worm-infested beam used by Oscar to support the edifice of his sexual philosophy. They had met the year before, Bobbie told me, when Bosie went to Oscar for help with a blackmailer. In fact, the night John Gray came to Bobbie's rooms, howling that another man had usurped him in Oscar's affections, it was none other than Bosie Douglas he was referring to. And though Oscar had evidently tried several times over the ensuing year to rid himself of Bosie, sensing Bosie's fatal destructive power, Bosie hung on like some evil germ burning and multiplying in his blood. Oscar, thus infected, lost the will to cure himself while he still could, and gave himself up with dark fatalistic joy to the disease.

They were not, however, a couple, in the sense that the two Charlies were, tender and solicitous of one another's welfare. Oscar (earning, according to Bobbie, a hundred pounds a week from *A Woman of No Importance*) was keeping the spendthrift Bosie, but he had moved on, with Bosie's help, to a more 'advanced' kind of love-affair: they now shuttled boys back and forth between them as though they were passing sticks in a relay race. A fierce sexual competition now formed the basis of their 'romantic' liaison.

My health had not been good that summer, and Dr Symes Thompson had forbidden wine and spirits; over dinner at Willis's Bosie was continually exhorting me to drink, and scoffing at my temperance while he, Oscar and Bobbie threw back glass after glass of champagne until their eyes were puffy pig-like slits. I wanted to join them, enter into what was rapidly becoming a Dionysian revel, but dared not. Too clearly I saw the great Oscar turn into a fatuous fool, Bobbie into a fawning sycophant, and Bosie into a stupid cruel schoolboy, the sort who derives pleasure from hurling fledglings from their nest and setting fire to kittens.

Oscar had by then seen several of my drawings for *Salome*,

and though he claimed to admire them, saying they represented 'something entirely new and deliciously poisonous', I knew that the drawings troubled and annoyed him; his taste in the visual arts, despite his reputation as a connoisseur, was utterly conventional. I had drawn him as Herod, as Herodias, and as The Man (or Woman, as Bosie gleefully pointed out) in the Moon, looking down on the proceedings from the sky over Judaea. Lane, acting on the advice of George Moore, and claiming it could not be used as an advertisement in the windows of booksellers, had made me redraw my frontispiece of a nude boy praying to a glaringly hermaphroditic herm, and another of the naked Princess Salome at her toilette. It was all part of my scheme to make the pictures equal to the text rather than subordinate to it: my personality as artist was not to be usurped by his as writer, and Oscar sensed this.

'I like you, my dear Aubrey,' he said, drunkenly grasping my thigh and emitting a whiff of his favourite white-lilac perfume, 'but I had no idea that you were such a seasoned murderer. With your uncanny drawings, and Bosie's superb translation, my little *Salome* is certain to create a stir among the Philistines.'

'I did not know Bosie was to do the translation,' I said.

Lord Alfred's drink-sodden eyes pounced suspiciously on mine. 'And why should I not do the translation?' he said, his voice slurred yet sharp. 'My French is perfectly adequate.' He turned to Oscar for confirmation.

'Your exquisite lips, dear Hyacinth, were fashioned by the gods themselves for French usage,' Oscar drawled complacently.

It was no answer, but Bosie turned to me with a look of triumph, as if to say: 'You see?'

The play was in progress as we entered Oscar's box at the Haymarket, but that did not prevent the drunken revellers from making a noisy entrance. Every eye in the theatre was upon us as we took our seats, and though I enjoyed the attention I was quite well aware that not all of it was favourable. Max and Billy smiled at me sympathetically from the pit after glancing at the others. Oscar was sitting like a stupefied Queen Victoria as Bosie whispered and giggled into his and Bobbie's ears; and I, to one side, was only too glad to be spared the intelligence of what were undoubtedly nasty comments about me.

*   *   *

My work on the *Morte*, which had started out so joyously, was rapidly becoming the death of me. I was obliged by my contract with Dent to provide a certain number of drawings at specified periods so that he could get them into production for the next instalment. Unutterable boredom set in; the time and lucubrations required to replicate a thousand times over a false medievalism in which I no longer believed, and which hampered the development of my own style, made me impatient and irritable. I faltered, I lost interest and inspiration, and put off the work as long as possible so that I could devote my time and energies to *Salome* and the myriad new projects offered by John Lane and other publishers. Lane had been so smitten with my ingenious cover and frontispiece designs (an ornate key with the author's initials embedded within it) for a sensational feminist novel called *Keynotes* that he and his partner Elkin Mathews decided to publish a whole series of modern novels using my 'keynote' as the series colophon.

Starting a new project, dear Father, is infinitely more exciting than finishing it. The raw howling birth of a vision is far purer than its exhausted demise. To be modern is never to have enough time, and now I had more work to do than time to do it. I slaved from morning to night, sleeping badly, worrying incessantly. Despair set in when I saw the proofs of the *Morte* drawings and realized how much of my fine linework was lost in the reproduction. Why continue it at all? I threatened to throw it over, which set off fierce battles with Mother. She, of course, knew of my frustrations with the *Morte*, but became a shrill harpy on the subject of Duty and Responsibility. As each deadline drew near she would pester and nag, demand to see the drawings, ask how many I had left to complete, until finally I would explode or – a tactic which I had used from earliest childhood, and which was more effective when it came to punishing her – retreat into silence.

What I could not bear to admit was that my health was breaking down again – now, of all times, when I had so much to accomplish! That dark worm in my cornucopia was burrowing to the surface, leaving a trail of fever and effluvia in its wake. The Cough – short, dry, insistent – returned. Yet, if anything, the disease made me feel wild and reckless. I was simultaneously tormented by a fretful energy and a persistent unlocalized drain upon my vitality. A perverse increase in cerebral activity kept me too excited to rest. I would lie in bed, burning and tossing like St Lawrence on his gridiron. Finally the disgusting oral menses began, the haemorrhages that convulsed my body and paralysed me with fear.

How well I knew Dr Symes Thompson's consulting-room by then, and his patient unvarying routine of listening to the whistles and wheezings of my chest cavity, tapping me between my shoulder-blades, taking my pulse and temperature, and – most frightful of all – recording my weight, which kept dropping. He was slow, methodical, utterly useless, and every time he spoke his breath was like a gust from an open sewer.

'Does the fever ever leave you?' he asked me that August, just before my twenty-first birthday, as I stepped off the scale with a horrid sense of failure. Instead of gaining weight I had lost it.

'No. I am constantly burning.'

'Are you still suffering from bouts of pessimism and depression?'

'I shall never be well, shall I?' I said, perilously close to tears.

'Pessimism is a popular sickness these days, amongst the young.'

'Do you have any idea, Dr Thompson, what it feels like to be so young and yet so old at the same time? Death preys incessantly on my mind. I cannot stop thinking about it, being afraid of it.'

His cloudy eyes were kind, but I never sensed that he saw me, *me*, the essential unique soul that made me different from his hundreds of other patients suffering from the same disease. 'Are you prepared for it, my boy?' I held my breath against the stench of his own.

'Is one ever prepared? No, I am too busy; I have too many things to do, too much work, and social obligations.'

'Besides your tuberculosis, my boy, you are suffering from the times. The *fin de siècle* has created a certain *mal de siècle*. Did you know that? Yes, I am certain it is true. Have you ever asked yourself why so many people are ill these days? It is because the nervous system is overloaded as never before. We are all of us overexcited.'

'Yes,' I admitted, 'I am either exhausted or excited all the time. I cannot stop my brain. And my sexual organ, Dr Thompson – it seems to be—'

'Overstimulated?'

'Yes.'

'A penis in a continual state of irritable longing, what we call *orexis*, is a pathological condition common to consumptives. But you must not give in to the morbid instincts of an enlarged member, my boy. Sexual erethism must be fought by complete rest and mental discipline. You must at all costs keep yourself pure. The nerve tonic I prescribed for you, have you been taking it?'

'Yes. But it only increases my nervousness.'

'I want your mother to paint your chest with iodine. And I want you to go to the country.'

Panic thrummed in my nerves when I heard this. 'No, I cannot leave London; I have far too much work to do.'

'The climate of Haslemere is good for drying out excessive moisture in the lungs, and I know of a resort where you will be comfortable.'

'I am not going to a sanatorium!'

'A few weeks of complete rest—'

'I am not going to a sanatorium!' I repeated. 'I am not so ill, and I could not bear to be confined to a bed – I must be up and about – a sanatorium would kill me—'

'On the contrary, sunlight and inactivity are precisely what you need, my boy. I am going to recommend a course of copper salt treatment along with oxide of zinc—'

'No, no, no, no!'

But Mother, of course, was on Dr Thompson's side, and so alarmed at my condition that she immediately fell in with his plans. I resisted her every step of the way; I was not going to give in so easily. Indeed, to hear our rows you would have thought we were the bitterest of enemies. No matter – the haemorrhages continued and she won: I spent my twenty-first birthday in a damp hotel bed in Haslemere, staring out into the sodden landscape that was supposed to dry out my lungs.

My enforced inactivity was unbearable; even the sight of birds in flight roused my anger. Enormous flies buzzed impatiently in the window-panes, waiting for me to become carrion. I dreamed horribly of the sheep in the slaughterhouse being hurled down into the pit where the men with knives were waiting; I was one of the sheep, being jostled forward, towards the ledge – and woke just as I was about to be pushed over. The terror! God, how I cursed my patrilineage, that murky flow of diseased blood that was inexorably pushing me towards the final ledge of the slaughterhouse.

Mother's attempts at cheerfulness, her little presents and 'surprises' were meant to reduce me to a state of infantile dependence that I found intolerable. Twice a day she brushed on the iodine until my chest looked like that of a Red Indian – or should I say a roast fowl. With joyful precision she weighed out and mixed the drams and scruples of zinc and copper salts that left my head aching and my tongue numb. Was she actually humming? I was *entirely hers*, and she devoted herself to me with that terrible pleasure a captor finds in a captive. It was humiliating, demeaning, boring, and I was paying for it all. I made her life there as miserable as I could, until finally, after a week, she repented, broke down in tears, was forced to concede defeat and returned with me to the lovely fogs and grime of London. There, at least, I knew that I was still alive.

By November, Salome was on the brink of shedding her final veil, and the dance I had seen evolve from its slow sensual beginning erupted into a final bitter bacchanalian frenzy. I was thoroughly disgusted with Bosie Douglas by then, and it was with the greatest of difficulty – and only for the sake of helping Mabel with her theatrical career – that I maintained cordial relations with Oscar Wilde.

You see, when Oscar finally put his moonblind eyes in his pocket and read Bosie's translation of the play in the cold light of day, it became embarrassingly apparent that his cruel darling Hyacinth's command of French, regardless of the shape of his lips, went *de mal en pis*. It was a joke! Oscar winced, I groaned, and John Lane quite rightly refused to publish it.

What I found particularly intolerable was the way Bosie Douglas's *feelings* were so constantly kept in view. Oscar was positively afraid of the violent tantrums Bosie threw every time he was crossed; by then it was quite apparent that, like his tiresomely mad father, Bosie

271

throve on quarrels. Bobbie Ross, eternal pacifier and intermediary, interceded on Bosie's behalf and told Oscar that Bosie's life would be scarred for ever if all his hard work on *Salome* was returned to him like a mere schoolboy's assignment. Art is art, I said, and an artist stands or falls by what he produces; the artist's *emotions* are superfluous. What was to be done? I had the answer for that: let me do the translation.

At first Lane and Oscar agreed. I had no time, but I made time – this literary opportunity was too precious to squander. Meanwhile, behind my back, the Oscar-Bosie melodrama remained in its perennially heated third act. Bosie, when he got wind of the new scheme, was a perfect maelstrom of malevolence and accused Lane of stirring up trouble; what he said about me I shall leave to the darker caverns of your imagination. Oscar then unjustly rejected *my* translation and began a translation of his own from Bosie's translation. I said it would be dishonest to use Bosie's name as translator when the final work had been so much altered by Oscar. Finally a ridiculous truce was reached. Rather than have Bosie's name appear on the title page as translator, Oscar proposed to *dedicate* the book to him as translator. By then their hysterical public parade of emotion in a matter that should have been settled privately, between professional *artists*, had thoroughly sickened me.

I had faced enough artistic problems with *Salome* to justify some resentment, but I still knew it was a book that was going to attract comment – and probably censure. Three of my designs, returned as indecent, I replaced with stunning and deliciously irrelevant new ones, while over the cock of Herodias's naked page I merely *tied* a fig leaf. Aymer informed me to my great satisfaction that Oscar, snuffling about for sympathy, had taken several of the drawings, including the ones that caricatured him, to the two Charlies, complaining that they were too Japanese, while his play was 'Byzantine'. The two Charlies, bless them, found the drawings brilliant, original and evocative.

Salome was scheduled for publication in February 1894, and the final instalment of *Morte D'Arthur* in April. In London and Paris my name was already well enough known to provoke Whistler's jealousy. Word got back to me that when asked his opinion of me Whistler replied: 'He seems to me like one of those men who stand idle in the market-place because no man hired them.' I, standing idle? The Master was obviously groping in the dark for his insults. People in London thought the caricatures I drew of him (and his fat wife) malicious, but really I did take the greatest care to make sure they were recognizable.

The year 1893 was drawing to a close; and, even though the new year promised many exciting new projects, I must confess, Father, that I was frequently prey to a curious sense of doom. It was not my health, tho' that remained uncertain. No, it was a queer mental oppression, difficult to identify; perhaps a fear that from too much good something bad must result.

I remember standing with Bobbie Ross in front of the Albemarle Hotel one freezing winter's night – it must have been in November – as that dark fatalistic sensation descended. We had been out carousing, dining with Count Stenbock at Jimmy's in Piccadilly (where the Count picked up the bill *and* one of the notorious young ladies – in fact, young men – who liked flouncing through the restaurant in all their finery) before going on to the Café Royal for a glass of Château de Mille Secousses. Perhaps it was the sight of Oscar, drunk, holding forth to a group of what looked to me like adolescent blackmailers, that depressed my thoughts. Perhaps it was my unending virginity, or merely the despairing burden of my *Morte* work. Bobbie and I were called over to Oscar's table to meet his 'exquisite Aeolian harps'.

'Does that mean they hum before they are plucked?' I sardonically asked Bobbie afterwards.

'Oscar is becoming careless,' Bobbie said. 'It's useless to say anything, yet it does worry me.'

Bobbie was a worrier. If he did not worry on his own account, he worried for others. His hairline had suffered as a result, and he had great bags under his eyes. Throughout the evening, as I complained about my *Morte* work, telling him I was sick unto death of it and longed to be released from Dent's contract, he pressed me to continue. When we left the Café Royal, he wanted to go on to the Crown in Charing Cross. 'I would just like to see if Bosie is there,' he said.

The Crown, Father, is situated between the stage doors of the Alhambra and the Empire, and many a Greek liaison has been forged

273

in its raucous smoky confines. Bosie, to my relief, was nowhere to be seen; and Bobbie, for a reason as yet obscure to me, looked crestfallen.

'Bobbie, what is the matter?' I asked.

'Nothing – only . . . Oh, do come to my new rooms for a nightcap, Aubrey. You haven't seen them yet . . . and I hate being there by myself.' When I agreed, he asked if we could stop at the Albemarle first. 'Just for a few minutes, I promise you.'

'Bobbie, what is going on?'

As we stood in the freezing drizzle, Bobbie plaintively looking up at the red-curtained windows of the hotel, he told me. Bobbie had recently fallen in love with the son of an army colonel, a 'wonderful' sixteen-year-old schoolboy called Philip Danney whom Bobbie had known since he was fourteen and had recently met again in Bruges. Bobbie had invited Philip to visit him in London, which Philip had done. 'I thought I would die of happiness,' Bobbie said. 'Never in my life have I been so close to a union with my soul's most perfect desire.'

With the giddy joy of a bridegroom, Bobbie wrote to Bosie, then staying in the country with Oscar, telling him about Philip. And what did Bosie, that evil foul-blooded aristocrat, that dear friend over whom Bobbie had always taken such infinite pains, do? He took the next train to London, whisked the impressionable Philip back to the country, and buggered him. The next day he turned the youth over to Oscar, who buggered him. Then Bosie brought his conquest back to London and was keeping him here, at the Albemarle, at Oscar's expense!

It was too squalid for words, and I could only marvel that the heartbroken and utterly betrayed Bobbie still could not bring himself to break with Bosie and Oscar. They remained, despite their treachery, his dearest friends. Staring wistfully up at the windows of the Albemarle, Bobbie drunkenly murmured: 'The only person I have ever loved – besides Oscar – is even now behind one of those curtained windows.'

'With the one person I shall never respect and now regard with even more contempt than I did before.'

'I wonder which window is theirs,' Bobbie said. He gave me a wan smile when I put a sympathetic hand on his shoulder. 'Come, let us go to my rooms for a last drink. You must be freezing, Beardsley.'

'No, I am always burning.'

Bobbie had recently moved from Church Street to Upper Phillimore Gardens in Kensington, and his new rooms were notable for their spacious disarray. We chatted amiably about art matters. That indefinable sense of doom glowered deep in my thoughts, and I sought to dispel it with lightheartedness; Bobbie, manifestly morose, tried to do the same.

As I walked about his rooms my glance happened to fall on his letter-strewn writing-table and a familiar piece of stationery. Quickly I moved closer. The address at the top was 114 Cambridge Street, the handwriting my mother's. Without Bobbie seeing me, I extracted the letter and read it:

'The way Aubrey is treating Mr Dent over the *Morte D'Arthur* makes me exceedingly uneasy. I was horrified to hear him propose throwing it over entirely. That he should even contemplate behaving in such an unprincipled manner is monstrous. If his "Morte" work is a little unequal, that is his own fault. He has always been wilful enough not to exert himself over what he pretends he doesn't like. But he undertook to do it, and Mr Dent and the subscribers have spent money over it, and it will be disgraceful if Aubrey gives it up . . . Please, I beg of you, use what influence you have over Aubrey to make him see the enormous risk he would be taking if he broke his contract with Mr Dent, what it would mean in terms of his reputation and future work not only with Mr Dent, but with all publishers . . . PLEASE DON'T BETRAY ME BY LETTING HIM KNOW I HAVE WRITTEN TO YOU.'

The treacherous bitch! Writing secretly to my friend, exhorting him to act against me on *her* behalf, so that she could continue to reap the rewards of *my* hard labour! Reduced to a naughty ungovernable boy in the eyes of my friends – the humiliation! My very manhood was called into question. I was consumed in an inferno of rage. I stuffed the letter into my pocket, not knowing what I would do but knowing I must somehow punish her for this unpardonable transgression.

I left Bobbie, who was by then staring morosely into his brandy, no doubt torturing himself with lurid visions of Philip Danney taking Bosie's prick up his sweet little bum, and drove back to Cambridge Street by cab. Cabs, once an unimaginable luxury, were now part of my daily life as a successful man. The clouds had parted, and a freezing wind blew; ancient, enormous, mysterious London sped by to the hypnotic sound of horse's hoofs; row after row of dark houses gleamed in the moonlight; the streets were empty, except for – here and there – clustered around cabmen's shelters, or gathered near a rubbish-fed fire, frost-bitten whores and vagrants. The struggle to stay warm, to stay *alive*, even when life was sheer degradation and unending misery – how strange it all seemed in the comfortable midst of my bitterness.

The scandal broke soon afterwards. Doom appeared on the horizon. Philip Danney, returning three days late to his school in Bruges, was severely questioned by the headmaster and tearfully admitted to carnality with Bobbie, Bosie and Oscar. When the boy's father, Colonel Danney, heard about it, the police were called in. Bobbie and Bosie, gibbering with terror, and in an attempt to smooth matters over, made a quick trip to Bruges. Bobbie returned his fickle sweetheart's letters. Bosie claimed the story was a complete fabrication. The Colonel was going to prosecute, and Bobbie and Bosie were actually on the verge of being sent to prison, when old Danney realized that his son would be liable to a six-month sentence himself. He dropped the case, but not before Bobbie's mother and sister in London had been informed.

Poor Bobbie! He who was so solicitous on behalf of others was now reviled as a disgrace to his family and unfit for human society. His health broke down, just as it had at Cambridge when he was subjected to such merciless persecution. He was sent off to Davos; and Bosie, through Oscar's intervention with Lady Queensberry, was shipped off to Cairo. Oscar escaped entirely: Bobbie and Bosie had done everything in their power to keep his name out of it.

As for me, I left Mother's letter to Bobbie lying where she would be certain to see it. When next she saw me she had a stricken look on her face. I said nothing. Indeed, for days on end I said nothing. I ignored her entirely, turning my face to the wall whenever she entered. She sent Mabel to make an appeal on her behalf. Finally I relented and we worked it out in the course of a fearful row. Mother, in tears, promised she would never do such a thing again. I promised I would complete the *Morte* only if she ceased her nagging.

Mother of course knew nothing about the Bobbie scandal, and Mabel and I kept her in the dark about it. It wasn't until my own life was torn to shreds eighteen months later, and hers along with it, that she came to realize the true nature of persecution.

Meanwhile, to Oscar, I remained 'dear Aubrey'.

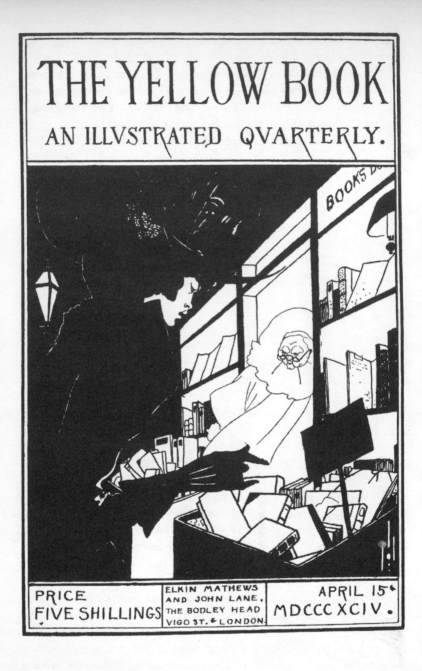

THE YELLOW BOOK

AN ILLVSTRATED QVARTERLY.

BOOKS D

PRICE
FIVE SHILLINGS

ELKIN MATHEWS
AND JOHN LANE,
THE BODLEY HEAD
VIGO ST. & LONDON.

APRIL 15&
MDCCC XCIV.

XIII

UR JOURNEY TO the City of Light has been postponed for a day or two, Father, owing to Mother's sciatica. Truth to tell, my own fears about making this trip are growing as well. My first enthusiasm for the pneumothorax cure has been tempered by hearing reports of others who have died or whose condition rapidly deteriorated during the course of treatment.

To be permanently one-lunged, like a bird clipped in the wing, forever earthbound – the idea fills me with a

279

lop-sided terror. If it is so difficult to draw a deep satisfying breath with two lungs, how much worse must it be with only one? It fuels my abiding fear of suffocation. And then the journey itself, in my present condition, gives rise to apprehensions of another sort. At the same time, I know I must leave St-Germain if I am to get well; St-Germain has exhausted me, and I it.

If this next journey should prove to be my last, Father, I want to begin it with a cleansed soul. With this in mind, it seems wise to continue the story of my life without interruption or delay. It is a way to calm and recollect myself amidst the turmoil of packing and the fret of the future . . .

If every artist has one great year, one *annus mirabilis*, in which he finally pecks his way through the hard shell of public indifference and stands before the world with wings stretched and ready for flight, that year for me was 1894. Not three years past, yet how distant it seems already, that glorious *Yellow Book* year, that year of recognition and success. The memory of it sits on my palate like a sweet red wine. London was mine then; for sixteen months I was as happy as a sovereign assuming his throne. Yet in the very sweetness of my success there lurked a curious malignancy, at first unseen, later ignored, and finally, when it was too late, denied.

Despite a bitter yellow fog that enveloped London, turning the city as dark at noon as it was at midnight, the first day of January 1894 was an auspicious one. Mabel and I had invited Henry and Aline Harland and Netta Syrett to a New Year's Day tea. Harland, another barnacle in the colony of writers and artists who had attached themselves to John Lane and The Bodley Head, had become a fairly good friend by then. We were both patients of Dr Symes Thompson, a specialist in consumptive disorders, but quickly realized we had in common far more than our diseased lungs. Mabel and I frequently attended Henry and Aline's Saturday soirées, which featured coffee, cigarettes, Aline warbling at the piano, and endless excited talk amongst a congregation of amusing, ambitious and sometimes *outré* guests.

Harland had dropped his American name, Sidney Luska, and

traded his American accent for a British one. Like many talented *arrivistes* he felt it his duty to mint an exotic and quasi-aristocratic background for himself and made it a point to know everyone in artistic London. In the Harlands' tongue-pink drawing-room in Cromwell Road, with its Persian carpets, its modern pictures and old comfortable furniture, I had met everyone from Edmund Gosse to Count Stenbock to dear old Verlaine, who had come over to London the previous November on a visit sponsored by Billy Rothenstein and Bobbie Ross. Only once, when the poet Théodore Marzials bent one of her finest heirloom soup-spoons to cook up an injectable batch of morphine, did I see the *fausse-bohémienne* Aline Harland upset by the sometimes odd behaviour of her guests.

One could say anything at the Harlands' – indeed, one came armed with subjects to be attacked. Our common goal was to rid a dying age of its sentimentalities and hypocrisies and to establish fresh standards of beauty and sincerity in art. We warmed ourselves in the fire of subversion. Or so I thought. When the crisis came, Harland and all the dedicated decadents who gathered for comfort at Cromwell Road revealed themselves as the frightened complacent *poseurs* they really were.

For some time Harland and I had amused ourselves by tossing about the idea of establishing a new literary and artistic journal, a publication that would appeal to the *Zeitgeist* and, not co-incidentally, further our careers. Harland, with the despair that comes from losing one's God, had slowly lost his faith in the novel as an art form. The future of fiction, he believed, now lay in the short story, at which, so far, only the French were masters. Our new journal must thus champion the cause of short fiction by publishing at least one of Harland's stories in every number.

I, on the other hand, wanted to stretch my boundaries as an artist with pictures that stood alone, without an accompanying text, or with a text of my own devising. To remain a lowly handmaiden to the empress of language did not suit my burgeoning ambitions. Aubrey Beardsley the illustrator should be Aubrey Beardsley the artist. The *modern* artist, who drew with mechanical reproduction in mind yet lost none of his power to amaze.

These dreams suddenly coalesced on that foggy first day of January, as we gathered around a hot coal fire at 114 Cambridge Street. Aline,

Mabel, and Mabel's schoolmistress friend, the clever Netta Syrett, stood in a group, avidly discussing the Woman Question and new fashions for female cyclists. Miss Syrett, always in the vanguard of liberating trends, had in fact pedalled through the dense London fog, clenching a damp cigarette between her teeth like a carriage lamp, to join us – or to join Mabel, I should say, since no one but my sister seemed to exist for her; everyone else in Netta's sharp, dark, jealous range of vision was viewed as an interloper. And, like a woman who wishes to inflame her lover's ardour, Mabel would now and then glance coyly from Netta's eyes to my own, a secretive smile playing on her lips, knowing full well the furious distress it could provoke in me.

Trying to ignore her, I sat and listened to Harland, who was waving his spectacles and shortsightedly holding forth on the hearthrug. 'The truth is, most of our very best writers today cannot get their work published because there is no vehicle for it in the market-place,' he was saying. 'Anything that is not considered topical enough, or that is considered too risqué, will never be published.'

'This is where the French beat us hollow,' I concurred.

'The French understand art,' said Harland, carefully scratching his head to avoid inadvertently smoothing his carefully unkempt hair. 'One need only to look at the number of literary journals published every day in Paris to see that. What have we here? *Punch, Pick-me-up*, the *Quarterly Review* – all of them dedicated to ridiculing anything progressive and defending the old order.'

'Down with the old order,' said Miss Syrett in her low smoky voice, raising her teacup. The ladies had abandoned their discussion of cycling bloomers and now migrated towards our conversation.

'What we want, then, is a literary and artistic quarterly for everything that is fresh and unconventional,' I said. 'Something fervently modern.'

'A *Zeitgeist* of our complex age,' agreed Harland.

'After all, not to be new is, in these days, to be nothing,' I said. And I, to be sure, was new: my *Salome* drawings, due for publication the following month, would be ample proof of that. 'Ours, after all, is the decade of a thousand *isms*, isn't it? Impressionism, Naturalism, Realism.'

'Aestheticism, Darwinism, Socialism,' nodded Harland.

'Feminism!' shouted Miss Syrett, gazing at Mabel.

'Symbolism,' added Mabel.

'Modernism,' put in Aline.

'Vitalism,' said Harland.

'Individualism!' bugled Miss Syrett.

'Diabolism,' I enjoined.

'Subjectivism!' cried Aline, as agitated now as a player in charades.

'Onanism,' I said before I could stop myself, then added, rattled by a sudden cough: 'Pessimism.'

'Aubrey . . . ?' Mabel enquired solicitously.

But I was not to be stopped by my fretting lungs. The fever that had been toasting my blood suddenly began to boil, and I leaped up, seeing clearly, for the first time, what our quarterly would be. 'Look here,' I said excitedly, 'in general get-up it should look like an ordinary French novel.'

'With a yellow cover?' Mabel said.

'Yes, a yellow cover with a frightfully clever design by me.'

'Delightfully shocking,' said Miss Syrett.

'The artwork must stand on its own and not be mere illustrations to a text,' I insisted. 'We shall find brilliant story painters and amazing picture writers. Champion youth and thumb our noses at superannuated Puritania. We shall confuse and confound and astound, Harland.'

'If we could do it, it would simply make our names,' said Harland, catching the hot flush of my enthusiasm.

'And our fortunes,' I said.

'What will you call it?' asked Mabel.

Yes, what would we call it? The importance of a name! I looked out into the yellow fogs of London, my head spinning. I thought of yellow, notorious and unavoidable yellow, sun-blinding absinthe-blending yellow, full, rich, fiery, defiant, revealing and concealing yellow, gay and god-like yellow, the favourite colour of Regency dandies.

Like every question that is difficult, the answer was amazingly simple. I turned to our guests. 'It is to be called *The Yellow Book*,' I announced.

Oh, the grinding joys of *The Yellow Book*! The hard work – the pleasure in conspiracy. Who was accepted, who was not. Harland

and I set to work at once, knowing full well that our idea was a timely one and a perfect publishing project for John Lane of The Bodley Head. After all, most of the advanced writers and artists in London known to Harland and myself were also known to Lane; he was one of the few publishers interested in new ideas, and had recently started to make a name for himself precisely because of it. What better idea, then, than to publish a literary and artistic quarterly featuring the works of the very artists he represented, and whose work he fostered? It would help sales all around.

Lane invited Harland and me to the Hogarth Club the very next day to discuss the project, and within half an hour had consented to publish it. Harland was to be literary editor, and I the artistic director. We were awarded generous salaries, and promised Lane the very best; to prove our point, Harland left the table to telephone Henry James and solicit a story for the first number. It had the queer sense of ease that had accompanied other turning-points in my life, as though one were somehow made complicit with fate simply by trusting it. How could I have known, sitting there in a comfortable leather chair in the smoking-room of the Hogarth Club, that the colour yellow would be my undoing? Yellow, the colour of pus and piss.

Lane took advantage of Harland's absence to tell me about the progress on *Salome*. He was a bearded, pot-bellied, cunning-eyed man, short in stature but a giant of willpower and egotism. When he was thirteen he'd been sent to work for the railways, but somehow, through sheer dint of self-interest, had also started trading in rare books. He'd mysteriously elbowed his way into a partnership with dull Elkin Mathews of The Bodley Head, and was now the driving force behind it. There was something slightly illicit about Lane and his bullying vitality, and I suppose that was why one couldn't help liking him.

'*Salome* is certain to create a furore,' Lane said, rolling his fat, ever-present Havana cigar between pursed lips. 'Of course Piggot's decision to ban the play was the best piece of publicity we could have hoped for, and that's how I'm advertising it − as the play the Lord Chamberlain refused to license. Brilliant, if I do say so. But Oscar, you know, is not very happy with your illustrations,

284

Mr Beardsley. They make no sense to him. He feels they undermine the beauty of the text.'

'They complement Oscar's play perfectly,' I said sweetly. 'They *reveal* it for exactly what it is.'

'And people will *revile* them for that very reason,' said Lane, smiling at his own wit. 'Now, Mr Beardsley, you know in what high regard I hold Oscar. But – let me be frank – his reputation in certain circles is suffering a sea-change.'

'Perhaps,' I said, 'you mean a sex-change?'

'Will you and Harland want him to be associated with *The Yellow Book*?' Lane asked carefully. 'He's certain to find out about it immediately.'

What did I owe to Oscar? I asked myself. I had managed, like a determined dog, to clamp my teeth into his coat-tails and shake loose the *Salome* commission. But my pictures were hardly adoring. From the whole artistic fray I emerged as Oscar's equal, and that was what he could not bear. His behaviour with Bosie Douglas and the stable of young louts with whom he now consorted was embarrassing and dangerous. That was what Lane was complicitly warning me about. A spark of hubris, my own, suddenly ignited in my veins, and I decided on the spot that Oscar would be excluded. It's ironic, of course, that *The Yellow Book* and its association with Oscar – an association that led to my own ruin – never published a word by Mr Wilde.

I delighted in the outrage that attended the publication of *Salome*. I knew, because of it, that I had hit my mark squarely in the John Bull's-eye. Mother, on the other hand, was visibly alarmed, and would come racing up to my studio as each new review appeared.

'Someone else is attacking you,' she would say, breathless with fear and indignation, waving *The Times* or the *Saturday Review* or whatever newspaper was frothing with rage that day.

And when I would laugh Mother would turn on me with the ferocity of a Philistine. 'How can you laugh at these attacks on your work?'

'What does it matter what old John Bull and Mrs Grundy have

to say about my work? They hate art – and they know absolutely nothing about it.'

'It *matters*, Aubrey,' Mother would insist. 'A reputation once destroyed cannot be put together again.'

She was thinking of her own reputation, probably, tarnished on Brighton Pier those many years ago and which led to her downfall through marriage. Something else was on her mind, too, but she was obviously reluctant to reveal it.

'Yes, Mother, what is it?' I said impatiently. 'I have heaps of work to do on these new commissions from America and have to meet Harland in two hours' time for lunch.'

'I wish, Aubrey, that you had not accepted the *Salome* commission,' Mother said finally. She wilted under my glare. 'I am afraid something awful may come of it.'

'I am an artist, Mother. If I spent all my time fretting about what the critics thought of my work I would never put pen to paper. And then', I said pointedly, 'how would we live?'

'I did not mean to—'

'Mother, please, I am busy.'

I was. My workload was overpowering. I was illustrating two volumes of Poe for an American publisher, designing and soliciting work for *The Yellow Book*, while drawing my own contributions, and finishing up borders and chapter headings for the final instalments of the interminable *Morte D'Arthur*. Another recent and rather more jolly commission had come from the American actress Florence Farr. Miss Farr wanted an eye-catching poster and programme cover for a new play by George Bernard Shaw that she was producing at the Avenue Theatre. At last I was to be on the streets – on hoardings!

I suppose snobs would consider it a dubious achievement, something *déclassé* and indicative of a low character, but I am proud that I changed the face of poster design in England. What had we before I came along? The Beggarstaff Brothers, direct and artless. In Paris it was a different story, of course. The French allow beauty to permeate all aspects of their life, right down to the *affiches* lining the Boulevard de Clichy. I had noted carefully the posters of Cheret, father of the contemporary *affiche*. The problem, as I saw it, was lack of outline: everything was a fizzle of gay abandoned movement. My poster creations, on the other hand, move with severe deliberation.

286

Billy Rothenstein and I went to the opening night of *Arms and the Man* by courtesy of Miss Farr, who was playing Louka. Shaw had given the play to Miss Farr to help her avert bankruptcy from her last theatrical fiasco – she had produced Yeats's poetic but unplayable *The Land of Heart's Desire* – and because he was, I suspect, like Yeats, a little in love with her. The emancipated Miss Farr, when she was not acting and managing her theatre, also served as a priestess-scribe for the Order of the Golden Dawn, an occultist group based in Bedford Park; and it was in this latter capacity, I suppose, that she had earned her reputation as something of a sacred prostitute. Shaw once told me that she had had no less than fourteen lovers by the time he met her in '94.

My cab dropped me at the Thames Embankment near Charing Cross, and as I walked up towards the theatre, passing a dozen or so leering whores, I saw my poster. There she was, the woman behind the green dotted curtain. I had not signed the poster, but everyone knew it was my work.

Waiting for Billy, I watched people as they wandered up to look at it. 'Aubrey Beardsley,' said a few of the women knowingly, pointing. Their husbands or escorts for the evening usually gave a disgusted sniff. 'See his nonsense everywhere,' one said. 'His art is the talk of London,' said the lady with him. 'He illustrated Oscar Wilde's *Salome*, and just today I read an interview with him in the *Sketch* about a new quarterly called *The Yellow Book*.' Her husband was superior and dismissive: 'All I can say is, a *man* wouldn't put his name on such rubbish.' 'No,' said another top-hatted gentleman beside them, 'but a *Mary-Ann* would.' The two men enjoyed a good laugh.

I felt vindicated somehow – elevated – and rather dream-like; anonymous, but hearing myself talked about. I cared not what they said, only that they said something. When people passed the poster without so much as a glance I fell into a quiet rage. Once inside the theatre, I saw people looking at my programme cover – the same lady behind a curtain, only reduced – with interest, glancing through its pages and then back to the front cover. Billy, I knew, was envious of my success.

In *Arms and the Man* Shaw saw through the bloated militarism and jingoistic rattlings of our age, our need to usurp and conquer everything in sight, and his truth-telling caused something of an uproar that opening night. Much of the audience – including the Prince of Wales – sat in stony silence, unable to bear the thought that his Majesty's army was being portrayed in such a ludicrous and unflattering light. The rest of us laughed and cheered. In one damning line, a nervous actor substituted 'British' for 'Bulgarian', and was greeted with a storm of boos. When he came out for his curtain call, Shaw was loudly hissed by the same gentleman who had reviled my poster outside the theatre. 'My dear man,' said Shaw, silencing that boor at once, 'I quite agree with you – but who are we against so many?'

The day is for the head, the night is for the senses. I became an *habitué* of the music-halls, finding in those raucous smoke-filled environs relief from the nervous worries that accompany success. As dusk deepened to dark, I would put my work aside and abandon myself to the night. Evening clothes were my pleasure. I could afford to dress with exquisite care; padded jackets gave my stooped shoulders a firm sense of purpose, and in the toe of my patent-leather pumps I could see Narcissus himself peering up from a shining black lake. At last I was a gentleman of means.

In matters of love I appeared as vain and experienced as Casanova. In truth, I was still a virgin.

Beneath my veneer lurked the insatiable venereal. Wallowing in the swamp of my fever, which rose predictably in the late after-noon, were impossible fantasies of sexual encounters with panting, leg-spread, full-hipped, sharp-nippled women – imaginary women of all shapes, ages, classes and colours: furious Amazons, amiable dwarves, frightened virgins, indolent Negresses, fiery Jewesses, bored countesses, penniless flower-sellers, actresses, whores, nuns, sisters . . . This sexual erethism could not be controlled, Father; the more I attempted to restrain my immoral desires the quicker they would rise up in big steamy bubbles from my inner effluvia. It was not controllable by my will, whatever you would have me believe.

I have, of course, been told by various doctors since then that such teeming passions are felt by many consumptives; that the disease is, in fact, one of inner repression seeking release in action. Count Stenbock told me there are doctors who recommend a kind of sexual therapy for consumptives. 'They actually believe,' he said, 'that fucking can cure you.'

That may be true, but certainly fucking never cured Count Stenbock, who died with only his monkey at his side. It did, however, fascinate him, and it was the Count who helped introduce me to that indecent world of under-the-counter literature as personified by Leonard Smithers, my present publisher.

Bobbie Ross was serving out the terms of his penance in the yodel-filled valleys of Davos, no doubt pouncing on the Swiss boys as they tobogganed down the snowy mountainsides, so it was Max or Billy who generally accompanied me to the halls. The Oxford was Max's favourite: he had fallen quite in love with Cissy Loftus, a fifteen-year-old singer with straight hair and unpainted face, who was just then conquering London. I preferred heartier fare, Marie Lloyd singing 'You Cannot Tell Cigars by the Picture on the Box' or my other favourite, 'Oh! Mr Porter'. Dan Leno kept us in stitches.

It was a place for boisterous forgetting, the music-hall, a gallery of dark mysterious profiles seen in silhouette against the glare of gas-jets, a house of artifice where class was forgotten and Respectability eagerly nuzzled the delightfully dirty shoulder of Ill-Fame. Whores flitted in and out with the rank persistence of my fever-cooked phantasies. It was at the Tivoli, in fact, that I caught my first glimpse of Penny Plain.

Afterwards Max and Billy and I would go somewhere to talk about our amazing careers over jellied eels. Both Max and Billy would be appearing in the first April number of *The Yellow Book*, Max with a clever essay on cosmetics, Billy with two portraits. Lane, smartly capitalizing on the leering success of *Salome*, had launched an enormous 'publicity campaign' (as the Americans call it) for *The Yellow Book*, and my posters could now be seen in bookshop windows all over London: THE YELLOW BOOK SOLD HERE.

But Max and Billy were essentially timid creatures, and crept home virtuously to practise the five-fingered exercise in their solitary beds. Saying that I was going to find a hansom on the Embankment, I would leave them in the West End and begin my nocturnal prowlings.

Leading out of the Strand was a certain street, dark as pitch, where one black midnight I had wandered quite by chance, and been startled by the sight and sound of a whole row of pissing doxies. Pressing myself into the angle of a wall, I was able to watch the whole fascinating process. They were like cats with an accustomed place, and would generally arrive in pairs, one acting as sentry and screen while the other squatted to fill the gutter with a gush of stale beer. It was a charming and tender scene. Chattering like ladies during a theatre interval, they would then change places and the other would hoist her skirts. Impossible to imagine Mother or Mabel relieving themselves in like manner!

I loved to walk along the Embankment, its pavements glittering with fallen rain. Cleopatra's Needle and the two sleek Egyptian sphinxes conferred an ancient yearning mystery on that riverside promenade, where centuries of Londoners like myself, in moments of triumph or despair, had gazed out over the great dirty Thames, flowing like life itself on its way to the Eternal.

Yes, Father, there were women down there, women whose purpose was made manifest by their brazen glances and slow calculated steps. I let them tease me and teased them back, glorying in my proximity to this lowest rung of society. And it was here, one misty night along the Thames Embankment, that I saw again the girl from the Tivoli, Penny Plain she was called, and resolved to speak with her.

Now that she was moving in my artistic circles, Mabel's humdrum life as a teacher at the Polytechnic had become unbearable to her. More than ever she was convinced of her calling as an actress, and more than ever she was quarrelling with Mother about her future in the theatre. Mother hid her old-fashioned moral objections to the stage under the practical cloak of finance. When that didn't work, she proceeded to attack and undermine Mabel's abilities and harp on about her inexperience. Mabel, however, remained steadfast, and eventually Mother was forced to capitulate.

Behind my back Mother wrote to Bobbie Ross, asking him to speak to Oscar Wilde about Mabel's acting career. She did not approve of Oscar, mind you, but she knew quite well that he was quickly becoming the darling of the theatre world. Bobbie did as Mother asked, and Mabel was given a part in the touring production of *A Woman of No Importance*. I was white with rage when I learned what Mother had done. I had no intention of ever going to Oscar again, for anything; but there was Mabel to consider, and Oscar was – I hated to admit it – always generous in such matters: recently, so that I could make a drawing of her, he'd even taken me backstage to meet Mrs Patrick Campbell after a performance of *The Second Mrs Tanqueray*. I continued to see Oscar – there was no way around it given our circle of mutual friends – but I found him increasingly abrasive and irritating. His endless brilliance roused a kind of jealous anger in me, and my growing fame acted as a kind of irritant to him. Gradually we began to spar with words.

Before she left on her tour, Mabel pestered me day and night to help her with her lines. Now that she had achieved her goal, the poor darling was tremulous with fear that she would not succeed. She had given notice to the Polytechnic and was now faced with the consequences of her decision.

'What if I fail?' she moaned, nervously rocking Nip in her arms as she tortured herself with visions of jeering theatregoers.

'Then, you had better learn to dodge the tomatoes,' I said.

'Aubrey, I'm so frightened.'

Like a little girl she sought comfort in my arms. 'There, you mustn't be afraid. The point is, you are doing it, you are following the truth of your nature.'

'But I *am* afraid,' she insisted.

I stroked her hair and whispered: 'What do you wish for?' This was always my way of getting her to muster her disaster-plagued thoughts.

Mabel thought for a moment. 'Pearl ear-rings and a gondola on the Grand Canal.'

Venice was out of my reach, but I was able to present her with the ear-rings before she left for the station. One pearl was white, the other black. 'They are called the Venus ear-rings,' I said, affixing them to her blushing ears. 'The Goddess of Love wears just such a pair in a painting by Rubens.'

'I love you, Aubrey.'

'I love you, Mabel. I want your happiness above everything else.'

'You'll take good care of Nip?' she asked, lapsing into a little-girl voice. 'He wikes his tea at four o'cwock, you know.' She kissed the cat's sleek black head and deposited him in my arms as tenderly as if it were our child.

'Be brilliant,' I said. 'You have my reputation to uphold.'

'I promise I shall be brilliant.'

'Mabel?' Mother was standing at the doorway to my studio, pulling on her gloves, ready to accompany Mabel to the station.

Mabel's voice was low and tremulous as she bent to kiss me. 'Goodbye, darling.'

I wanted that kiss to go on for ever, but waved her off cheerfully. Mabel stopped once on her way out to look at me again, fondling the bijoux of Venus and blowing me a secret kiss. That vision of her, so radiantly innocent and so darkly knowing, poised on the threshold of her new, independent life, nearly stopped my heart.

The Yellow Book was an immediate sensation and sold out its first edition of 5,000 copies in less than a week, forcing Lane to order a second printing, and then a third. An American edition, published in Boston, was equally successful. The critics, naturally, were outraged, dipping their pens in vitriol before hurling them in the direction of The Bodley head.

Most of the thunderbolts were reserved for me and my drawings, but Max's superbly comic essay 'In Defence of Cosmetics' was reviled as 'pernicious nonsense', and Henry James's story, 'The Death of the Lion', was called 'mincing'. Of the kind of harsh notoriety that frightened Max and the highly respectable Henry James, however, I could not have enough. Like one of the martyred saints in Aymer Vallance's rooms, I merely smiled as the boiling oil was poured over my head.

I hired a press-cutting agency to keep me informed of my enormous success with the critics. There was the *World*: 'Who wants these fantastic pictures, like Japanese sketches gone mad, of a woman with a black tuft for a head, and snake-like fingers starting off the keyboard of the piano she is playing in a field . . .?'; and the equally generous *Westminster Gazette*: 'As regards certain of his inventions in this number, especially the thing called 'The Sentimental Education', and that other thing to which the name of Mrs Patrick Campbell has somehow become attached, we do not know that anything would meet the case except a short Act of Parliament to make this kind of thing illegal.' Wedmore in the *Academy* called my work 'meaningless and unhealthy', and Henley of the *National Observer* drew attention to my 'audacious vulgarity and laborious inelegance'.

But none of this mattered: the fame of *The Yellow Book*, with its 'hue of jaundice', spread through the bookshops like a delightful disease. To celebrate its inauguration, Harland and I planned a dinner in an upper room of the Hotel d'Italia in Compton Street for all contributors. Harland and I sat at the head of the table with Elizabeth Pennell between us. My mouth was dry from the fever that had been rising all afternoon, and the noise and excited talk jangled my overwrought nerves to a painful degree. An uncomfortable swelling in the sides of my neck was a distant bugle-call of the disease that I feared would any moment engage me in battle. But now that I had fame, dear God, I wanted to live for ever.

Harland rose, swept off his spectacles, and speechified about the distinction and modernity of our creation, in which art and literature were equal partners and every contribution was judged solely on the merits of its workmanship. 'Hear hear!' Glasses were raised. 'To *The Yellow Book*!' When it was my turn I rose very calmly and astonished them all by saying: 'I wish to speak on a most interesting subject: myself.'

My social success following publication of the first *Yellow Book* was, to put it mildly, overwhelming. Invitations and *cartes de visite* simply poured in, and I was constantly in demand. London had a new scandal to celebrate, a new style to fawn over, an intriguing new personality to discuss. Door after door opened in a perpetual social enfilade, and I flew from one smart gathering to the next with hardly a breath to spare.

Never alone, I was always lonely. I longed for a woman, Father, and drew them incessantly, as though I might this way find solace for my anxious desires. I drew women of the night, no more than faint outlines of white in a sea of black, trudging through the dark whore-filled peripheries of Leicester Square. I drew tired coquettes preening in their mirrors, and pert knowing girls winking at the viewer. I drew the New Woman, and women golfers, and women reading. I drew actresses – Mrs Patrick Campbell and Letty Lind and the great French actress Réjane. I made all these women my own, and they were seen in *The Yellow Book*, and as posters on hoardings, and on the covers of popular journals. London could not get enough of the Beardsley Woman, and Beardsley could not get a woman at all. Or at least not one who satisfied his desires.

I was, of course, an object of the greatest curiosity and speculation. People wanted to look at me – as they had when I was a child at the piano – to behold the prodigious wonder. Tricked out in my evening clothes, my fringed hair severely parted, dark hollows under my eyes, I raced about London charged with the task of being unforgettable. When you are successful, Father, you must always have something to say – especially, perhaps, when you have nothing to say. I indulged myself in talk on all subjects, and liked to give my conversation a suggestive edge.

What were my tastes? People supposed me naughty from my pictures, and I hadn't the heart to disabuse them. (I attended church regularly, Father, like all good hypocrites.) Many assumed that I was an invert, for the bearded and manly elders of *Punch* and other periodicals hinted broadly that my work betrayed an unwholesome effeminate tendency. In any case, my character was presumed *risqué*, even *roué*, and I now became aware of the remarkable seductiveness bestowed upon the successful consumptive.

For there were women, Father, who with a knowing arch of an eyebrow, a coy smile or an adoring gaze let me understand that success would follow pursuit. I could have had my pick of any number of them, but the idea of beginning a furtive and exhausting middle-class liaison filled me with a curious repugnance. I preferred, instead, to dabble in the mud of the West End.

One night, after a spirited smoker in Lane's chambers at The Albany, I made my customary way to the Embankment, emboldened by the two glasses of port I had consumed. A slurring mist thickened the air, muffling the light of the gas-lamps and erasing outlines. Sounds were curiously enhanced, yet queerly remote: a hansom as it clopped and rattled down the street, a sudden wail or gin-sodden laugh rising from an unseen doorway.

I saw her at once as I passed the naphtha-flare of the cabmen's shelter near Charing Cross pier. A damp murmuring crowd was gathered near a fire, eating sausage pies and drinking tea from the vendor's urn. She had been warming her hands, and turned to walk along the Embankment a few paces in front of me.

She stopped when she heard my footsteps and seemed to be waiting for me. 'Good evenin', sir.' Her voice was ripe and delightfully bold.

'Good evening,' I said, tipping my hat. I wondered if she could hear my heart, which had set up a sudden pounding clamour.

'Didn't see you at the 'alls tonight.'

'No, I had an engagement elsewhere.'

'Looked, but I didn't see you,' she said playfully.

'You keep an eye out for me, do you?'

'I allus look. No 'arm in it, is there?'

'You're shivering.'

'It's a cold night, sir. Change of season. I'm allus cold these days.'

'You should be wearing a heavier cloak.'

'Ain't got one, sir,' she said, casting down her dark eyes. Tiny beads of moisture hung on the tips of her lashes.

'If you had one, would you wear it?'

She looked at me with sudden hopeful surprise. 'Oh, sir, course I would.'

'This should be enough for a warm three-quarter-length.'

She stared at my proffered note with a kind of alarm. 'So much! Cloaks ain't that much, sir, even at the Stores!'

'Take it,' I insisted. 'I can afford it.'

The money emboldened her. 'Can I 'ave a new 'at as well? This old thing . . .' She rolled comically contemptuous eyes up to the little narrow-brimmed toque trimmed with dirty and rather exhausted-looking artificial flowers that sat high upon her frizzled red hair.

'So long as it's becoming. A charming face deserves a charming hat.'

'Charming . . . ?' She repeated the word with disbelief.

'What is your name?'

'Well, sir, I've got a few of 'em,' she admitted. 'Most gen'lemen call me Penny Plain.'

'Why is that?'

' 'Eard the sayin', "Tuppence coloured, penny plain", ain't you, sir?' Now she lifted her chin and pushed her face rather defiantly towards mine as if to give me a better look at her lineaments.

Admittedly, there was a blunt coarseness to her features, and no man would ever call her beautiful, but there was a pert exciting liveliness about her that by-passed aesthetic considerations and went straight to my cock. I could not help myself. I touched her damp hair. Penny Plain sensed my arousal.

'There's a decent place just ten minues' walk from here,' she whispered. 'I wouldn't take you nowhere dirty, sir.'

'What if that were precisely what I wanted? Something dirty.'

'Then, I know 'nother place,' she smiled, taking my arm.

My work as art director for *The Yellow Book* was frightfully time-consuming; but my health withstood the test, and besides other commissions, mostly for posters and book covers, I made certain that I had several drawings in the July and October numbers.

Harland, already cringing under the blows of the critics, decreed that I must 'tone down' my contributions. No ladies of frayed hem, no winking girls must ruffle the dust-filled balls or brains of the paying public. *The Yellow Book* had already acquired a reputation for being decadent, meaning French, which was why it was so successful; but the cowardly Harland was determined to emphasize the serious over the sinful. Had not old Sir Frederick Leighton, whom I had solicited for a drawing for our first number, in order to lend respectability to the enterprise, refused any further association with us?

Harland knew full well that it was my artwork, however reviled, and not his precious short stories, that made people put down their five shillings. It wasn't Harland they were paying for, or the boringly eminent Sir Frederick Leighton with his studies of classical draperies – it was Aubrey Beardsley.

The audacious Lane had by this time broken with Elkin Mathews and taken The Bodley Head sign, imprint and most of its authors to new quarters in Vigo Street. Lane put me up for the Hogarth Club, where he had always liked to conduct business, and I also began regularly to attend meetings of the Rhymers Club at the Cheshire Cheese in the Strand.

There, in an upper room, with its sanded floor and grime-dark panelling, the Rhymers conducted their search for modern subject-matter, modern forms, modern emotions. Yeats, with his gaunt frame and greasy swept-back hair, was the most interesting of the lot. He read his poems in a harsh, high-pitched, hierophantic chant, sway-ing like a priest about to be overcome by the incense of his own words.

I liked Yeats despite or perhaps because of his endless gabble about diabolism and the occult. When he was not ruthlessly pulling every possible string he could to advance his career, Yeats cosily lounged with his fellow-priestess Florence Farr in a world of mystic reverie and the black arts. Both were high-ranking officials in the Order of the Golden Dawn, and Miss Farr had reputedly gone so far as to summon the spirit of Mercury himself.

Is there another world, Father? An old demon world, deeper than this one, something tucked away in a fold of mankind's ancient consciousness and pre-dating time itself? Being so finely attuned to death, and the dissolution of the darling here-and-now, my mind often wanders to such possibilities. What is beyond this life we lead? What is underneath it all? What explains it, and all that happens to us?

Spirits of another sort moved the Rhymers to ever-greater displays of eloquence. After adjourning one whisky-sodden meeting it was agreed that we would regroup at the nearby rooms of Arthur Symons in Fountain Court, the Temple. Laughing and stumbling, we started down the Strand but had not advanced more than a few paces when a familiar figure stepped back into a doorway.

'Gentlemen, gentlemen,' I said, drunkenly gaining their attention, 'I would like to introduce you to a young lady of the halls.'

Penny Plain, wearing a new three-quarter-length cloak of Bedford cord and a charming new hat, eyed me like a suspicious but hungry cat.

'Gentlemen, this is Miss Plain. Miss Plain is charming, and I think that she should join us in our revelries.'

The timid expressions of the Rhymers could not hide the sudden hunger in their eyes. Perhaps it was one of the devils or pagan spirits hovering about Yeats that prodded me to action, or perhaps it was a desire to reveal satanic urges of my own. In any event, after a round of bawdy badinage, Penny Plain took my arm and accompanied us to the Temple.

The poetry bewildered her. Symons, as he stoked up the fire, was excitedly chanting some lines of his idol, Verlaine:

> 'I am the wound and the knife!
> I am the blow and the cheek!
> I am the limbs and the rack!
> Both the victim and the torturer . . .'

'What's 'e goin' on about?' Penny Plain asked. Simple things of the earth, such as the fire in Symons's grate, interested her more than the occult and intellectual. And it was her lack of mental apparatus that delighted me. 'Ooh, that's lovely,' she said, putting out her red frost-nipped fingers. 'I'm allus cold, even with me lovely new cloak.'

'Will you join us in a drink?' Yes, Father, I asked because I knew what happened to her when she tasted spirits. They caused her to abandon every last vestige of civilized restraint, marginal at the best of times, and reveal the deep, innocent, insatiable cupidity that lurks in the hearts of us all.

She drank whisky and when that was gone she drank gin. The Penny I had found in the Strand sang bawdy cockney songs in a strident ear-splitting voice and, like a cockney Salome, shed her garments one by one until she was dancing naked before the fire wearing only her mud-sputtered high-heeled boots. She seemed perfectly at her lascivious ease; it was the poets, rather, constantly seeking new sensations, who were discomfited by their lust. The whole company reminded me of schoolboys with their noses pressed to the glass of a sweetshop they had been forbidden to enter.

So, like a chairman introducing acts in an obscene music-hall, I continued to direct the proceedings. My drunken plain Penny now lay stretched out on the hearthrug, a Venus savouring the heat of the flames on her pagan flesh and dreaming of dark pastoral perversions. Her close-set eyes darted hungrily from one face to the next as I whispered in her ear what my plan was.

'But I get paid extra for each of 'em!' she growled, finance immediately taking precedence over romance.

'You shall have a golden sovereign,' I assured her.

'All right, then.'

Like a cat preparing to leave a comfortable fireside, she gave one long, luxurious feline stretch before sitting up. Then a nervous silence fell upon us all as Penny Plain led us, one by one, from the flickering hearth into the darkness of the room beyond.

I was the last, by choice, and by the time my turn came I was half-delirious with excitement. Bacchus had crowned me with vine leaves. I was a sovereign of the underworld. The constant suppression of natural instincts, that which gives us the quality of refinement, gave way to the rutting fury of Priapus. Penny Plain's flesh, as she emerged from the darkness with another exhausted Rhymer, was ruddy from fucking, her hair tangled with the knots and twists of abandoned ardour. I would have done anything, followed her into the portals of Hell itself, had she asked. But she said nothing – only held out her hand and looked at me with a mysterious smile.

A confession, Father, must have no omissions. It is the emissions, rather, that must be recounted. I took her hot damp hand and let her lead me into the Cave of Love, stupefied by the glory of her form and the knowledge that it was now to be mine. She was filled with the spunk of my friends, poets who had stopped worrying about metre and rhyme and given themselves over to nothing more than hoarse carnal gruntings. It teased my fevered preliminaries to imagine them spending in her, sliding in the hot slippery dews of her pasture, moaning the ancient worldless paean of love.

'I wants me golden sovereign,' she whispered, pressing herself to my naked flesh. 'Ow!' She started. 'You're burnin' up!'

I reached for her, pulled her close, forced open her lips with my tongue.

'I wants me golden sovereign,' she insisted, pulling away.

'I am your golden sovereign!'

'You!' Her laugh was foul, abusive, and her resistance to my embrace a further goad to my passion.

299

I took that little hand and pressed it to my Turk's rapier. 'Here is your sovereign. Here is your slave.'

'Oh, my.' She rolled her eyes up to mine. 'That weren't there the last time.'

But I could wait no longer. I greedily began to suck on her wide round nipples, teasing them to renewed life. The smell of her flesh and its salty flavour awakened me to a dark new world. Something in me wanted to cry in gratitude, and disgorge at the same time a flood of obscene prayer to the holy cunt.

'You're 'ot as fire,' she murmured, pulling me down to Symons's bed. 'Go on, then, 'ave at it, yer rile 'ighness.'

The invitation was clear. My sceptre was drawn. Her red-haired cock-chafed muff glowed like a mysterious fissure in the cave of Venus, full of fertile promise and amazing revelation. I dove hard into the goddess and drove and drove, and spent my glorious gushing litany of praise in her honour.

XIV

DA LEVERSON'S MESSAGE from the penny-in-the-slot devil stated, quite unequivocably, *Bravery will be required.* And mine? When I inserted my penny and the devil spat forth his communication it said only *Beware*.

'Oh dear,' said Ada subduing the mirth we had shared a moment earlier. Her pale sparkling eyes, usually so mischievous, betrayed a sudden squinting anxiety.

'Written, no doubt, by Henley of the *National Observer*.' The evil little piece of paper stuck to my fingers, and I could not quite bring myself to release it – afraid in some dark superstitious part of me that dropping it into the filthy street would bring even more bad luck. Finally I slipped it into my waistcoat pocket, my evening ruined.

'I must make one further enquiry of the devil,' Ada said, dropping another penny into the machine's gullet, 'for a friend who refuses the advice of mere mortals.' She meant Oscar, of course.

We waited for the prophecy, but none was forthcoming. The devil refused to answer. A sudden gust of wind blew, so strong and piercingly cold that passers-by groaned, and with it came the thick wet snow that had been falling off and on all day, turning the streets to mud.

For a moment Ada looked uncharacteristically discomfited. 'What does one do?' she asked, peering at the machine with helpless alarm as the snowflakes caught on her dark brows and formed drifts in the landscape of her hat.

'You might kick it,' I suggested. That was what I wanted to do.

'Oh, no! One must never—' Then, remembering her manners, her credo of being unfailingly amusing, the Sphinx turned to me with her generous smile. 'When the devil himself goes on strike, Aubrey, striking the devil is never a good idea.'

'No doubt he considers himself a gentleman,' I complained.

'Indeed, yes. And what does a gentleman do when he has been struck? He proposes a duel. And when would I have time to cross swords with the devil?'

We started back for the St James's and the opening night of Oscar's new play, *The Importance of Being Earnest*. It was the eve of St Valentine, 14 February 1895.

Despite the weather the St James's was packed, and a perfumed palpable air of excitement filled the theatre. Oscar's last play, *An Ideal Husband*, had opened only a month before and was playing to capacity at the Haymarket; this one, a farce, was rumoured to be his best, and was billed as 'a trivial comedy for serious people'.

But no one looked very serious that night, despite the in-convenience of the mounting blizzard, and people stared as Mrs Leverson and I, greeting the friends we encountered, made our way through the glittering crowd of first-nighters to her box. Were we not 'close friends' of the celebrated Mr Wilde? Ada, Oscar's adored

'Sphinx', was rumoured to have written *The Green Carnation*, a tittering 'insider's' satire on the inverted Wilde-Douglas set, which had been published the previous autumn. I, of course, had drawn the unforgettable pictures for Oscar's *Salome*. How far I had come, I thought, from that nervous boy meeting Oscar for the first time in Burne-Jones's garden! Here was I, now considered a member of his 'circle', decked out in evening clothes, my toes pinched in pointed patent-leather slippers, carrying an ebony cane, a celebrity in my own right. Mabel, who was doing a walk-on elsewhere, was to join us later.

As Ada, comfortably enthroned, began to receive the stream of young courtiers who surrounded her wherever she went, I slipped out of the box and anxiously paced the corridor, fishing the devil's message out of my vest pocket. *Beware.* Simple and direct. But what was I to beware? There were so many possibilities.

My health was the first consideration. For months I had been feverishly dancing on the precipice, working myself to exhaustion, rarely turning down a social invitation, sleeping fitfully or not at all. Never had I felt so burningly alive, cherished so much the pleasures of success. When I was not holding forth at a smart soirée or spooning up consommé next to a duchess at an elegant dinner-party, I prowled the dark streets of the West End, like a bobbie on a beat in Hell. I consorted with the notorious Count Stenbock, and enjoyed the little museum of erotica hidden away on the upper floor of Smithers's shop in Arundel Street. To satisfy my amatory needs I could always find my pretty plain Penny Plain, though fear of the pox kept me from broaching her sweet little cunt as often as I desired.

Then, the previous November, I had suddenly haemorrhaged, and in a fit of terror allowed myself to be shipped off to Dr Grindrod's Hydropathic Establishment at Malvern Wells. When Death doffs his hat, Father, and smilingly presents his card, you submit to anything, even the torture of a water cure, rather than accept it.

If it is true, as Mr King used to tell us in science class, that the human body is 98 per cent water, then I am certain that by the time I left Dr Grindrod's clinic my personal fluid quotient had increased to 99. The aquatically minded Dr Grindrod was convinced that transmogrifying ailing mortals into mermen and mermaids was the surest road to health.

Groaning with fever, I was submersed in an icy pool and left there, despite my screams and chattering teeth, for what seemed like hours. Other prime examples of diseased flotsam thrashed and floated around me, determined, as I was, to endure Dr Grindrod's unending series of water tortures if only they would lead us to the goddess Hygeia.

A disciple of Priessnitz and the Teutonic school, Dr Grindrod had a predilection for imprisoning his patients in small enclosed chambers where he could more conveniently observe their discomfort. In one such chamber, my burning, aching body was suddenly bombarded with stinging jets of ice water. In another, called the compressed-air bath, I and a dozen others were forced to sit in an iron closet as the good doctor, peering at us through a glass panel, increased the air pressure half an atmosphere until our eyes bulged.

Wrapped in damp towels, I would be wheeled out to dehumidify in the freezing open air, and made to choke down food that was indistinguishable from a poultice. And through it all, while being dosed with pusatillas of the twelfth potency and duodecillionths of ipecacuanha grains, I was forced to consume bucketfuls of the warm chalky Malvern waters, whose curative effects, according to Dr Thompson, who owned a share of the clinic, rivalled those of Evian and Apollinaris.

But lying in my room at night, cut off from my friends, fretting about my work, listening to the hollow graveyard coughs and sudden cannon-shot belches of my diseased and dyspeptic compatriots, I became frantic, and thought only of escape. I loathe all sanatoria and clinics, for they seem to me like animated charnel-houses, and I preferred to die at my drawing-table, surrounded by what I loved, rather than in some wet lonely water-closet.

After two weeks I left the clinic, despite Dr Grindrod's admonitions, and returned to the acrid fogs of London. Oh, the teeming majesty of it all! The noise and trance-inducing bustle of the great metropolis! The strange ingredients that bubbled in London's rank wonderful stew, waiting to be fished out and savoured! The joy of being amongst the living instead of the half-dead!

Dr Thompson said positively that there was no disease, and that if I rested at home I could get quite well. But I did not rest, I could not, for Volume IV of *The Yellow Book* was due in January, and my other commissions required immediate attention as well.

Was this what I should beware? The nervous strain of too much work on my health? If that were so, why did I now feel so well? So well, in fact, that I had spent part of the Christmas holidays with Max at Windermere, and was considering an offer to accompany Lane to New York the following April, there to give a series of lectures on my work.

You will no doubt call attention to the moral error of my attempt to interpret the penny-in-the-slot devil's warning that night, and ascribe it to a misguided and unholy superstition. But, in fact, it acted as a goad to my conscience, and forced me to examine my recent history in the manner I am relating to you here.

I wondered, for instance, if it was my choice of friends that I was to beware. Would my associations lead me to ruin? I was not unaware, Father, of a certain notoriety that had attached itself to my person. That I had enemies there was no doubt. In the great whispering gallery that is London one is always hearing low-pitched revelations intended for ears other than one's own. I knew, for instance, that Mabel and I were suspected of being lovers. I knew, too, that I was presumed by many to share with certain of my friends a taste for the male bum.

I let them think what they liked, and made no public attempts to defend my character. To the critics I was Weirdsley Daubery, Awfully Weirdley and Daubaway Weirdsley. Well, then? It amused me to give them a leg-up. A hoax I had perpetrated in the last two numbers of *The Yellow Book* had freed me from concern for the critics for ever. Using assumed names, I had published two drawings executed in a style far less original than the one I was known for; as usual, the critics pounced like hungry locusts on the drawings signed with my real name, mocking and reviling my efforts. The two pseudonymous drawings, on the other hand, were praised. At last I knew that personal spite and not aesthetic criteria moved the pens of my critics.

Beware. Yes, I was trespassing across certain social boundaries, but what is life for, I wondered, if not to experience everything one can? Those who stepped deeper into the forbidden possibilities of experience were the ones who intrigued me the most. One such, of course, was Count Stenbock.

Count Eric Magnus Andreas Harry Stenbock had a face as flat as Estonia, his place of birth. He had been brought up in England, at Thirlestaine Hall near Cheltenham, studied at Wiesbaden until he was seventeen, and then gone up to Oxford, where his gifts for poetry blossomed. The Queen's Jubilee moved him to write a set of popular verses which began: 'There is a thing which no one knows/How the Queen looks without her clothes.' He had also paid Hatchard's to publish two melancholy volumes of pederastic love-poems.

Practising debauchery from a very early age, the Count had perfected his methods during a sojourn at his estates in Kalk, and was a confirmed werewolf, or so he claimed, by the time he returned to London in 1887.

Werewolves are transformed by the moon; Count Stenbock was transformed by opium and alcohol. Secret rites of all kinds were what he lived for; witchcraft and demonology the topics he preferred to discuss. Occultists, I have since learned, are prone to moroseness, if not downright gloom, but Count Stenbock took this propensity to its farthest limits: he was in love with Death itself.

By the time Mabel and I made his acquaintance he had published two cheerful stories – 'The Shadow of Death' and 'Studies of Death' – in Bosie Douglas's *Spirit Lamp* at Oxford, and had become a public invert of the most amazing stripe. His thin yellow locks were regularly curled and worn shoulder-length, and his sartorial colour schemes could be judged successful only by their flaming excess. A green suit with an orange silk shirt and a loose red tie could not but excite interest.

After attending one or two of our Thursday at-homes, the Count invited us to dine with him. His home, at 21 Gloucester Walk, had been purchased, I believe, with an eye to the nearby barracks in Regent's Park.

We had heard that the Count was a zoolatrist, but this had not prepared us for the menagerie that joined us for dinner. An enormous tortoise painfully inched its way around the carpets, ignoring the excited yaps of a dachshund named Trixie, and a chattering smelly monkey decked out in a Slavic costume leaped back and forth from the sideboard to the table, snatching food from our plates and shitting in the soup-tureen. Count Stenbock unperturbedly ate his milk-sopped bread – a diet imposed upon him by a seriously enlarged liver – as an eight-foot snake slithered around his neck and chest.

'You've hardly touched your food, Miss Mabel,' the Count said at the end of the fourth course.

'Forgive me, but I am not terribly hungry,' Mabel said, prising the monkey's hand from her ear-ring.

'More wine?'

'Yes, please.'

'I wonder, has either of you ever celebrated a Black Mass?' he asked as our wine-glasses were refilled.

'Have *you?*' Mabel countered.

The Count's gelid, heavily lidded eyes dropped, and he let out a small high-pitched laugh. 'Do you think, Miss Mabel, that I could ever pray to a God who created something like me?' His thick jewelled fingers stroked the snake slowly slithering around his neck. 'I wonder – would you care to see my aesthetic chambers?'

He led us up to a suite of rooms at the top of the house. The sitting-room, papered in a hellish red, was furnished with oriental cushions, thick patterned Persian rugs, and a variety of monstrous-looking hothouse plants. Mabel, peering into a large aquarium, gasped when she saw that it was filled with toads and horned lizards. In the bedroom, painted peacock-blue, the Count bade us be seated. 'It's quite all right,' he said to Mabel, whose experience of male boudoirs was limited to mine. 'I promise I shan't eat you.'

What he intended to eat was opium, and as he prepared his pipes I wandered about the room taking stock of its contents. A bronze statue of Eros stood in one corner, behind a brazier that burned a heavy scented resin. Aesthetic paraphernalia of the sort that Oscar had championed in the eighties, but which was now *passé*, added to the morose languor of the place. Naturally I was drawn to the bookcases, where I saw several volumes of *Sittengeschichte*, those enormous pseudo-pornographic tomes which are such a curious speciality of the Germans, as well as books of a more openly erotic nature: *Gynecocracy*; a *Narrative of the Adventures and Psychological Experiences of Julian Robinson (afterwards Viscount Ladywood) under Petticoat Rule, Randiana; or, Excitable Tales, The Convent School; or, Early*

Experiences of a Young Flagellant, Teleny; or, The Reverse of the Medal; A Physiological Romance of Today. Many of the books I recognized from Smithers's shop in Arundel Street.

'What is that?' Mabel asked, pointing to a design painted on the ceiling over Count Stenbock's bed.

'A pentagram,' he said. 'It keeps the evil spirits at bay.'

'Are there many evil spirits in Regent's Park?' Mabel asked.

'My dear, they are legion.' When we politely declined his offer of opium, the Count sighed and lit his first pipe. He had, at dinner, quaffed an enormous amount of wine, and his face was greenishly mottled, as though some preliminary rot were taking possession of his flesh.

The Count's elaborate mirrored toilette-table was covered with flagons of the powerful scents with which he liked to douse himself, as well as other curious ointments and unguents. Mabel was examining this stock of feminine oddments when she caught sight of something in the mirror and whirled around with a cry of surprise. 'There's a creature in that corner!' she ejaculated.

There was indeed. In my initial fear I thought it was a homunculus conjured during one of the Count's Black Masses. Dressed in evening clothes, it was lying on the floor beside the Count's bed.

Count Stenbock, sinking into the netherworld of opium dreams, was rather startled by Mabel's outburst, but began to laugh when he realized what it was that had frightened her. 'Have I not introduced you?' he said, pulling the manikin – for that is what it was – beside him on the bed. 'This is *le petit comte*, my son and heir. When I die, he will inherit everything I own.' The doll was amazingly life-like, handsome as the Count was not. 'I created him,' the Count said, stroking the doll's black hair. 'He accompanies me when I travel.'

And I, too, began to accompany Count Stenbock, not often, not everywhere, and generally late at night, when the first round of London's night-time revelries had ended, and the next, darker round was about to begin. Neither his painfully engorged liver nor his chronic spermatorrhoea nor his constitutionally melancholy temperament was allowed to interfere with his search for suitably unsuitable entertainments. The Count was interested to a degree in amatory unorthodoxy.

When, in a club, he ordered 'a boy' one could never be certain if it were a male youth or a bottle of champagne he was requesting. Often it was both. The Count, despite his title and wealth, revered the sons of toil, and was amazingly democratic in his tastes. He sought out the company of Guardsmen, dockworkers, sailors, navvies, the stronger and more abusive types being his favourites, and savoured the discipline of the birch, especially when it was administered by his inferiors. Indeed, merely thinking about a little amorous *fessée* sent a delicious tingle of apprehension down to his flabby buttocks. I look back now, from my bed in St-Germain, and wonder if it was audacity or a fascination with perversity that led me to join him.

It was not that I participated, Father, but I did look on, in a kind of greedy stupefied wonder, as he made his sad debased way about London, reeking of scent, his thin yellow curls hanging flaccidly about his flat, ugly Slavic face.

One night, at his suggestion, we dressed in shabby labourer's clothes and bought caps near the docks so that we could wander freely through the rank dangerous warren of streets in Limehouse. It was a curious thrill to discard identity and see life as it really was, in all its coarse brutality. Count Stenbock took me to a low filthy inn called the Failure, a particular favourite of his, and there I watched as he purchased a supply of opium and consorted with the natives.

There were other adventures, sordid and thrilling at the same time, and I witnessed the steady advancement of his depravities until they ceased to fascinate and began instead to depress me. There came a time when at last I saw clearly that Count Stenbock was no more than a rich, miserable, talentless fop who hid behind his bizarre affectations like a child hiding behind his mother's protective skirts. Anyone with sufficient means may cultivate exotic and forbidden experiences for their own sake; the French call this *le culte du moi*; but lying here in the bitter shreds of my own life and ruined reputation I have learned that experience means nothing if it isolates one from one's fellow-man.

Count Stenbock flirted with pain and Death because life held no joy for him; life held no joy because he had nothing to offer it. He sought annihilation in opium and alcohol because every time he sat down at his crowded toilette-table and looked into the mirror he saw reflected the *horror vacui* of his existence: no reflection at all. Whilst I, who knew the terrain of the Valley of the Shadow quite intimately, had no desire to join the other shades in their endless procession to nowhere. Death kept my ambition on the move.

It was in the midst of these private cogitations prompted by the penny-in-the-slot devil's communication that I ran into Bobbie Ross, quite out of breath and with an anxious look on his permanently worried face.

'Aubrey!' he exclaimed, shaking my hand. 'Have you seen Oscar?'

I said that I hadn't and asked him why he was so agitated.

'You've not heard? Oh, my dear, such ructions!'

The Marquess of Queensberry, Bosie Douglas's mad violent father, had earlier appeared at the theatre with a giant bouquet of vegetables, which he was planning to hurl at Oscar during his curtain speech. Luckily Oscar heard about it in time and was able to have Queensberry stopped at the box office and refused admittance. Oscar was terrified, apparently, because Queensberry, convinced that his son was being publicly corrupted, and furious over Bosie's inability to take a university degree, which he blamed on Oscar, had made a number of threats over the past several months, and had even had Bosie and Oscar trailed by private detectives. Bosie, quite as mad as his progenitor, had done everything in his power to incense the Marquess. 'I shouldn't be surprised if it ended in a duel!' Bobbie said.

'It's difficult to imagine Oscar with a pistol,' said I.

'I meant a duel between Bosie and his father,' Bobbie said. 'Bosie has taken to carrying a revolver around with him.'

He quickly related to me the curious recklessness that had taken possession of Oscar; not that I hadn't heard the rumours myself. 'He refuses to listen to his friends, and treats it all as a kind of dangerous game,' Bobbie reported.

'But, Bobbie, life *is* a dangerous game. You of all people should know that.'

'Yes, yes, but Oscar is being careless. A game has certain rules.

A man in his position, at the very pinnacle of his career, must be concerned for his public reputation.'

The five-minute bell rang, and Bobbie and I parted amidst a crush of box-holders making their way to their seats. I was about to enter Ada's box when I heard Oscar's voice from within.

'. . . allow a boor and a bully like Queensberry dictate my conduct?'

'Yes,' came Ada's murmured reply. 'I have been hearing some rather unpleasant stories about him.'

'The man is utterly mad, which of course explains his mania for eugenics. Those with tainted blood are always the first to insist on the need for proper breeding.'

Ada made an indistinct response, and then asked if Oscar had seen the latest number of *The Yellow Book*.

'Yes, dull and loathsome; a great failure, I'm happy to say.'

'Then, you did not approve of my story in it?'

'Forgive me, Sphinx, I'm certain your story was brilliant. I only hope that Aubrey Beardsley did not provide an illustration for it.'

'It was he who asked me to contribute,' Ada replied. 'You were once fond of Aubrey, were you not?'

My ears burned as I heard Oscar say: 'I invented Aubrey Beardsley. He would be nothing without the notoriety he achieved at my expense. Yet have I once been asked to contribute to this malarial *Yellow Book*, by this board of editorial adolescents who learned about Art from me?'

The rumour, then, was true. Oscar was boasting that he had 'invented' me. I had heard of this from others, but assumed it to be malicious gossip. Their voices dropped again, or perhaps I could not hear them for the rage that coursed through my veins. Finally Oscar said: 'You know how I am always superstitious on opening nights. Today I went to see Mrs Robinson the palmist.'

'What did she say?'

' "I see a very brilliant life for you up to a certain point. Then I see a wall. Beyond the wall I see nothing." ' He gave a curious mirthless laugh.

'London is a dangerous place for you just now.'

'Yes, my dear Sphinx, London is very dangerous. Writters come out at night and writ one, the roaring of creditors towards dawn is frightful, and solicitors are getting rabies and biting people.'

'*Fin de siècle*,' said Ada.

'*Fin du monde*, Sphinx.'

'You have many enemies just now. Your boys provide ammunition for your critics—'

'I know what you are trying to tell me, Sphinx. But I would sooner have fifty unnatural vices than one unnatural virtue. I want the passion of love to dominate everything in my life. And now, my dear, I must retire backstage.'

'You'll return later, Oscar?'

A rustling. I flew down the corridor and hid myself as Oscar emerged and disappeared down a passageway.

The play, of course, was brilliant – even in my simmering fury I could see that. Never had wit and paradox been taken to such hilarious and absurd heights. The audience began to laugh almost as soon as the curtain rose, and before long the playhouse was roaring. Oscar had triumphed with his trivial comedy.

Mabel, her cloak soaked through, her hat dripping, the hem of her gown spattered with mud, her evening slippers quite ruined, joined us towards the end of the first act. 'What beastly weather!' she moaned. Beside Ada, calm and dry and sparkling in her satin and diamonds, poor besmirched Mabel looked like a dishevelled flower-seller – and knew it. 'The snow has blocked all the streets, and it was simply impossible to find a cab.'

Just as she was about to take a seat Oscar entered the box.

'Oh, you mustn't sit on the same chair as Aubrey, my dear,' he said. 'It's not compromising.'

His physical presence was always overwhelming, but never more so than that night when he was at the zenith of his popularity. Bronzed to the colour of clay from his recent sojourn in Algeria (where Bosie had remained), his hair waved, white gloves in hand, wearing a coat with a black velvet collar, and with an array of seals on a black moiré watch-ribbon hanging from his white waistcoat, he towered above us like some ancient emperor in modern dress – a *nouveau* Nero. A green carnation – symbol of his cult – blossomed in his buttonhole; two emerald rings flashed on the little fingers of his manicured hands.

'What a contrast the two are,' he said, surveying Mabel and me with a coy smile as he puffed nervously on a gold-tipped cigarette. 'Mabel a sweet fresh daisy, and Aubrey – dear Aubrey – the most monstrous of hothouse orchids.'

I forced myself to be civil, but my tone must have betrayed the true nature of my sentiments. 'Congratulations, Oscar. You look as though you might crow at any moment.'

'I never crow,' said Oscar, 'I swan.'

Ada, who usually enjoyed and encouraged raillery, perhaps sensed the friction between us and redirected Oscar's attention to where he most enjoyed it: himself. 'What curious rings, Oscar. They appear to be covered with symbols of some kind.'

'This,' he said, raising his left hand, 'is the cabbalistic sign of all joy, and this' – flashing the emerald on his right hand – 'the symbol of all misfortunes.'

'Are you not tempting fate, then, by wearing the one on the right?' Ada asked.

'One needs misfortunes to live happily, Sphinx, just as one needs joy to understand sorrow.'

'I'm afraid I missed the first act,' said Mabel. 'Has your new play a philosophy?'

'Yes – that we should treat all trivial things seriously, and all the serious things in life with a sincere and studied triviality. My goal, really, is simply to make dialogue as brilliant as possible.'

Dear Mabel, ever loyal to my cause, asked if Oscar had seen *my* brilliant drawings in the most recent *Yellow Book*.

He wavered for a moment before answering. 'Absinthe is to all other drinks what Aubrey's drawings are to other pictures. It stands alone. It shimmers like southern twilight in opalescent colouring.'

'Adorably sweet of you to say so, Oscar, but I really have no great care for colour. My art, like my life, is a tension between black and white.'

'Absinthe is just like your drawings, Aubrey. It gets on one's nerves and is cruel. Baudelaire called his poems *Fleurs du mal*. I shall call your drawings *Fleurs du péché* – flowers of sin.'

'I know *péché* when I hear it, Oscar.'

'Yes, dear Aubrey is always *too* Parisian. He can never forget that he has been to Dieppe – once.'

'I believe,' said Ada, 'that the curtain is about to go up. Oscar, will you stay here for the next act?'

'Did you tell Oscar about his fortune?' I asked Ada, knowing how superstitious he was, and went on before she could reply: 'Mrs Leverson consulted the Devil on your behalf before we came in.'

'The Devil?'

'He refused to answer,' I said, 'but here, take mine.' I dug out my fortune and handed it to him. Our hands briefly touched.

Oscar quickly read the message, smiled, and tore it in two, handing half of it back to me. 'Friends should always share, Aubrey,' he said with elaborate courtesy. 'When it comes to bad news, one should never be selfish.' He bowed to Mabel, kissed Ada's hand, and was gone.

The memory of that night remains with me for ever, Father, haunting me with its presentiments of the catastrophe that was to destroy us two months later. The raging blizzard without, the glittering crowd within; the sense of danger lurking in an overripe atmosphere, of demons being spawned and released by our own wilful actions. It was the height of civilization and the end of civilization, the shining moment of triumph when the public stands in homage to its artists – before tearing them to bits.

At the time I did not see it in this way. It was simply another first night – a time to see and be seen, flatter and be flattered. But there was one thing that set it apart even then: from that time forward I regarded Oscar Wilde as my enemy. His claim to having 'invented' me grew like a tumour in my soul; the more I thought about it – and I thought about it incessantly – the larger and more disfiguring it grew. I attempted to lance it, to lance *him*, in caricatures; and when his name came up in conversation, as it always seemed to, my tongue became forked and poisonous.

Through the next two months I worked at my usual feverish pace, preparing Volume V of *The Yellow Book*, and even went so far as to begin a play with Brandon Thomas, author of the popular

Charlie's Aunt, hoping in this way to prove myself Oscar's equal in wit and stagecraft. He, of course, was one of the play's leading characters, lampooned as a fraud, and Mabel was to have a leading role.

My social obligations continued apace. I regularly met the Rhymers, and publishing magnates, and attended the theatre or caroused in the music-halls with Max and Billy Rothenstein. Our Thursday at-homes were by now popular enough to attract a whole new stratum of society.

Mabel, now a PB (Professional Beauty, Father), was developing a reputation of her own, though it did not lead to as many professional engagements as we hoped. I worked incessantly on her behalf, using my name as bait, and she tirelessly made the rounds of theatre managers' offices and cultivated as many high-placed theatrical people as possible. But no important roles were forthcoming, and the small ones filled her with despair because they were generally so poorly written.

When she did find work, she inevitably found herself cast as a brittle Modern Woman with advanced views, a rich man's spoiled mistress, or a scheming trollop. To salve her wounded *amour-propre* she adopted a rather nervous, high-flown manner, but she tempered this – at least, among our closest frends – with a growing delight in telling risqué stories when Mother was not with us, or was out of earshot.

Surrounded by a crowd of young, adoring, but maritally unavailable men, she would make them rock with laughter as she related, for instance, a story involving Sarah Bernhardt:

'The Divine Sarah, when Paris rejected her, wisely took herself off to reap the fame and fortune that foreign places can provide. Thus she found herself in Brazil, where she enjoyed a success far greater than any she had known in her homeland. The students adored her, and unhitched her carriage so that they could drag it themselves from the theatre to her hotel. Once there they formed an honour guard along the staircase, and made a carpet for her with their jackets. "Pizez là-dessus!" they cried, which in their Brazilian accent means "Put your feet here". Sarah, however, thought they were saying, 'Pissez là-dessus" – "Piss here" – and was so astonished by their request that she could only murmur in reply: "Dear boys, that is something I reserve exclusively for the Paris newspapers." '

There were many pleasures in those two precious months that remained of my reputation. We were often, Mabel and I, in the company of Ada Leverson, whom I adored despite her intimacy with Oscar. Dear Ada, renowned for her lively wit, brilliant parodies, and abundant intelligence, sought out the more exotic fauna of London to grace her salons and *soirées musicales*, and moved with ease amid the various warring tribes of the metropolis. She reverenced superior minds, but had a curious propensity for falling in love with wayward men who could never make her happy. Her husband, Ernest, twelve years older than she, was a humourless bore who worked in the City and generally ignored her. Ada had long since ceased to love him, but she was unequal to the task of making him unhappy; and, although for all intents and purposes they lived separate lives, a separation was unthinkable because of her horror of scandal.

Not long after the opening night of Oscar's play, Ada sent round a note inviting me to tea. We were quite intimate by then and enjoyed exchanging secrets and confidences. She had recently moved from Courtfield Gardens in South Kensington to an exquisite little Regency house in Deanery Street, Mayfair. There, in her blue and white drawing-room decorated with silk fans painted by Charles Conder and bowls of smilax and carnations, Ada greeted me.

She was wearing a white chiffon tea-gown edged in sable, and a rather melancholy, enigmatic smile. Her hair, though beautifully curled, was never abundant; and there was, too, because of her heavy dark brows, a masculine cast to her face when you studied it in isolation: not manly, but boyish – and of boys Ada was particularly fond. Her own had died, and perhaps that was why she always welcomed me with such direct openheartedness.

'You look positively *ravissante*, my dear,' I said.

'Oh?' She coloured with pleasure and stroked the sable of her gown. 'In what sense – ravishing or ravenous?'

'I suppose it depends on how hungry you are.'

'I'm quite famished,' she said, pouring out the tea and dismissing the maid.

'And – forgive me – somewhat *triste*?'

Ada sighed. 'Nothing is as important to happiness as the temper of those we live with.'

'Ernest again?'

'How wicked of you to guess. Ernest is a remarkable man, you know. He cares nothing for me until something goes wrong; and then, when it does, he finds me an indispensable conduit for his rage.'

'Money?'

She shrugged. 'I suppose so. One never knows with Ernest.' Suddenly she laughed, the sound low and mysteriously feminine. 'He's quite mad on electricity these days and is constantly going to a doctor for shocks.'

'What ails him?' I asked.

'What ails so many people these days?' Ada said, rising and pacing to the window. Outside there was a steady clatter from the hansom cabs and carriages that used Deanery Street as a short cut to Park Lane. 'Can it be put into words? Some queer sense of devitalization, of fear even, as this old century grinds to its conclusion.'

'Do you fear it?'

'I?' She turned to me with that same curious smile. 'Nothing tires me more than the doomsayers. One can find fault with every age, for every age has its faults. Is it not more important to live while we live?'

'Yes, to taste everything we can in the short time given to us.'

The last of the early-spring light was pouring through the window, clear and bright and hopeful. I thought in that moment that I should like to live for ever as I was living now. Ada came round behind me where I sat and put her hands on my shoulders. What beautiful hands they were: perfectly useless for the meaner tasks of life.

'I shall always be grateful to you, Aubrey,' she said.

'Whatever for?'

'For asking me to contribute to *The Yellow Book*. I think you don't know what it meant to me to be asked. To be able to sign my name to my work after years of enforced anonymity. You and Oscar have both helped me to define myself as a writer.'

The moment I heard his name coupled with mine I rose from the divan and walked away from her.

'Aubrey?' She came to my side, stood close, looked up at me with trepidation. 'Have I said something to upset you?'

'No,' I lied. 'Nothing.'

Again she touched me – this time tracing a line along my ear. 'I think you are one of the most attractive men I have ever known.'

'That, my dear Ada, is only because you've never seen me naked.'

She was startled, but that was what she loved; to be shocked out of the complacency of her class and sex. I could sense that she was aroused, for she drew in her breath and moved closer. 'If I were to see you naked, I might find you even more attractive than you are clothed.'

'Clothes make the man, my dear.'

'And removing them makes the lover.' She was suddenly in my arms, looking up at me with a tender, trusting, compliant expression. 'Would you believe it, Aubrey, my husband can execute the entire sexual act without kissing me once?'

'Perhaps he's been shocked once too often,' I said.

'Or not shocked enough.'

Her eyes drew me in like a net, and those red lips were offered in a way I could not refuse. The wise, witty, wealthy Ada melted in my embrace. When I left Deanery Street an hour later, Oscar's Sphinx had one more secret.

I suppose there is some unwritten natural law that the depth of one's fall is commensurate with the height of one's ascent. The higher one climbs, the deeper one plummets. For a moment we are allowed to sip the nectar of the gods and breathe the crystalline air of the empyrean; having done so, we are tossed to the dung-heap, slaughtered like sheep. What a curious network of cause and effect rules our lives, Father. Laws we rightfully scorn suddenly scorn us. At times there even seems to be some inevitable pattern to it all – but, if there is, it is only that genius must suffer so that mediocrity can triumph.

Father, even you will know the story of Oscar's sudden nightmarish downfall – at least, as it was reported by the newspapers. In the spring of 1895, London became the scene of a spectacular *auto-da-fé*. People demanded sacrifice. There was a blind consensus that some inner corruption – personified by Oscar Wilde – was eating away the moral fabric of English civilization, and that it must be excised, destroyed before it spread further. That, on the face of it, was the justification for what transpired. But, in fact, the whole sorry story was nothing more than the blood malice of two madmen – a father and his son – that was conveniently transformed into a 'cause'.

As the events began to unfold and the warring camps began their manoeuvres, I found myself, somewhat to my surprise, sympathetic towards Oscar. In March he had taken rooms at the Avondale Hotel in Piccadilly, where Bosie Douglas proceeded to run up yet another enormous bill and even insisted that Oscar put up a new boy at his expense. When Oscar refused, Bosie accused him of cowardice – his favourite taunt – and moved out. The Marquess of Queensberry, like a dog who has scented blood, then appeared at Oscar's club, the Albemarle, and left a card accusing Oscar of 'posing as a somdomite'. This public – if misspelled – accusation forced Oscar into a corner. If he did nothing, Queensberry's allegation would be broadcast as true, and Oscar subject to arrest. If he sued for libel to protect his name, he would have to prove that the allegation was false.

The story comes from Bobbie, who was present at each important juncture. Oscar, having received Queensberry's accusation, returned to the Avondale determined to flee to Paris. But, thanks to Bosie's spendthrift ways, Oscar could not pay the hotel bill. Indeed, he had no money at all, and his luggage was impounded by the management. There followed a midnight meeting with Bobbie, who told Oscar to take no action. Together, Bobbie and Bosie went the following day to Humphreys, the solicitor, to see what could be done. The despicable Bosie was overjoyed – at last his hated father had put something in writing, and could be prosecuted.

Humphreys took Bosie's side. Bosie insisted that his brother, Lord Douglas of Hawick, and his mother, Lady Queensberry, would pay all court costs and, like his father, forced Oscar into a corner. He accompanied Oscar to Marlborough Street police station where Oscar signed his life away by swearing out a warrant for Queensberry's arrest on the charge of publishing a libel.

Edward Carson, once Oscar's fellow-student at Trinity College, Dublin, was retained as Queensberry's barrister. He told Queensberry that the case was too weak and further evidence would be required to make Queensberry's plea of justification stick. At this point, two actors who bore a personal grudge against Oscar because he had once made them rehearse on Christmas Day happily supplied information about Oscar's friends. Private detectives hired by Queensberry tracked down a male brothel frequented by Oscar and Bosie, broke in, and found the names and addresses of several boys Oscar had used. The boys were rounded up and, to save their skins, gave evidence against their former benefactor. Oscar and Bosie had no idea what was happening.

Public sentiment against Oscar, even at this early stage, was overwhelming. His friends – Frank Harris and George Bernard Shaw – urged him to drop the case and go with Constance to Paris. Oscar was on the verge of following their advice when Bosie appeared and began to scream at them that they were no friends of Oscar's. Oscar, the poor muddled fool, agreed with Bosie and refused to leave London. He thought he was infallible – until he and Bosie were shown the list of boys. Suddenly it was no longer a trial for libel. Oscar was accused of soliciting a dozen boys to commit sodomy, and in two separate counts he was charged with immorality for publishing *The Picture of Dorian Gray* and a piece called 'Phrases and Philosophies for the Use of the Young'.

The first trial opened at the Old Bailey on 3 April. Bosie, Oscar's insatiable tutor in corruption and the instigator of Oscar's lawsuit, was presented by Carson as a young innocent led dangerously astray by Oscar's domination. What a mockery of the truth! The black-mailing boy-whores were continually referred to as homeless and helpless lads forced to succumb to Oscar's carnal advances against their wishes.

Two days later the Marquess of Queensberry was exonerated and it was ruled that Oscar's being called a sodomite was in the public's interest. His prosecution on charges of gross indecency was thus almost certain. Bobbie told me that the courtroom was filled with cheers when the verdict was read. Oscar had become a target for the mob.

But still he refused to take the advice of his friends and leave the country. Even Queensberry said he would not prevent Oscar's flight – unless Oscar took Bosie with him, in which case Queensberry promised to shoot Oscar 'like a dog'. Instead, Oscar went with Bobbie to the Cadogan Hotel, where Bosie was staying, and drank and vacillated. 'The train is gone,' he mumbled when Bobbie told him to catch the next boat-train to Calais. 'It is too late.'

It was. Early that evening a reporter from the *Star* informed Bobbie that a warrant had been issued for Oscar's arrest. Oscar's face went ashen when Bobbie told him, but he stubbornly settled himself in a chair and said: 'I shall stay and face my sentence, whatever it may be.' An hour later the fateful knock was heard at the door. And then it was that my fate was sealed with Oscar's. Oscar gathered up his stick and gloves and coat and, it was everywhere reported, a copy of *The Yellow Book*. He was handcuffed and led down to the police van.

Outside the Cadogan Hotel pandemonium reigned. A kind of mass hysteria had taken hold of the eagerly waiting crowd. Oscar was called every vile name in the language. Illiterate whores and tramps joined hands, chanting abuse and dancing in the mud. It was a London Walpurgisnacht. And then someone saw what he was carrying. '*A Yellow Book!* The sodomite's got a *Yellow Book*!'

There was no stopping them by now. The fire of their hatred spread throughout the streets of London. A mob gathered outside The Bodley Head in Vigo Street, where *The Yellow Book* was published, and began to hurl stones through the window. The next day the headlines of the papers gleefully proclaimed: 'OSCAR WILDE ARRESTED WITH YELLOW BOOK UNDER HIS ARM.'

John Lane was in New York – on the very excursion I had decided against making – and Harland was on holiday in Paris. When Lane's terrified assistant cabled him that several *Yellow Book* authors under the moral leadership of the mediocre Mrs Humphry Ward demanded my head on a platter, Lane – the coward – acquiesced. I was immediately given the sack from the periodical that I had founded.

Oscar at least had the benefit of a trial – two more trials. I was simply judged and found guilty by association. Suddenly I was an unemployable pariah.

XV

N THAT FIRST moment of calm after a catastrophe, Father, the brain goes blissfully numb. One cannot register the full extent of the cataclysm all at once. Only by terrifying increments does the horror that has befallen reveal itself.

At first I simply refused to believe the news. Even as word of my dismissal spread through scandal-mad London I maintained that a mistake had been made; Lane must see that I had nothing to do with Oscar and his troubles; once the hysteria had died down, surely he would reinstate me as art director and my salary would resume.

But, in fact, the hysteria was not allayed. Instead, it grew to monstrous proportions, fanned by the daily newspapers and popular press. Articles damning *The Yellow Book* as 'the Oscar Wilde of Artistic Quarterlies' and claiming that 'Uncleanliness is next to Bodleyness' sidestepped personal libel but still managed to couple Oscar's name with my own. I refused to respond to this scurrilous misrepresentation until an article appeared in *St Paul's* declaring that Oscar Wilde and Aubrey Beardsley did not represent the glorious traditions of English art since, 'having no manhood', our work was 'effeminate, sexless and unclean'. Sick with anger, I wrote an aggrieved letter to the editor, ending with: 'As to my uncleanliness, I do the best for it in my morning bath, and if your art critic has really any doubts as to my sex, he may come and see me take it.' Of course it did no good, and the letter was never printed.

Meanwhile, Oscar went to trial on charges of gross indecency. It is quite impossible, Father, to convey the atmosphere of London during that time. One half-expected to see witches flying past the chimneypots and people being burned at the stake in Trafalgar Square. People became beasts. Everything that had been progressive and modern in the world of art and literature was suddenly suspect. Those who had never read a story or looked at a picture now fulminated against the vile decadence which had overtaken their culture. Old-fashioned 'wholesome' values were preached from the pulpits. The ruling Philistines saw a 'plot' to undermine their sacrosanct society and demanded a return to the old order.

Panic spread amongst the inverts of London. Today it was Oscar, but who would it be tomorrow? If evidence had been obtained by threats, bribes, blackmail and stolen address-books, who was safe? What other names would come out in cross-examination? Incriminating letters were burned, certain books and well-thumbed journals disposed of, bachelor households dissolved, and hasty marriages arranged. Those who could afford to fled the city. The boat-trains to Calais and Dieppe were filled with nervous gentlemen whose blood turned to ice every time they saw a grim-faced official. Bobbie left, and so did that cowardly Caligula, Bosie Douglas, whose evil machinations had brought all this about. Indeed, half of my friends were suddenly out of the country.

Another ominous event added to my mounting unease, and seemed to foretell even worse events to come. Word came that Count Stenbock had died on the very day of Oscar's first trial, and the two events will be linked in my mind for ever.

Count Stenbock, his yellow curls faded, his face blotched, unable to concentrate for the amount of alcohol and opium he had imbibed, had looked very ill the last time we met, on the eve of his departure to the Riviera. Madness set in almost as soon as he left England; he was racked by terrifying delusions – those demonic creatures he was always trying to invoke in his Black Masses now descended upon his weak fevered brain and tormented him with hellish persistence. He would not be parted from his doll, *le petit comte*, insisting that it was his son and would protect him. In this pathetic condition he was brought back to his mother in Sussex and confined like a madman to his room, with only his monkey as company. By this time, however, he could not live without drink, and after obtaining some he fell into a drunken rage and attacked his stepfather with a poker. Toppling headlong into the grate, he split his head open, and died the same day. The monkey, his fur matted with blood, was found sitting on his master's sunken chest. At last poor Count Stenbock had consummated his marriage with the great love of his life, Death.

On 25 May, Oscar was found guilty of gross indecency, sentenced to two years' hard labour and moved to Pentonville prison. He was forced to walk a treadmill for six hours a day, and to pick oakum until his fingers bled. He went from gold-tipped cigarettes, Trimalchian feasts and champagne to a meagre daily ration of rancid skilly; from luxurious hotel beds to a bare wooden plank; from holding forth with brilliant unrestrained wit in the drawing-rooms of London to brutally enforced silence in a small cold cell: thus was England's greatest living dramatist brought to his knees for the sin of sexual non-conformity. The press was ecstatic.

Oh, I pitied him, Father – yes, quite as much as I hated him – and I hated him from the deepest cavities of my festering soul. And I hated him even more as the consequences of that one damning act – carrying a *Yellow Book* with him to the police van – pitilessly revealed themselves.

The current of my previously hectic social life ebbed to less than a trickle. All those fashionable wealthy hosts and hostesses who had besought my presence in their salons and at their supper-tables now ignored me entirely. Publishers who, two months earlier, were willing to pay great sums to have their books graced by my pictures now passed me over in favour of less 'dangerous' artists. Commissions dried up entirely. With no market for my work, I could not work. Each blank sheet of paper taunted me, dared me. My hand faltered.

It seemed best to be away from London when Volume V of *The Yellow Book* appeared. Lane had quickly recalled the entire edition so that my pictures could be purged. Harland was distantly sympathetic, but would do nothing to endanger his own position and continuing salary. From the beginning, of course, *The Yellow Book* had been considered mine, for it was my art that distinguished it and made it so eagerly sought after. Harland's jealousy had been tempered by our enormous success; now he saw his chance to remake *The Yellow Book* in his own bland image. To spare myself further humiliation I went to Paris.

But some vital force had been knocked out of me, and my joy had withered in the frosts of public contempt. The depth of the mob's hatred had shaken me to my roots. Even Paris could not help. All the beauty and civilized grace of that great city meant nothing to one who now stared into the abyss of utter ruin. What was to happen to us? How would I now be able to support Mother and Mabel? I walked the quays, unknown, alone, pondering my fate, and at night frequented the Chat Noir in pursuit of forgetfulness. But I could not forget: as I stared at Willette's wall painting of the Pierrots and Pierrettes descending from the youthful Bohemian gaiety of Montmartre to their final plunge of despair into the darkness of the Seine, I seemed to see a terrible allegory of my own situation.

Worse still, my illness, like some internal vulture feeding on the carrion of despair, began to pluck and scavenge within my body. I could feel it in there, feasting on my lungs with the pleasure of an insatiable *gourmand*. My night fevers returned, my coughing resumed, I was racked by queer sudden pains and a terrifying breathlessness. No amount of tooth powder could erase the sudden pestilential foulness of my breath, which always acts as a barometer to the state of my lungs.

There was nothing for me but to return to London and raise some capital. But from whom? Mabel suggested Marc-André Raffalovich, a rich untalented dilettante whom we had met the previous year. Raffalovich would surely be sympathetic to someone who had been ruined by Oscar Wilde. Oscar, once his lover, was now his worst enemy in the world.

André's house in South Audley Street, Mayfair, had once been pointed out to me by Ada Leverson, who was a neighbour. André was a friend of hers, but this had never prevented her from spearing him on the point of her delightfully barbed tongue, and he had often been a general source of merriment between us.

André, as I have already related, had come to London with his English governess, Miss Gribbell, determined to be a great social success. Unfortunately, for all his cash he had no cachet. When he was not hosting gala soirées, and nervously introducing people to their own husbands and sisters, he liked to preside over 'octets' — eight-course eight o'clock dinner-parties for eight people. His guests, in true London fashion, accepted his lavish hospitality, then mercilessly ridiculed him behind his back.

André was known to me, too, because of Oscar's undisguised contempt for him: 'as ugly as Raffalovich' was how Oscar described anything that displeased his aesthetic sense. Stories of their feuds and Oscar's withering *bons mots* at André's expense regularly flew about London. Before Oscar's imprisonment their mutual loathing had reached the point where André refused to sit next to Oscar at Trumper's, the barber in Curzon Street where they both had their hair cut.

I arrived at South Audley Street early in the morning, having travelled through the night from Paris, only to be informed by the butler that Mr Raffalovich was out on an early call. 'I shall wait, if I may.' The butler showed me to the drawing-room.

The room was exquisite in its understated simplicity, not what I had expected at all. Bouquets of cut flowers, their ripe scents spicing the air, frothed from Japanese vases. Books of a mystical nature, mostly in French, were precisely stacked on a polished rosewood table, a pearl rosary carefully laid out beside them. On one wall, above a rather self-conscious prie-dieu, hung a jewelled crucifix and a collection of valuable Russian icons, the stern unyielding faces of the Fathers of the Church highlighted by gold leaf. Hanging opposite – quite surprisingly, given the sacerdotal air of the room – was a Gustav Moreau watercolour of Sappho. This immediately claimed my full attention, and I was studying it when André entered.

'Mr Beardsley, this is quite a surprise.' André's first language was French, and though he had worked diligently over the years to rid himself of an accent he had not quite succeeded.

'Mr Raffalovich.' He put down the books he was carrying and we shook hands. 'I do hope you'll excuse this intrusion.'

'Do you like the Moreau?' he asked.

'Very much.'

'I cannot yet bring myself to part with it.'

'Why must you?' I asked.

'Let us say that my tastes are changing. Subject-matter that once inspired me no longer does so.'

'You are redecorating your soul,' said I.

He fussed with some flowers. 'One could put it that way.'

He was not quite as affable as I had hoped; remained somewhat distant, almost cold. A small man, he dressed with the severity of a priest and attempted unsuccessfully to hide his effeminate mannerisms with a strict stiff demeanour. André, with his sharp little nose, had the look of a peregrine falcon, and I could not help imagining him with a bit of bloody entrail dangling from his beak. His hair was jet-black, as were his eyes, which shone with a brooding intensity and bespoke the Russian Jewish heritage he had in every other way attempted to eradicate. His smooth tight flesh had the pale yellowish tinge of a lemon ice. Ada had told me that he affected various nervous maladies and used too much glycerine on his face.

'I am sorry I was not here when you arrived, but I had an appointment with Father Sebastian Bowden. Do you know the church of the Jesuit fathers in Farm Street?'

'Where the fair sinners of Mayfair meet? Yes, I know it.'

'That is where I was baptized.' He gestured to a chair, and I sat. 'I am pursuing my religious instruction there. The good fathers have been most helpful to me. Their library is one of the best in London, you know.'

330

'Mr Gray, I understand, is in Berlin.'

By now, everyone in London knew that André had established a strange liaison with the poet John Gray. According to rumour, John Gray had suffered a complete nervous breakdown, even threatened suicide, after his break-up with Oscar. André took him up – and in, providing a smart little house for Gray in nearby Park Lane. Gray had subsequently undergone a religious conversion, become a Roman Catholic, and was now a practising celibate and seriously contemplating entering the priesthood. Miss Gribbell had also converted; and André, third of the Holy Trinity of South Audley Street, went over to Rome not long after she did.

'Yes, we felt it would be for the best,' André said. 'I shall be joining him there in a few days' time.'

'The Continent has suddenly become extraordinarily attractive to unmarried men.'

André studied me for a moment, perhaps trying to gauge my mood. The last thing I wanted was to appear grim and desperate. 'We retained a barrister to hold a watching brief for Mr Gray at the . . . recent trials,' he said. 'Given our past experience with Mr Wilde, it seemed the wisest course of action. So many names named, so many lives ruined on that man's account.'

'Yes, so many,' I said.

'The papers in Europe say, "So this is how you behave to your poets," and the papers in America say, "So this is how your poets behave". Shall I tell you something shocking, Mr Beardsley?'

'Please do.'

'I have not the slightest sympathy for Oscar Wilde. I found him to be a coarse and bloated sensualist, quite lacking in any of the higher spiritual qualities.'

'Oh, come, Mr Raffalovich, Oscar was often so full of spirit that he could not stand straight.'

A humourless man, he refused to smile at my joke. 'This horrid affair has galvanised every level of society. Suspicion and ignorance walk the streets hand-in-hand, thanks to that man. He has set the clock back fifty years.' His face constricted, and I could see a rising tide of bitterness in his lineaments.

'I had hoped that artists at least would stand together in the face of this,' I said.

'True artists, Mr Beardsley, those of us who attempt to instil culture in a society and thereby elevate its tone, are in constant danger of misrepresentation. It takes only one man – one immoral fraud, who was not so much an artist as a vulgar showman – to topple the entire fragile edifice we have so carefully built up.' Was he wearing a corset? He looked most uncomfortable and sat with great care, a pinched look on his face, as though he might explode at any moment. 'Coffee?'

I said no. 'I shall come to the point of my visit, Mr Raffalovich. You have no doubt heard that John Lane has relieved me of my duties as art director of *The Yellow Book*?'

'Ah, *The Yellow Book*,' he said, tapping his fingertips together. 'Yes, Mr Gray and myself had at one time hoped to be included as contributors. Our poems, however, were summarily rejected.'

'Mr Harland was in charge of the literary contents,' I said.

'We found it odd, Mr Gray and I, given our literary reputations, to be passed over in favour of so many mediocre talents.'

I could not let his personal pique stand in my way and plunged on. 'To be quite frank, Mr Raffalovich, I find myself very hard up at the moment. As you know, I have a sister and a mother to support, and now that my salary has gone it has become impossible to make ends meet.'

André ceased tapping his fingers together and began instead an intricate series of hand movements. He pressed his palms flat together, then locked his fingers in what looked like prayer; opening his hands again he stretched his fingers apart and pressed his palms one against the other, back and forth, as though forming something with dough. 'And all because of Oscar Wilde,' he said slowly.

'Yes, unfortunately.'

'I, too, have suffered at the hands of that beast.'

'Of course I shall continue with private commissions, but those are at present somewhat uncertain, and my health is unfortunately not good.'

He narrowed his eyes and pursed his thin lips in what might have been concern or envy. 'Ah, yes, health. My own constitution is a constant source of concern to Mr Gray and Miss Gribbell. I suffer – and I always begrudged my pain until I learned how to offer it up to Christ. That is a secret I have recently learned: unhealthy habits of thought contribute to physical illness.' He gave a delicate cough. 'All the vitalizing magnetic currents in the world, Mr Beardsley, will not, in the end, help a person whose moral will is impaired. Good health begins in the soul.'

'Are you suggesting that my disease is self-imposed?'

He sat for a moment in silence, contemplating me from his chair. 'I have always thought highly of your work, Mr Beardsley,' he said, beginning the hand movements again, 'though I sometimes thought your drawings showed a rather . . . dangerous cleverness, a stylistic tendency towards the obscene.'

'I merely depict life as I see it, the interpretation I leave to others. If my work makes people uneasy, perhaps it is only because it exposes their complicity with their own sexual natures.'

With this he rose and began a circuit about the room, stopping at one point to gaze up at the ferocious portraits of the Fathers of the Church as he surreptitiously plucked at something in his clothing. 'When one accepts Christ as one's saviour, one is forced to refashion one's personal behaviour. One begins to see the world in a new light.'

'And perhaps, in the process, loses one's unique vision,' I countered. 'That which made one an artist in the first place.'

'A Christian artist does not lose his vision, Mr Beardsley; he only enhances it by acknowledging its source.'

'There are many sources, Mr Raffalovich; your own poems, if I may so, have often been inspired less by love of Christian virtue than by love of other men.'

'That is true,' he said, turning to face me. 'I have not yet won my freedom from the snares of the flesh. However, I shall. In time, believe me, I shall.'

'May I count on you for help? Any small commission—'

'Perhaps a sum of money would be more useful to you just now.'

'Yes, but I should like to offer you something in return.'

'That may be possible as well,' he said. 'My new book of poems requires a frontispiece. May I tell the publisher that you will provide it?'

'Of course. It would be an honour.'

André went to his desk and extracted a cheque-book. 'Would twenty guineas be sufficient for now?'

'Thank you.'

333

He tore off the cheque and handed it to me, his dark eyes glowing. 'Artists should stand together in the face of a common threat, Mr Beardsley. When may I see you again?'

'Whenever you like.'

'Soon, then, I hope.'

He stopped me as I was about to leave. 'May I ask one of the priests from Farm Street to call on you, Mr Beardsley?'

'No priests, Mr Raffalovich. Not yet.'

'Then, I shall pray to the Blessed Virgin for you.'

'Thank you,' I said. 'And when you pray would you kindly do so at the top of your voice?'

I suppose one is always looking for consolation, some soothing balm to reduce the endless frets and miseries of existence, and to disguise its more naked horrors. André found his consolation in God. I looked for mine in the pleasures of the flesh, and filled my glass as often as I could with the wine of forgetfulness.

Once I had not cared tuppence for what people thought of me. I had even enjoyed letting them think that I was an invert, for in that fleeting halcyon period before Oscar's trials there was a tacit belief in the art world – at least, amongst the fashionable and the educated – that inverts constituted a special artistic class and set the most advanced standards. There was acceptance, sympathy, curiosity and, with these, an increasing willingness amongst inverts themselves to come out from behind the cloak of secrecy and stand in the full light of day.

All that had changed. People scurried back into their holes, not wishing to confront the fury of the mob. In the end it is the mob that rules us. Once I had not minded; now it was intolerable to be unfairly damned and branded as less than a man, as something sexless and unclean. When André's publisher rejected my frontispiece because it contained a nude male Amor, I knew that one phase of my artistic life was over; everything I drew was now suspect, assumed to contain hidden messages and inducements to sin.

I was trapped and I knew it. Drawing – the one thing that had always given me the greatest pleasure and shielded me from the mockery of the world – was no longer possible. By deadly increments I descended into a pit of despair.

I wanted to defend myself, but how could I? To whom? Only the whores parading along the Strand offered me the opportunity to prove my manhood. Drunk, feverish, pale, coughing, I pursued them with an insatiable and perpetually unsatisfied lust. Penny Plain became my consort as often as I had half a crown to spare; gone for ever were the days of golden sovereigns pressed into an amazed strumpet's dirty palm.

Drink fuddled me, but I drank, and when I drank I whored, and when I whored my prick stood stiff, and when my prick stood stiff I could, for a few moments anyway, attack my attackers.

A few times I went off my head completely. One bleary morning, after a night of debauched forgetting, I turned up at Yeats's door in Bloomsbury with Penny Plain. I was drunk, and my mind was running obsessively upon my dismissal from *The Yellow Book*. Yeats, pen in hand, was in his dressing-gown but invited us in.

' 'e's in a state,' said Penny Plain, advancing towards the solid security of an overstuffed chair. 'Oh, me poor bleedin' 'ead.'

'You're working,' I said to Yeats in an accusatory tone. 'I am not. My drawings – you've no doubt heard – are sexless and unclean, not fit to be published anywhere, by anyone.'

Yeats was obviously disturbed by our untimely intrusion but did his best to make us welcome. With his long dressing-gown, embroidered with what looked like cabbalistic designs, greasy unkempt hair, and gold pen, he looked like one of my own drawings of Merlin in *Le Morte D'Arthur*. 'I was defending you last night,' he said, 'in the only way it is possible to defend you, by saying that all you draw is inspired by rage against iniquity.'

'Even if it were so inspired,' I said, 'the work would be in no way different. Willy, I shall never draw again!'

'Nonsense,' said he.

'Is it?'

'And, even if it were true, the work you have already done will never be forgotten. You have never done anything to equal your Salome with the head of John the Baptist. That one work alone—'

'Salome!' I groaned, reminded of Oscar and the chaos he had caused

335

in my life. In my drink-sodden state all the loathing I felt for Oscar gathered itself up into a bitter poisonous lump that pressed against my brain. Then and there I began to curse Oscar, curse my fate, curse life. 'When I was a child I was a musical prodigy!' I cried. 'When I walked into a room people stared at me! I still need to be stared at!'

'Leave off,' complained dear tarnished Penny, holding her head as though it would topple from her shoulders. 'You think you're the only one in this world who's got problems? The 'ole bleedin' world's got problems!'

But I had seen a mirror and moved unsteadily towards it, determined to see the truth of my reflection in the light of day. God, what an appalling image confronted me there! My immaculate person gaunt and dishevelled, my eyes red and sunken, my wasted flesh green with putrefaction. 'Yes, yes, I *look* like a sodomite,' I said, 'but I am not that. I am not that!'

Penny Plain cackled from her chair; and Yeats, dear man, came up and put a sympathetic hand on my shoulder.

'Willy, we are losing our house,' I said. 'We are losing everything.'

On a rainy afternoon in June I sat in my bare studio staring out of the window in a kind of exhausted trance. The house was no longer ours, and we were splitting up. Mother and Mabel were going to lodgings in nearby Charlwood Street, and I had found cheap furnished rooms in Chester Terrace. Everything, it seemed, was at an end, and I went about the grim business of life as if I were attending to the details of my own funeral. That, I was certain, could not be distant. The haemorrhages had returned, and I was spitting blood – *chucking a ruby*, as we lungers say.

'Aubrey?' Mabel knocked and came in carrying a wrapped parcel. 'Another package from André Raffalovich.'

'You open this one. I am too tired.'

'Divine-looking chocolates,' Mabel said, trying to tempt me.

'Have the carters removed everything?'

'All the rooms are bare. The new tenant can move in at once.'

'Mabel – I'm sorry – about the house.'

She came to my side, caressed my hair. 'There's nothing dis-honourable about moving back to lodgings.'

'I had hoped this would be our home. Finally. Something that belonged to us, where we could do our work and live our lives as we pleased.'

'We've had two years of happiness,' Mabel said. 'I shan't forget. Thursday at-homes, passing tea and cakes to every smart young man in London. And the look on Mother's face when you had your studio painted bright orange and black.'

'And our Christmas tree. I wonder if we shall ever have another Christmas tree.'

Mother, grimly officious in her apron, joined us. 'Aubrey, the most beautiful flowers have just arrived from Goodyear's. Here is the card.'

'I know who they are from.'

'Mr Raffalovich,' said Mother. 'He has become a generous friend very quickly, yet you've told me almost nothing about him.'

'There's nothing to tell, Mother, except that he's as rich as Croesus and an artist must never discourage the attentions of a potential patron. Especially an artist who suddenly has no patrons at all.'

Suddenly she began to weep, and then Mabel, too, burst into tears. And though I, the responsible party, was too sick and exhausted to weep I felt a keen sense of failure and humiliation at letting them down. Poor Mother had come to love the excitement of our lives; the suppressed Bohemian in her nature, the girl who wanted to enjoy life, had blossomed in the last two years – only, in the end, to be trampled down once again. The common ruin we now faced reminded her of the grinding misery she had endured with my father, and would have to endure again, perhaps until the end of her days. Such pleasure it had given me, to provide her with a home and money. I think my heart ached more for her and Mabel – cast adrift in this sea of scandal and penury – than for myself.

'I must go find Nip,' Mabel said, drying her eyes.

When we were alone, Mother said: 'Forgive me, dear. This is not a time for tears.'

'Mother.' I drew her close and put my arms around her. She smelled of soap and polish. 'I promise I shall make it up to you.'

'There is nothing to make up, Aubrey. What is important now

is that you rest and get well. I know this has been a trying time for you. Your health has suffered because of it.' She sighed and went to open the wndow, staring out at the rain with a look of such terrible sadness that I wanted to cry out at the injustice of life, the bitterness of fate. Downstairs I could hear Mabel calling her cat. 'Tea,' said Mother firmly, turning to me with a smile. 'Before we leave, we shall have a proper tea. You would like that, wouldn't you?'

I nodded and watched her leave. A moment later Nip, Mabel's black cat, appeared in the doorway and stared at me with accusing eyes. I tried to coax him over to me. 'Well, Nip, it's all over. You know that, don't you?' The cat, usually so purringly affectionate, remained in the doorway.

'Nip? Nip, where are you?' Mabel was climbing the stairs. 'There you are, you naughty kitty!' She rushed after him, but the cat darted into my studio before her and with a graceful leap disappeared through the open window. 'Nip!' Mabel was horrified. She ran to the window crying out as if her heart would break. 'Nip, come back! Come back!'

'He'll find a new home,' I said, trying to rise so I could comfort her. A spasm shot down my back, and with a groan I fell back into my chair. 'Mabel,' I gasped, 'the medicine – the syrup—' I doubled over as the coughing began, searching my pockets for a handkerchief.

'Aubrey!' Mabel ran from the room. 'Mother! Mother!' In the hallway she collided with Arthur Symons. 'Oh! I'm afraid Aubrey is not well enough to receive visitors, Mr Symons!'

'Aubrey is well enough,' I gasped, for by this time the coughing attack had subsided and all that remained was to regain my breath.

Symons and Mabel, their faces a double mask of surprise and concern, looked in as I slowly sat up and adjusted my tie. 'Arthur, do come in. I'm sorry I cannot offer you a chair. Mabel dear, would you bring us some tea?'

'Are you sure?' she asked.

'Quite sure. Arthur, please do come in.'

He was a disgusting picture of health, with his fair hair and pink and white cheeks. Born in Wales of Wesleyan-worshipping Cornish parents, Symons was the last person one would suspect of arch-aestheticism – yet so it was. Of all the Rhymers, it was Symons I responded to most sympathetically, for he had as deep a love of France and modern French poetry as I.

'I have just come from a meeting with Leonard Smithers,' he said, cautiously advancing into my studio as if afraid I might drop dead in his sight.

'The remarkable publisher of Arundel Street?' I could not bear his gaze; I knew how I must look, and forced myself to be lively.

'Beardsley – good news! Very good news!'

'I am dying of suspense, Arthur.'

'We've finally come to an agreement. I had to tell you at once.'

'I wish you would.'

'Smithers is going to finance a new quarterly. We're going to call it *The Savoy*. A good name, don't you think?'

'Very good.'

'Suggestive of opulence, magnificence, modernism.'

'And expensive hotels,' said I.

'Yes. I am to be the literary editor.'

'I do hope you won't publish anything Harland may submit.'

'We'll publish everyone who's been drummed out of *The Yellow Book*. Without you, *The Yellow Book* is nothing, Smithers and I both agreed on that. And you, Beardsley – we want you to be art director.'

I could not speak for surprise; I dared not, lest I weep.

'Will you? You'll have a free hand. From the artistic side, you understand, *The Savoy* will be a vehicle for your magnificent drawings. Will you?'

'They shan't make me disappear quite so easily as they think,' I murmured. 'I shall give you scorching drawings, Arthur.' I began to laugh.

'Let us shake on it, then.'

I put out my hand, and Symons took it. 'Repeat after me, Arthur: Piss on *The Yellow Book*.'

'I beg your pardon?' he said.

'I said: Piss on *The Yellow Book*!'

In my glory days I remember seeing a play, the name of which now escapes me, in which there was a comic character who brought the house down because of the way he said a certain line: 'Smythers, please, not Smithers; Smithers is a different party, and moves in quite a different sphere.'

I have in these letters, Father, alluded several times to my current publisher, Leonard Smithers, usually with a mixture of contempt and regret. At this juncture I must of necessity bring Mr Smithers more fully into the picture, for whether I like it or not he figures prominently in the history of my life and the education – or debasement – of my soul.

If any one person may be said to possess two separate and distinct personalities, it is Leonard Smithers. On the one hand he is a man (I cannot say gentleman) of considerable erudition, a Latin scholar and an authority on Napoleon and the French Revolution. On the other, he is a rank vulgarian who indulges in the grossest excesses of the flesh, collects brass pigs, and calls himself, after one of his fictional heroes, Mr Fuckwell. Unfortunately it is the Fuckwell side of him that has steadily gained the upper hand.

This Jekyll and Hyde quality extends to his publishing ventures, for Smithers the lover of beauty and art is responsible for the production of some astonishingly beautiful *livres de luxe*, created with the greatest care and finesse. From the very outset of his publishing career he showed remarkable courage and a sincere interest in new ideas, and was willing to take on writers other publishers would not touch. As a dealer in rare books, he can wax ecstatic over a tooled leather binding or an old Sarum missal. But in his felt-hung back room he also keeps a double-crown Wharfedale printing press to multiply that other speciality of his: pornography. His bookshop in Arundel Street, just off the Strand, had a tiny upper floor that was a veritable museum of erotica. Now that he has moved to the Royal Arcade, of course, his choicer specimens of the fleshly school are never displayed except by special appointment.

Smithers is a Yorkshireman – he was a solicitor in Sheffield before coming to London – and can drink any ten men under the table. Whoring is his other great pastime, although he is happily married to a broad good-natured ex-trollop, and he has a mistress in every postal district in London. Between the brandy, and the whores, and the chlorodyne to which he has now become addicted, his constitution has suffered grievously. He has a pitted doughy face and sunken eyes; his hands twitch from constant nervous excitement and excessive stimulation.

Billy Rothenstein once said that Smithers was an evil influence, and I suppose in many respects he was right. But at that juncture of my life – sacked from my job, shunned by respectable publishers, reviled by the public, homeless, ill, wretched – Smithers appeared like a god sent from the Underworld to bring me back to life. His giant Rabelaisian nature appealed to some defiant part of my own that wanted to fight back, to show my detractors that I was still alive and kicking. I had every intention of shocking them rigid.

André was by this time courting Mabel and me with gifts of money, walking-sticks, theatre tickets, chocolates, flowers, first editions and pious tracts. He loved to be seen with both of us, or with me alone, at private views and first nights. It grimly amused me to re-enter the public arena on the arm, as it were, of this small, rich, effeminate man who eagerly inhaled the attention that was paid me, and who was intent on converting me to the true faith. He was as unlike Smithers as an orchid is to an oak, and, as I quickly discovered, jealously despised my new publisher for usurping his proprietary claim to my soul.

Smithers, at least at the beginning of our relationship, was almost as generous as André. We struck up an agreement by which, for a weekly salary, Smithers would own the rights to all my drawings. Most of these would be published in *The Savoy*. But Smithers, buttering his bread on both sides, held out additional inducements: he had a regular clientele with somewhat irregular tastes, and prevailed upon me to extend the limits of my creativity to satisfy them. 'Try your hand at it,' he suggested. 'I should be able to pay you a not inconsiderable sum for a piece of prose erotica. You could illustrate it yourself.' If this did not appeal to me, perhaps I would consider illustrating other classic works – he had just commissioned translations of Juvenal's *Satires* and the *Lysistrata* of Aristophanes.

André was forever dangling the prospect of a regular allowance before me, but he wanted me to rest my hand and refashion my subject-matter. In short, he wanted to control me and control my art. 'Your art is a result of your illness,' he insisted. 'Your fevers call up an unhealthy world, a demonic universe.'

341

'And who's to say that it's not the demons who are in charge of our earthly affairs?' I said, deliberately provoking him.

'If you would rest – do nothing – regain your health – pray, and listen to wise spiritual counsel, you would realize the error of your ways. Your art would then become infused with a new Christian radiance.'

What he never understood was the hard-edged spirit of satire and mockery that has always ruled my intellect. 'Now you sound like Edmund Gosse. He once told me I should turn my hand to worthier projects like *The Rape of the Lock*.' Gosse's suggestion, in fact, had interested me.

'It would suit your talents admirably.'

'Yes. Perhaps I could interest Smithers in publishing it in an *edition de luxe*.'

Every time I mentioned Smithers, André's visage would turn sour and peevish.

Smithers, at any rate, did not seek to control me. He sought instead to free me from any last vestige of respectability. Like an obscene father, he guided me to those forbidden places where the spirit has ceased to struggle with the flesh, and the flesh is free to revel in its own dark lubricious juices. With my body sending me such frequent reports of its progressive dissolution, I wanted to taste as much of life as I could before the only taste left to me was the wormy earth of the grave. It was not the Virgin Mary to whom I wanted to pray, but the Great Whore of Babylon.

The heady charms and excitements of London, which I had so dearly loved when I was in the thick of it, were now lost to me – perhaps for ever. Where once I had been embraced, I now received nothing but snubs and the cold shoulder. The city had turned its back on me, shown me its fickle heartlessness. Now when I walked along the Embankment, where once my feet had trod so triumphantly, a heavy sense of desolation overtook me, and I felt utterly excluded from the endless bustle and business of ordinary life. So I was determined to leave London for as long as I was able. Symons and I decided to meet in Dieppe to work on *The Savoy*. It was cheaper than London and, more importantly, it was not London.

There were few calls to make before I left. Ada was one of the few people who would still receive me. We spent a quiet hour together before my train, talking in the low voices of people who have mutually suffered a great calamity. We did not talk about the most talked-about man in London, whose portrait in the hall was shrouded in black crape.

I knew, of course, that she had sheltered Oscar between his trials; for this simple act of human kindness she had risked her entire social reputation. It had forced her to confront her greatest fear – scandal – and I thought I detected a quiet new strength in her demeanour as a result. Only by facing our greatest fears can we ever hope to overcome the power they exercise over us.

She had lost something of that gay frivolity which Oscar, like a magician, had conjured up in her. Of course she was impeccably ravishing, in a gown by Worth, but its subdued cut and sombre colours suggested mourning. Before I left she said she had something she wished to give me, and pressed a small package into my hand. 'Do not open it now,' she said. 'Use it however you like, and remember me always.'

'Ada—'

'Life is full of such curious turnings,' she said, her eyes filling with tears. 'Strength is required, Aubrey. At those times when we feel weakest and most vulnerable, some inner strength becomes available to help us through our trials. Now kiss me, please, before you go.'

In the cab on the way to the station I opened the package. Inside there was a large emerald. I have long since been forced to sell it, but Ada I have never forgotten.

The steamer emitted one final lugubrious shriek as it cut off its engine and glided past the two giant crosses that mark the entrance to Dieppe harbour. The gentle cliffs of the coastline rose up white and pure against a blue balmy sky, and my heart, so sick and heavy, felt some dim stirring of new life. For most of the summer and early autumn, Dieppe was to be my home. Yes, I was going into exile of a sort, but I resolved that my exile should have the exciting piquancy of a holiday.

Symons and Smithers were waiting for me at the landing-stage, Smithers with a quite appalling hag on his arm. Her welcoming grin revealed several gaps in her teeth. She was the first of dozens that I would meet in the coming months.

Symons had booked a room for me in the very heart of town, beside the Église St-Jacques, a venerable old structure built in Flamboyant Gothic style. St Jacques, the patron saint of fishermen, leaned upon a staff in the arch of the doorway. All around the church there was a lively noisy fair going on. In the peepshows you could view scenes of the murder of Monsieur Carnot, your French President, stabbed in Paris the previous year, and the degradation of Dreyfus. There was a transformation show of Joan of Arc, flying wooden horses, and a *salon de tir* where a pretty girl loaded your musket and you took shots at dancing bubbles on a fountain. Barrel organs ground out waltzes, and bands played tunes for dancing. The delicious smells and overall hubbub went to my head at once, and I told myself that I was glad to be away from grey grimy London.

We immediately set up a programme of work, meeting every morning at the Café des Tribunaux in the Grande Rue to consolidate our plans for *The Savoy*. While Symons and I discussed contributors, layout and all the artistic details of the new enterprise, Smithers drank and kept an eye out for 'fuckables' as he called them. 'There's a pretty little cunt,' he would say appreciatively, ogling some passing maid, or 'That one's just ripe for a good rogering from Mr Fuckwell'. In a crowd he was forever 'accidentally' bumping into women and seizing a sly pinch before the startled lady knew quite what was happening. 'These French doxies love to take cock on the sly,' he insisted. 'Their cunts have a good hard grip, and suck you in to the very root.' He was obsessed, and his endless obscene observations and blatant attempts to pick up women provided cynical amusement rather than embarrassment.

In the afternoons we stayed apart. While Symons worked on his poems or essays, and Smithers went prowling, I would generally take myself off to the peppermint-coloured Casino built above the *plage*. I loved the Casino and its endless parade of the fashionable and the ridiculous. There you could see the distinguished likes of Massenet and Saint-Saëns basking on the parapet, or Cléo de Mérode, an old beauty of the Opéra, strolling by with a pug dog and a parasol, or social luminaries like Comte Robert de Montesquiou and the Comtesse de Greffulhe, whose morning pearls created a sensation. The notorious Marquise de Mornay, who dressed as a man and looked like an ancient paederast, hobbled along the promenade with the rest of the decked-out English and French inverts.

Below, on the part of the beach reserved exclusively for subscribers to the Casino, an equally engaging pageant of colour and movement helped one to forget the dreary wreck of one's own social life. All day long the privileged subscribers moved up and down the wooden staircase from terrace to beach and along the boards that formed an intricate pathway over the pebbles. A line of private boxes stood in front of the double row of bathing machines, and there sat all the smart women and *beautés de plage*, wearing their best hats and smiles, pretending to read and sew when, in fact, they were there to flirt and chatter and exchange comments on the bathers. In England, of course, women were not allowed to bathe with the men. Here the sexes freely mingled. Women wearing white *peignoirs* could be seen hurrying from the bathing machines to the sea's edge, where they would drop their gowns, reveal their figures (often corseted, I noted) in dark bathing costumes, hesitate a moment and then delicately wade into the water.

In the Casino itself you could dance, listen to music, write letters in the reading-room, or gamble. The chandeliers, hung on ribbons, never ceased to fascinate me. I liked to walk through the large rooms when no one was there, when the entire place contained the sense of frivolous things caught in a moment of suspended life. My drawing was in a similar state of suspension, and so I wrote instead, taking myself to the reading-room to work on a novel that had taken possession of me and which Smithers promised to publish. This was the story of Venus and Tannhäuser, in which I extolled in beautifully wrought prose the endless perversities enjoyed in the Cave of Venus. Around me fashionable ladies and gentlemen scratched out their letters to mothers, fathers, sisters, brothers, lovers. They had no idea of the obscenities I was quietly inventing in their midst.

At night I was drawn like a moth to the Casino where I studied the gamblers at *petits chevaux* with hypnotized fascination. Gambling provided the secret heartbeat of the place; all the rooms, all the garden paths led inexorably to the central room with its green tables surrounded by avid circles of people throwing down and scooping up five-franc pieces as they discussed lucky numbers and watched the little coloured horses race towards the winning-post. I had never gambled, and could not for some time work up my nerve to participate, though Smithers was always encouraging me to try. When finally I overcame my scruples and placed my first bet I felt something within myself give way. The sheer intoxication of abandoning myself to Fate, of kicking away the bourgeois restraints that held me in check, worked like a dark tonic on my spirit. As the summer wore on I found myself at the tables nearly every night, as superstitious with my lucky numbers as anyone there. I lost more than I won, and had to cable Smithers, when he was back in London, for fresh funds.

Symons went off for a spell to Paris, but I lingered on alone, working on *Venus and Tannhäuser* in feverish bouts that left me both exhausted and exhilarated. I wanted to take my prose to places where prose had never been for fear. Defiance and my implacable hatred of the Philistines moved me to write that obscene work, Father – and something in my own nature, too, some hungry desire to experience everything that was forbidden, even if the experience was vicarious and imaginative.

Dieppe was a centre for French and English artists of all kinds, and I made the acquaintance of several of them. Jacques-Émile Blanché, who knew and admired my drawings, painted my portrait. He enquired constantly about my work, and I peevishly said I could draw only in London. I did make one or two attempts and even went so far as to prepare a canvas for a picture – never painted – in his studio; it was to be called 'The Little Horses'.

In late August I returned to London to settle my affairs. I gave up the lease of Chester Terrace, put my Japanese prints and first editions at Smithers's disposal, and took new rooms at 10 St James's Place. Oscar had once rented the same rooms, and it gave me a curious sense of satisfaction to take over what had once been his. While Oscar tramped the prison yard and shivered in his cold cell, I entertained André, Smithers and those few friends I still had. Lane, feeling remorse for his shameful treatment of me, threw a few commissions my way, and some others came through the Smithers connection. I started to draw again, but my work was going in a new direction.

So was I. In September I once again left London and set off for Germany. An inner voice bade me postpone no longer my desire to see all the visible glories that remained to be seen.

IT WAS NOT exactly pleasant, after the sunshine and hard-working frivolities of Dieppe and my brief tour of Germany, to return to the anti-light — anti-Enlightenment, one might say — of England. But the first number of *The Savoy* was to appear in early January 1896, and all my energies were required in London. I was determined to make it a success and to show the world that Aubrey Beardsley, far from being repentant and ruined, was working at the top of his quite unrepentant powers.

I was impatient for this opportunity to show my detractors how far I had advanced as an artist.

For the prospectus I drew a magnificently fat John Bull – none other than dear Leonard Smithers himself in the guise of an average Englishman – striding forth on to a brilliantly lit stage to announce the first number. Smithers had proudly sent out some 80,000 of these before George Moore, a prospective contributor, noticed a little pictorial joke that Smithers had overlooked, no doubt because I hadn't pointed it out to him: by the insertion of one deftly suggestive line in his trousers I had given John Bull a cockstand. Of course, only those who knew what cockstands were, and looked for evidence of them everywhere, would see it.

Moore, I suppose because his novel *Esther Waters* had been prosecuted for obscenity a couple of years earlier, was hyper-sensitive on such matters, and he quickly called a meeting of other contributors to denounce John Bull's prick and demand its withdrawal. Since the prospectus had already been sent out and nothing could actually be done about it, Smithers readily agreed. However, I was forced to castrate Mr Bull in a similar drawing to be used on the magazine's title page – a task I performed unwillingly but not without a certain unpatriotic pleasure.

Objections were also raised to my brilliant cover design. This showed a horseless lady holding a riding crop in a dense, mysterious, classical landscape. The smiling lady towered above a charming little putto pissing – quite appropriately, I thought – on a copy of *The Yellow Book*. She was Authority – always ready with the whip – and the putto was that untrammelled impish spirit known to schoolboys and artists. But Smithers, not wanting to raise the hackles of the paying public, forced me to expunge not only the putto's piss but his *petit* penis.

Rather hypocritical such artistic censorship seemed to me, especially since our publisher was producing all manner of pornographic novels and photographs in his own back room, but I suppose he was right in wanting to emphasize the artistic and literary merits of the new periodical, and to keep his two markets distinct. In my own defence I can only say that I was still burning with indignation over my fall from grace, and wanted to strike back at the hypocrisy of my persecutors with the full sting of my mockery. If they were so thoroughly frightened of me, regarding me as some kind of erotomaniac, then I wanted to give them something to be frightened about.

Castrations aside, I was wonderfully represented in the first number, not only with pictures but also with words. For some time I had been hard at work writing and illustrating my libidinously romantic tale of Venus and Tannhäuser; a tamer version of it had been promised, in fact, to John Lane while I was still with *The Yellow Book*, and Lane had actually announced its publication. Now, understandably, I had no intention of letting that traitor publish my work, even if he thought he retained contractual rights to it, so I changed the title to *Under the Hill*, altered the names of my chief characters from Tannhäuser and Venus to the Abbé Fanfreluche and Helen, and told Smithers to publish several chapters in *The Savoy*. My pungent text, with its veritable cornucopia of beautifully described perversities, had to be severely expurgated, of course, but even in its caponized version I was mightily proud of my literary achievement, and just as proud of my illustrations, which were filled with a new richness of detail. My style was changing.

Behind my back, Symons had objected to *Under the Hill* and my other literary contribution, an illustrated poem called 'The Three Musicians'. I suppose it irked him, as it would any lesser talent, that I had gone beyond mere picture-making and was trespassing on his literary territory. But people were talking of *The Savoy* not because of Arthur Symons's contributions, but because of Aubrey Beardsley's reappearance. It was our first falling-out as co-editors, and the beginning of my disenchantment with him as a friend.

Soon after the first of the year *The Savoy* appeared in the bookshops, very pretty indeed, and quite unmistakable, with my adorable cover design printed in black on pink boards. Everyone except the critics – unanimous in their preordained disdain – agreed that it beat its rival, *The Yellow Book*, hollow. There were literary contributions from George Bernard Shaw, Max, Symons of course, Ernest Dowson, Yeats, Havelock Ellis and Aubrey Beardsley. The artists were Aubrey Beardsley and his friends Joseph Pennell, Billy Rothenstein, Charles Shannon, Max Beerbohm, Charles Conder, and his enemy, the famous James McNeill Whistler – whom I had temporarily forgiven in order to get a drawing for our inaugural issue, no mean feat given his stinginess and his antipathy towards me.

To celebrate, Smithers hosted a supper-party for all the contributors in a private room at the New Lyric Club. His tiny heavy-bosomed wife, Alice, the ex-whore, was the only woman present, and did the honours. Mrs Smithers was accustomed to entertaining men, but artists and writers were somewhat beyond her intellectual capacity. Still, she made a valiant effort, puffing about the gathering to drop inane pleasantries about the weather and exclaim endlessly over the bamboo wall-covering: 'Quite original, is it not?'

As we stood about the supper-table waiting for the signal to be seated, I noticed Yeats passing a letter to Symons. Symons, evidently finding its contents amusing, announced: 'Gentlemen, a friend of Mr Yeats, an Irish poet, has sent us this congratulatory letter. "*The Savoy* is the organ of the incubi and succubi—"' Before Symons could finish, Smithers shouted, 'Give me that letter, I will prosecute that man!' and tried to snatch it from Symons's hand. An undignified scuffle ensued, but Symons managed to hold on to the letter and continue: ' "I shall never see *The Savoy*, nor do I intend to touch it. I have no wish to be allied with people possessed by a sexual mania like Beardsley, Symons or that ruck." ' Laughter ceased, and a sudden embarrassed silence filled the room. I was aware of people wanting to look at me but avoiding my eye. ' "It is all mud from a muddy spring," ' Symons read, ' "and any pure thought that mingles with it must lose its purity." '

'Oh dear,' said Alice Smithers, 'it does not sound terribly congratulatory.' She turned to Yeats. 'I always say, if you can't find something pleasant to say, it is better to say nothing at all.'

My honour and reputation lacerated by the vehemence of this stranger's denunciation, I stood as dumbfounded as Marguerite Gautier in *La Dame aux camellias* when she has been publicly humiliated by Armand. A sensitive nerve had been touched; my shell was thinner than I thought.

'Gentlemen, please be seated,' said Alice Smithers.

To ease the strain that had fallen over the company, I did my best to seem jolly and unconcerned, and soon the supper room was filled with wine, laughter and merriment. Yet I could not help observing that the atmosphere was different from the dinner that had inaugurated *The Yellow Book*, and this, I think, was because of Smithers. For, no matter how much the assembled group of young British authors and artists wanted to see their work in print, they were well aware that the man responsible for their publication was a secret pornographer, a man of the lowest and most disreputable morals – a man with no social standing whatsoever, a man one would avoid under any other circumstances. In short, our host was an embarrassment.

And so, in some respects, was I, as the letter from Yeats's friend made perfectly clear. Yet what could I do? I had need of Smithers's weekly cheques, and an even greater need to be in the public eye. As an artist I was impotent unless people saw my work, which was gaining daily in power and mastery. My desire to astonish people by the sheer force of my grotesque vision became a kind of aching mania that visibility alone could satisfy. Smithers regarded me as a genius and offered opportunities no one else did, so I had to love him at least a little. And his unabashed sexual lubricity, before it began to disgust me, was something I admired and even aspired to.

Therein, Father, lay my concern and my dilemma: my soul and my body were at odds with one another, divided by the sharp dark knowledge of my mortality. The fever that hummed strange mournful lullabies in my blood as it nudged my cradle towards the abyss forced me to consider that invisible world beyond this one, where purity was supposed to be rewarded and sin punished. At the same time, with the dizzying chasm of eternity looming always so near, it was this world – the seen world, the world of physical sensation, of soft hot flesh and the fiery tumult of passion – that I clung to. And Smithers, his cock a perpetually burning arrow, was my guide to that world, the best bad influence a fellow could have.

André Raffalovich, on the other hand, seemed determined to obtain as exclusive a contract to my soul as Smithers had to my drawings. In his self-appointed office of cicerone to the spiritually dispossessed, it became increasingly apparent that Brother André hoped to snare my wayward personality and chloroform it with the beauty of self-denial and piety. He was joined in this venture by John Gray, whose anaemic poetry, now that he was on the road to priesthood, emulated that of decadent French divines instead of devine French decadents.

It annoyed and bewildered me, the way the pair of them were constantly hovering around like mystical waiters eager to serve up a holy dessert wafer on my outstretched tongue, but I subdued my uncharitable feelings because their hospitality was so generous and sincere, and in André's home I was always made to feel specially welcome. In my kinder moments I even found something touching in their shared life and mutual dedication to higher religious principles.

Every time I looked at John Gray, however, I was reminded of that night in Bobbie's flat, when Gray stumbled in drunk and hysterical because Oscar had dropped him. He was now so self-possessed, so quietly strong and certain in his faith that I could only wonder whether it were a deliberate pose induced by personal embarrassment or an actual benefit of his conversion.

A mysterious man, the handsome John Gray, always in the background of André's life yet dominating it by the sheer force of his character. Like Mary Magdalene, his favourite saint, Gray had sacrificed his considerable physical beauty by turning it from profit to priestliness. The ambitious poet who had calculatedly fucked his way to publication was no longer a notorious courtesan of the literary world; no hand but God's now touched that sudden saint John Gray.

André, on the other hand, was not above a certain peevish spitefulness and jealousy, perhaps because he still preferred a hairy chest to a hairshirt. Gradually I was becoming better-acquainted with my strange little benefactor of South Audley Street. Countless hand-delivered notes written on lilac paper in his spidery feminine scrawl continued to invite me to luncheons, dinner-parties (those 'octets' he was so fond of), first nights, and concerts – most of which I attended – and a bewildering variety of religious services, which I did not. His luxurious carriage was always at my disposal, and I grew to enjoy those frequent drives between my bachelor rooms in St James's and André's house in Mayfair. Luxury is something I have always instinctively appreciated, and I must say that André has impeccable taste when it comes to creature comforts. That's the glory of the Jesuits, after all. None of this Aunt Pittish self-denial; they revel in the glory of gold and know the solace it brings.

* * *

As soon as word got round that I was leaving London again, the inevitable invitation appeared from South Audley Street inviting me for tea. I had not informed André that I was leaving, so of course his brotherly interests were aroused.

It was a wet blustery day in early February, and despite my burning brow I was grateful for the hot wood fire in the drawing-room grate. The damp wrought havoc with my lungs, so that my every breath was a shallow gasp. During the Christmas season André had set up an evergreen tree in this room and decorated it to rather showy effect with rare orchids set in glass vials; we called it the Holy Ghost Tree, because from a distance it appeared to be covered with tiny white doves.

That afternoon in February, though, I only noticed that another Russian icon, fiercer than all the rest, had been added to the collection above the prie-dieu and Moreau's watercolour of Sappho had been removed.

'My dear Aubrey, how too good of you to come round in this beastly weather,' André said. 'Mr Gray and Miss Gribbell are both attending Mass, so this afternoon I shall have you all to myself. I hope you don't mind?'

'Of course not,' I said, wondering if he had somehow planned this tête-à-tête in advance.

Joseph, his giant blue-eyed Swiss butler, entered with tea. When he left us, André said in a low voice: 'I told you, did I not, that Joseph has finally decided to become one of us?'

'One of us?'

'A Catholic. Dear boy, at first he was as stubborn as only a Swiss peasant can be. Calvinist, you know; desperately suspicious of priests and Pope. I can't begin to tell you the number of ridiculous objections he had and the countless arguments he used before he saw the light.'

'Yes,' I said, 'It's amazing the number of dreary hopeless creeds people believe in.'

My ironic tone was lost on Raff. 'Towards the end he even voiced an opposition to the Jesuits who had saved him, and said he preferred the Dominican order. 'Can you imagine?'

'What's wrong with the Dominicans?'

'The Dominicans are preachers – *frères prêcheurs* – and arguers. Mass is not central to them, preaching is. It's not the altar they emphasize, but the lectern. And then, my dear, something worse – no decoration. Their churches are as bare as Golgotha.'

'And how was this miraculous conversion finally achieved?' I asked politely.

'Patience and persuasion,' André said, pouring out the tea. 'I hope I do not sound boastful when I say that I was instrumental in the whole process. One begins merely by setting an example.'

'Conversion by gratitude is very effective, I'm told.'

My host allowed himself a faint superior smile. 'You enjoy spiting me; but, I assure you, the joy I feel in bringing even one soul back to its true mooring is genuine. In any case, Joseph will praise God in the end, not me.' He pursed his lips, demurely crossed his ankles, and proceeded to heap our plates with sweet French pastries. 'You are leaving London?'

'For a while, yes.'

'On the advice of your doctors?'

'On the advice of my purse.'

An annoyed look, instantly subdued, troubled his face. 'I have asked you over and over again to come to me – like a brother – whenever you felt anxious over money.'

'I feel anxious about everything these days, André. Money is only one part of it.'

'Then, your health is not good?' His black eyes glistened with hunger for details of my mortal illness, of which he could never have too many. Like me, Raff had enjoyed a sickly childhood but, try as he might, as an adult he could never be as ill as I. I was the undisputed victor there. 'Are you haemorrhaging?' he asked bluntly.

'A little,' I said.

'Where are you going?'

'To Paris.'

'Ah. Your mother will be accompanying you?'

'No!'

'Would it not be wise if she did?'

'Finding wisdom in a mother is like finding saintliness in the Devil,' I said.

356

'Yes,' said André thoughtfully. 'Mothers can be trying, but you must admit they are terribly useful. 'I don't know how I should run this household without Miss Gribbell.'

'You've never told me anything about your real mother.'

André's smile was terribly sweet and terribly false. 'Very beautiful and very cold – at least, to her ugly little son. I once heard her refer to me using those very words. I think in some strange way it made me love her all the more.'

'What we cannot have is generally what we most desire.' I was thinking as much of John Gray as of Madame Raffalovich when I spoke, but it suddenly struck me that perhaps this was indeed the strange paradox that ruled human passion, the one universal truth, the great lesson that taught us nothing and in the end rendered us all fools.

'Yes, curious, is it not?' André said.

'My own dear mother has always been rather too approachable,' I said. 'Do you know, André, these few months that I have been living in St James's Street represent the first time in my adult life that I have lived without her? I wish it could stay that way for ever. How can a man truly live like a man with his mother forever hovering near with her exhortations to be good, to be careful, to be temperate?'

'In your condition you must be careful,' André said.

It was the voice of a doctor, and it enraged me. 'That is the last thing I want to be! God, how sick I am of carefulness and respectability. Don't you ever want to throw it all over, André? Curse and fuck and spit in the face of all the world's bloody timidity and self-righteousness?' He said nothing, but looked at me with fear and a kind of wonder, as though I were a prophet whose teachings echoed so strongly in his heart that he dared not listen. 'I do!' I exclaimed, rising, wafted aloft by the fever dancing through my veins, making me lightheaded and careless. 'Whatever is forbidden, that is that I want, that is what I crave.'

'And that is what you must renounce,' he said with sudden vehemence. 'You must rid yourself of that obscene devil.'

'No, I must dance with him – right to my grave.' With cruel pleasure I watched the colour rise in his small lemony face and the sudden nervous twiddle of his dainty little foot. 'Nature never tires

357

of killing, André, but I am tired of her killing me. I ask you, how can I die without living first? And this filthy disease, it makes me hate myself because I can never be rid of it.'

'Not in your present state, no.'

'Not in any state!' I shouted. 'Every time I look in a mirror I see it. And everyone else sees it as well. Everyone expects a beautiful dying, with no bitterness and no regret. Fear they understand, for all men fear death, but the daily weight of it they do not know. It drives me mad, the way they look at me, watch me to see how I am dealing with it—'

'Looking for an example,' said André. 'Who can teach us about dying except the dying?'

'I am not dying!' I cried, surprised by my own vehemence.

'Of course not,' André said quietly.

'Perhaps I should oblige them, since everyone seems to love a dying boy. They love to measure their own state of health against mine.'

'If your spiritual constitution can be changed, Aubrey, so can your health.'

'That is rubbish! Do you think I haven't prayed? I have prayed until my soul bled. I have prayed for health, and it has never been given to me!'

'You must not pray for your body, you must pray for your spirit,' he insisted, half-rising from his chair. 'Pray for a spirit that is unafraid of death and strong enough to withstand the temptations of the flesh. Pray with me now,' he said, impulsively reaching out for me with a hairless claw-like hand. 'I will help you to call upon the saints. They will intercede on your behalf. Illness is an act of God, Aubrey, and it can only be cured by a life of righteousness.'

I avoided his grasp. 'You mean self-righteousness.'

'Your sickness is a sign of disobedience to the law.'

'What law? My sickness is a gift from my father. It's the only thing he ever gave to me. We're constantly talking about the spiritual fathers, André, and never about our real ones. Why?'

André carefully eased himself back into his chair and was silent for a moment. 'I suspect it's because we both hate them so much,' he said finally.

'Ah, so you finally admit to a human failing,' I said, wanting to torture him with sarcasm. 'Hate. Delicious, isn't it? And much stronger than love.'

'Much easier anyway.'

'You know what it is to be hated, and to hate in return.'

'But I try always to love,' he insisted, wanting to believe this, a pleading look in his eyes.

'Loving one's enemies is unnatural,' I said coldly. 'Let us be frank. Neither of us, for instance, loves Oscar Wilde.'

Before its publication in France I had read André's most recent book – or pamphlet, I should call it – *L'Affaire Oscar Wilde*, in which he gave full vent to the virulent rage that Oscar inspired in him. Even I, who had lost everything because of Oscar, was amazed and a little disgusted at André's method of attack and the lowness of his blows. The pamphlet revealed the workings of a very small and very vindictive mind.

André's head was bowed – perhaps under the sudden weight of his conscience – and he now looked up at me like a little boy shy of some naughtiness but wanting to confess it and be forgiven. 'Dear brother, I suffer from many human failings,' he said. 'Hate is perhaps the least of them.'

He told me then, as the rain silvered the windows and the fire crackled in the grate, about his life before his conversion, how he had given himself up to cynicism and lust, caring for nothing but the satiation of his basest carnal desires. He bought a magnificent yacht, had it painted black, named it *Iniquity*, and sailed from one Mediterranean port to the next, feasting like a hungry whore on the local merchandise. A harem of dark-skinned boys was kept to supply his every wish, no matter how debased. The jewelled ciborium purchased from impoverished monks at an ancient monastery he used not for Communion wafers but for cakes of hashish, which he smoked from an ivory pipe while stroking his boys with hot scented oil and inserting a gold coin into the arses of the ones he favoured. And thus with the debauched splendour of a late-Roman emperor this effeminate, slightly built, velvet-eyed Russian Jew, whose paternal ancestors had fled a pogrom in St Petersburg and ended up the richest bankers in Paris, spent his days with the curtains drawn against the hot fiery glare of southern skies and his nights in the hot fiery arms of olive-skinned strangers. It was not love, though at first he mistook it for love.

But the more he gorged his sensual appetites, the hungrier he became – ravenous, insatiable, with a hunger that sickened him by its very excess. Meaning dissolved in its grip; a black despair overtook him, then a fearful depression which nothing on earth could alleviate. He drew back the curtains and looked at the shimmering radiance of a sun-licked sea, thinking that the light would revive him, shake him back into life, but the light seemed to accuse him, and he could see nothing in it save the nullity of his own existence.

'The dark night of the soul,' André said, with a shade too much drama in his voice. He stared into the fire, obsessively tapping his fingers on consecutive beads of the rosary beside him. I wondered if he was counting his money or tallying up his sins. 'When life is ashes, and God has no meaning. What then is left? The hellish daily grind of misery, of something deeper than misery. Of utter futility. It is the lowest circle of Hell, Aubrey; one can descend no further.'

'And what did you do?' I asked, not without interest. 'How did you escape it?'

'One morning I prayed, and the catastrophe was over. The pessimism that ruled my life was gone.'

I found this simple-minded answer maddeningly vague. 'So with all your good health and the vitality of money you leaped across the chasm of pessimism and found yourself in the arms of God. Some of us cannot make that leap, André, but I am happy that you did.'

'You, too, could find comfort in the Church, Aubrey. Only the Church offers a true remedy against the disease of pessimism and the sickness that comes in its wake. Only the Church can save and cure you.' His dark eyes glittered with fanaticism.

I did not want to be snared, and yet I did. Some primitive part of me wanted to be taken out of myself, relieved of the sodden weight of sin and self. But the artist in me reared up like one of those wild Dartmoor ponies that refuse the bums and bridles of man. Giving up my selfhood, however wilful and vagrant it might be, meant giving up my art, my only freedom, my only truth.

'I'm certain you did find comfort in the Church, André,' I said, adding spitefully, 'but tell me, isn't there a danger for you in loving the church men more than the Church?'

He glared at me, twisting suddenly in his chair, and his hand flew out, knocking the pearl rosary from the table to the carpet. 'You have a vulgar streak in you, Mr Beardsley,' he said, stiffly bending over to retrieve his beads. But, as he did so, I heard some funny little popping sounds and what sounded like the snap of an elastic bandage, and saw André poised, halfway down, looking round in alarm, 'Oh!' he said in a high startled voice. He righted himself with a jerk and grabbed his stomach as a curious bulge strained the fabric of his tight black waistcoat.

'André, what is it?' I asked, hurrying to his side.

'Nothing . . . nothing,' he groaned.

'What has happened?'

'My corset . . .'

I had to turn away to keep myself from laughing. 'But, André, you've already fasted yourself to skin and bone. You're nearly as thin as I am. What need have you of a corset?'

'Look!' he said.

I turned and was confronted by a strange sight. André, like a martyr proudly showing the wound that killed him, had unbuttoned his waistcoat and shirt. Something horribly black and hairy protruded from the gap. 'What is it?' I said.

I watched as he slowly pulled the vile thing out; it was like watching someone giving birth to a monster, or exorcizing a demon from his stomach. His eyes sparkled with pain, a tortured and triumphant grin stretched his lips. When he had extruded the beast he laid it like a quilt across his knees. 'You think I don't take my renunciation of the flesh seriously,' he said. 'As you can see, I do.'

'My God,' I murmured. 'A hairshirt corset. Do you really hate your flesh so much?'

'I wear this not because I hate my flesh, but because I love it too much.'

I saw now that the corset was covered on both sides with short stiff bristles and had a pouch that fastened over the genitals like a codpiece. 'It must certainly make masturbation a scream,' I said.

'Can you never cease your sexual flippancies?' he cried.

'No,' I said, looking him squarely in the eye. 'Nor do I care to. I enjoy sex, André, and I think of it incessantly.'

'Because of Smithers,' he accused. 'That man is a vile influence.'

'He took me on when no one else would.'

'He encourages you to excess,' André cut in.

'And he pays me.'

'I will pay you!' he said. 'I have in mind a regular allowance for you – let us say a hundred guineas a quarter. Would not such a sum allow you to rest and cease working for Smithers?'

'I am an artist. I must work, André. I'm going to Paris to work, not to rest.'

'Your work you will no doubt find on the rue Monge, with all the filthy whores of Paris.'

'They're cheaper than the filthy whores of London.'

'Sexual love debases man by bringing us down to that very state of nature it is the aim of culture and civilization to abolish.'

'You're confusing culture and civilization with religion and theology,' I said. 'They are antithetical concepts.'

'Why can I not make you see?' he moaned.

'I see all too well, André. And let us not forget that my vision, in my eyes, is as sacred to me as yours.'

'Sacred! Your vision is demonic, and so long as you remain with Smithers it will remain so.'

'My next work for Smithers is hardly to be demonic, André. Even you could not object to it.'

He asked me what it was, and I told him: I was to illustrate Pope's *The Rape of the Lock*. André immediately wanted to hear all the details; but I refused to satisfy his curiosity, for I did not like to talk about my work before I had completed it. It was a little superstition I had.

By now the sky had turned black, the wind had picked up, and the lamplighter was making the rounds of South Audley Street. Joseph came in to draw the curtains and remove the tea-tray. I thanked André and said I must go. 'Will you let me know your address in Paris?' he asked.

How sad he suddenly looked, sitting so stiffly in his elegant chair, the hairshirt laid like a dead pet across his knees. A rich, unlovely, unloved man who indulged himself in the chocolate-box of prayer, thinking it would satisfy his craving for purely physical sweets. Something in me melted a little, for I knew that loneliness, that desire to give oneself up once and for all and be done with the endless pain and turmoil of life.

362

'I don't want you to think that your words always fall on such barren ground,' I said kindly. 'It's just that I'm not very fruitful soil for conversion. I melt only to harden again.'

'I think of you as a brother.'

'Then, we are brothers with very different philosophies.'

'We share the disease of pessimism,' he said.

'But we look for our cures in very different ways.'

'God hunts down the sinner, Aubrey. I know this from my own experience. He haunts him, won't let him rest, chases him to exhaustion. And the greatest joy a sinner can know is to let himself be captured.'

'Then Oscar must be terribly happy just now. Yet I somehow think he is not.'

'I was speaking of you,' André said.

'I know.'

'Dear brother,' he said, suddenly taking my hand. I thought he was going to shake it, but instead he turned it over and stared intently into the maze of lines in my palm. 'A hand is a map,' he said.

'I shouldn't be surprised, given the amount of travelling I'm forced to do.'

'All that we are and will be is here. A map,' he said, pulling my palm closer. His eyes became black mysterious slits as he examined it. 'Full of bright thoroughfares and dark evil little alleys where one can easily become lost. All the verdant paths and wrong turnings are here.'

'I thought the Church forbade palmistry and fortune-telling.'

'This is an inherited gift,' he said in a low voice. 'Something I did not choose and rarely exercise. Ah, what a hand is this,' he murmured, gazing deep into the design etched in my palm. With the tip of his fingernail he slowly traced a line in the upper quadrant and then stopped and looked up at me as if I were some awesome wonder in a temple.

'What is it?' I asked.

'Your life line.'

'What do you see?'

'Dear brother,' he said, bending his head like an acolyte before a high priest. He kissed my hand and folded it in his own. 'Think on the ways of God before it is too late.'

Starving people hallucinate food, and men dying of thirst dream they are gulping down cold clear water. Is it so unusual, then, for someone in the grip of a mortal disease to imagine that he will live a long life?

The rasping murmur of my rotting lungs was like the voice of some obscene muse heard far below the surface of the earth, but so long as I was working I could ignore it, make plans for the future, believe that a full span of years would yet be mine. How could I otherwise complete all I had to do? In a room in the Hôtel St-Romaine in the rue St-Roche my undistracted powers flamed to life and the set of drawings for *The Rape of the Lock* fairly leaped off the golden tip of my pen. The intoxicating delirium of creation, of hot-handed connivance with one's own brilliance, made those weeks in Paris something like a dream.

For some time I had been studying eighteenth-century French engravings, finding in the work of Watteau especially something that beckoned to my spirit. It was a period of such graceful indecency and melancholy eroticism that I could not resist it. And as my *Rape* drawings miraculously appeared, one after another, they captured the spirit and stylistic essence of that *ancien régime*. The drawings were engravings, saturated with a painstaking perfection of form and detail. I was triumphant with my achievement, for each straight line defied the cough and hectic fever shaking my frame. Each line was a solid refutation of my own weakness.

Smithers, shuttling back and forth between London and Paris, waxed ecstatic once he saw the drawings and announced the book for April.

I lived the life of a hardworking hermit, but allowed Smithers to coax me out of my lair whenever he appeared. These days he was often in the company of Ernest Dowson, a young poet whose sordid appearance never failed to irk me, and Yvonne, a straw-haired cross-eyed tart he had picked up in the Empire music-hall. Yvonne had a friend in Paris named Rayon, and the five of us, or just Smithers, Dowson and I, would carouse in the wilder cafés of the Quartier.

'If grapes grew in England,' Smithers would say, gulping down another glass of wine, 'what a different land it would be!'

'We should have bacchanals in Trafalgar Square,' Dowson agreed.

They dragged me off to meet Gabriel de Lautrec, a French man of French letters, where I was induced to take hashish for the first time. Smithers had procured some chlorodyne for himself, and Lautrec mixed up a concoction of ether for Dowson and himself. The three of them grew more Bacchic by the minute, but I felt no effect whatsoever. 'If this is all there is to hashish,' I complained, 'I hardly wonder that it has such a bad reputation.'

From Lautrec's we went on to supper in a private cabinet at Margery's, Smithers all the while rhapsodizing extempore on the glories of French women. 'Ah, how the mademoiselles of the Grandes-Boulevards love a good solid English cock stuffed up inside them, with what delicate fervour they die as our good English spunk squirts up inside them and their cunts liquidize in rapture.'

When Yvonne and Rayon appeared, Smithers called for more oysters and wine. 'Gentlemen,' he said, 'consider the amazing similarities between one of these' – picking up an oyster – 'and one of these.' Yvonne let out a loud squeal as he grabbed her between her legs. 'An oyster and a cunt, gentlemen. You open the shell to expose the salty flesh within and then, gentlemen, you eat.' He stuck out his fat tongue, tilted back his head, and slid the oyster down his throat.

It was then, when I was least expecting it, that the hashish took effect. I began to laugh. How hilarious the world was! The hot pandering tongue of the Devil himself was mine as I matched and then exceeded Smithers in his erotic monologues. Soon we were all behaving like imbeciles. We asked the women to bet which of us had the biggest prick, and the girls felt us up quite openly.

'This one is a dirty little weasel,' Yvonne said, pinching a red-faced Dowson between the legs. 'And this one is a little worm,' Rayon said of Lautrec, but looking at me. I began to cough with excitement as she came over and began to stroke me. 'Bah,' Yvonne said, throwing a mock-contemptuous glance at Smithers's quite obvious engorgement. 'This one I know all too well – it is as small as a herring and swims just as fast.' Smithers let out a roar and pulled her to him. I stared into Rayon's deep blue eyes as she fondled me with the finesse of Cleopatra. 'Now, this one,' she said, 'this one is as strong as a lion.' It wasn't true, but Rayon's busy fingers and adorable smile almost made me believe it was.

In February an event was announced which had all of Paris buzzing. A. M. Lugné-Poe was producing the first performance of Oscar's play *Salome* at the Théâtre de l'Oeuvre. The news brought with it a curious welter of emotions, most of them unpleasant, but in the end my curiosity got the better of me and I booked seats.

Dowson went with me. As usual he stank like a polecat and looked more like an itinerant drunk than an itinerant poet. He was a good poet and a congenial companion, but his self-neglect filled me with revulsion – the stained rotten teeth, the dirty scraggle of beard on an unwashed face, the filthy sweater and trousers shining with grime. He drank incessantly, and belonged to that throng of self-destructive Bohemians descending to madness and despair in Willette's painting in the Chat Noir.

We took our seats in the tiny theatre with the rest of artistic Paris and waited for the curtain to rise. My stomach was in a knot when it finally did and I heard the first line of dialogue in French: 'Comme la princess Salomé est belle ce soir.'

A flood of memories swept over me. I thought of the beautiful drawings I had done for the play, and how eagerly I had sought that commission; the fatal ease with which it was given me; the joy with which I allied myself to Oscar even as I mocked him in my drawings. And then I remembered the battle I had waged with Bosie Douglas over the English translation; and how furious I had been with Oscar's favouritism. The critical furore when the book was finally published – when I still found scandals delicious – had filled me with childish glee.

How much had happened in three short years! Everyone in the audience knew that the playwright was serving time in an English prison; it added to the excitement and savoury poignancy of the event. But no one knew of the injustice that had befallen *me* because of my alliance with Oscar. The sting of memory was all the greater because I saw with a horrible clarity how I had, quite unwittingly, brought all this to pass.

Nemesis delights in trickery, Father. With the blackest irony she could muster she had reunited me with the source of my ruin here in this tiny theatre in Paris.

And what was it, I wondered, that had led me down this dark pathway I was following? How was it that I found my way to Oscar and from him to a business alliance with a pornographer? Was some inherited twist in my intellect responsible for my sex madness, or was it the result of the inferno kindled by consumption, that inner fire which could never be doused and kept my imagination boiling? I began to fear there was something in my blood even worse than the disease that was killing me.

The performance of *Salome* was a triumphant one, but even more triumphant was the one I gave afterwards, drinking and cavorting with Dowson despite a raging fever, and bedding down with Rayon while my soul was as dark and heavy as lead.

In March, Smithers returned to Paris and our night-time revels continued. It was more and more difficult for me to keep up with him, but I did so to spite the cough and humour the fever that was now like a kettle permanently on the boil.

Unable to complete all the work I had promised Smithers for the next issue of *The Savoy*, I was desperate to maintain the closest possible contact. The man was my saviour: that drunken insatiable lecher with piggish eyes sunk deep in bruised sockets held my future in his hands. He was the only one who would present my work to the public, the only one who would pay me a regular salary. A man who collected pigs was responsible for my immortality.

And I could not trust him. I wanted to, desperately, but signs were appearing – like buboes on a plague victim – that all was not well with him. The true state of his business affairs was always something of a mystery, but when I began to receive those post-dated cheques with mysterious instructions for cashing at strange out-of-the-way places I grew a little alarmed. Any business setbacks he might have would place *The Savoy* and, more to the point, *The Rape of the Lock* in jeopardy. The thought of once more being without a publisher or source of income was terrifying to me. There would be nothing left! I would be a pauper.

To protect myself I began to accept small commissions, mostly of an erotic nature, but I had to keep them a secret since my contract with Smithers was an exclusive one.

Smithers hid any business fears he had and did his best to alleviate mine, but my unease persisted. The constant uncertainty of my future was a fretful torment. I wanted straight lines, definite facts; but Smithers, cloudy and raucous with drink and whores, gave me nothing more than indefinite scribbles. His erotomania was beginning to disgust me; the loveless sensual pleasures he seemed to live for were nothing more than insatiable addictions, joyless habits that obliterated any finer instincts.

But I needed to be with him because he was my artistic link to London. Now that I was in exile I craved news of the city I hated and loved. It was a way of clinging on, of believing that my work still carried weight and importance.

At the Café de la Paix, before leaving for Brussels, Smithers finally admitted to me that *The Savoy* was already in trouble. 'We are having problems with distribution,' he said, 'and distribution is everything.'

The problem was W. H. Smith, the largest booksellers in England. Smith's controlled all the bookstalls at the railway stations, where it was essential to have copies of new magazines displayed because that was where they sold best. But they refused to display any copies of *The Savoy*. Their long-standing commitment to protect the morals and religious beliefs of their customers, they said, prevented them from distributing any magazine containing the work of Aubrey Beardsley.

Symons, once he heard this, dashed down to confront the manager of Smith's. He pressed the man to point out one drawing in *The Savoy*, just one, that could be viewed as in any way morally reprehensible or just cause for refusal. The man, angered by this intrusion on his moral authority, flipped through the pages until he came to an illustration which, he said, proved his point. 'You must remember, Mr Symons, that we have an audience of young ladies to consider.'

'But that is a drawing by Blake,' Symons said. 'Blake was considered a very spiritual artist.'

The manager, who obviously had never looked at a piece of art in his life, who couldn't tell a Blake from a Beardsley, refused to bend, and *The Savoy* was denied distribution. But he stopped Symons as Symons was storming out of the door to say: 'If, contrary to our expectations, *The Savoy* should have a large sale, Mr Symons, we should be very glad to see you again.'

'Will it fold?' I asked, terrified. 'Do you mean to tell me that the opinion of one ignorant Philistine can destroy all of our hard work?'

'It will not fold,' Smithers assured me. 'Far from it. Symons tells me *The Savoy* would do better as a monthly than a quarterly, and I am inclined to believe him.'

'Yes, make it a monthly,' I said.

'Could you . . . keep up?' he asked.

'Of course. I will work harder than ever,' I promised. 'I shall pray to the patron saint of keeping things up.'

'Who is that?' Smithers asked, smiling as he did whenever he knew I was about to blaspheme.

'Priapus.'

Smithers laughed. 'Priapus!'

'Patron saint of cockstands.'

'Getting one?' Smithers asked. 'Or keeping one?'

'If you pray hard enough at his shrine, Len, he lets you keep it up once you've got it up.'

'Ah, you do have a wit to your wickedness, Mr Beardsley. And I have a train to catch.'

'I shall accompany you to the station, Len. I wouldn't want my dear publisher to lose his way and end up on the rue Monge.'

On the way to the Gare du Nord I kept him in such foul good humour that he begged me to go with him to Brussels. 'We'll line up all those Belgian whores and give them the good fucking they deserve,' he said. I protested, saying I had no change of clothes, and hadn't paid my hotel bill, but Mr Fuckwell obliterated all my objections with an intoxicating recital of the carnal delights waiting for us. We drank more, until we were screaming with laughter. Why not go to Brussels? The idea was delightful. I made up my mind as the train was pulling out of the station, and Smithers pulled me up into the compartment. I was as light as a feather.

We drank and staggered about all the next day and far into the night. Never in my life have I given myself up to such utter moral chaos as I did there in Brussels. I broke free of every last restraint and unleashed at last the full mad power of Dionysus. The tethering realities of money and disease and reputation were burned away in the flames of strong red wine and the hot arms of five-franc whores.

As the night wore on I began to feel peculiar, and then horribly bilious. Smithers laughed as I vomited into a gutter, and asked the whore he was with if she was hungry. I had fallen on my knees, and when I tried to raise myself found that I could not do so. My chest was swollen with pain, and the fever so high that I was dripping with perspiration. 'Smithers,' I gasped.

'Up, up, up,' he drunkenly chanted.

I shall die, I thought. Here in a foreign gutter, covered with vomit, I shall die. I tried again to stand, but the effort ignited the pain in my chest to such a degree that I doubled over gasping. 'Smithers, for God's sake!' I whispered.

I felt his hand on my arm and was pulled to my feet. There was an explosion in my chest, and as the blood poured out of my mouth I remember thinking I must look like a grotesque gargoyle spewing sewage.

I had intended to stay in Brussels for no more than two days, but ended up staying there for nearly three months. Those hideous days and nights at the Hôtel de Saxe I came to regard as the fateful turning-point of my life. I had a sense that, no matter what I wanted, my condition was irrevocable. No cures would cure me. Death was licking me with his foul black tongue.

Smithers had returned to London, and I lay in the shivering half-stupefied agony of mortal illness, wishing only that the incessant pain and fever would end. My bedclothes were perpetually soaked. The Belgian doctor blistered me, which gave me a dreadful pain in the spine, and any sudden change of position gave me beans. He put me on a diet of fruit and milk and forbade me to draw. I was furious, but what did he care? He was healthy.

By late April I could walk without a stick, but stairs were the very devil. I was a prisoner, tied to a mattress which soaked up the sweat and the sterile seeds of wet dreams. For these continued unabated, Father, and mocked my new dilemma: I was mentally randy but physically impotent. My prick, my staff of life, my pen and my power, it was dead.

The breathlessness – God, the horror of suffocation.

When Smithers sent me a copy of *The Rape of the Lock* I wept, for I thought I should never again see work of mine published. The book was as beautiful as I had imagined it, and I forgave Smithers everything.

I kept the seriousness of my situation from Mother for as long as I could. Sick as I was, the idea of returning to the life of an invalid under her care was the final sign of defeat. I knew she disapproved of Smithers, and I knew that she disapproved of the way I had chosen to live my life, and I didn't want to answer her inevitable enquiries. I dreaded seeing her again.

Instead, I asked Mabel to come and spirit me back to London. She, however, had a small but regular theatrical engagement and risked losing her place if she left. She was perfectly willing to do so, but I would not let her. Mother would have to do.

Before Mother came, the doctor gave me a complete 'clean-out' with creosote, followed by acetate of lead – regarded, he said, as invaluable in checking expectorations.

'I don't expectorate anything but the best from you, Doctor,' I said.

One small miracle – for so it seemed. Rayon came all the way to Brussels to see me. She was concerned. It seemed she had even fallen a little bit in love with me. Love! Was it still possible?

I lay back and let her work her wiles on me – darling Rayon of the downy upper lip. She did her utmost – a perfect Venus to my wasted Tannhäuser – to tease my flaccid prick back to life. And I grieved – my body ached for a full communion with hers, and I knew I should never have it. I could not. The fever hummed in my ears, in my heart; I was aflame for her; and I could not, and never would have her – have anyone. I was doomed. There was no hope for me, no chance to enjoy the bliss of marital tenderness and satisfaction. The disease had claimed me for its own – I was its lover; it would suffer no other.

Mother arrived in early May, ill and exhausted herself, and together we crawled back to London. Immediately I went round to Dr Symes Thompson, who pronounced very unfavourably on my condition. He and Mother immediately conspired to ship me off to Crowborough, where the air was fresh and earthly temptations few.

I couldn't stand Crowborough, and I couldn't stand Mother. The two of them together were enough to drive a reasonable man to despair. I could share neither my work nor my life with her, and was expected always to be the dutiful dying boy.

What did I care about the beautiful Sussex landscapes she constantly exhorted me to enjoy, as if there were some benefit to be gained from staring at a 'lovely scene'? That natural world she and the doctors are always praising has never inspired me or influenced my drawings one jot. Under the sunlit surface they know and love I see quite another world lying in wait: a ravenous mother, queen of the beetles and the worms, eager to devour me, horrifyingly maternal in the way she chews up life and reduces it to the dark Ur-broth of her womb.

I am against Nature. And I was definitely against Crowborough. The hatred I felt for it, and for her, my maternal guardian, was so great that I had to punish her.

It was an old game, and one in which I was always the victor. The only rules were my rules; what I wanted must prevail. To gain my release I simply turned my face to the wall every time she entered the room, and said nothing. A man must stand up to his mother, after all, or risk annihilation.

In June, so that I might sip a more beneficial air, I was moved to the Spread Eagle Hotel in Epsom. I remembered the town from my boyhood, when we had briefly lived in Ashley Road. It was here, when I was eleven, that Lady Hentietta Pelham had given me my very first commission for drawings.

My work now was very different from those childish Kate Greenaway place-cards. In Epsom, with the doctors' assurances that I was making progress, I drew like a demon on a new set of drawings for Smithers.

You will never see my *Lysistrata* drawings, Father. They would shock you to the depths of your gentle celibate soul. There is nothing morally reprehensible in them, yet they celebrate the rampant carnality of Aristophanes's play with a frankness and comic gusto unmatched since antiquity.

As drawings they are superb. I dispensed with all the painstaking background perspectives and details I had mastered in *The Rape of the Lock* and concentrated my characters instead in pure outline on a flat white surface. Greek vases and the old Greek satyr plays provided my aesthetic inspiration, and the physical circumstances of my captivity provided the imaginative.

What was more appropriate to my situation, after all, than this play in which the men of Sparta and Athens are forbidden their carnal rights? I, too, was now forbidden the fulfilment of sex. I was no more than a bawd in a gelded cage. My cock, like the ones I gave the Greek men, was a giant ache in want of relief.

It seemed tied up with the disease somehow, this constant irritable longing of my sexual organ and sexual imagination. Tormented by visions and memories of Rayon, Penny Plain and all the girls I had wantonly fucked or imagined fucking, I frigged myself with a violence that shook the bed and left me gasping for air and drenched with sweat. But to no avail. I could not come. The disease was supping on the very root of my manhood.

Smithers was planning to publish the *Lysistrata* in a very limited edition of a hundred copies for private distribution only (yes, with Smithers I had gone from *Under the Hill* to under the counter). We both knew that, if sold openly, the drawings would be classified as obscene, so worked on the project with the utmost secrecy.

At first I was nervous and self-conscious about this obscene commission. Defiance and a continuing need to prove myself drove my pen. Then, as the drawings actually took shape, and the combustive elements of creation ignited, I slipped into a divine state of knowingness, and saw how revolutionary the drawings were. Some would call them pornography; to me they were simply gorgeous grotesque drawings that fitted Aristophanes's text perfectly. Some would call me a pornographer; but as I drew I felt like a saint. My gold pen became the instrument of my martyrdom, killing me with the proud feverish ecstasy of my art.

Of course I would not let Mother see the beautiful hairy cunts and cannon-sized phalluses in my *Lysistrata*. She knew I was drawing, which the doctors had forbidden, but she dared not reproach me for fear that I would again turn away from her. Nor did I tell André what I was doing, except by oblique reference. His censure might lead to a withdrawal of support, and it seemed wiser to indulge him in the fantasy that I was reading all his pious books with the greatest of interest, and conversing deeply and with serious religious intent with the priests he sent to call on me.

My spirits remained tolerable so long as I could draw and believe that I was getting better. In August, however, the month of my twenty-fourth birthday, the haemorrhaging returned with a foul vengeance. Doctors and more doctors. Whispered consultations with Mother, just beyond my hearing. Coughing, pain, fever, diarrhoea, vomiting, blood. Finally I was told that my left lung had broken down completely, and the right was becoming infected.

I lay then in a seething whirlpool of dread. I was dying. I would be judged by the work I left behind. Where was I going? What terrors and mysteries would be revealed to me in that world beyond the grave? Debts remained to be paid – my hotel room in Paris – the smallest and most trivial details vied for attention with that other one, the great one, the certainty of my death.

I had to prepare for it, be ready for it at any time. But I was not ready. There was too much I had yet to do.

With Smithers as witness, I signed a will naming Mabel as the sole executrix of my estate.

Though the distance between us made my sister a rare visitor, she was always in my thoughts. I had hoarded nearly a thousand pounds for her, money she would find useful as she pursued the vagaries of a theatrical career. Mother, I feared, would prove unequal to administering my artistic remains. For one thing, she might be faced with the bawdy drawings I had done as private commissions for Smithers or, secretly, for Herbert Pollitt. Confronting the reality of my underground existence would cause her so much pain and bewilderment that I thought it better to spare her. Mabel, however, was too broad-minded to be shocked, we kept no secrets from one another; and she would be a shrewd negotiator, better able than Mother to deal with any posthumous sales, contracts or rights to do with my work.

Mabel came to visit when I was moved again, this time to Boscombe, in Hampshire, and found rooms for me overlooking Southampton Bay in a villa called Pier View. If it was sea air that I needed, I wanted to go to Brighton, with its Regency charm and lively throngs of visitors. I knew Brighton, and found a curious comfort in the idea of returning home. But Mother and the doctors said no. Absolute rest and absolute quiet were essential, and God knows Boscombe was quiet. It was a place for cast-offs, for lonely old ladies and retired colonels, a place not for the living but for the dying or already dead.

Mabel stayed a week before Mother came. I dreaded her departure, fearing I would never see her again, and followed her every movement with the eyes of a jealous keening puppy. I hungered for the touch of her cool white hand on my burning flesh.

Darling Mabel, how I loved her. I hoarded up impressions of her as a miser does his gold. By living independently my sister had by now liberated aspects of her character and demeanour that for many years had remained quiescent. She now spoke freely, even boldly, and expressed opinions that even the newest of New Women might find *outré*. Stylishly flamboyant, determinedly Bohemian, she favoured mannish clothes when she was off the stage and out of the public's eye. Her tall willowy figure now had the wilful touch of an Amazon in it.

At times I felt almost as if our roles had been reversed, that I was now nothing more than a weak helpless girl and Mabel my strong older brother. I could rest in her strength, and bathe in her tender solicitude.

Yet, for all her showy vitality and bold-spirited charm, she remained tortured by a secret guilt, some oppressive weight that never allowed her to stop examining her spiritual conscience.

Mabel understood me in a way Mother never could. She kept nothing from me, and regaled me with stories of backstage life in the theatre, of gossip and scandal and all the things that make the cauldron of London life so delightful and irksome. Drawn into the Catholic trinity of South Audley Street, she frequently saw André, John Gray and Miss Gribbell. The Church tempted her, and she confessed that she had actually gone to confession. She was, in fact, being coached for her new role of convert by Father Sebastian Bowden, André's favourite priest.

'It is such a beautiful religion,' she explained, 'and it answers so many questions.'

'Yes, all very neat and tidy; but, my God, Mabel, one must give up so much for it. Free will! I'm not ready to renounce my past as sinful – it would be like condemning everything I had done, and saying it had no value.'

She paused, nervously touching her hair, and then sat down beside me with downcast eyes. 'Our past *was* sinful, Aubrey.'

'How can you say that!' I cried, straining to sit up in the bed. I took her hand and put it to my hot face and kissed it. 'Mabel, we are different.'

'Yes, I know,' she said quietly.

'An ordinary life has never been ours. From the time we were children playing the piano for the Duke of X.'

She started at the mention of his name. 'That beast.'

'It all started with him, didn't it? In some strange way.'

'I've never told Mother,' Mabel said.

'It was Mother who allowed him to molest us.'

'Aubrey, how can you say such things? That is not true!'

'It was Mother who took us there. We had no choice but to do the things we did. We had to perform, always, and everywhere, and with everyone. It was the only way we could have their love.'

'Their hypocritical love,' Mabel said dimly.

'We did the best we could, Mabel, under very difficult circumstances.'

'They've become no less difficult, I find.' To keep herself from crying she quickly rose from my bedside.

'Do you still love me?'

'Oh, Aubrey.' Her face crumbled, and she ran back to me, sobbing.

'Perhaps there's a different philosophy for people like us,' I said, happy now that I could stroke her hair and have her in my arms. 'Something that explains but does not condemn.'

'I wish we could have a little house together,' she whispered in my ear.

'We will, darling, we will.'

'Do you remember how happy we were? Is that all the happiness we shall ever have? I can't bear to think so.'

'Where should our little house be?' I said, changing my tone to that of a father speaking intimately to his daughter. 'In Pimlico?'

She caught on to my game at once. 'No,' she said, pouting like a little girl, 'not in 'imlico.'

'Where, then?' I whispered.

Her eyes grew round as saucers. 'In Wegent's Pahk.'

For the first time in months I laughed. Mabel could always do this to me, and it was one of the reasons I loved her so. With no one else could I be so freely myself, and indulge my taste for verbal games and absurdities. She laughed, too, but quickly grew serious again.

'There's something I haven't told you, Aubrey.'

I saw my future with her wiped out. 'You're getting married.'

'You know I would never do that,' she said, staring at me as if the idea was monstrous. 'No, it's something else. I may be going away. There's a chance that I might be offered a tour with Bourchier's company.'

'Where?'

'In America,' she said, avoiding my eye.

'So far!' was all I could say. The thought of her proceeding with her own life, when mine was now circumscribed to this one dismal room, added to the weight of mortality already crushing my chest. Thoughts like this were constantly torturing my mind, reminding me that with my death only my life would end, while others would continue through future years without me.

'I shan't go if you think—'

'Of course you must go. When?'

'In December.'

'And for how long?'

'Six months,' she said.

I wondered if I would ever see her again. 'You must go,' I said.

*   *   *

In December she returned to say goodbye before sailing from Southampton. When Mother left the room, Mabel held me with the passion of Venus, Isolde, Guinevere. I could feel her very essence blend with mine. And when she had gone I was seized with a frantic need to see her ship actually sailing away. Why it seemed so important, I do not know, but so urgent was my desire that I got out of bed and dressed with a speed I had not been able to muster for weeks.

'Is it wise?' Mother kept asking, infuriating me. 'Is it wise?' She was frightened and barely had time to pull on her coat and hat if she wanted to keep up with me.

There is a high seaside promenade in Boscombe Gardens, ideal for watching the boats leaving Southampton Bay. There I climbed, seeming to know the path by instinct though I had never been on it before. I thought of nothing except that I must see Mabel's ship. My breath was high and shallow in my lungs, never quite as deep as I wanted it to be. Mother followed, breathless from the rapid ascent, calling after me, telling me that I must slow down.

At the top of the cliff a view so spectacular met my eye that I stopped in my tracks, struck dumb with what I can only describe as rapture. After nearly four unending months of confinement in my sickroom, all at once I saw eternity. The sun was the colour of a blood-soaked wafer being dipped into the chalice of the sea. Far far out, yet perfectly clear, was Mabel's steamer, on its way to New York.

'Mabel!' I cried, waving frantically. 'Mabel!'

The next moments are difficult to describe. I felt the blood rushing up from my chest to my throat and stumbled in alarm as it gushed out of my mouth. I was afraid to breathe, lest I suffocate on it, yet I had to breathe, for I was being smothered. The sheer force of it was as strong as a blow from within, and to my horror the blood would not stop, but kept pouring out in peristaltic waves.

Mother was stunned and didn't know what to do. I heard her crying my name, and then weakly calling out for help. We were alone on the cliff. 'Aubrey,' she whimpered, trying to staunch the flow with her absurdly tiny handkerchief. 'Aubrey darling.' My body might have been broken on the wheel, so limp was it. Mother tried to raise me but could not. 'Dear God,' I heard her say, and then call again for help. She tried to lay me out on the turf, but the position made me choke and clutch frantically at the air. 'I must go for help!' She wrapped her cloak around me and hurried off.

It was the queerest thing, Father. I was suddenly floating in a warm pool of perfectly quiet light. I had never seen light so beautiful, or felt such calm. When I looked down, I saw my body, quite plainly, lying like a broken doll on the grass. I felt nothing for it – it was simply a body, sloughed off like the shell of a snail. Where I was looking from I cannot tell you. But I then saw Mabel's boat, and then the deck of the boat, and then Mabel herself, standing alone and staring back towards the land with a look of such deep sorrow that it grieved me. I wanted to go to her, tell her not to weep, but the light suddenly began to vanish, or be pulled back within me, and I was conscious of myself on earth once more, in pain, the blood-stained grass by my face, and knew that I would die if I did not rise and find water. I was not yet ready for the warm light.

I shall not bore you, Father, with more details of my illness. It is my mental state that I am now examining. The life of the mind is the life of the soul.

My soul, by the end of the year 1896, was seemingly dead. A stagnant pond. I had nothing to celebrate. My health was gone. All the old fears I had about Smithers had returned. *The Savoy* was dying. Worse still, publication of my *Book of Fifty Drawings* was delayed because of Smithers's business mismanagement. That book meant more to me than anything else. I wanted it to be an entirely pretty monument to my career, showing the progression of my work from *Morte D'Arthur* to the *The Savoy*. I desperately needed to know exactly when it would be out; but my cleverly evasive publisher, in letter after letter, would never let me know where the project stood.

As I got sicker and sicker, fewer and fewer of my drawings appeared in *The Savoy*, usually with an accompanying note that owing to illness, etc. etc. It was horrible to see those public statements announcing, for all intents and purposes, my death. Even my drawings seemed to announce the fact. One was called 'The Death of Pierrot', and showed Pierrot's body in bed and his collapsed spirit in a chair. Another one, 'Ave Atque Vale', accompanied my translation of Catullus' Carmen CXI, in which a youth comes to say hail and farewell to his brother's ashes.

All through those Boscombe months I had in fact been drawing whenever I could. New ideas were constantly agitating my thoughts. My work was all I had left, all that made my exile tolerable, the only thing that kept me from dwelling too much on my deteriorating condition. When Smithers finally announced that the December issue of *The Savoy* would be the last, I let it be known that all the artwork in the final number was to be mine, just as all the writing was to be Symons's.

Music had returned to me, and I put it in my drawings gratefully. Little Chopin waltzes I had played as a boy began to haunt my memory and inspired me to complete my two Chopin drawings. I read the score of Wagner's opera *Das Rheingold* as though it were a novel, and heard as I never would in life the mystery of its prelude, which seemed to rise up from the very mud of the Rhine. Wagner is one of my heroes, and I drew the mythical creatures of the Rhine as a homage to him. There was Wotan, King and Father of the Gods, proud and majestic in a black cape, and Erda, the Earth Mother, rising from her primeval sleep to utter a warning. The charming Rhinemaiden Flosshilde swam through my pen, and Alberich, the bound hairy dwarf shaking his fist with rage, was none other than the imprisoned Oscar. Loge, the god of fire, was my favourite, and I drew his essence with an insider's knowledge: his body, like mine, was ceaselessly consumed by a sheet of flames.

For Smithers I began a set of drawings for Juvenal's *Satires*, which he wanted to issue, like the *Lysistrata*, in a private edition. The drawings were far more corrupt than the ones I had done for Aristophanes, and were meant to show the joyless degradation into which Roman society had fallen. I pictured the Empress-whore Messalina, wife of Claudius, stealing off to the rank whorehouse she frequented at night, and returning home the next morning to her unsatisfied place at the Emperor's side. I showed Juvenal scourging a woman rammed down on a giant pole.

When the Juvenal project broke down with Smithers, I offered my illustration of 'The Impatient Adulterer' fiddling with his foreskin to my secret and *sympathique* patron, Herbert Pollitt, thereby gaining a few extra guineas. Pollitt was always on the lookout for erotic drawings which suited his inverted temperament. He was an odd and amusing chap who had created quite a stir at Cambridge by performing a Loïe Fuller dance in full drag. (*Drag*, Father, is a word coined by inverts; it means 'dressed as a girl'.) Perhaps that was why he was so eager to receive the two additional drawings I offered him. These showed the effeminate Roman dancer Bathyllus, described by Juvenal, performing his lewd rendition of 'Leda and the Swan'.

I also drew Pierrot, over and over again. At last I understood him, that thin white clown with the thin tragic face. I understood his exhaustion. It was my exhaustion, and the exhaustion of the whole nineteenth century as it drew to a close. It was the knowledge of mortality, his own and that of a civilization grown stagnant and corrupt. The degeneration of the entire human species, grown evil not by design but by the progressive debasement of its blood, stares back at Pierrot from the darkness on the other side of the footlights.

Pierrot knew, as surely as I did, the terrifying value of each grain of sand as it dropped through the hourglass.

AUBREY BEARDSLEY

I

XVII

BARELY MADE IT to the New Year of 1897. *This* year, Father, just five endless months ago. In January I lay between life and death. The disease was apparently spreading rapidly, and as my left lung grew purulent and began to disintegrate I spat it up in bloody coughing attacks that exhausted me to the point of delirium.

I must have looked like a vampire in dire need of blood as I lay there in a troubled feverish swoon, skeletally thin, my lips cracked and swollen, and my

383

eyes staring out from black craters. The deadly sin of Vanity had no place in those days.

Old friends came to visit. To say goodbye. Bobbie Ross. Aymer. Others. I craved news of the world, of London, of anywhere beyond that tomb-like room with the dreadful wallpaper whose pattern swirled through my dreams. Yet in some curious way none of it seemed to matter. The consuming flames of my disease had burned through my connections to the world. I had sloughed off human emotions, discarded them like a useless skin.

I was too ill to work, but my imaginative powers remained unimpaired. If anything, they grew more violent – accelerated, I suppose, by the very fear of their annihilation.

By the middle of the month my condition was critical, and it was decided that a move to some more vigorous climate might prove beneficial. A dead whale was washed up on Boscombe beach on the very day I was borne off. A closed heated carriage took me the two miles to Bournemouth, where I was installed in yet another hideous room, this time in a guest-house called 'Muriel' on Exeter Road.

A ghastly monkey-puzzle tree in the front of the house became an omen of death to me. All day long enormous black rooks darted in and out of it, cawing with demented laughter as they feasted on some unseen carrion hidden within the darkness of its ugly branches. I hated that tree, yet it was all I could see from the window.

Still, the neighbourhood was livelier and less morgue-like than Boscombe, and I dreamed of attending symphony concerts in the Winter Gardens Pavilion nearby. The new doctor, Dr Harsant, said that Pier View had been quite the wrong place for me, and that the move to Bournemouth had probably saved my life. Ah, why do we keep paying doctors if not to hear that our lives have been saved by coming to them?

Still, even Dr Harsant talked of the necessity of a milder climate, which meant out of dear damp England. Yet another move. Where? Knowing I had not many months now to live, I needed to settle on one fixed place. But there were so many to choose from, each offering its own special wine of air and atmosphere. Kreuznach, Soden (close, I believe, to Gommorah), Bagnères-de-Bigorre, Luchon, Cannes, Luxor, Menton, Biarritz, Davos, Monte Carlo. Was I to spend my last days in the frigid air of the Swiss Alps or in the mummifying

384

blaze of an Egyptian desert? Was I to sniff the soft ozone-laden zephyrs along the southern coast of France or inhale vapours in some place as yet undiscovered? Air, never enough air.

In March another haemorrhage occurred, spurred on by a bitter wind blowing across the bay. Now I was not only chilled to the marrow, but my hands were transparently blue and my perpetually aching teeth chattered with the cold. Even sitting up was forbidden. What an ignoble existence, alternately freezing or burning under the bedclothes! All I wanted was London – dear city of triumph and tragedy – and a little house where Mabel and I might live and work when she returned from her American tour.

She had left Bourchier's company, by the way, and joined up with another headed by none other than Charley Cochran, my old friend from Brighton Grammar School. Charley, who had introduced me at the age of thirteen to the sin of Onan, frigging himself in comical poses under the old pier, had emigrated to America where he had become C. B. Cochran, Theatrical Management. From Mabel's lively accounts, I gathered that Charley had gone from hand to mouth, as it were, and now had one ravishing *ingénue* after another glued to his lips.

As the weeks wore on, Dr Harsant began to speak of the necessity of a long long rest on the northern coast of France. He put me on gallic acid and ergotine, but still the bleeding continued. After a thorough examination of my sunken chest he concluded that, whatever the situation in the left lung, the right one had deteriorated no further and would not, if I left England.

As soon as I felt reasonably assured, the blood made its appearance again – this time out of my bum. Spitting blood is one thing, shitting it quite another. Dr Harsant, in whom I was fast losing confidence, suggested it came from the liver.

Through all those months, no matter where I was, André kept in daily touch with me. He never deserted me. Accustomed as I was to holding him at arm's length, as it were, it took me some time to discern that his brotherly solicitude was genuine. His concern for my welfare began at last to touch some part of me I had thought to be frozen.

His spiritual advances I continued to resist, but even that was becoming more difficult. I considered conversion from a purely

385

financial standpoint, of course, but as a genuine solution to a need in my soul it remained impossible. By a simple renunciation of my past and a promise to abide by the rules of the Church in the future I could wipe the slate clean. My soul would be a sheet of virgin vellum. But to renounce my past was to renounce my art. If I denounced my erotic drawings as wilfully obscene, I denounced my self, the self I had exercised with free will and a determination to abide by no rules save those I myself created.

Along with André's generous gifts of pious books, hothouse fruit, bouquets of flowers, and boxes of chocolate, there arrived one day a small vial of water from Lourdes. It frightened me. What was I to do with it? Drink it? Bathe in it? Pour it over my head? It was on my bedside table when André himself came to visit.

That was the last time but one I saw him. Mother ushered him in with a reverence she had never showed to Smithers. André's dress was more severely clerical than ever, but stylishly so, for he is a perfect martyr to fashion. A white gardenia was fixed in his lapel, and he had put on his magnetic rings to ward off the rheumatism that made his tiny hands ache so. I noticed that he was carrying an intriguingly shaped parcel and wondered if it was for me.

André started when he saw me, but was too polite to comment on my altered appearance.

'Aubrey, my dear friend,' he said in gentle sickroom tones, 'you are looking better.'

'No, I'm not,' I said.

Mother fussed over me as if I were a doll. 'My little white mouse remains impossible, Mr Raffalovich,' she confided playfully to André, snaring his attention with a sad sympathetic glance. The glance of the living, I thought. 'Temper tantrums.'

'How tired I am, André, of hearing my lung creak all day, like a badly made pair of boots.'

'We are following the doctor's orders exactly,' Mother said quickly, as if she were afraid of being charged with neglect. 'It was too good of you, Mr Raffalovich, to send Dr Harsant to us.'

'Dr Harsant's treatment is only making me worse,' I grumbled.

Again I saw that glance pass between André and my mother. Sharing the secrets of the living.

'Father Bearne tells me that you have been talking with

him,' André said, taking the visitor's chair beside my bed. 'That pleases me.'

André had been sending priests to me for some time now, all of them Jesuits of course. Intellectually I enjoyed their company, even looked forward to it after one too many dismal conversations with Mother. Yet I always knew, or at least suspected, that they were being charming only because their underlying goal was to woo me over to the Church. The greater the beast, the greater the conquest. What I *was* meant nothing to them; their sole concern was what I would be.

'They have good libraries,' I admitted.

'The Jesuits never allow one who belongs to them to lack anything,' André assured me.

It was impossible, of course, to have any real conversation with Mother hovering near, and I was glad when André finally asked her if he might speak to me alone. Mother practically curtsied to him before she left.

'How is London?' I asked.

'Oh, we scurry on through the season.'

'I don't know which is worse, to be in London or away from it. It's a confounded nuisance to have to conduct all one's business by penny post.'

'I'm told Smithers is close to bankruptcy,' André said pleasantly.

'That's a lie. In fact he's bringing out my album of drawings any week now.'

'I shall look forward to seeing it, of course.' He paused to brush a hair from his trousers. 'John Gray passed by Smithers's new shop in the Royal Arcade the other day, did I tell you? He noticed that one of your drawings was in the window. For sale.'

I hid my jolt of apprehension by asking how much Smithers was asking.

'I do not know – quite a lot, I believe. I assume he shares with you any profits he may make on your work?'

'Of course,' I lied.

'Are you working now?' he asked.

'Yes, but I'm torn between illustrating *Mademoiselle de Maupin* and *Les Liaisons Dangereuses*. Which do you think would be more improper?'

'Both would suit you,' André said wearily.

The Devil himself must have inspired me to ask if he had seen my new illustrations for the *Lysistrata*. I pulled out a copy hidden away in my bedside table and watched with interest as André examined the drawings.

He showed no trace of emotion as he handed the volume back to me. 'Why must you abuse your talents this way?'

'I have so little else to abuse down here.'

'I know pornography when I see it,' he said.

'And I know a weekly cheque for twelve pounds when I see it.'

'It is what one would expect. Pornographers produce pornography.'

'It is not pornography! It is my work, what I am paid to do. It is my life, and I am in no way ashamed of it, André. Living in your somewhat rarefied world, you may not realize that it costs money to die.'

'Money again!' He threw up an exasperated hand. 'You continue to take Smithers's foul coin yet you reject mine! Why? With a quarterly allowance you could rest.'

'I'll be resting soon enough, André. While I'm alive I need to work and to have my work published, to be an everlasting annoyance to the people of Philistia. For the little time that is left to me I want to be out among people, in the brightest, warmest sun I can find, not huddled up in some dark damp church muttering unheard prayers and promising to give up chocolates for Lent.'

'Prayers never go unheard,' he insisted, as he always insisted.

'I am prey to very black moods, André. I pray, but the prayers mean nothing. I feel nothing except depression and fear.'

He reached over to me. 'Then it is time, my dear brother, to give yourself up to God.'

'I am an artist. Piety and belief are stumbling-blocks to an artist. They stand in the way of expression. An artist must go as far as he can—'

'Like Monsieur Wilde?'

'Yes, unfortunately. Each in his own way.'

'The fear and depression you describe are a malady common to our age,' André said. 'We all feel it, especially the upper classes. At certain moments in history, when civilization is coming to an end, a spiritual nausea seems to prevail, and a weariness with existence. A constant sense of foreboding. I have felt it myself.'

'But you overcame it,' I said bitterly. 'You managed to escape its grip by turning your will over to God. And I would, too, André, if I only knew how. How?' I asked, or pleaded, rather, for at that moment I was overcome by a strange longing for peace.

His dark eyes blazed, kindled by my sudden earnestness. 'There are two ways of ridding ourselves of a thing which burdens us,' he said, moving closer. 'One can cast it away, or one can let it fall. To cast away implies a certain interest, a certain animation, even a certain fear. But to let fall is absolute indifference, absolute contempt. Believe me, Aubrey, use this method and Satan will flee.'

I said nothing, but could feel movement from somewhere deep in my bowels, something dislodged, sparked into life and struggling to be free.

'Listen to me,' he said, his voice altered by deep emotion. 'I suffered as you do, from a kind of blindness. I, too, failed to realize that we must live in mystery.'

'We live by chance,' I weakly insisted.

'No, but if chance existed it would be even more mysterious than Providence.'

'Yes, it all sounds adorable, but as a philosophy of life it must end in a kind of fatalism.'

'Faith in our Lord is not fatalism!' he said, taking both my hands. Mine were so cold and sore, his so warm. 'Free will always remains free. You can continue to reject His offices, Aubrey, but you do so at your peril.'

'I hate the idea of redemption!' I cried. 'I find it utterly middle-class.'

'But you have always been fascinated by the spiritual life,' he said, speaking a truth I did not want to hear. 'Like me, fascinated and fearful of it.'

Then I told him, as I had told no one else, of my boyhood vision, of the cross with the bleeding Christ which had appeared on my bedroom wall. André listened with the rapt intensity of one who craved miracles.

'It was a sign,' he whispered, 'don't you see?'

'It had no meaning that I could understand,' I said.

'A man – a God – dying on a cross for your sins, giving Himself to you, out of love, asking only for your love in return, that is the meaning of the Cross,' André said. His falcon head with its sharp hooked nose was poised over me as if I were a feast, and he looked into my eyes as if he wanted to begin there, to pluck out and devour my vision. 'You know the meaning of that cross,' he insisted. 'You know it as well as I do.'

'Sometimes I think it is I hanging on that cross.'

'Yes, it is you, in His sacred heart – you, Aubrey, whom He loves.'

'I am unworthy,' I said, speaking from a place I had left long ago, some hidden crevice of my soul that remained clear and white amidst the blackening rot around it.

André squeezed my hands to his chest. 'It is the unworthy who are the worthiest,' he whispered, an emotional dew filling his eyes. 'Aubrey, it would be the happiest moment of my life if you threw off this malignancy of pessimism and accepted the generous love of Christ. Now. This very minute. You can rest in him.'

'I can never rest,' I said, still determined to resist him. 'I must drive myself to the limits of my endurance.'

'But why?'

'Because I haven't got long to live! I know my disease cannot be cured. I shall not live longer than Keats did. And I have a mother to care for. My tailor, Doré, has just served me with a writ for payment. I cannot return to France for the number of creditors there. And on top of these material worries I have my art to consider. That is why I cannot rest, André.'

'But suppose – just suppose – you had an allowance, a regular quarterly sum sufficient to pay for all your expenses. Let us say a hundred guineas a quarter, with the understanding, of course, that if this amount is not adequate you will inform me and it will be increased.'

How tempting it was, Father. A regular income for doing nothing. A spiritual advance payment. 'What are your terms, André?'

'Only that you rest, and stop your incessant worrying about money.'

'I shall continue to work,' I insisted.

'Of course,' he agreed, 'but perhaps this sum – if you accept it –

will allow you to stop providing Smithers with certain kinds of work.'

The rasping laughter of the rooks filled me with apprehension. 'I will consider it, André.'

'Dear Brother!' he gasped, beside himself with joy.

'I make no promises, but I will seriously consider it.'

With trembling hands he offered me the package. It contained a large, exquisitely wrought crucifix.

'I came today praying for a miracle,' André said.

'I am sorry to disappoint you.'

He ignored my dry tone and paced excitedly back and forth beside my bed. 'You understand, don't you? You spoke of seeing a cross, and I have brought you one. A miracle. Our sympathies are in perfect accord. We are twin souls.'

Why should it mean so much to him? I asked myself that question again and again. And was it true? Was his life for me the pure love of brother for brother? Or was there something else in it, some redirected desire of the John Gray kind?

After all his hard work I wanted to give something in return, and I knew that what he wanted more than anything else was intimacy. Someone with whom he could share his soul and indulge his generosity. What more does any of us want?

The crucifix was pleasantly heavy, but wonderfully slender and elegant. I was taken by its design. I laid it down on my chest and motioned for André to fetch my drinking-glass and the holy water from Lourdes.

He watched with greedy eyes as I poured out the water. My own heart was pounding, for I was terrified of a miracle. 'Our Lady's bathwater,' I said, toasting André and drinking it down in a gulp.

Now I motioned for him to come closer. 'Dear Brother,' I said, 'will you help me to pray?'

They were like trance words. André's eyes closed immediately, he bowed his head and began to say a Hail Mary. I joined him, and as I prayed I could feel that strange warmth moving again in my bowels. 'Pray for us sinners, now and at the hour of our death.' The moment I had finished saying the words I knew what that strange warmth was, and I turned my eyes to heaven as the blood bubbled from my arse like a hot blasphemous spring.

*　　*　　*

One day, soon afterwards, I decided to live. I gave myself one more year. And from then on I believed that I was recovering, and getting better by the day.

Thanks to André, a move was now being planned. I had decided on the south coast of France, but Dr Harsant forbade travelling further than Paris. There were worse places to die, the guest-house 'Muriel' being one of them, and the idea of Paris never failed to arouse my excitement. It was settled then, but did not give me as much joy as it might have done, for I knew that I would never see England again.

One delicious treat was allowed me before I left. With Dr Harsant in attendance, I heard a symphony concert at the Winter Gardens Pavilion. My ears, starved for music, sucked in each note, each chord, each progression, theme and coda, and I tried to keep from weeping as the old ineffable bliss of music travelled one last time up what was left of my spinal cord.

André made sure that my last days in England were comfortable. Every foot of the journey from Bournemouth to London was planned for us, expense being no object. How delicious it was not having to count every ha'penny, and to know again the charming comforts made possible by wealth.

Mother and I travelled first class to London, and were met at Charing Cross with a lovely padded Bath chair. My withered corpse of a body was propped up and wrapped round with heaps of thick woollen blankets to keep out the sharp London winds. No walking was necessary; I was *wheeled* out to André's waiting heated carriage.

From Charing Cross we were driven to the blessedly modern Hotel Windsor with a blessedly modern lift in it. Flowers, chocolates and a heap of pi books, including John Gray's new volume called *Spiritual Poems*, waited for us in our charming sitting-room. I was curious to see what John Gray, the sinner-turned-saint, had to say about the soul.

I could barely move, my chest ached, and there was a stinging halo of pain round my fundament. Yet I was almost happy. I was back in London – back in the filthy, wet, noisy, eloquently squalid city that I so loved.

We saw André, of course – it was the last time I saw him – and John Gray came for a brief visit. He was mysteriously shy about his book, and said he had definitely settled now on taking holy orders. André had himself joined the order of Little Oratorians. He was now relinquishing all worldly ties, he said, by giving up what had meant the most to him: his writing.

That's a relief anyway, I thought. His last pamphlet, published in France and called '*'Uranisme, Inversion Sexuelle Congénitale*', had been a bizarre study of inversion. The condition, he maintained, was a congenital one, an inherited propensity. Who knows? Perhaps it is.

Mother enjoyed tea with Miss Gribbell, who spoke unendingly of Mabel. Mother, in turn, spoke unendingly of André. Ironic, how little they actually knew about either.

Raff's private physician, Dr Phillips, whom you have heard me mention with fondness and respect, and who just came to examine me here in St-Germain, gave me a thorough examination. My left lung, he said, had consolidated generally, but there was no cause for immediate alarm. I begged him to tell me how matters stood, preferring truth at this point to the comforting lies other doctors had given me.

'I am telling you,' he said, 'that given proper treatment an entire recovery is not impossible.'

I'm certain those frank eyes of his could not lie, just as yours could not, and I searched them fearlessly for the telltale sign of falsehood but found none.

Before we left I had my hair cut. I brushed my fringe to the sides and exposed my burning forehead to the air. Then I had myself 'photoed', the last photograph of me to be taken in England. The photographer was able to 'touch up' my wasted features. André's carriage returned us to Charing Cross, where he had taken seats on the boat-train to Boulogne. 'Are you comfortable, my dear?' Mother asked.

I didn't answer. Through the carriage window I was seeing London for the last time. My city. My true home, which would not have me.

The entire journey was supervised by Dr Phillips, who accompanied us, and was handled so judiciously, so expertly, that I almost enjoyed it. And then I was in Paris, dear Father, where through André's kind introduction I met you.

*   *   *

The mere sight of Paris was a blessed treat. We had rooms at the Hôtel Voltaire, where Wagner had once stayed, and a view over the Seine to the Louvre. You know, dear Father, the miraculous resurrection I experienced there. For the first time in four months I was able to go out walking. My eyes watered at the sight of the delicious tender green on the trees. Paris, the city of satisfying proportions, and such a joy after the horrid squareness of England.

Yes, just a month ago I felt as fit as a fighting cock, and walked the streets as pertinaciously as a tart. Only, to avoid haemorrhage, I was carried up to my rooms at night.

Mother, however, could not abide Paris and was utterly British over everything. 'They really have no courtesy here,' she complained, 'none whatsoever. Every one of them is a thief or a trollop or an anarchist.'

'Or an artist,' I said dreamily. We were sitting near the fountain in the Palais Royale. The sun was setting with that soft subtlety and sublimity known only to Paris in the spring. The colours were superb. A few wisps of cloud high above were stained as red as a consumptive's handkerchief, but everything else was quietly shaded in gradations of pink, yellow and lavender. This Nature-worship was quite a new thing for me. I was also hatching schemes for new drawings and anticipating the evening ahead. I was meeting some new friends for supper in the Quartier and we were going on from there to the Gaîeté, where Yvette Guilbert was singing.

It would have been almost perfect if it hadn't been for Mother.

'I hardly know why I am here,' she said, furiously rolling up a spindle of embroidery thread, 'when you spend so little time with me.'

'Mother,' I said, 'I am well. I want to be out and about.'

Her lips were grimly set, and she looked exactly what she was: a middle-class Englishwoman determined to hate Paris and make life a misery for her son.

'I have seen this before, Aubrey. A change of scene and a new set of drawings – it fills you with a furious energy. You then take on too much, spend far more time away from me than with me, when, supposedly, according to the generous terms of Mr Raffalovich, you are to be in my care.'

'Care, Mother, not grip.' I was determined to keep my temper, not to spoil my rare lovely mood, but as usual she was able to put me into a guilty fret.

She pulled her shawl closer, to ward off the evening chill before it arrived. 'Perhaps I should return to England,' she said, or threatened rather. 'My own mother is gravely ill and could do with my nursing, only I have told Mr Raffalovich that I will not leave you.'

'You have no life with me, and no life away from me,' I said wearily. 'Is that what you are trying to say?'

'The water is so ghastly here,' she went on, determined not to hear me, 'and the food, you know what it does to my gastritis. And of course they are cheating us at the hotel. *I* know who stole that hundred-franc note from your wardrobe.'

'Mother, I have an appointment and I must go.' I rose, still amazed that I could do so. 'I will see you back to the hotel.'

But she did not move. She sat there with an aggrieved look on her face. 'Shall I dine alone?' she asked, her voice querulous, pathetic. 'Again?'

'I don't know what time I shall return. Perhaps it would be better if you did.'

She gathered up her embroidery-bag with a sigh just loud enough to be heard. 'If you do not mind, I shall cut the pages of the little Book of Martyrs sent by Mr Raffalovich, and eat one or two of the chocolates he sent. That will be quite enough for me.'

She was beginning to enrage me. 'And, please,' I said, 'sniff the flowers as much as you like. I'm sure André would want you to.'

André, you see, had become her ideal son, the man whom I should in all ways emulate and never did.

'Have you been careful with your money, Aubrey?' she asked as we started back towards the colonnade. 'I should hate to have to pester Mr Raffalovich for more.'

'Don't be so concerned about money. André has more of it than you and I can even conceive of. He lives in a never-ending gush of it.'

'I do not know what we would do if he stopped his support,' she said. 'The money you receive from Mr Smithers is so erratic and uncertain.'

I stopped and turned her like a recalcitrant child to face me. 'Mother, I have been earning the living of this family, in one way or another, since I was eight years old. We have never lived in great comfort, but neither have we starved. I have seen to that always, have I not?'

'I know in times past you were rather careless with money.'

'Yes, dear, when I had some.'

She laughed a little, and for a moment looked almost like a girl, standing there in the soft rosy dusk, perhaps the way she had looked to my father when he met her secretly in the gardens of Brighton Pavilion. But now she had relinquished her beauty and all the sparkling little pleasures that make life such a feast. The face she generally wore was a tragic mask set in anticipation of nothing but pain.

My poor dear mother. How little I valued her. I saw her as an inconvenience, a sickroom appliance, an irritation, an eternal reproach.

'I know you are drawing again, Aubrey. Would Mr Raffalovich approve of these new drawings?'

My moment of tenderness passed. 'My work does not depend upon the approval of André Raffalovich, Mother. I am free, thank you very much, to work as I please.'

'As you please Leonard Smithers,' she said with disgust.

'What do you want me to do? Lie quietly and rot in your care? Stay in bed all day praying like your darling Mr Raffalovich?'

'Mr Raffalovich is a gentleman,' she said, turning from me and starting off. 'He does not pray in bed.'

'He prays everywhere!' I jibed. 'He even prays in his water-closet. He prays and prays, Mother, so he will not have to face the world as it is.'

'He is a kind and generous man,' she said, quickening her pace.

'Mabel will never marry him, you know.'

That stopped her. 'If that is so,' she replied, 'it might be wise for you to accept his offer.'

'You want *me* to marry André?' I hooted with laughter. 'Mother, he hasn't asked me.'

'Stop making a game of what I say, Aubrey. You know what I mean.'

'You mean the hundred guineas a quarter. I know exactly what you mean. You mean sell my soul to André Raffalovich.'

'Yes, instead of to Leonard Smithers.'

I hailed a cab and stuffed her into it despite her vehement protests over the cost. I was too angry to escort her myself for the short distance to the hotel. Another precious day spoiled. Another spiteful reference to Smithers, with whom I had to deal if I wanted to see my *Book of Fifty Drawings*, and for whom I would continue to draw, no matter what his reputation, so long as there was any hope in heaven for the work's publication.

'Good night, Mother.'

She leaned out of the cab window, desperate now that she faced my actual desertion, the time when I would no longer be her prisoner and she my warden. 'I did not mean to anger you, darling.'

'Mother, I did not come to Paris to stand beside the Louvre and have a row with you,' I said calmly.

'Forgive me,' she pleaded.

'I have an appointment and I shan't be returning for dinner, and perhaps later I will go to the Opéra or the theatre.' I knocked for the driver to go.

Mother settled herself back in the cab with a tight-jawed determination not to enjoy the ride. 'I cannot believe you are well enough,' she said bitterly.

I couldn't, either. But, strangely enough, all the assorted squalors of Paris, all those frightful sins just waiting to turn the soul of a proper young Englishman black, no longer had any appeal to me.

I preferred to wander alone along the quays. Ridiculously hopeful thoughts strayed through my head. I would go to America with Mabel. Begin a new life. Find a new publisher. Be cured. Become a Catholic.

We talked of it so often, Father, when I came to call on you at the Jesuit house on the rue de Sèvres. My return to health I took to be a sign that I was ready to make the great decision. I had paid my debts, and taken leave of the Aubrey that I was.

All that remained was my confession. But then I became ill again, and was quickly moved here to St-Germain.

That final task, my confession, which I once regarded as well-nigh impossible, I think I have now accomplished in these letters to you. Of my past there is nothing more to tell. I stand naked now in the eyes of God, my outline clearly revealed. I have drawn myself not as what I should be, but as what I truly am, a great artist and a great sinner.

Tomorrow, Father, when I return to Paris, I pray that you will cover my wasted and shivering body with the warm cloak of the Church.

May 1897,
Hôtel Foyot, rue Tournon,
Paris.

Y DEAREST BROTHER,

Very many thanks for your recent kind thoughts and assurances.

This morning I was received into the Church by dear Father Coubé. Unfortunately I was not at all well and could not risk the inclement weather, so the beautiful church ceremony that I had envisioned and hoped for was after all impossible. The Blessed Sacrament will be brought to me here, tomorrow, I hope.

Forgive a very dry account of what has

been the most important step in my life. You will, I am certain, understand fully what my simple statements mean.

The pneumothorax treatment proved to be unwise, and we have now been ordered off post-haste to Dieppe for the remainder of the summer season. The bacilli evidently flourish rather too giddily in the sodden Parisian air.

Your letter and splendid present – the cheque for £90 – have just arrived. I am more deeply touched and honoured than I can say. André, there is no way I can ever hope to repay your many kindnesses. I have been cruel to you in the past, but it was the cruelty of a child, and I ask for your forgiveness. Your friendship has come to mean more to me than I can ever hope to recount.

Yes, I agree that the remaining £10 would be more useful in the form of a note. I can that way apply it to our immediate expenses in Dieppe. We will be staying at the Hôtel des Étrangers, and I shall look for your next letter there.

Goodbye, dear André; and again most heartfelt thanks. Pray for me with special fervour at this time. With the greatest love,

I am, dear Brother,

Your very affectionate
AUBREY BEARDSLEY

ALBERICH

September 1897,
Casino de Dieppe

DEAR PÈRE COUBÉ,

It is with considerable urgency that I send you this account of a meeting that has left me reeling with both anger and remorse. Now, when what little strength I have must be so carefully husbanded, I am faced with a turmoil so great that I feel it has ruined any hope of a possible cure while I remain in Dieppe.

Let me recount the events, and perhaps cool my agitation.

Escaping from Mother's penetrating

eye, I had for one blessed hour been sitting by myself under an umbrella on the terrace of the Hôtel des Étrangers, sipping a milk and soda – the lunger's version of an aperitif. My new *Volpone* drawings were preoccupying me, and I was idly sketching out my plan for them when I heard a terrifyingly familiar voice:

'Aubrey! My dear boy!'

I turned and there he was, staring intently – wondering, I suppose, if he dared to smile and show his blackened teeth.

How much of a man can one see in a moment? All of him, I'm afraid, when what one sees has been irrevocably altered. The gods had revoked Oscar's citizenship in the pantheon. He who had been a giant among men was now an ordinary mortal. Less than ordinary – he was a convicted criminal.

Gone, the vibrant elasticity of his frame; now he looked slightly stooped, as if some psychic punch had knocked the wind from his lungs and he could not regain it. Gone, the smooth, fat, ruddy flesh of the perennially feasting glutton; his skin, dry and lustreless, had taken on the greyish hue and texture of cheap porous paper. Gone, the dark curling hair that had once been fashioned tiara-wise against his forehead and brushed back on his head; his locks, where they escaped from his hat, now hung limply, shot with grey. And his eyes – ah, those were the most changed and terrifying of all. The exalted light that once shone in them so clearly, so brilliantly, had been dimmed, perhaps extinguished for ever. I fancied I could see in the devitalized orbs a dog-like yearning for affection of any kind.

And, while I, in that first moment, saw all this in Oscar, I wonder now what he, in that same moment, saw in me. For I had changed, too. Like him, I had been toppled from my pedestal. I, too, was a spectre of my former self. What magnificent failures we had both become!

Then a cough took me by surprise, and I twisted away, shamed by the hacking obviousness of my disease and my own speechless surprise at his appearance.

I hoped he would disappear. There was too much between us ever to say it all, and his very presence called up in me a bitterness so intense that, until that moment, I had not known how utterly it had penetrated my being.

When my spasm passed I sat, unable to look at him. There was

406

a sly hard edge in Oscar's voice as he said: 'From the way you are behaving, Mr Beardsley, one would think that you were English. Not even a *crumb* of greeting for the pariah dog of the nineteenth century?'

Oscar's assumed identity as Sebastian Melmoth fools only those people who don't matter; those who do, know exactly who he is. He is, after all, not a man to be lost in a crowd. His physical presence demands attention. Now, of course, it is all negative attention that he receives.

'Look at them,' he murmured, casting his eyes round the terrace; he must be a very strong man, for I could not look into eyes as murderously unforgiving as those now focused on us. 'Look at them, how they turn away, harden their eyes. Smirk. The very same who once besieged me with invitations.' With that – in defiance, I think – he abruptly sat down beside me and called to the waiter.

'Monsieur?' The waiter, I could see, had quickly been informed of Mr Melmoth's other and more notorious persona. Suddenly he didn't know if it was appropriate to fawn.

'Bring me a glass of absinthe,' said Oscar, half-turning towards me. 'I wish to look into its cloudy opalescence and read my future with Aubrey.'

The waiter's voice was precise and unnerving in that way mastered only by the French. 'Are you a resident at this hotel, monsieur?'

'You know perfectly well that I am not,' said Oscar.

'I cannot serve you, monsieur, if you are not a resident of the Hôtel des Étrangers.'

The waiter's manner infuriated me, and I brought him up short in his game by saying: 'Bring Mr . . . *Melmoth* . . . what he has asked for.'

The waiter was dumbfounded. 'But, monsieur . . .'

'Do as I say! You may put it on my account.'

In a huff of outrage, the waiter flounced away.

Oscar's voice was grateful. 'That was very kind of you, Aubrey.'

I was locked into battle at once. 'One can always be kind to people one cares nothing about. Your words, Oscar.'

He was silent for a moment, weighing the appropriate response, and in that moment of silence I knew I was waiting for his words

407

– waiting to hear the intoxicating phraseology and brilliance of utterance that were his alone.

Oscar said nothing. Instead, he did something extraordinary. He removed first one, then the other, of his soiled gloves, and laid his hands down on the table before me. I was forced to look; the gesture was so puzzling.

Oscar's hands were no longer fat and bejewelled; they no longer curled at his hip or waved languidly in the air to make a point. There on the table I saw the coarse hands of a convict. They were the hands of a man forced to pick oakum until his fingertips bled; the hands of a man with no water to wash in, so that filth became embedded in the very pores of the flesh and the crevices of the nails. The hands sparkled with mysterious wounds, the fresh skin of countless scars shining up and down his fingers like the pink tourmalines he once wore.

After silently displaying his stigmata to me, he put his gloves back on and said: 'It is curious how vanity helps the successful man and wrecks the failure. In old days half my strength was my vanity.'

'And now?' I asked.

'Now all I want is my artistic reappearance in Paris, not in London. It is a homage I owe to that great city of art.'

I kept my voice from expressing an iota of human concern. 'What will it be, Oscar? Another play? Another comedy?'

'No, no,' he said, shaking his head, 'I no longer see myself writing comedy. I suppose it is all in me somewhere, but I don't seem to feel it. My sense of humour is now concentrated on the grotesqueness of tragedy.'

I noticed the frayed edges of his jacket, the grime of his shirt-cuff, and I was moved – but not so moved that I could forgive what he had done to me. 'One must be sincere to write a tragedy, Oscar,' I said. 'Your greatest gift was always your insincerity.'

'In so vulgar an age as this, my dear boy, we all need masks. There is no way, otherwise, to disguise our suffering.' He sighed and stared for a moment out to sea. 'No, I shall not write another comedy. I am presently working on a poem – a ballad – did not Smithers tell you?'

'Smithers?' The last thing I wanted was to be warned of some new treachery on Smithers's part.

'He is the only one who will publish it.'

How hilariously perverse of fate, I thought, that we, the greatest of artists, the greatest of enemies, should end up with a pornographer as our sole means of publication. 'One hundred copies, you mean, for private distribution only?'

Oscar caught my meaning instantly. 'Yes, I'm afraid Smithers is so fond of suppressed books that he suppresses his own.' He dutifully waited for my laugh, and when it didn't come went on: 'A very limited first edition, shall we say? And, instead of the author's name, his prison number: C.3.3.'

Prison! A part of me longed to ask him what he had gone through, what horrors he had endured, what terrifying mysteries he had penetrated. But another part did not want to honour his pain and degradation by asking about them; I wanted rather to add to them, heap abuse on his head for what he had done to me. This man had ruined my life, and here was I offering him a drink at my expense!

'It should create some interest,' Oscar went on, the fire of his old enthusiasm much dimmed. 'You know, of course, that Smithers has been over to see me.'

Another galvanic current ran through me. 'No,' I said calmly, 'I did not.'

Again Oscar was a fellow-conspirator. 'Too awful for words, of course, but very good-hearted. Got up in a whole suit of French clothing from La Belle Jardinière; and, although it suits his particular *style*, one is not exactly proud of his companionship.'

'No.'

'He showed me your drawings for *The Rape of the Lock*. Obviously you resisted my suggestion to have nothing whatsoever to do with Pope.'

'I adore Pope,' I said grimly. 'I hope you will allow me my own tastes in poetry.'

'There are two ways to dislike poetry, Aubrey. One way is to dislike it, and the other way is to like Pope.'

My rage was mounting, dear Father. No one could kindle it as successfully as Mr Wilde.

'The penwork, I must say, was superb. A new style for you, was it not? The drawings — you will forgive my frankness, Aubrey — were no longer cruel, as your earlier drawings were cruel.'

How glad I was to know that he was still smarting from those caricatures in *Salome*.

'And with an eighteenth-century feel about them,' Oscar went on approvingly, patronizingly. 'And your drawings for *The Savoy*!' he exclaimed suddenly. 'I found them quite bizarre and astonishing. You have a great gift for the grotesque, Aubrey.'

'If I am not grotesque, I am nothing.'

'Yes, I often wondered why you had so little interest in beauty.'

'Beauty is the most difficult of things – and I sometimes think the world hardly deserves it. The grotesque is arresting and comparatively effortless – and it better describes my vision of the world.'

'Until recently I don't think I could have understood that philosophy,' Oscar admitted. But then he darted back to his favourite subject: himself. 'By the way, I spoke to your *owner* – Smithers – about your providing the frontispiece for my ballad when it is ready.'

With this impertinence I exploded. 'Never!' I fairly shouted. 'You see, as with Smithers, I'm not exactly proud of your companionship, either. Your companionship ruined me, Oscar, are you not aware of that? When you fell—'

'I was pushed, my dear boy—'

'—you took me with you, right down to the gutter. I could not defend myself because there were no actual charges brought against me. I was condemned on conjecture and insinuation. Whispers. Rumours.' For a moment I paused, knowing that if I were not careful I would be overwhelmed by such a magnitude of unexpressed emotion that I would be unable to speak at all. 'What an interesting study in contrasts, Oscar – your trivial comedies and your filthy life.'

To my surprise he did not try to defend himself. 'I am sorry my life was so maimed by extravagance,' he said, 'but I could not live otherwise. I, at any rate, pay the penalty to suffering.'

How dare he speak of *his* suffering, and ignore mine? Rage sent my voice up at least an octave. 'Do you, Oscar? Do you suffer now?'

'My dear boy,' he said, 'I have lost absolutely everything. Even my name. I am a bankrupt. My children have been taken from me, and I shall never see them again. I am simply a self-conscious nerve in pain.'

'I thought you were a wise man, Oscar, but you turned out to be nothing but a fool! For God's sake, you were given time to leave. You could have avoided everything! And, if you had, I would—' A coughing spasm left my sentence unfinished.

I would what? I ask myself now. If Oscar *had* taken the boat for Calais, slipped quietly over here, escaped England as pursued inverts have had to do for centuries, then what *would* my fate have been? Would I be still at *The Yellow Book?* Would my health be as tolerable as it was then? Would I be as revered as Burne-Jones? Would invitations pour in through the post, and commissions for new work keep my pen dipped in the ink-pot.

How could I ever know? The shifting winds of fate ceaselessly erase our footsteps in the sand. In the end we're left with nothing more mysterious than the moment at hand, and it's that we must make sense of. I had known suffering as great as Oscar's, and had known it because of him. And I knew that I was supposed to forgive him for what he had done to me; my new religion required that of me. But I could not, Father. My heart was stone.

Oscar sat back in his chair, and when he spoke his voice was annoyingly thoughtful. 'Yes, why is it, do you suppose, that one runs to one's ruin? Why has destruction such a fascination? Why, when one stands on a pinnacle – as I stood – must one throw oneself down? No one knows, my dear boy, but it is so.'

'I am not your dear boy,' I cried, hating every connotation that phrase exposed me to. 'I was never your dear boy. Nor was I ever your invention, as you claimed. To tell you the truth, Oscar, I never even enjoyed your company.'

His features blurred with pain, and I was glad – oh, yes, delighted – that my stiletto had plunged at last into his softest parts. I felt a kind of absurd triumph in piercing through the once impregnable armour of his intellect, and twisting the blade in his very human bowels. I think Oscar was surprised at the depth of my vehemence; perhaps until then he had assumed that I, like all the others, was blindly enamoured, infatuated as a schoolboy for his most inspiring teacher.

'Do you know my greatest tragedy, Aubrey?' he asked, his voice scraped clean of artifice. 'It is that I put my genius into my life, and I only put my talent into my work.'

'It hardly takes a genius, Oscar, to fuck stablehands and telegraph

411

boys.' I saw him wince, as much for my vulgarity as for the pain it caused him, and moved in for another strike. 'Your reputation destroyed my livelihood. I now live on the verge of a pauper's life – and death – and it's because of you. Now, please, do you have some exquisite *bon mot* with which to console me for my ruined life? Some trivial truth – or a paradox perhaps – that will give me back all I have lost because of you?'

'Because of me?' he said, leaning forward as if he had not heard correctly.

'Surely you knew at the time of your arrest that having a *Yellow Book* under your arm would compromise me? Did you really bear me so much ill-will?'

'You labour under a false impression, my dear . . . Aubrey. I carried no copy of *The Yellow Book* with me when I was arrested.'

Now I reeled under a blow. 'But it was reported—'

'Do you actually believe what you read in newspapers?' he said incredulously. 'I carried a book with me, that is true. It was an ordinary French novel, as I recall. Yes, very ordinary. It was, in fact, Pierre Loüys' novel *Aphrodite*.'

Imagine sailing along at full billow and then having the wind suddenly drop and your sails slacken. I sat in a stupefied numbness and managed only to say: 'I see.' At that moment I was sharply aware of the green and white stripes of the umbrella above our heads, and the suck and roll of waves on the shingle. I saw myself entangled in a fate that had once been understandable, but was now merely ludicrous.

'I once thought yellow was my lucky colour,' I murmured, more to myself than to Oscar. 'I see now that it is a colour of ill-fortune and irony.'

'Aubrey, I know now that much was wrong in my life. And I am most heartily sorry if my sins were added to your account.'

His face, formerly so bloated with egotism and self-engrossed merriment, now appeared harshly chastened. He looked like someone whose lineaments had aged and altered as the result of a great nervous shock. I thought I had seen this in that first moment, but I had not seen it clearly until now, when the whole animating force behind my hatred and desire for revenge had been sloughed off. Now I saw before me that most pitiful and unnerving of all the sights on the whole suffering face of the earth: a once-great man brought to permanent ruin.

'I suppose prison has a way of bringing out the repentance in one,' I said carefully.

'And strange truths. Things one would rather not know about oneself.' He fidgeted in his chair, I suppose because telling the unadorned truth made him uneasy. 'Things', he said, 'one would prefer to hide. Just as now I would prefer to hide the fact that I, too, am face-to-face with starvation.'

Before I could respond – if, indeed, any response was possible in the face of that naked, terrible admission – the waiter appeared, empty-handed, but full of a new gust of malicious authority. 'Monsieur, I must request that you leave this establishment,' he said to Oscar.

'Oh?'

'Several of our English guests have objected to your presence.'

Oscar signed to me not to get involved. 'I see. Well, dear England has done one thing,' he said, his voice rising with ire. 'It has invented and established public opinion, which is an attempt to organize the ignorance of the community, and to elevate it to the dignity of physical force.'

The waiter was relentless. 'Will you go, monsieur?'

'I will go. I will wander on.' Oscar rose slowly from his chair, unwilling to relinquish the old comfortable pleasures of sitting over a drink and hearing his own sonorous voice. But he rose slowly, too, I saw, because he was no longer the Oscar I knew. He was bereft of his vital energies. He was as I was, a discarded shell, doomed now to hear only the phantom whispers of the sea that once had been his element. The sight was unbearable, and I turned away from it.

'Misfortunes one can endure,' he said in a low voice that reverberated in my ears. 'They come from outside. But to suffer for one's own faults – ah! there's the sting of life.'

Fully erect, he faced – as an ex-convict – the hate-filled eyes of those around him, the people who had lived their lives without being caught.

'A hundred years from now, Aubrey, people will laugh at this age. A hundred years from now, life will be interpreted by physiologists in terms of nothing more than simple chemical actions. The guilt that tortures us will be gone.' He leaned close, as if to kiss me. 'And so will Art.'

Having told you this, Father, I must implore you not to mention any of it to André. It would upset him quite as much as it has upset me, and I shouldn't know how to explain the encounter to him.

We are, in any event, forced to leave Dieppe to avoid the possibility of another chance meeting. Mother is making the arrangements now. We are travelling south to spend the winter in Menton. The air there, I am told, is the best in Europe. Lemons and oranges can be plucked from one's bedroom window. I am certain it will be adorable, but cannot keep from hearing in my thoughts that old saw: 'Cannes is for living, Monte Carlo for playing, and Menton for dying.'

I shall write again when I have recovered from this blow to my nervous system. Goodbye, dear Père Coubé.

I am,

Yours affectionately,
AUBREY BEARDSLEY

January 1898,
Hôtel Cosmopolitain,
Menton

DEAR MABEL,

You must come at once. Aubrey will never be at rest until he sees you. The doctor pronounces – but I dare not say it. In frantic haste,

Your mother
ELLEN BEARDSLEY

Dear Père Coubé,

Thank you for your kind prayers. I have been too ill to write, although so often I wanted to.

Our hotel is situated amongst the lemon groves of the Côte d'Azur. The endless horizon of the Mediterranean and the curve of the Western Bay now constitute my sole view of the world. It is not unpleasant, even reminds me of Brighton if I let my thoughts drift off. One long wall of my room Mother has decorated for me with Mantegna prints. I call that my wall of reflection.

There is a slight, almost constant oozing from one lung, then the other. The new doctor has me bathing in turpentine – a somewhat ironic cure for an artist, don't you agree? As a result, my skin has become horribly inflamed and has broken out in a magnificent rash. Shaving is impossible. The doctor insists that my condition, though very grave, is still curable. I do not believe him.

Dear Père Coubé, I have almost found peace, but it still shames me to think of how rudderless and vain I was in the past. The result was certain drawings which I now regret. I am very anxious to efface all traces of a self that is no more. Yet once they leave the work-table my drawings can be reproduced endlessly by an unscrupulous character. There is quite literally no way to recall and destroy them.

What, then, am I to do? Any letter I write to Smithers and Pollitt on the matter is likely to meet with a response quite the reverse of the one I intended.

It pains me to give up my lewd monsters, for I have come to love them, yet I know that I shall not find my final peace until they are consigned to the flames. Pray that I find a solution to my dilemma.

You kindly ask about my new work. I am illustrating Ben Jonson's play *Volpone*. I find great opportunities for picture-making in this story of a man who was a fox. His pitiless unmasking at the end of the play reveals the tragedy that lends weight to comedy.

There is a soft velvety quality to these, my last drawings. I have put aside pen and ink for the subtlety of soft pencil work, and the shading in them is so fine that it becomes precious – a graphite nap on the paper, fragile and easily destroyed. For style I have chosen a voluptuous heavy-breasted Baroque.

Smithers is going to publish them in half-tone, which will capture their subtle, mysterious, mythical qualities to perfection.

I wish you could see them.

An armless and legless satyr sits on a herm, a hot cornucopia of life spilling out from his belly.

A tassel swings a silent death-knell.

A begemmed pachyderm with the majesty of his poundage raises an obedient leg.

A monstrous black crow wearing a jewelled tiara flaps through the sky.

These drawings are to be used for initial letters. V – my father's initial – is appended to the satyr. M – which calls to mind both Mother and Mabel – is affixed to a drawing of a childish Eros stretching out his hands to a welcoming goddess. Her eyes are fecund, tender, embracing, all-consuming. She sits on a soft bed waiting to clutch the eager child to her fertile breasts.

In my present state, the solid weight of the elephant appeals to my fancy, so I have given the letter V – the initial I share with my father – to it as well.

How the past crowds in when one is dying. How strangely clear the outline of one's life.

In the end all I can say is that I have given the world work that is unlike any other. I have followed my vision. That has been my strength, and my bitter consolation.

I have made mistakes, many of them. But I die as an artist should die, with a full body of work. Will it last? In future years will I have a reputation?

It no longer matters, dear Père Coubé.

Let them make what they will of all that I have left behind.

I am, dear Father,

Yours very affectionately
AUBREY BEARDSLEY

419

Dear Brother,

Mabel has arrived safely. I was afraid I should never see her again. A bone-chilling mistral is blowing across the bay, aggravating my lungs and my joints. I have, in consequence, been forced to set aside for the moment my drawings for *Volpone*.

Constance Wilde, who resides somewhere close to Genoa, recently came with her son Vyvyan to visit me. The boy looks a great deal like Oscar, though he claims to remember nothing of him. It made my heart glad to be able to tell him that his father was a brilliant man.

I enclose my most recent photograph, which you kindly asked for. Can you see your photograph on the mantelpiece? There is one of you, Richard Wagner and Mabel.

My sister joins me in sending warmest love to you, John Gray, and Miss Gribbell.

Affectionately
AUBREY BEARDSLEY

7 March 1897,
Hôtel Cosmopolitain,
Menton.

[Addressed to Leonard Smithers in Ellen Beardsley's hand]

Jesus is our Lord and Judge

Dear Friend,

I implore you to destroy *all* copies of *Lysistrata* and bad drawings. Show this to Pollitt and conjure him to do same. By all that is holy *all* obscene drawings.

AUBREY BEARDSLEY

In my death agony.

Dear Vincent,

I write to inform you of the death of our son Aubrey, who passed away early this morning. My darling boy will be buried here in a lovely cemetery overlooking the Mediterranean. A Requiem Mass will be held for him tomorrow in the Cathedral.

Only yesterday, he asked me, before I went out, to put his drawing-board, pen and ink beside his bed. Though drawing was forbidden, and indeed an impossibility, for him, I think he wanted, when he was alone, to see if he could still draw, but had not the strength to gather his materials. I had not the heart to refuse his request. When I returned he was lying with his face to the wall and he would not speak. This morning I found his gold pen sticking into the floor beside his bed. I think he must have flung it away, finding he could not draw.

His suffering was very great towards the end, but he was beautifully resigned and looked forward to eternal rest. The memories of our last few months together are too painful for me to recount in this letter. My darling boy and I were as one. He relied on me for everything. He was too good for this world.

My heart is broken, and I can write no more.

ELLEN BEARDSLEY

17 March 1898,
Hôtel Cosmopolitain,
Menton.

Dear Father Coubé,

My dear one has passed away. He died in my arms, full of love and sweet messages for all his friends.

He spoke of you so often, and with such gratitude.

This letter will not be long. I am too overcome by grief to write more than a few sentences.

My brother and I shared a love and understanding that can never be replaced. The battles we fought and won together shall now be mine alone. There can be no consolation except the hope that we will meet again. Then, I pray, he will bury his head in my hair, as he liked so much to do, and smile and kiss me and tell me, as he did when we were children, that I should not be afraid.

Pray for him, Father, and pray for us.

Yours sincerely,
MABEL BEARDSLEY

THE MARQUIS DE SADE
Donald Thomas

Few people know anything about the Marquis de Sade
(1740–1814), the man whose name is synonymous with
perverse cruelty and sexual depravity. Was he a monster?
Or was he simply a product of his time and class?

An aristocrat in an age of decadence, Sade attracted scandal in
the grand manner. Accusations of orgies in black-draped rooms,
whippings, poisonings and more extreme sexual crimes, led to
twenty-seven years of imprisonment under royal and
revolutionary regimes. Yet he became a judge in the
revolutionary government who opposed the guillotine, saved
enemies from prison and campaigned fearlessly against state
terror and injustice. His writings, which resulted in his
detention till death in the Charenton asylum and which even
today provoke violent condemnation, are considered by many to
be the work of a visionary whose ideas foreshadowed
twentieth-century thinking.

Following the storm of controversy surrounding the
re-publication of Sade's novels, *Justine* and *Juliette*, Donald
Thomas's timely biography presents a portrait of a complex
and contradictory man, unravelling his life against the
turbulent backdrop of revolutionary France, and assessing his
legacy in the context of our own time.

0 552 99499 5

BLACK SWAN

RHYMER RAB, ALIAS BURNS
An Anthology of Poems and Prose
by ROBERT BURNS

Edited by Alan Bold

The poems and songs of Robert Burns are known throughout the world. Yet few are aware of the wealth of writing of all kinds he left at his death in 1796. Now Burns authority Alan Bold brings together for the first time the finest of the verse with the best of the prose in an important new anthology which gives fascinating insights into the poet's complex and contradictory character.

Here are some of Burns's most revealing letters, ranging from formal appeals to aristocratic patrons, to bawdy accounts of sexual conquests; from the elevated passion of the famous 'Clarinda' letters, to the touching domesticity of notes to his wife and family; and from fiery political satire, to poignant pleas sent in the final days of his life. Here also are extracts from commonplace books, passages from travel journals and other significant pieces, including the complete text of the Autobiographical Letter, the poet's only personal account of his meteoric rise to fame.

With its masterful introduction, setting Burns's work in the context of his life and times, *Rhymer Rab, Alias Burns* allows you for the first time to experience in full the extraordinary artistic, intellectual and emotional range of one of the greatest and best-loved figures in world literature.

0 552 99526 6

BLACK SWAN

THE PAINTED WORD
Tom Wolfe

'WOLFE AT HIS MOST CLEVER, AMUSING AND
IRREVERENT'
Thomas Albright, *San Francisco Chronicle*

Tom Wolfe exposes the myths and men of Modern Art – from
the fuliginous flatness of the Fifties to the pop op minimal
Sixties right on through the now-you-see-it-now-you-didn't
Seventies – in an incandescent, hilarious and devastating blast.

'IF YOU HAVE EVER STARED UNCOMPREHENDINGLY
AT AN ABSTRACT PAINTING THAT ADMIRED CRITICS
HAVE SAID YOU OUGHT TO DIG, TAKE HEART. TOM
WOLFE IS ON YOUR SIDE . . . DON'T MISS IT. IT MAY
ENRAGE YOU. IT MAY CONFIRM YOUR DARKEST
SUSPICIONS ABOUT MODERN ART. IN ANY CASE, IT
WILL AMUSE YOU'
Judson Hand, *New York Sunday Times*

'*THE PAINTED WORD* MAY WELL BE TOM WOLFE'S
MOST SUCCESSFUL PIECE OF SOCIAL CRITICISM TO
DATE'
Christopher Lehmann-Haupt, *New York Times*

0 552 99370 0

BLACK SWAN

THE DEATH OF DAVID DEBRIZZI
Paul Micou

'HUGELY ENTERTAINING. AN ODD, COMPELLING BOOK
WITH A SUPERB TWIST, AND ONE WHICH SHOULD
CLINCH MICOU'S REPUTATION AS A WRITER TO BE
RECKONED WITH'
Carla McKay, *Daily Mail*

Pierre Marie La Valoise is incensed. He has just read with disbelief
what he considers to be a criminally unfair biography of David
Debrizzi, the renowned French concert pianist. He sees the book as yet
another self-serving attempt by its author, Sir Geoffrey Flynch, to take
credit for David Debrizzi's successes, and to glorify himself by his
association with his genius subject. Why else, wonders La Valoise,
would Sir Geoffrey's recollections be so at variance with the facts?

Resting comfortably on the terrace of a Swiss sanatorium, La Valoise
takes pen in hand to rebut Sir Geoffrey's *Life.* He weeds through its
distortions and omissions, its exaggerations and personal attacks, and
supplies the version of the truth that he had intended to incorporate
into his own biography, *The Death of David Debrizzi.* 'Never have I
begrudged you your *Life,*' writes La Valoise, 'any more than you would
deny me my *Death* . . . Given the state of my health, and the treachery
of my bastard of a British publisher – who loathes me merely because
I am French – I feel it is safe to say that your *Life* will stand alone on
the shelves for posterity, while my *Death* will remain untold.'

With abundant wit and verve, Paul Micou's third novel at last gives
La Valoise his say.

'IT IS SO FULL OF MUSICAL FEELING THAT EVEN THE
TONE-DEAF WILL FEEL THRILLED . . . ABOVE ALL, IT IS A
GOOD STORY . . . I HAVE NOT ENJOYED A BOOK SO MUCH
FOR A LONG TIME'
Oxford Times

0 552 99461 8

BLACK SWAN

LITTLE FOLLIES

The Personal History, Adventures, Experiences and Observations of Peter Leroy

Eric Kraft

'A REAL DELIGHT. PETER LEROY'S WORLD SHINES
THROUGH JUST LIKE CHILDHOOD ITSELF: BOTH TINY
AND ENORMOUS, FULL OF MYSTERY AND WONDER,
BUT WITH TERROR LURKING ALL AROUND THE EDGES'
New York Times Book Review

One cold winter afternoon in 1962, while dozing over a college
German lesson, Eric Kraft dreamed up a nameless little boy sitting
on a dilapidated pier, trying to bring the soles of his bare feet as
close as he could to the surface of the water without actually
touching it.

Eventually Kraft gave the boy a name – Peter Leroy – a family, a
hometown, a life. First published in the form of newsletters mailed
to friends, then as a series of novellas, then broadcast on American
radio, these magical tales of childhood have attracted a cult
following in the USA and wide critical acclaim.

The story of Peter Leroy's odyssey through a 1950s childhood in
Babbington, Long Island ('The Clam Capital of America') as
recalled, revealed, and somewhat revised by an older and more
reflective Peter, evolves into a saga as funny, touching, witty,
mythic, and multi-faceted as anything in contemporary literature.

'NOTHING SHORT OF BRILLIANT"
Armistead Maupin

0 552 99595 9

BLACK SWAN

MAYBE THE MOON
Armistead Maupin

'WONDERFUL, FUNNY, POIGNANT AND GUTSY . . . YOU
CAN FEEL THE AUTHOR'S HUGE AND HURT AND
LOVING HEART BEAT ON EVERY PAGE'
Anne Lamott, *Mademoiselle*

All of thirty-one inches tall, Cadence (Cady) Roth is a true survivor
in a town where – as she says – 'you can die of encouragement'.
Her early leading role as a lovable elf in a smash-hit American film
proved a major disappointment since moviegoers never saw the face
behind the rubber mask she had to wear. After a decade of hollow
promises from the Industry, she is still waiting for the miracle that
will make her a star. Through a series of bracingly frank journal
entries, Armistead Maupin tracks his spunky heroine across the
saffron-hazed wasteland of Los Angeles – from her infrequent
meetings with agents and studio moguls to her regular, harrowing
encounters wth small children, large dogs and human ignorance.
Then one day a lanky piano player saunters into Cady's life,
unleashing heady new emotions, and she finds herself going for
broke, shooting the moon with a scheme so hare-brained and
daring that it might just succeed . . .

Maybe the Moon, Armistead Maupin's first novel since his bestselling
Tales of the City series, is the tale of an outsider told from the
inside. It is a work that speaks to the resilience of the human spirit.

'DELIGHTS, AMUSES, MOVES AND ANGERS YOU WITH
THE LIGHTEST OF TOUCHES. IT IS, AS MIGHT BE SAID OF
CADENCE HERSELF, A SMALL MASTERPIECE'
Simon Callow, *Vogue*

0 552 99569 X

BLACK SWAN

SWEET THAMES
Matthew Kneale

'RAW IN CONTENT, ELEGANT IN TREATMENT . . .
RICHLY ENJOYABLE'
David Hughes, *Mail on Sunday*

It is 1849. A major cholera epidemic threatens London. Working
unsupported by employer or public authority, Joshua Jeavons,
engineer, is completing his great drain plan for the capital. When
the deaths begin, he works even more furiously, driven by a bold
vision – a London freed of rotting sewers, cleansed and reborn, and
he, Joshua Jeavons, hailed as the discoverer of the source of the
killer disease.

Then his beautiful young wife Isobella, a paragon of female virtue,
suddenly disappears and Jeavons must turn his attention to new
and even more perplexing questions. Why her coldness? Why her
absolute refusal of his attentions since the first night of their
marriage? Could certain unthinkable accusations, made
anonymously against Isobella in a series of letters, actually be true?

Jeavons' search for the answers to the mysteries that surround him
leads to the shores of the Thames where only sewer-scavengers
thrive; to glittering Haymarket cafés where high-class prostitutes
ply their trade; and finally to the dangerous heart of London's
slums. What he finds there, amid poverty, disease and death, will
shatter his ideals and strike at the core of everything he has ever
held dear.

'EXCELLENT . . . THE GRADUAL UNFOLDING OF THE
PLOT IS SUPERBLY DONE'
Mark Illis, *Spectator*

0 552 99542 8

BLACK SWAN

THE CAIRO TRILOGY
Naguib Mahfouz

The celebrated *Cairo Trilogy* tells the story of twentieth century Egypt through the eyes of the Al Jawad family. A sweeping family saga crossing three generations, the trilogy is set in the old quarter of Cairo, and spans the decades from the turn of the century to Nasser's historic overthrowal of the old regime in 1952.

Brimming over with warmth, humour and vivid description, *The Cairo Trilogy* offers a fascinating insight into this exotic, timeless city and into the mores of a culture so different from our own. Filled with compelling drama and earthy humour, this is an unforgettable story of the sometimes violent clash between ideals and realities, dreams and desires, which again displays Mahfouz's masterful storytelling talent.

'A MAGNIFICENT, TOLSTOYAN SAGA . . . UNMISSABLE'
Cosmopolitan

'AN ENGROSSING WORK, WHOSE AUTHOR CAN TAKE HIS PLACE ALONGSIDE ANY EUROPEAN MASTER YOU CARE TO NAME'
Sunday Times

'PROUST, TOLSTOY AND BALZAC ARE THE NAMES MOST FREQUENTLY FLUNG AROUND IN COMPANY WITH THAT OF MAHFOUZ'
Penelope Lively, *Spectator*

VOLUME I: PALACE WALK   0 552 99580 0
VOLUME II: PALACE OF DESIRE   0 552 99581 9
VOLUME III: SUGAR STREET   0 552 99582 7

BLACK SWAN

A SELECTED LIST OF FINE WRITING
AVAILABLE FROM BLACK SWAN

☐ 99526 6	RHYMER RAB: AN ANTHOLOGY OF POEMS AND PROSE	ed. Alan Bold	£6.99
☐ 99531 2	AFTER THE HOLE	Guy Burt	£4.99
☐ 99348 4	SUCKING SHERBET LEMONS	Michael Carson	£5.99
☐ 99587 8	LIKE WATER FOR CHOCOLATE	Laura Esquivel	£5.99
☐ 99563 0	SUNDAY TIMES BLACK SWAN LITERARY QUIZ BOOK	ed. Philip Evans	£3.99
☐ 99508 8	FIREDRAKE'S EYE	Patricia Finney	£5.99
☐ 99466 9	A SMOKING DOT IN THE DISTANCE	Ivor Gould	£6.99
☐ 99195 3	CATCH-22	Joseph Heller	£6.99
☐ 99369 7	A PRAYER FOR OWEN MEANY	John Irving	£6.99
☐ 99585 1	FALLING OFF THE MAP	Pico Iyer	£5.99
☐ 99567 3	SAILOR SONG	Ken Kesey	£6.99
☐ 99542 8	SWEET THAMES	Matthew Kneale	£5.99
☐ 99037 X	BEING THERE	Jerzy Kosinski	£3.99
☐ 99595 9	LITTLE FOLLIES	Eric Kraft	£5.99
☐ 99580 0	CAIRO TRILOGY I: PALACE WALK	Naguib Mahfouz	£5.99
☐ 99581 9	CAIRO TRILOGY II: PALACE OF DESIRE	Naguib Mahfouz	£5.99
☐ 99582 7	CAIRO TRILOGY III: SUGAR STREET	Naguib Mahfouz	£5.99
☐ 99391 3	MARY REILLY	Valerie Martin	£4.99
☐ 99469 X	MAYBE THE MOON	Armistead Maupin	£5.99
☐ 99461 8	THE DEATH OF DAVID DEBRIZZI	Paul Micou	£5.99
☐ 99536 3	IN THE PLACE OF FALLEN LEAVES	Tim Pears	£5.99
☐ 99504 5	LILA	Robert Pirsig	£5.99
☐ 99499 5	THE MARQUIS DE SADE	Donald Thomas	£6.99
☐ 99601 7	JOGGING ROUND MAJORCA	Gordon West	£5.99
☐ 99370 0	THE PAINTED WORD	Tom Wolfe	£4.99
☐ 99500 2	THE RUINS OF TIME	Ben Woolfenden	£4.99

NAME (Block Letters)..

ADDRESS ....

....